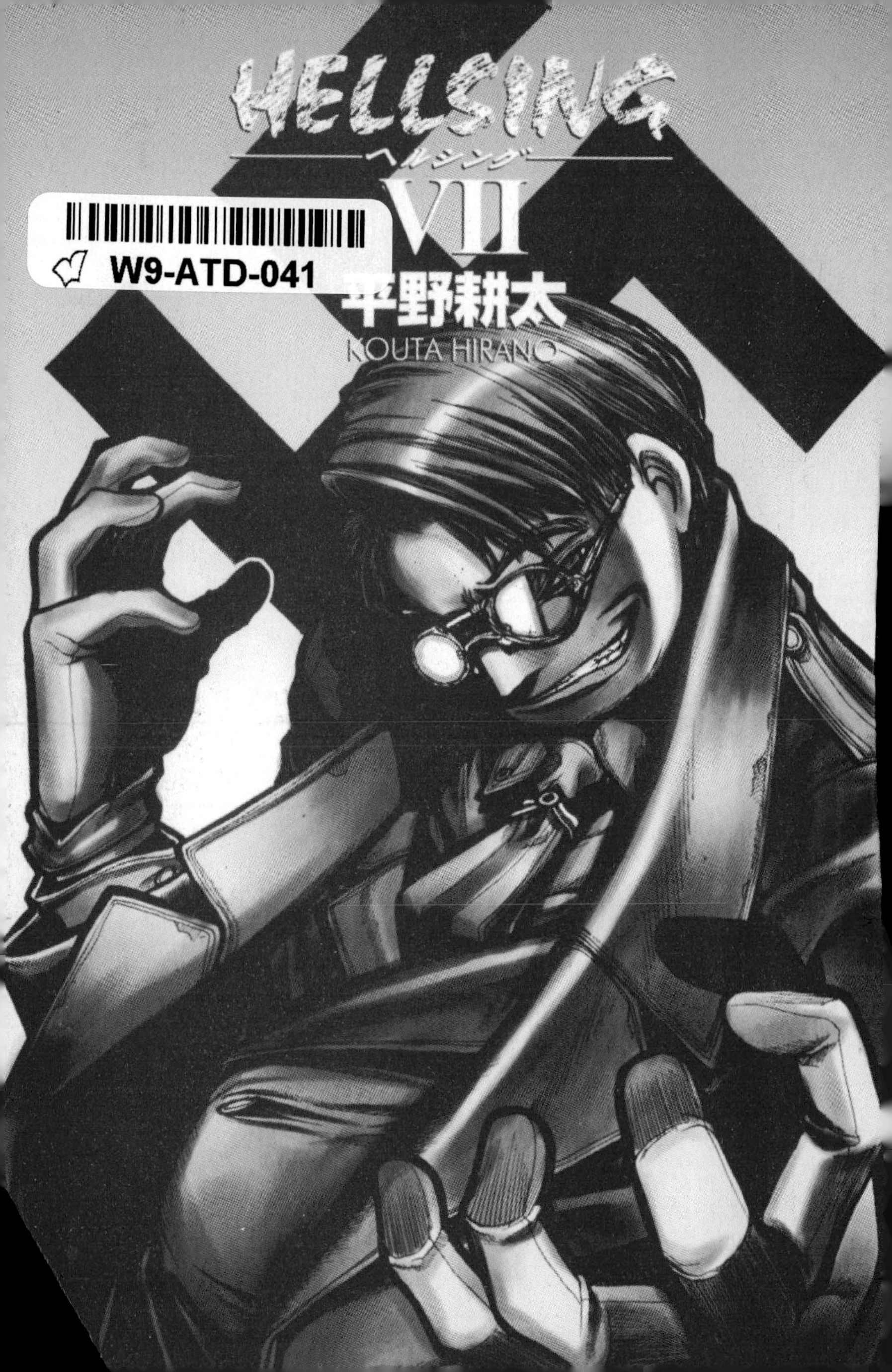
HELLSING
ヘルシング
VII
平野耕太
KOUTA HIRANO

HELLSING ⑦

ORDER 1

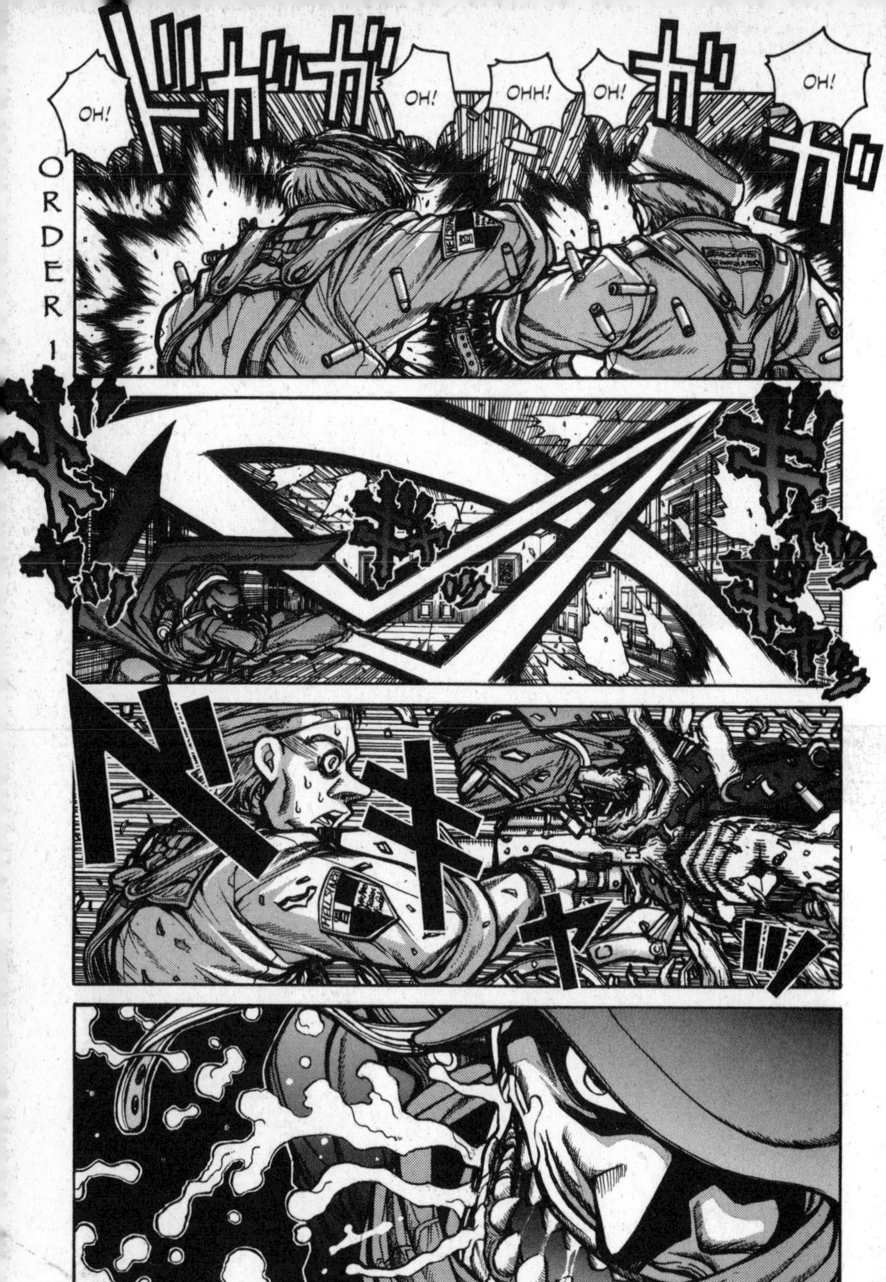

OH!
OH!
OHH!
OH!
OH!

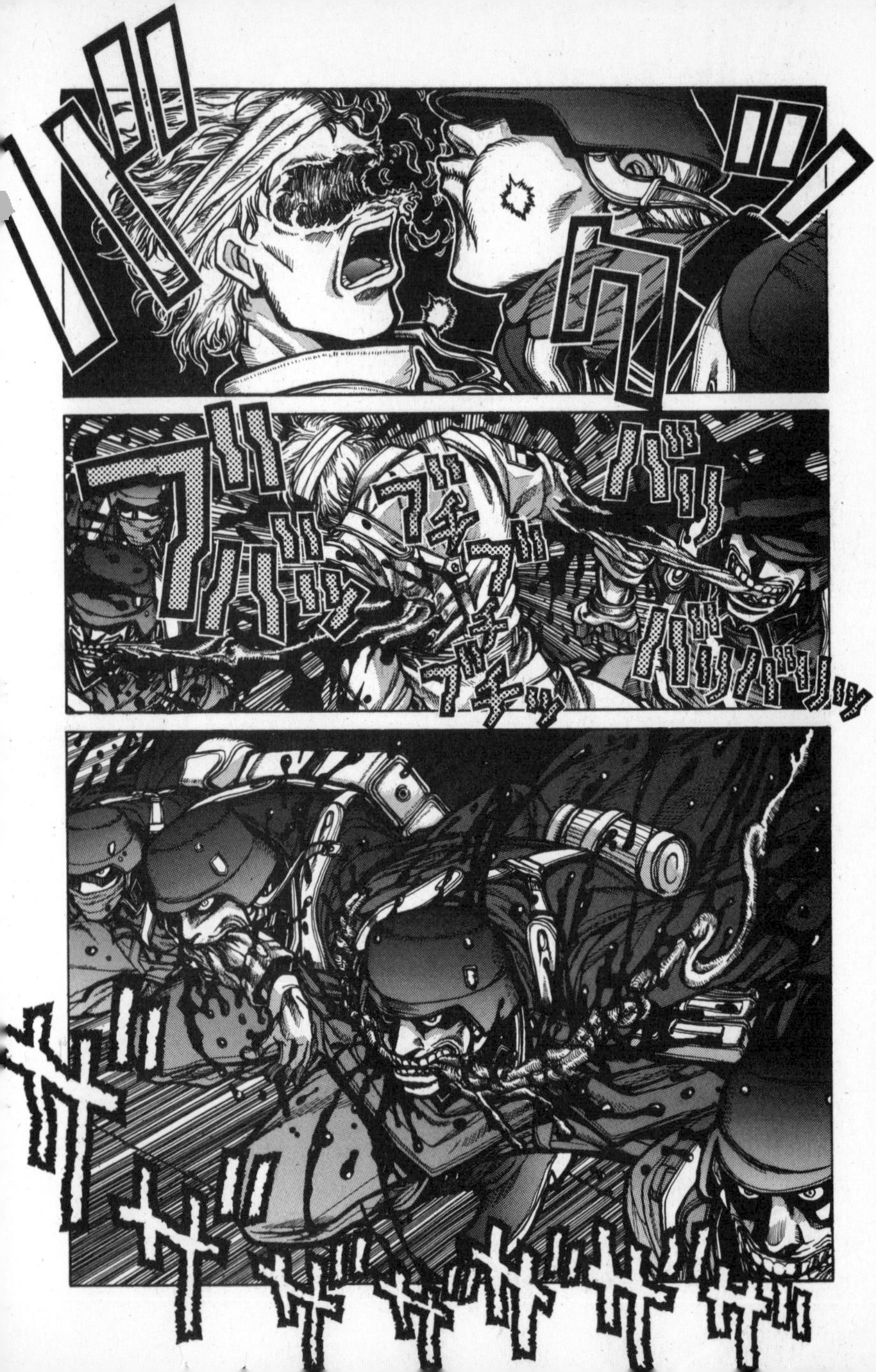
バリ
バリバリバリッ
ブチ
ブチ
ブチッ
ブバッ
ザザザザザザザ

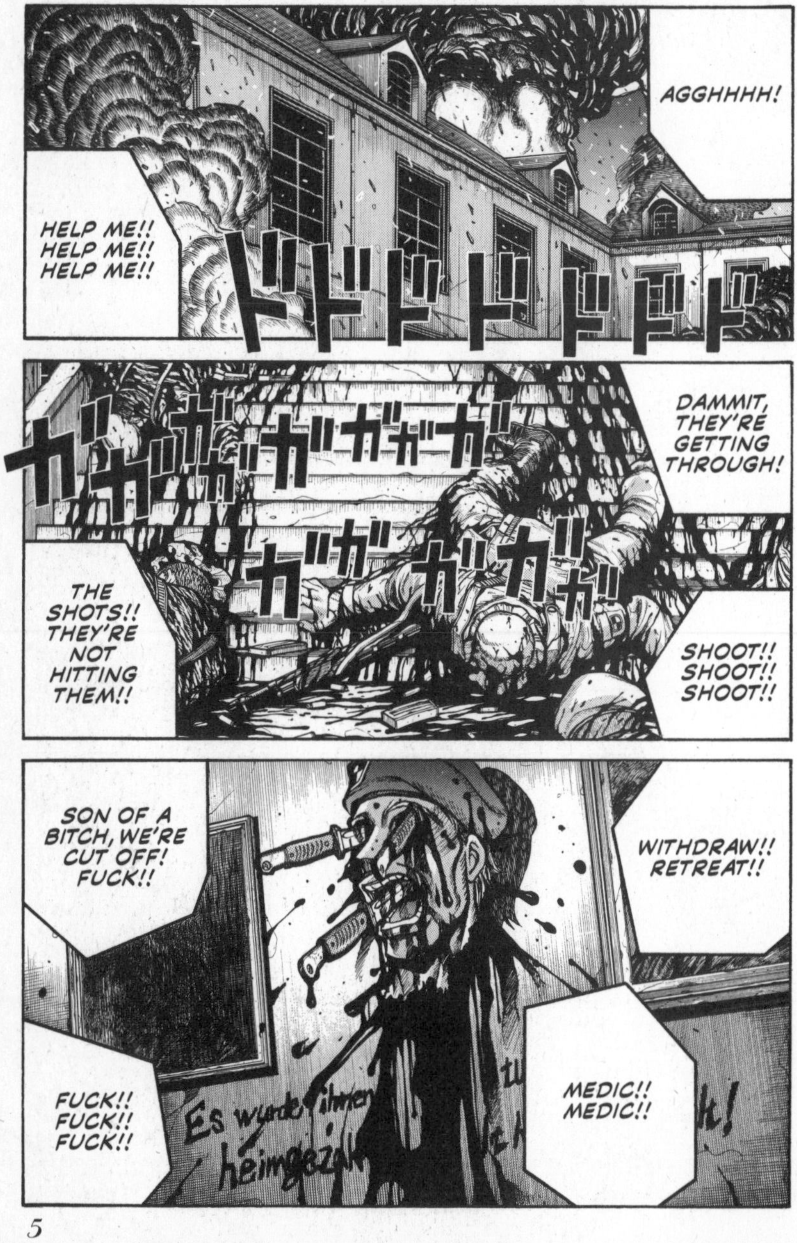
AGGHHHH!
ドドドドドドドド
HELP ME!! HELP ME!! HELP ME!!
DAMMIT, THEY'RE GETTING THROUGH!
SHOOT!! SHOOT!! SHOOT!!
カガガガガガガ
ガガガガガ
THE SHOTS!! THEY'RE NOT HITTING THEM!!
WITHDRAW!! RETREAT!!
MEDIC!! MEDIC!!
SON OF A BITCH, WE'RE CUT OFF! FUCK!!
FUCK!! FUCK!! FUCK!!

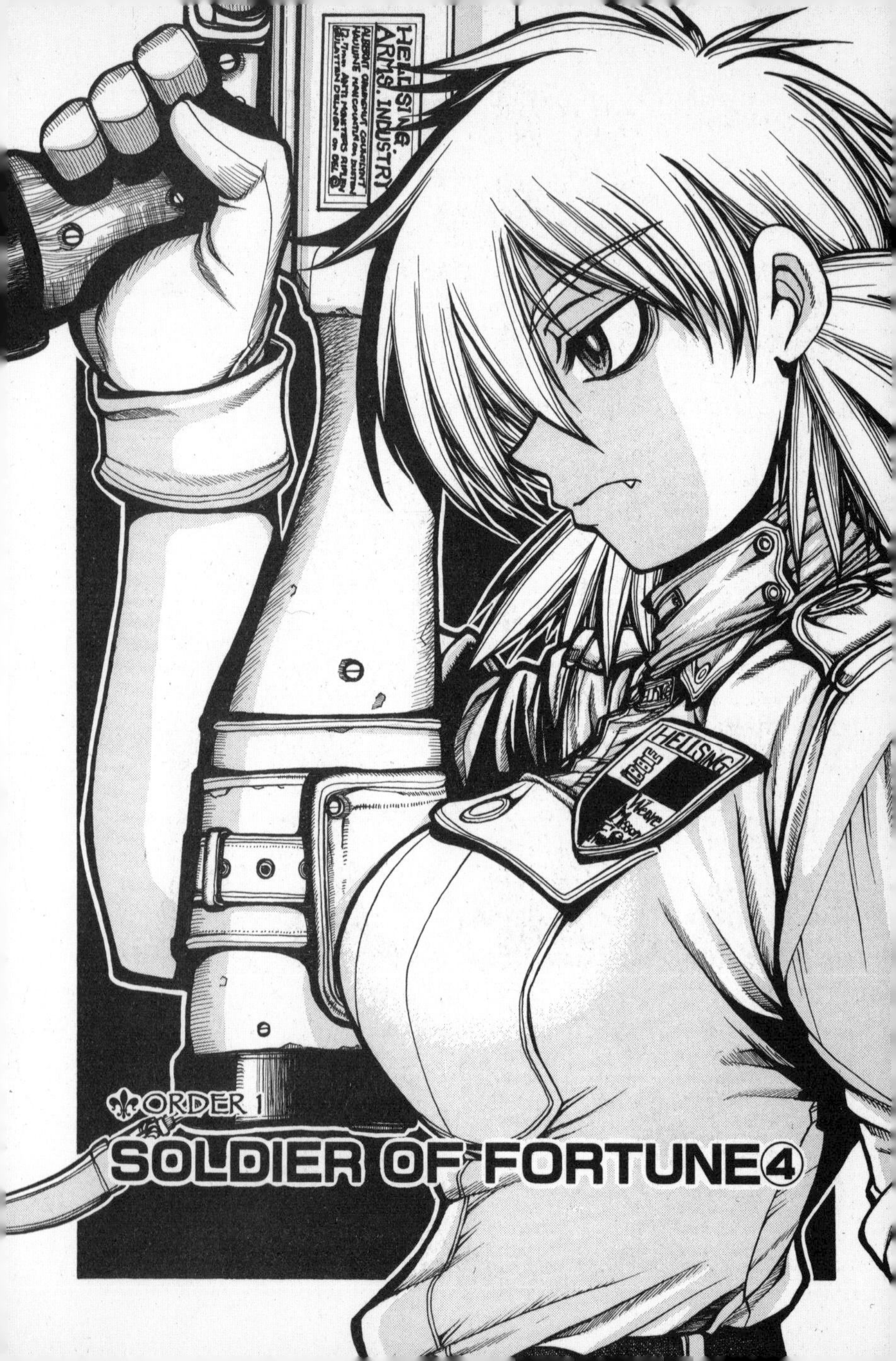
HELLSING ARMS. INDUSTRY
HELLSING
ORDER 1
SOLDIER OF FORTUNE④

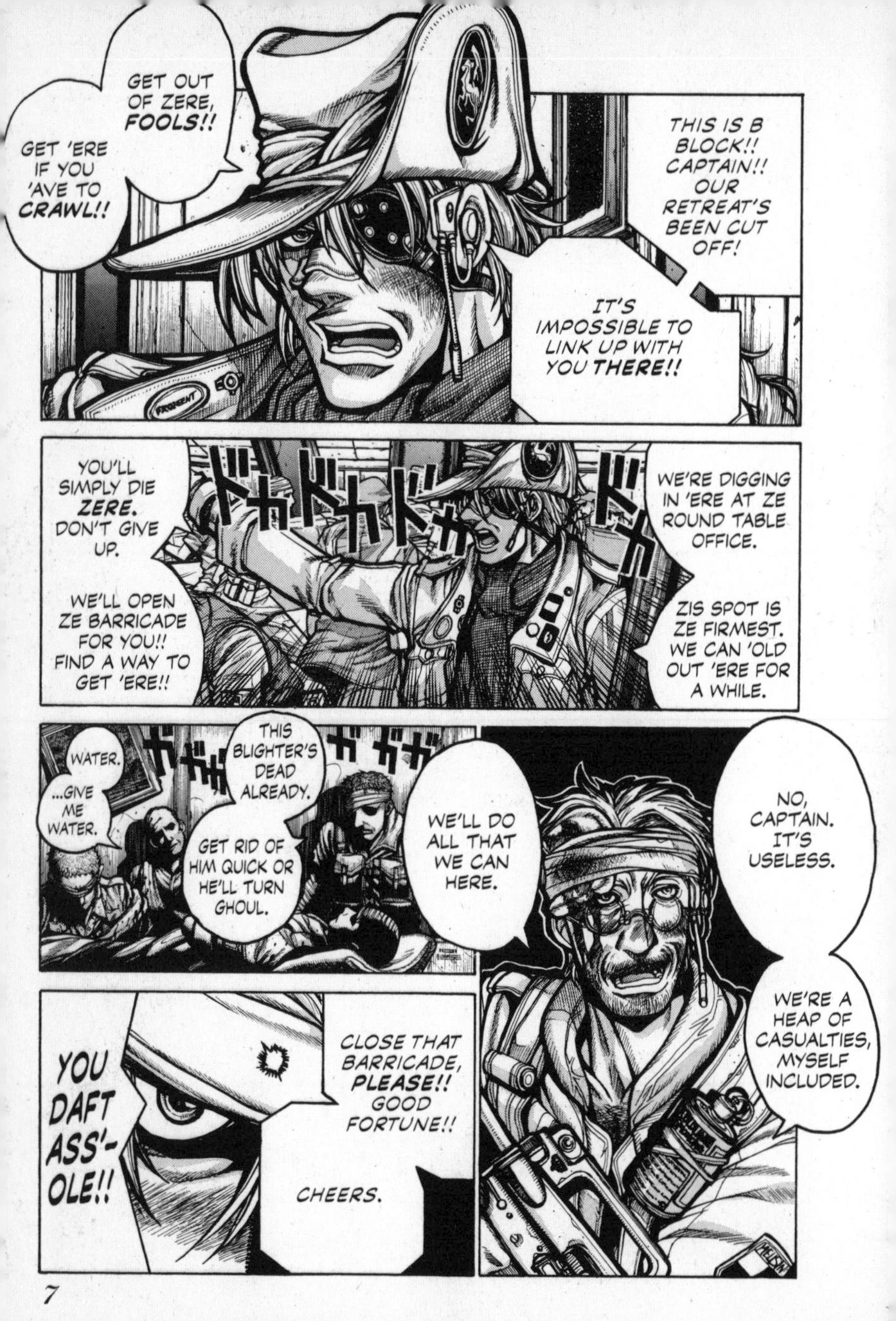
THIS IS B BLOCK!! CAPTAIN!! OUR RETREAT'S BEEN CUT OFF!
IT'S IMPOSSIBLE TO LINK UP WITH YOU THERE!!
GET OUT OF ZERE, FOOLS!!
GET 'ERE IF YOU 'AVE TO CRAWL!!
WE'RE DIGGING IN 'ERE AT ZE ROUND TABLE OFFICE.
ZIS SPOT IS ZE FIRMEST. WE CAN 'OLD OUT 'ERE FOR A WHILE.
YOU'LL SIMPLY DIE ZERE. DON'T GIVE UP.
WE'LL OPEN ZE BARRICADE FOR YOU!! FIND A WAY TO GET 'ERE!!
NO, CAPTAIN. IT'S USELESS.
WE'RE A HEAP OF CASUALTIES, MYSELF INCLUDED.
WE'LL DO ALL THAT WE CAN HERE.
THIS BLIGHTER'S DEAD ALREADY.
GET RID OF HIM QUICK OR HE'LL TURN GHOUL.
WATER.
...GIVE ME WATER.
CLOSE THAT BARRICADE, PLEASE!! GOOD FORTUNE!!
CHEERS.
YOU DAFT ASS'-OLE!!

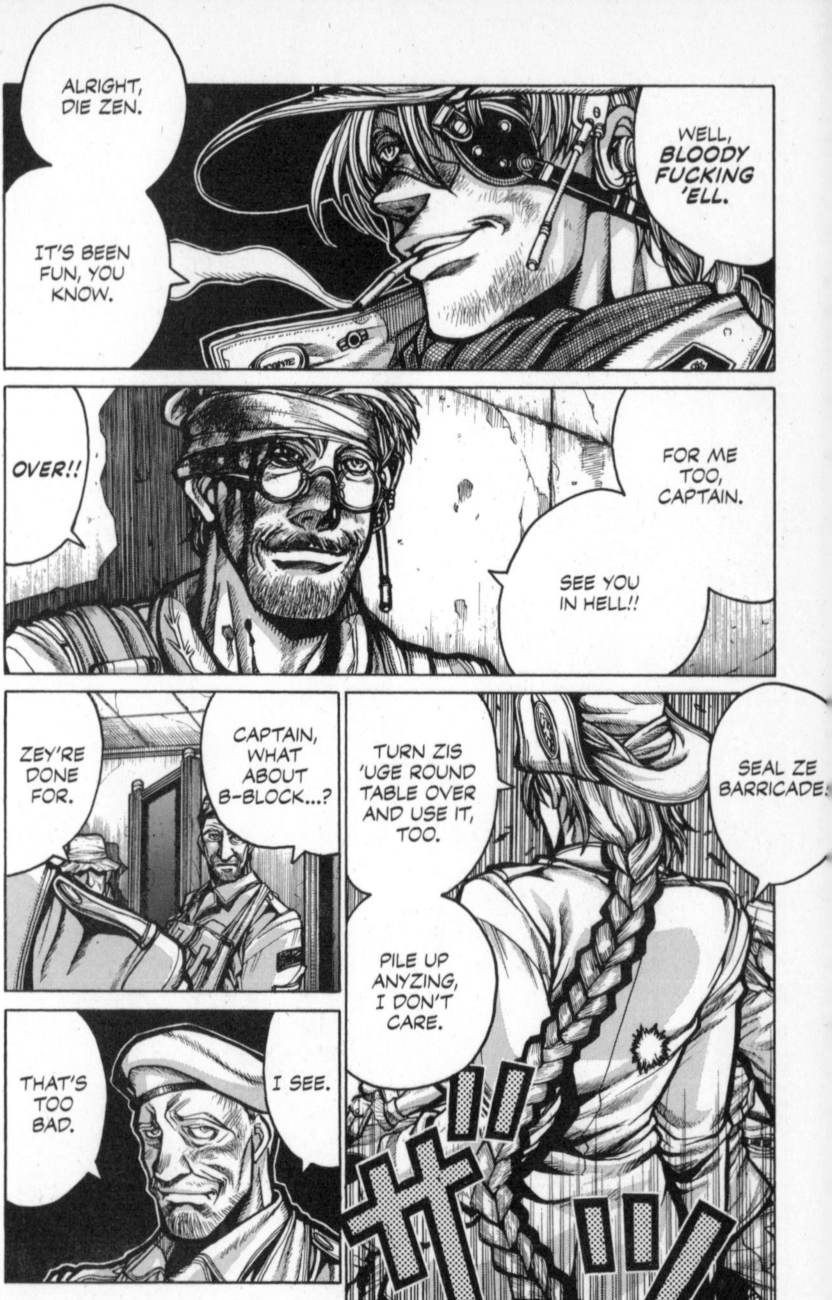
WELL, BLOODY FUCKING 'ELL.
ALRIGHT, DIE ZEN.
IT'S BEEN FUN, YOU KNOW.
FOR ME TOO, CAPTAIN.
SEE YOU IN HELL!!
OVER!!
SEAL ZE BARRICADE.
TURN ZIS 'UGE ROUND TABLE OVER AND USE IT, TOO.
PILE UP ANYZING, I DON'T CARE.
CAPTAIN, WHAT ABOUT B-BLOCK...?
ZEY'RE DONE FOR.
I SEE.
THAT'S TOO BAD.

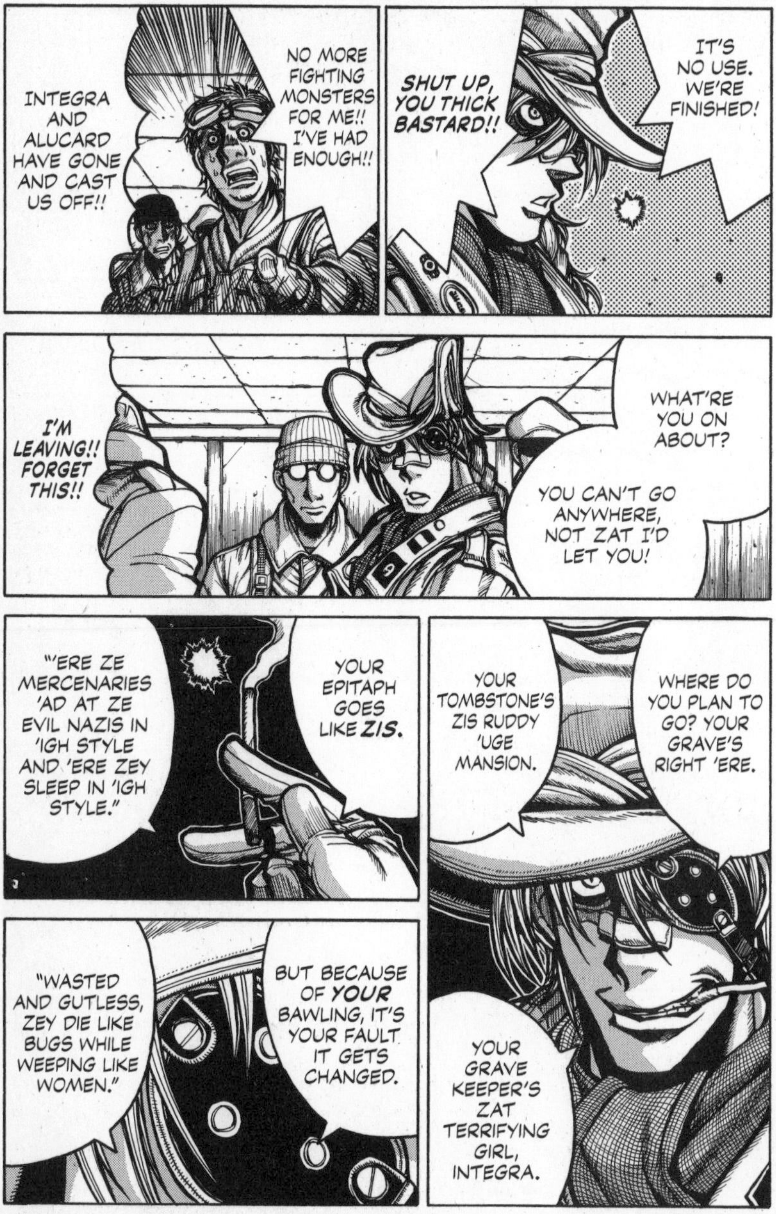
IT'S NO USE. WE'RE FINISHED!
SHUT UP, YOU THICK BASTARD!!
NO MORE FIGHTING MONSTERS FOR ME!! I'VE HAD ENOUGH!!
INTEGRA AND ALUCARD HAVE GONE AND CAST US OFF!!
WHAT'RE YOU ON ABOUT?
YOU CAN'T GO ANYWHERE, NOT ZAT I'D LET YOU!
I'M LEAVING!! FORGET THIS!!
WHERE DO YOU PLAN TO GO? YOUR GRAVE'S RIGHT 'ERE.
YOUR TOMBSTONE'S ZIS RUDDY 'UGE MANSION.
YOUR GRAVE KEEPER'S ZAT TERRIFYING GIRL, INTEGRA.
YOUR EPITAPH GOES LIKE ZIS.
"'ERE ZE MERCENARIES 'AD AT ZE EVIL NAZIS IN 'IGH STYLE AND 'ERE ZEY SLEEP IN 'IGH STYLE."
BUT BECAUSE OF YOUR BAWLING, IT'S YOUR FAULT IT GETS CHANGED.
"WASTED AND GUTLESS, ZEY DIE LIKE BUGS WHILE WEEPING LIKE WOMEN."

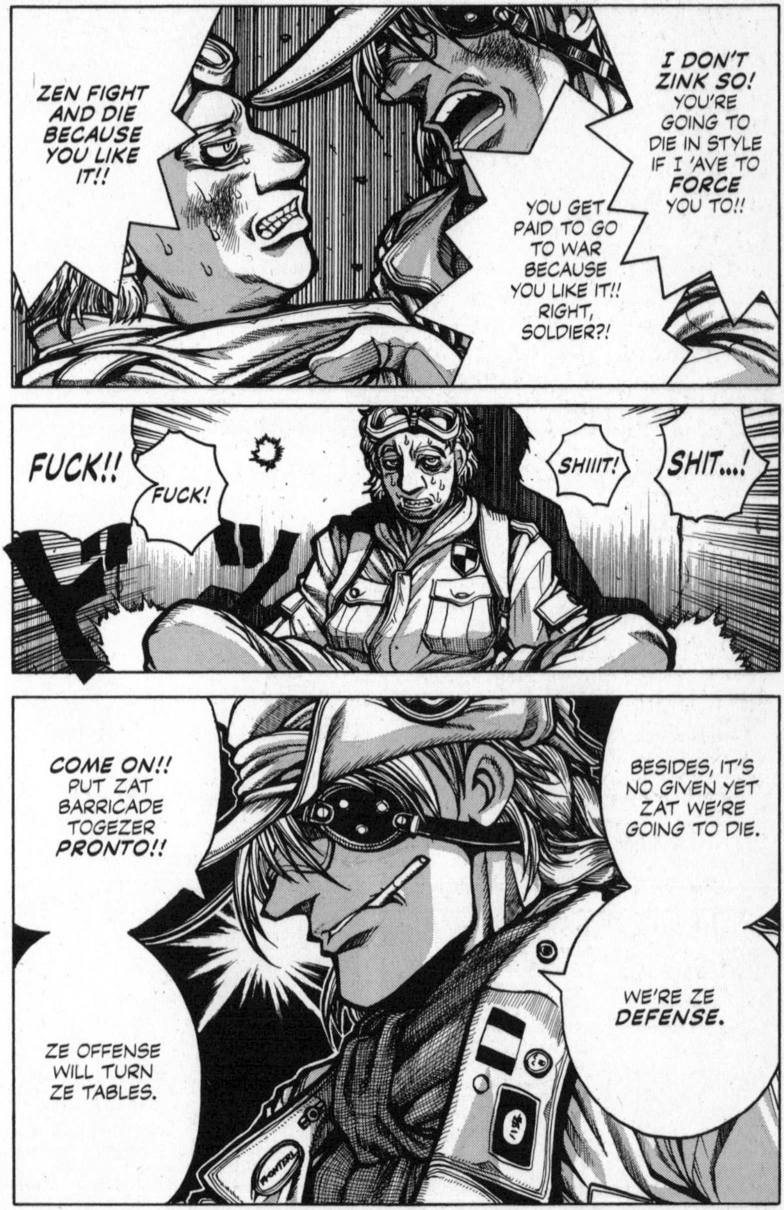
I DON'T ZINK SO! YOU'RE GOING TO DIE IN STYLE IF I 'AVE TO FORCE YOU TO!!
YOU GET PAID TO GO TO WAR BECAUSE YOU LIKE IT!! RIGHT, SOLDIER?!
ZEN FIGHT AND DIE BECAUSE YOU LIKE IT!!
SHIT...!
SHIIIT!
FUCK!
FUCK!!
BESIDES, IT'S NO GIVEN YET ZAT WE'RE GOING TO DIE.
COME ON!! PUT ZAT BARRICADE TOGEZER PRONTO!!
WE'RE ZE DEFENSE.
ZE OFFENSE WILL TURN ZE TABLES.

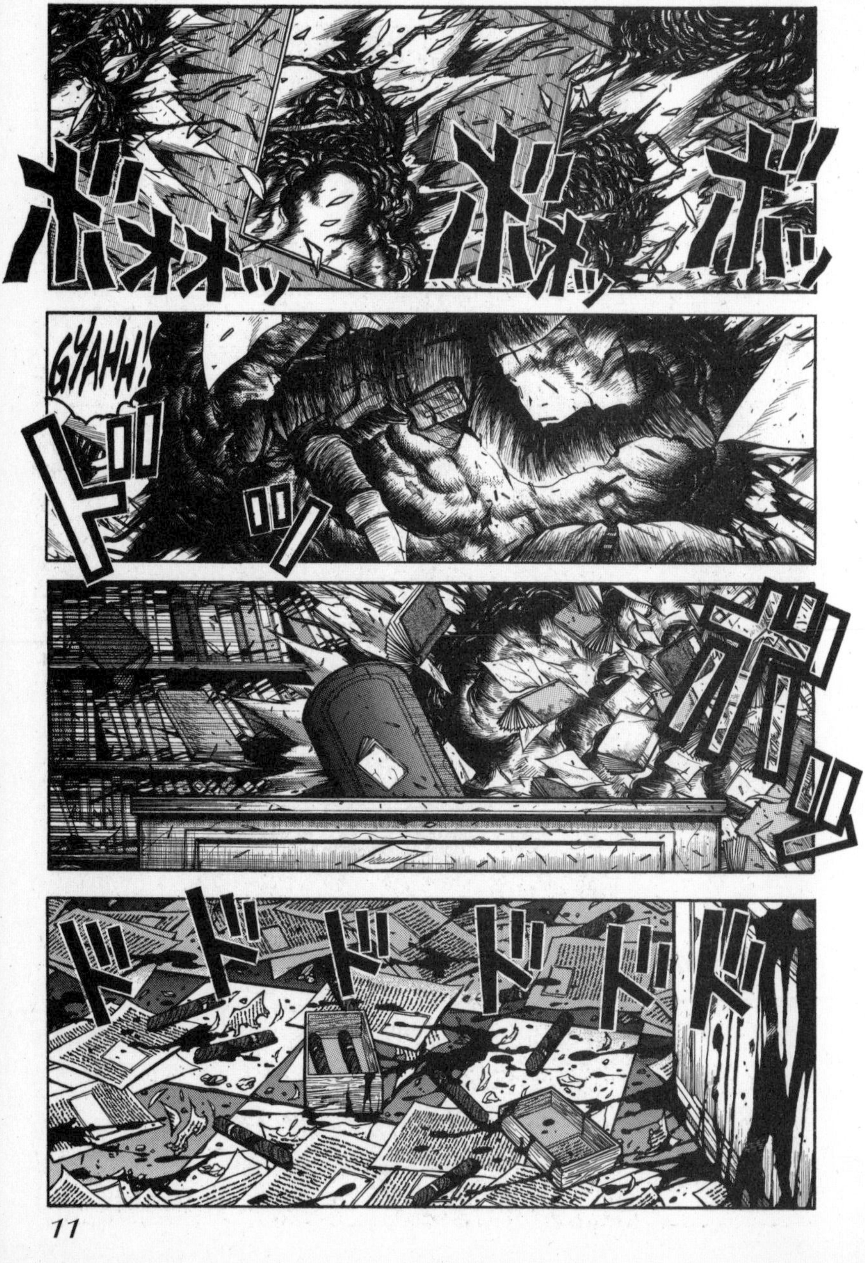
ボッ
ボォッ
ボォオオッ
GYAHH!
ドドッ
ボッ
ドドドドド

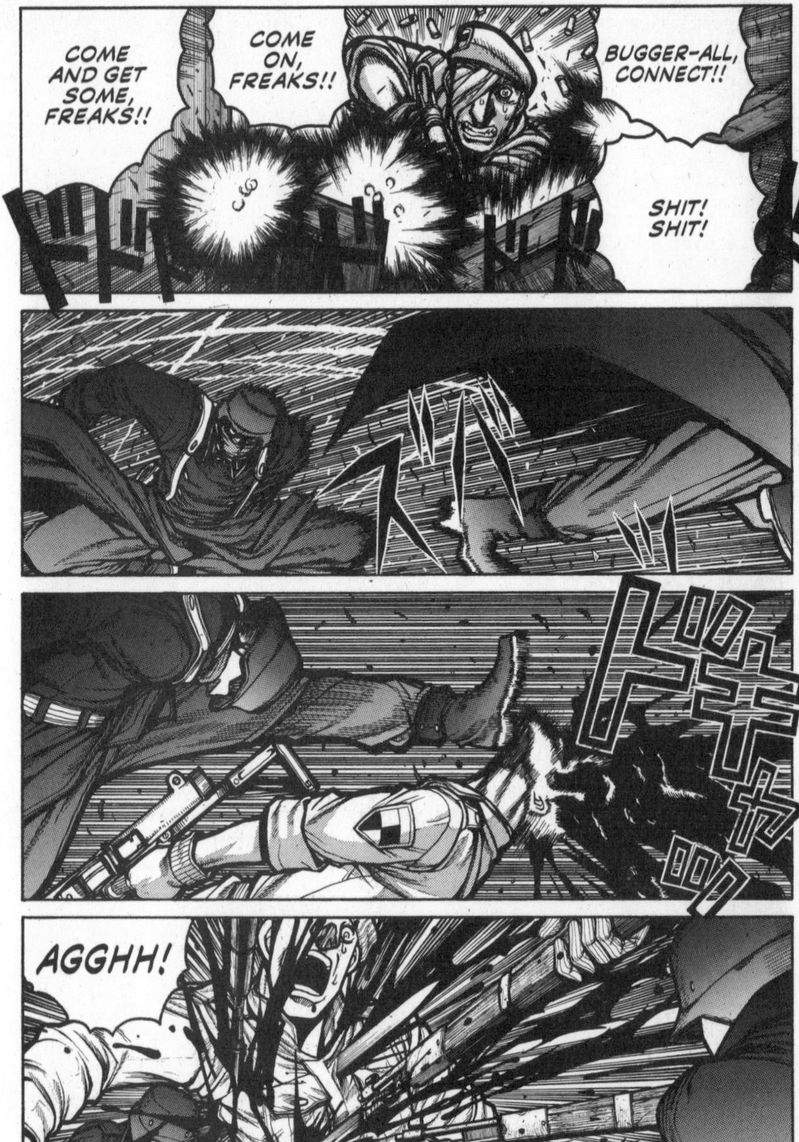
BUGGER-ALL, CONNECT!!
SHIT! SHIT!
COME ON, FREAKS!!
COME AND GET SOME, FREAKS!!
AGGHH!

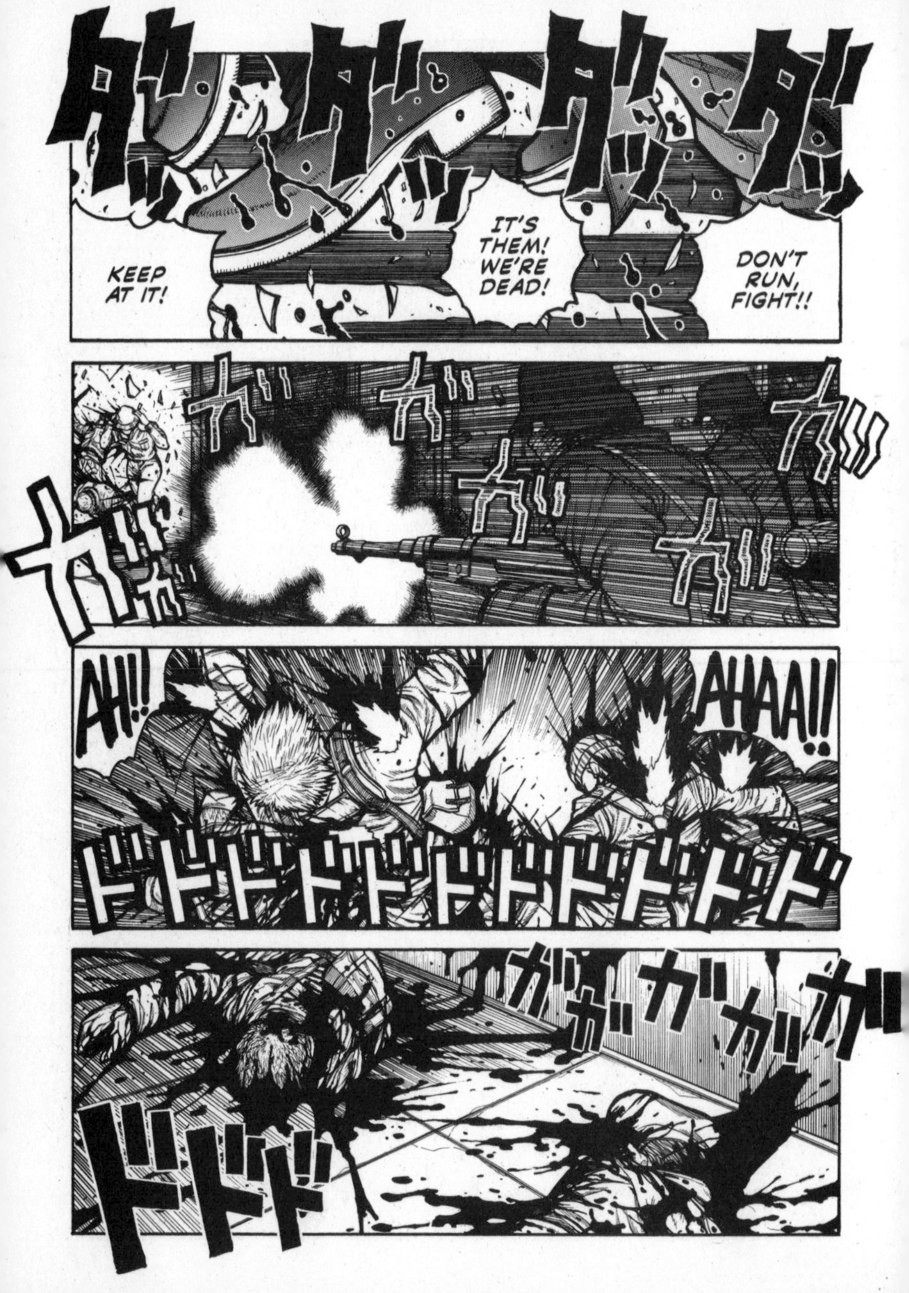

DON'T RUN, FIGHT!!
IT'S THEM! WE'RE DEAD!
KEEP AT IT!
AHAA!!
AH!!

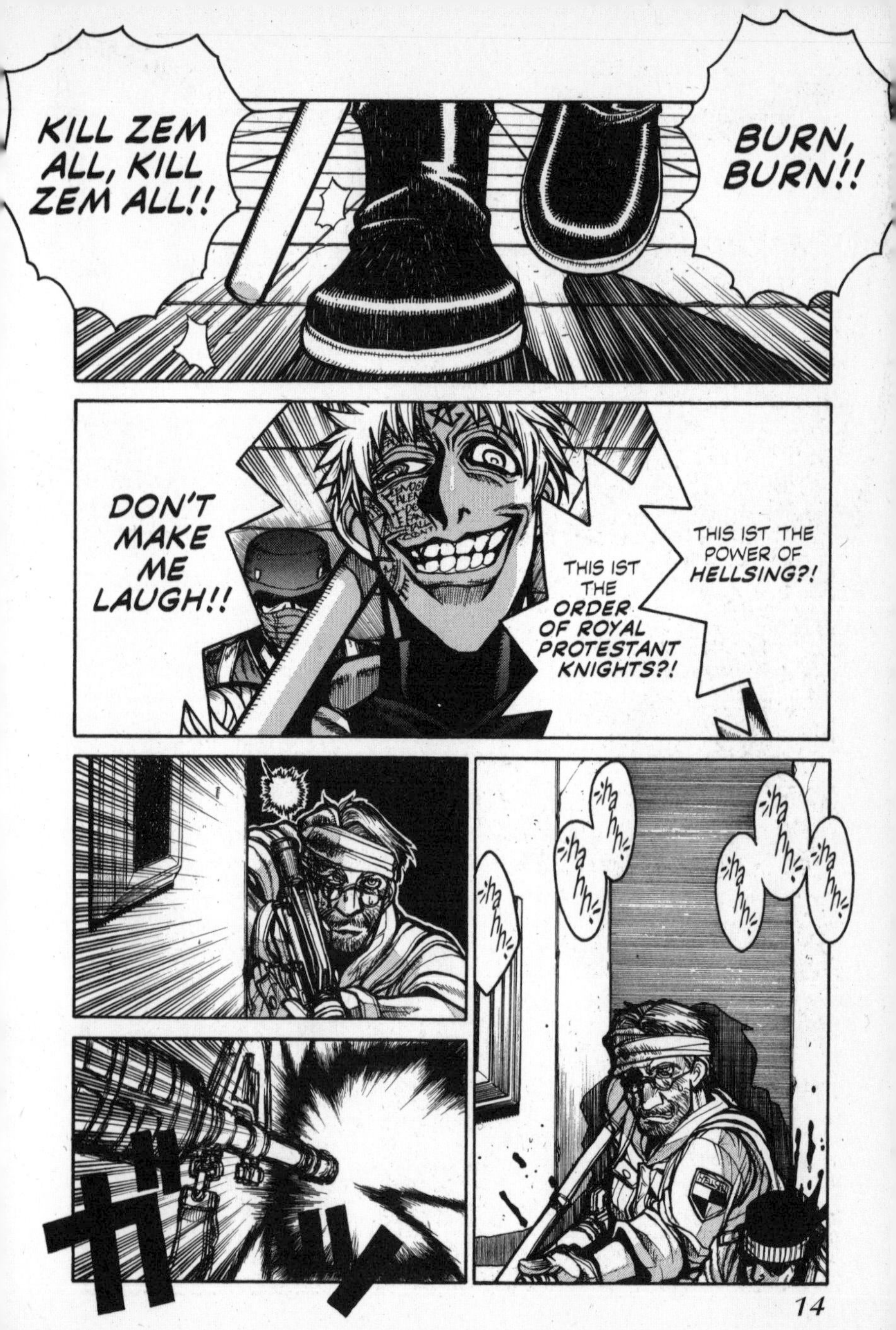

BURN, BURN!!
KILL ZEM ALL, KILL ZEM ALL!!
THIS IST THE POWER OF HELLSING?!
THIS IST THE ORDER OF ROYAL PROTESTANT KNIGHTS?!
DON'T MAKE ME LAUGH!!
hahh
hahh
hahh
hahh
hahh
hahh

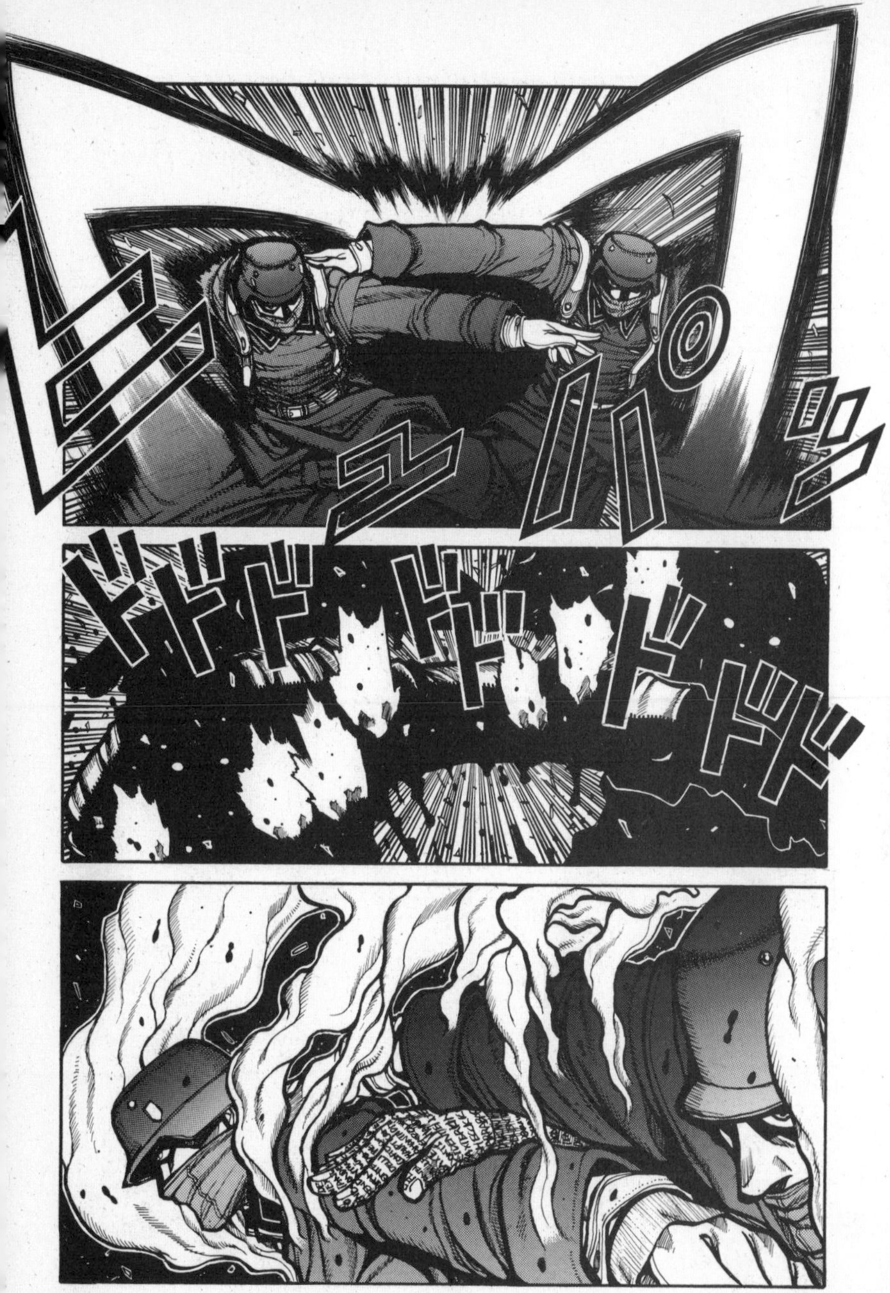

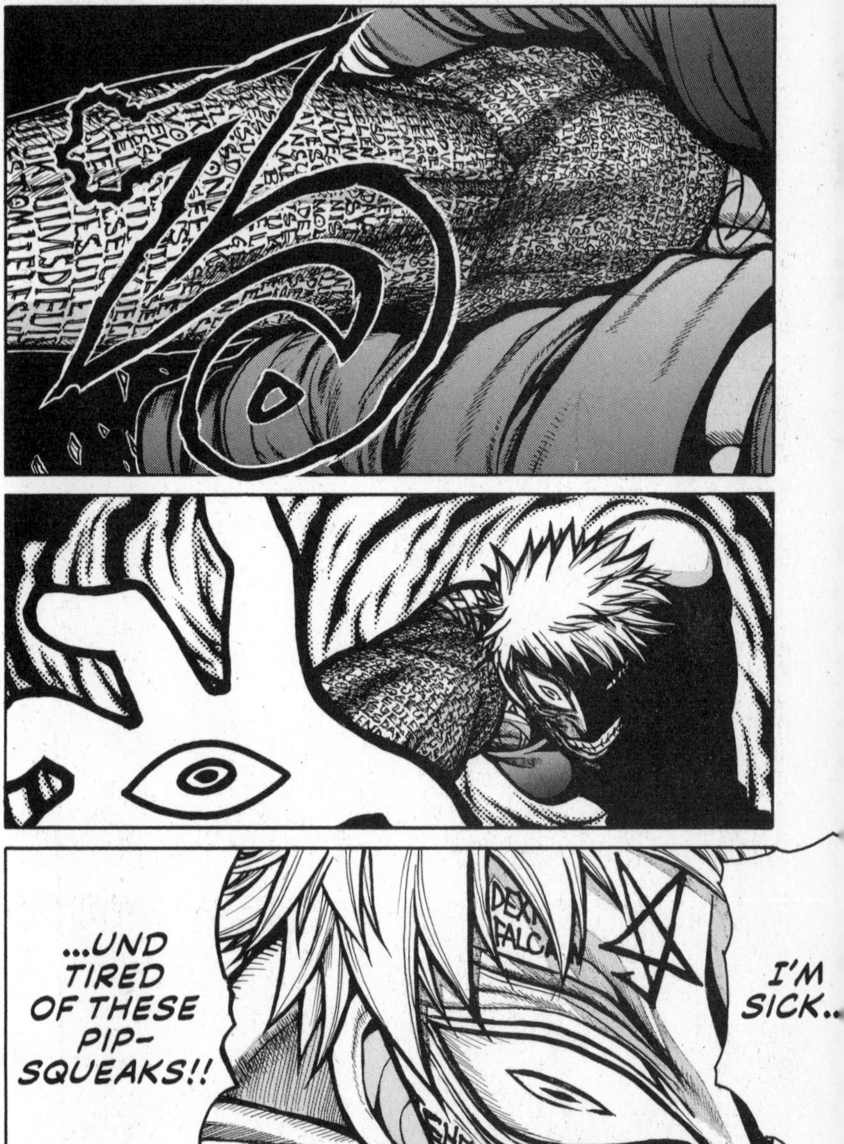
I'M SICK...
...UND TIRED OF THESE PIP-SQUEAKS!!

ズズズ
ズズズッ
ズアアアアア

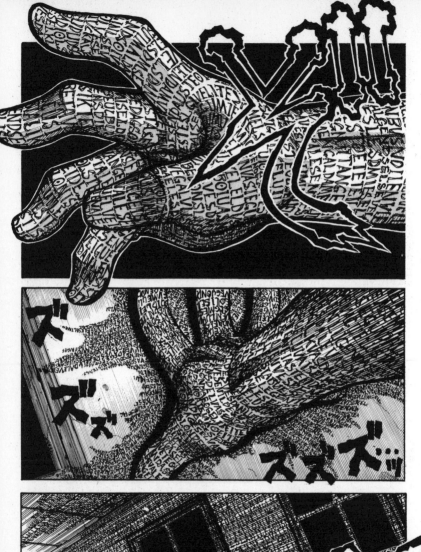

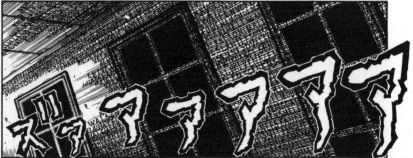

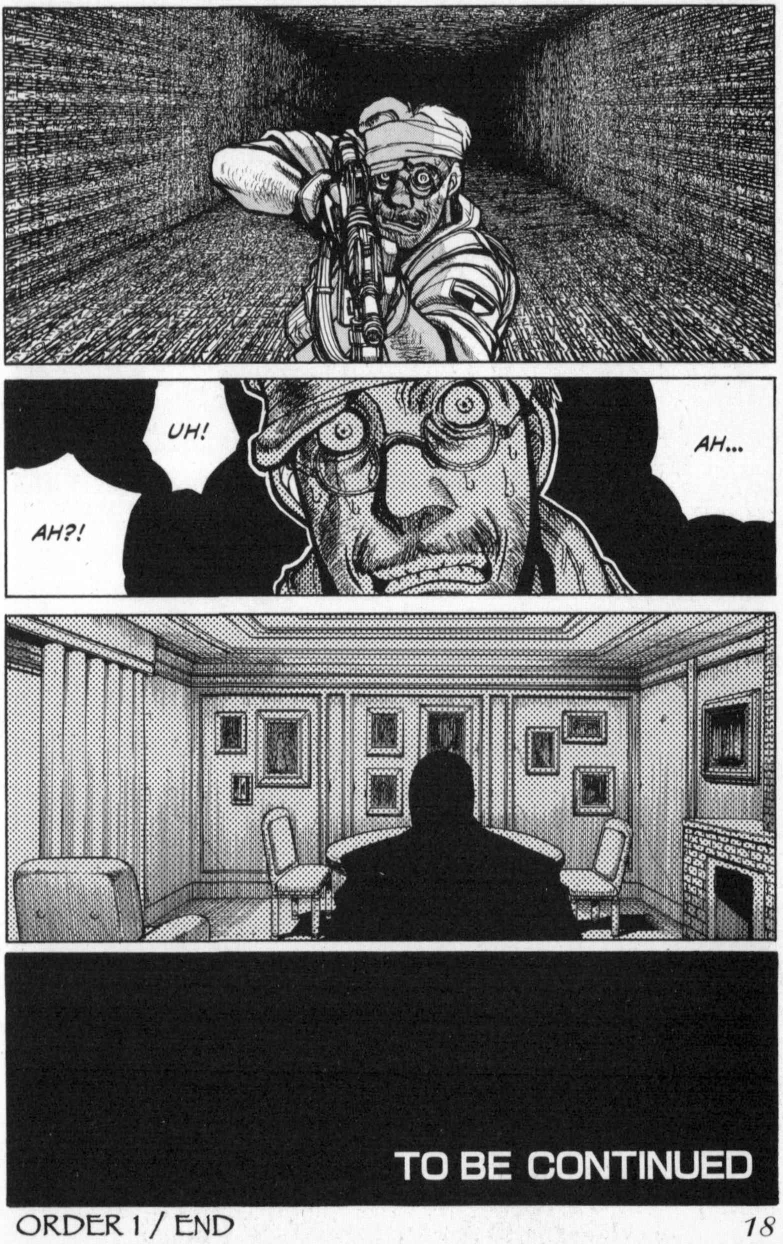
AH...
UH!
AH?!
TO BE CONTINUED

ORDER 1 / END

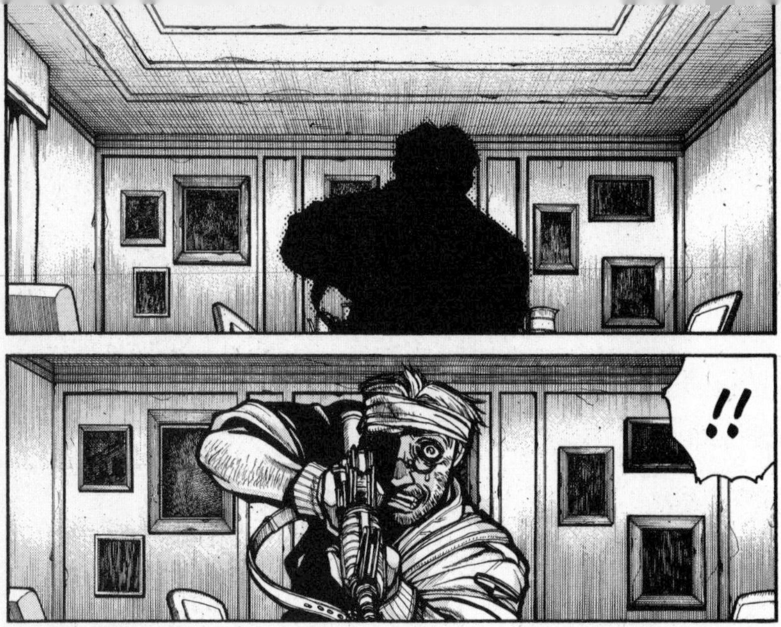
!!

⚜ORDER 2

SOLDIER OF FORTUNE⑤

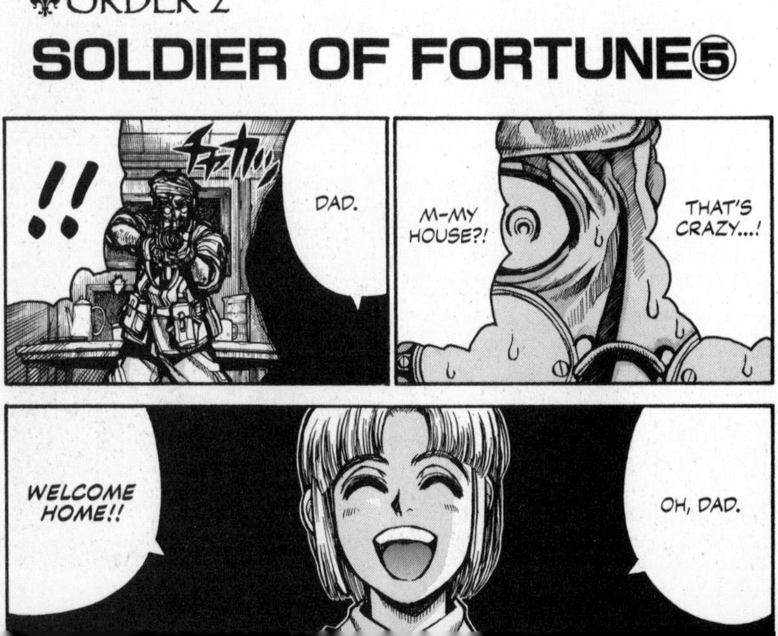
THAT'S CRAZY...!
M-MY HOUSE?!
DAD.
!!
OH, DAD.
WELCOME HOME!!

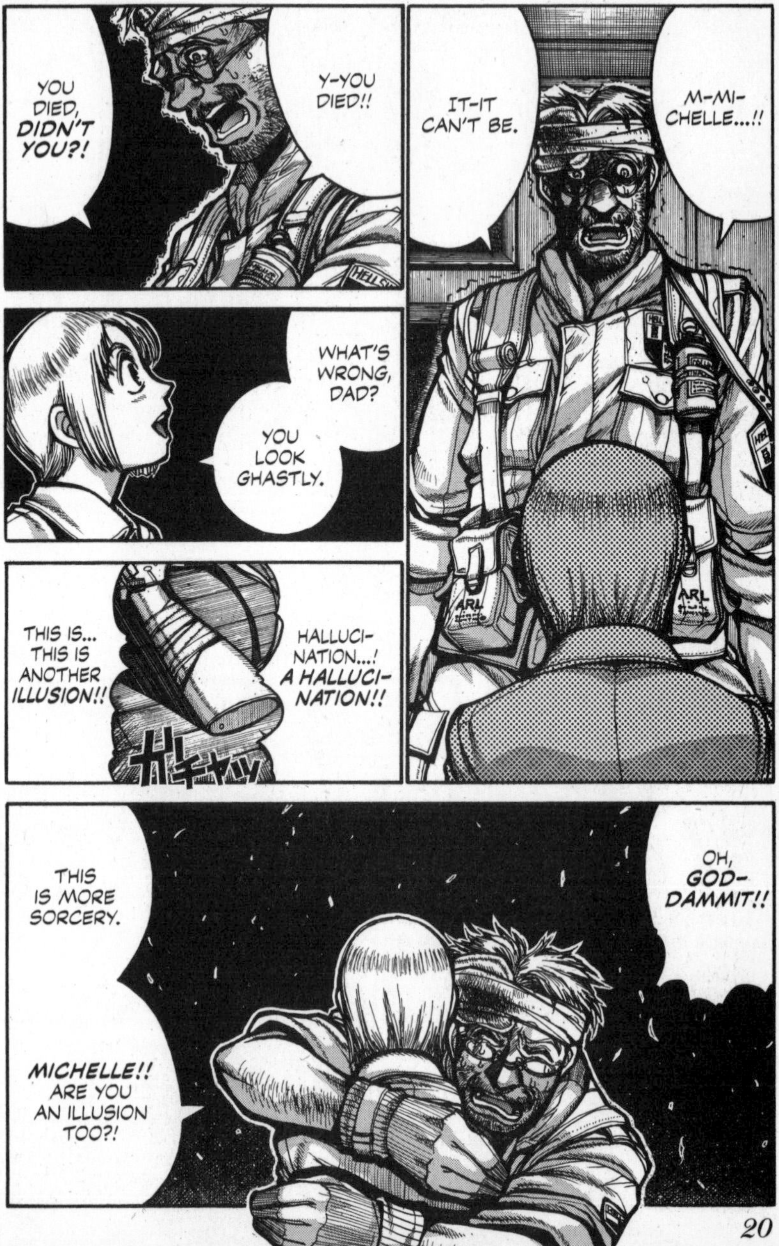
M-MI-CHELLE...!!
IT-IT CAN'T BE.
Y-YOU DIED!!
YOU DIED, DIDN'T YOU?!
WHAT'S WRONG, DAD?
YOU LOOK GHASTLY.
HALLUCI-NATION...! A HALLUCI-NATION!!
THIS IS... THIS IS ANOTHER ILLUSION!!
ガチャッ
OH, GOD-DAMMIT!!
THIS IS MORE SORCERY.
MICHELLE!! ARE YOU AN ILLUSION TOO?!

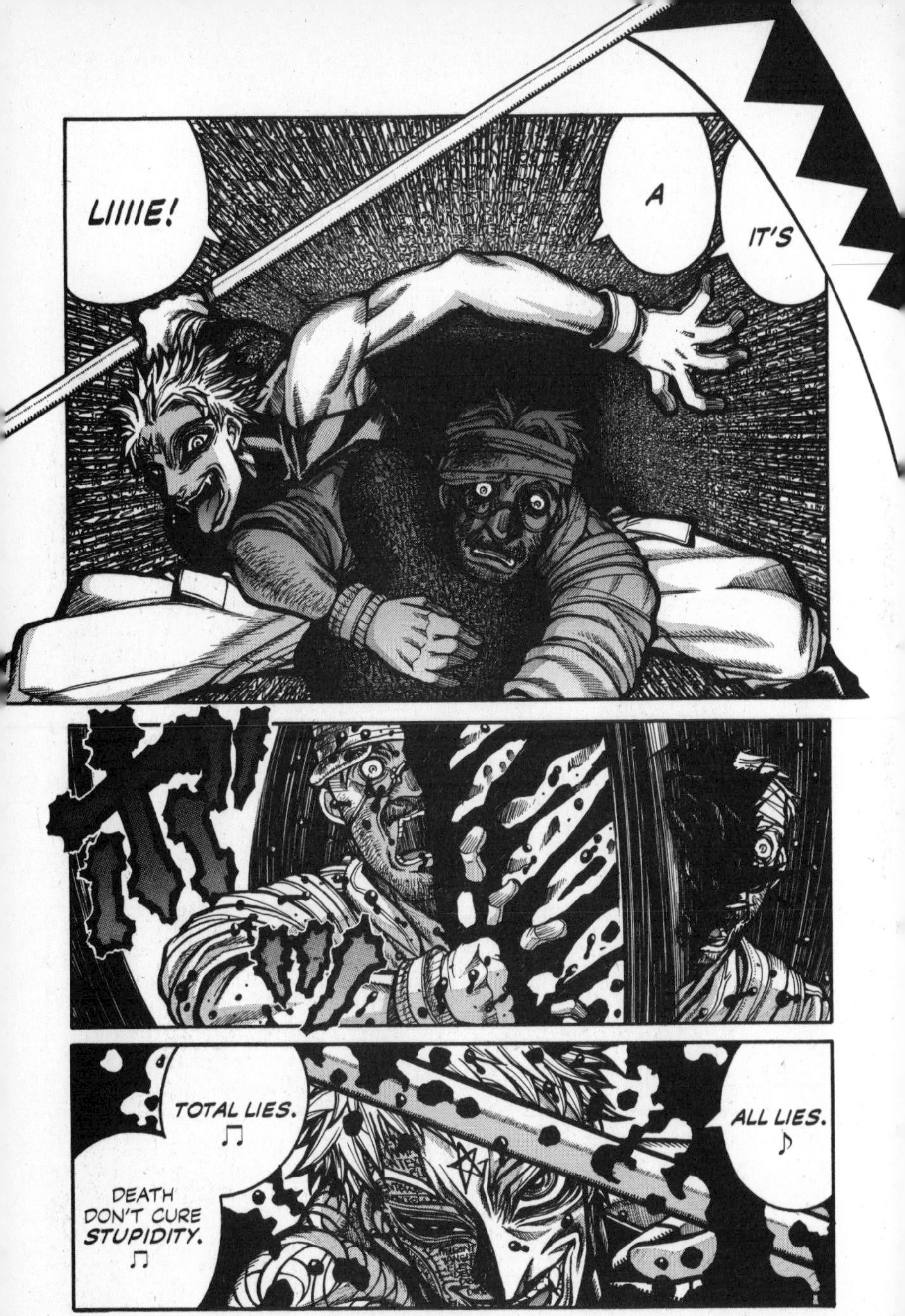
IT'S
A
LIIIIE!
ALL LIES. ♪
TOTAL LIES. ♫
DEATH DON'T CURE STUPIDITY. ♫

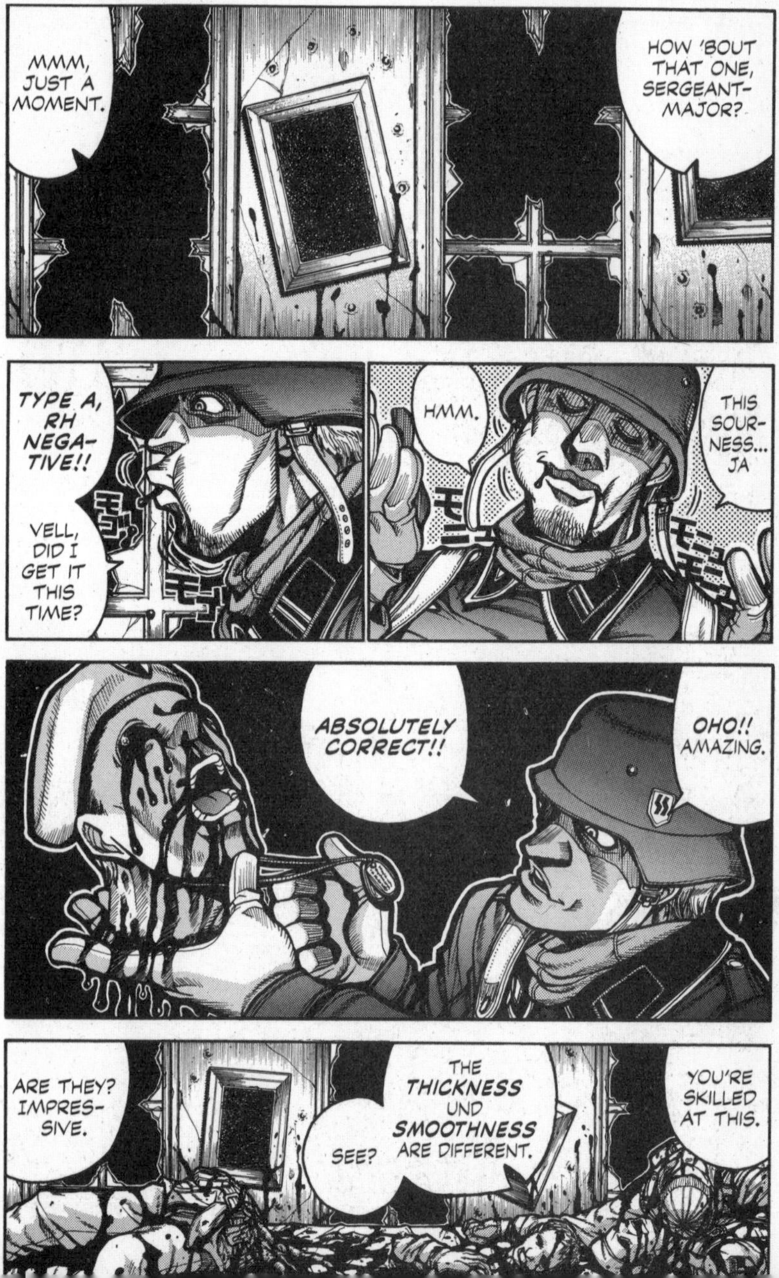
HOW 'BOUT THAT ONE, SERGEANT-MAJOR?
MMM, JUST A MOMENT.
THIS SOURNESS... JA
HMM.
TYPE A, RH NEGATIVE!!
VELL, DID I GET IT THIS TIME?
OHO!! AMAZING.
ABSOLUTELY CORRECT!!
YOU'RE SKILLED AT THIS.
THE THICKNESS UND SMOOTHNESS ARE DIFFERENT.
SEE?
ARE THEY? IMPRESSIVE.

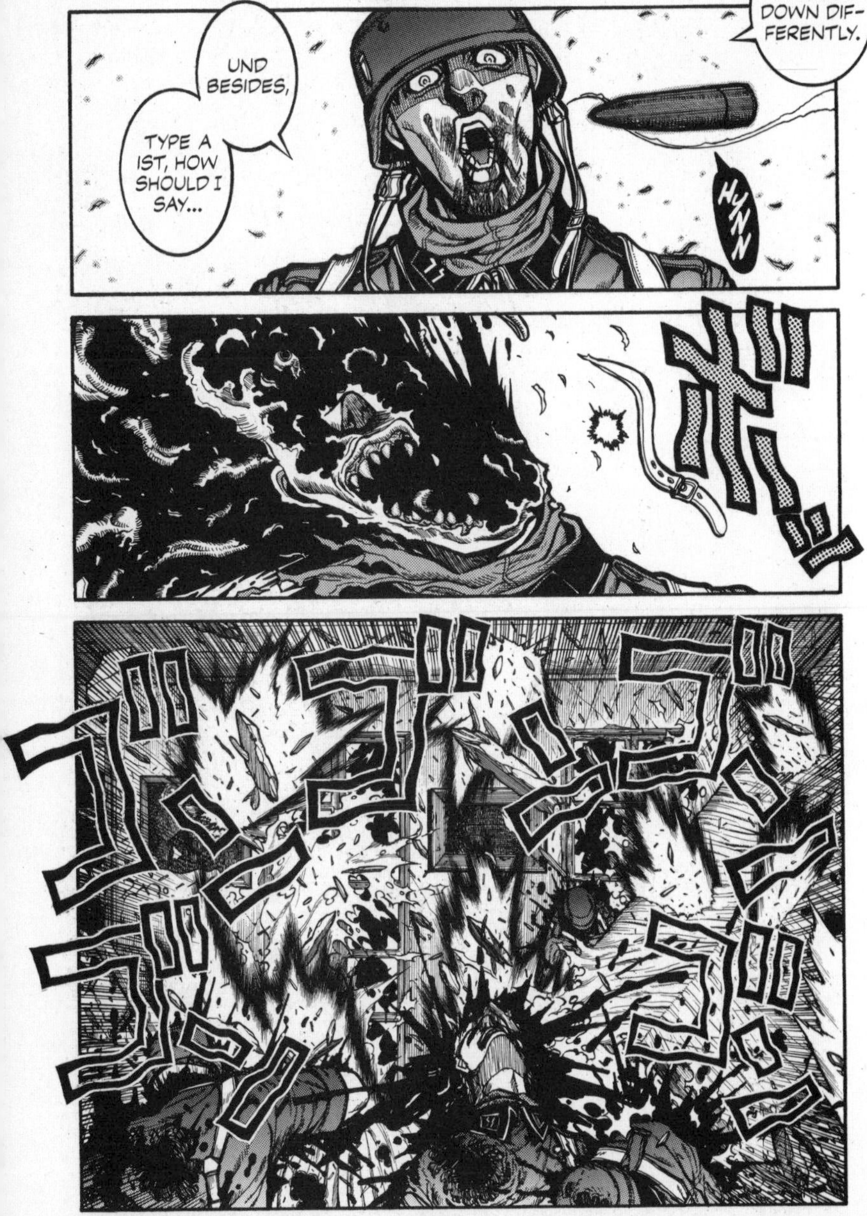
IT GOES DOWN DIF-FERENTLY.
UND BESIDES,
TYPE A IST, HOW SHOULD I SAY...
HUNN

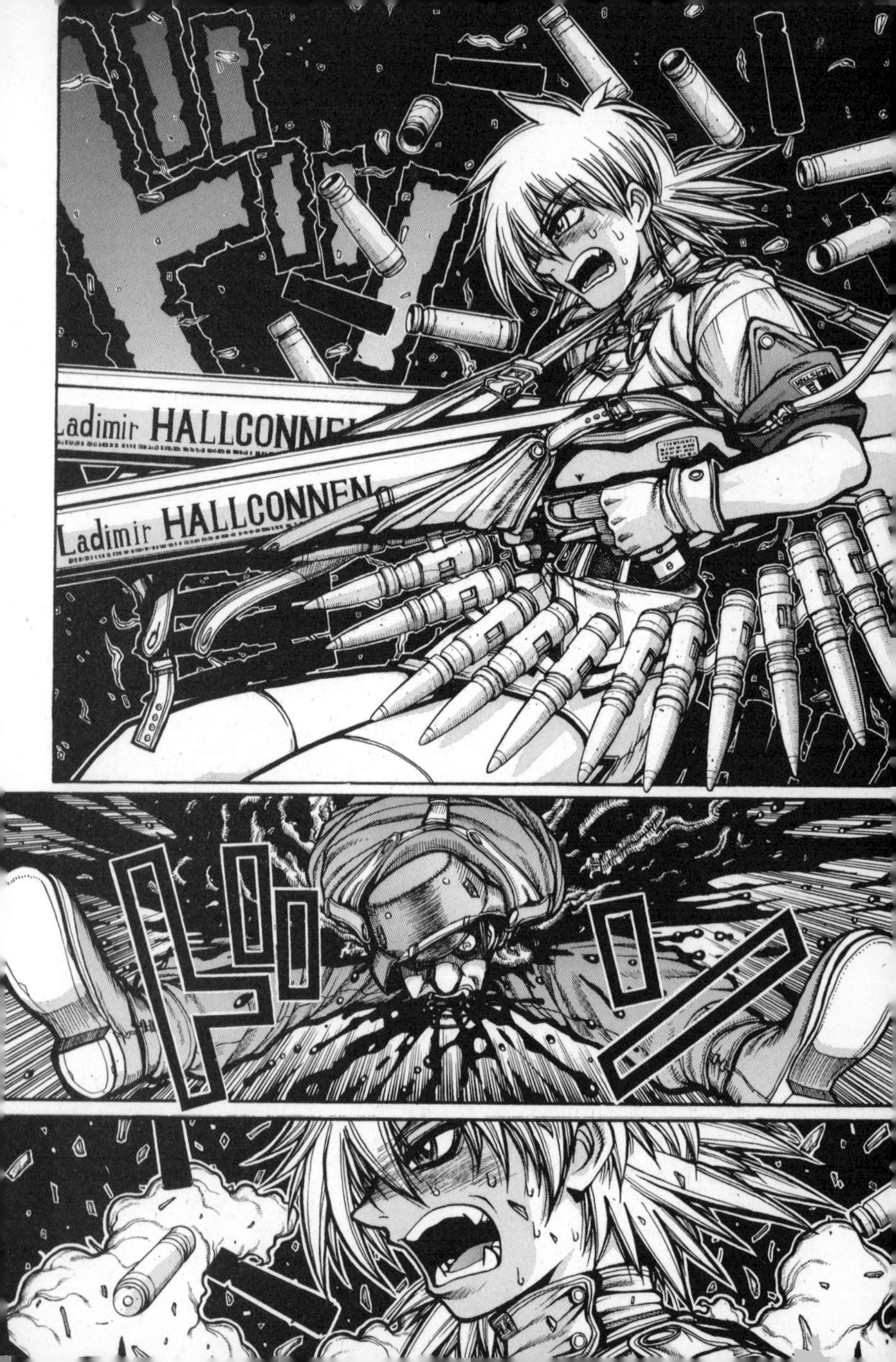
Ladimir HALLCONNE
Ladimir HALLCONNEN

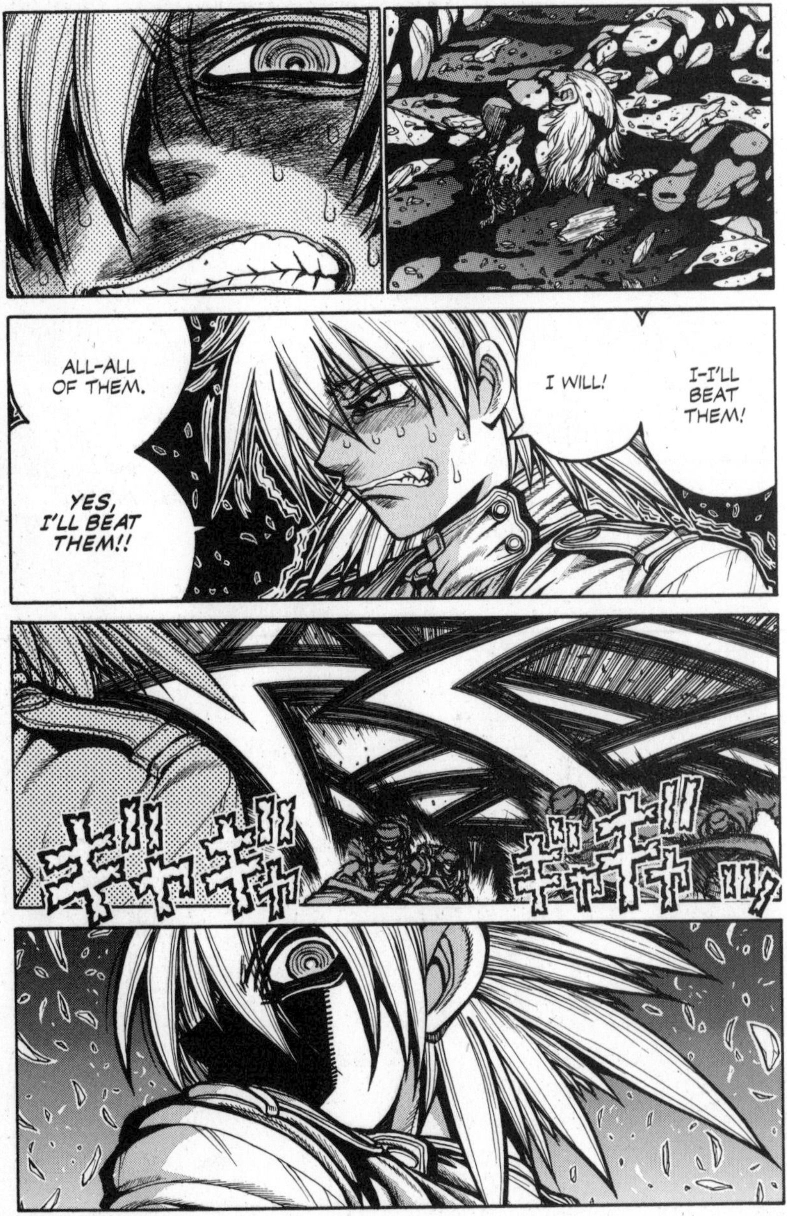
I-I'LL BEAT THEM!
I WILL!
ALL-ALL OF THEM.
YES, I'LL BEAT THEM!!

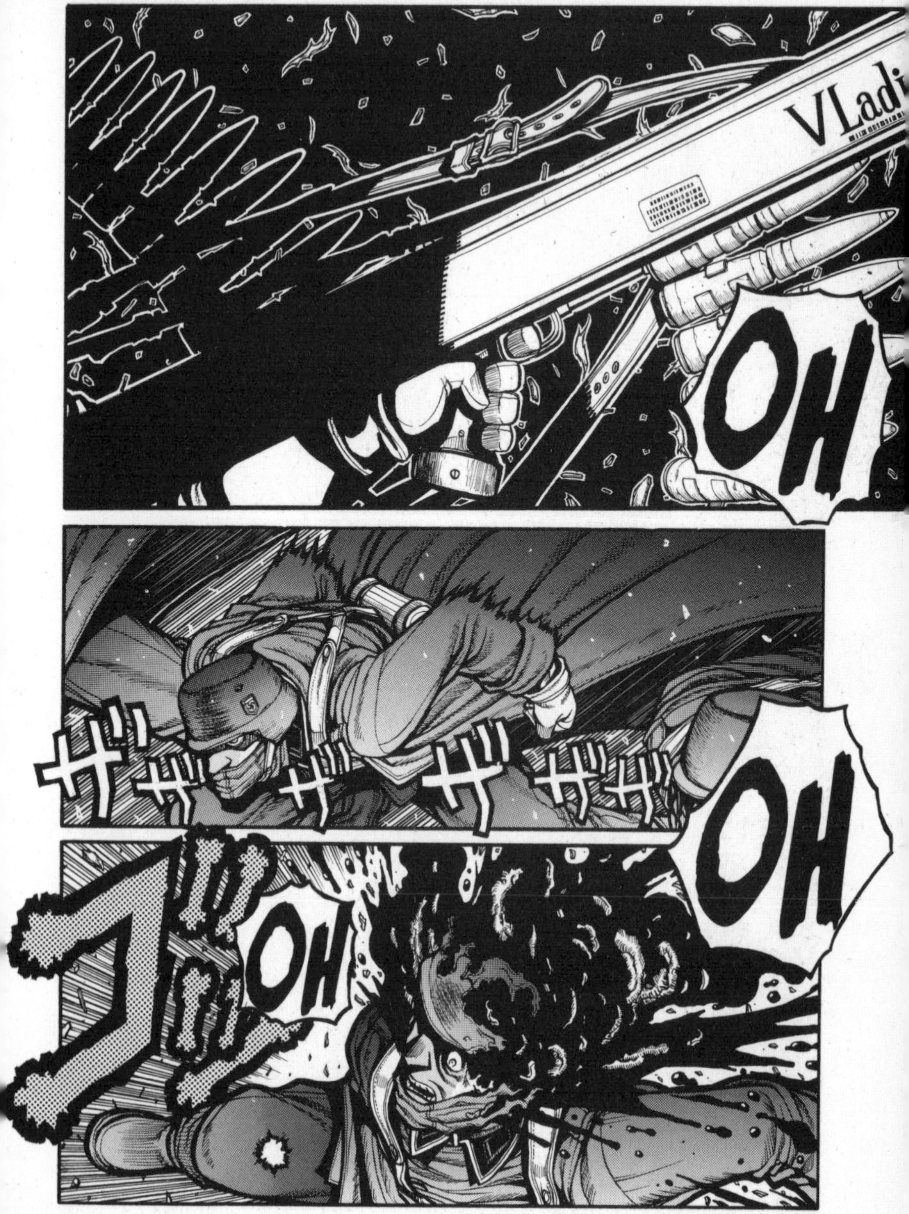
VLadi
OH
ギギギギギギ
OH
OH

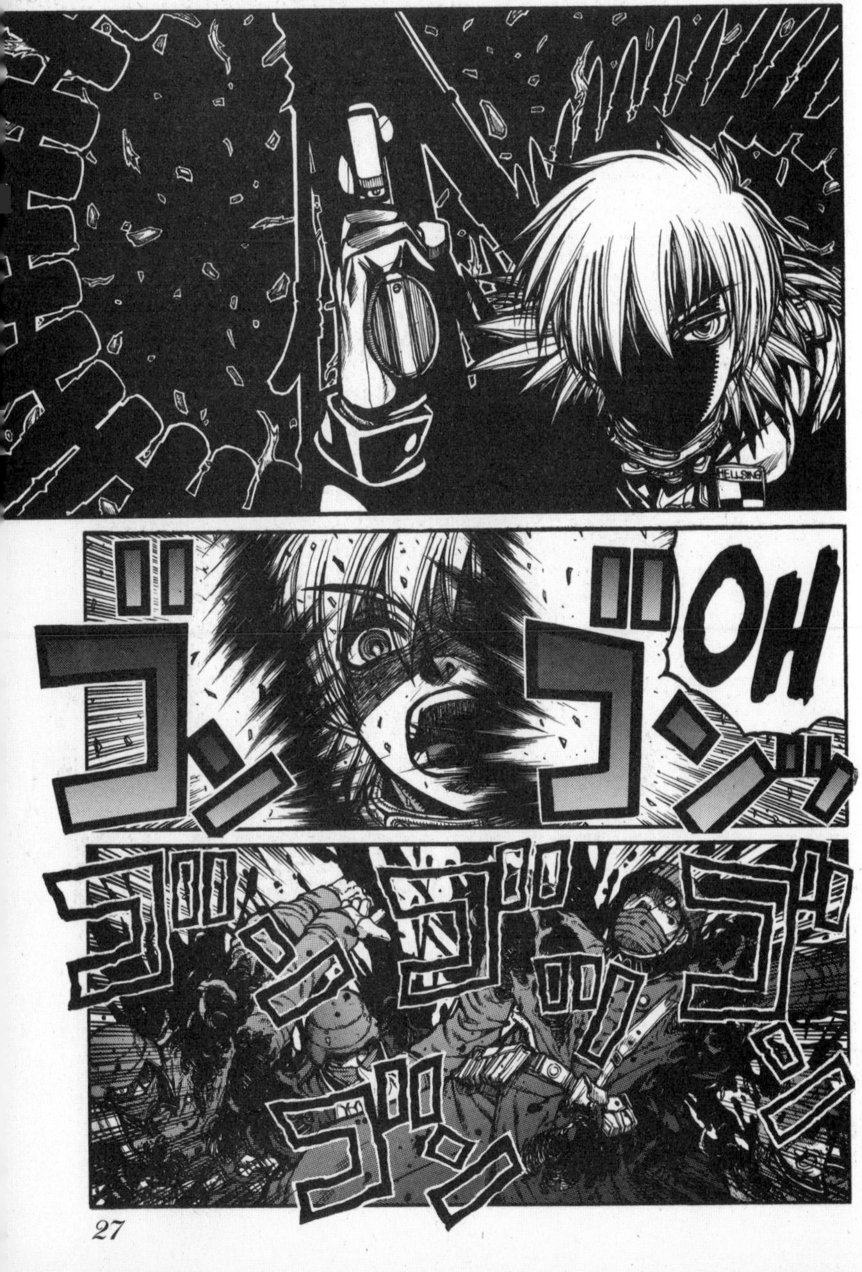
OH

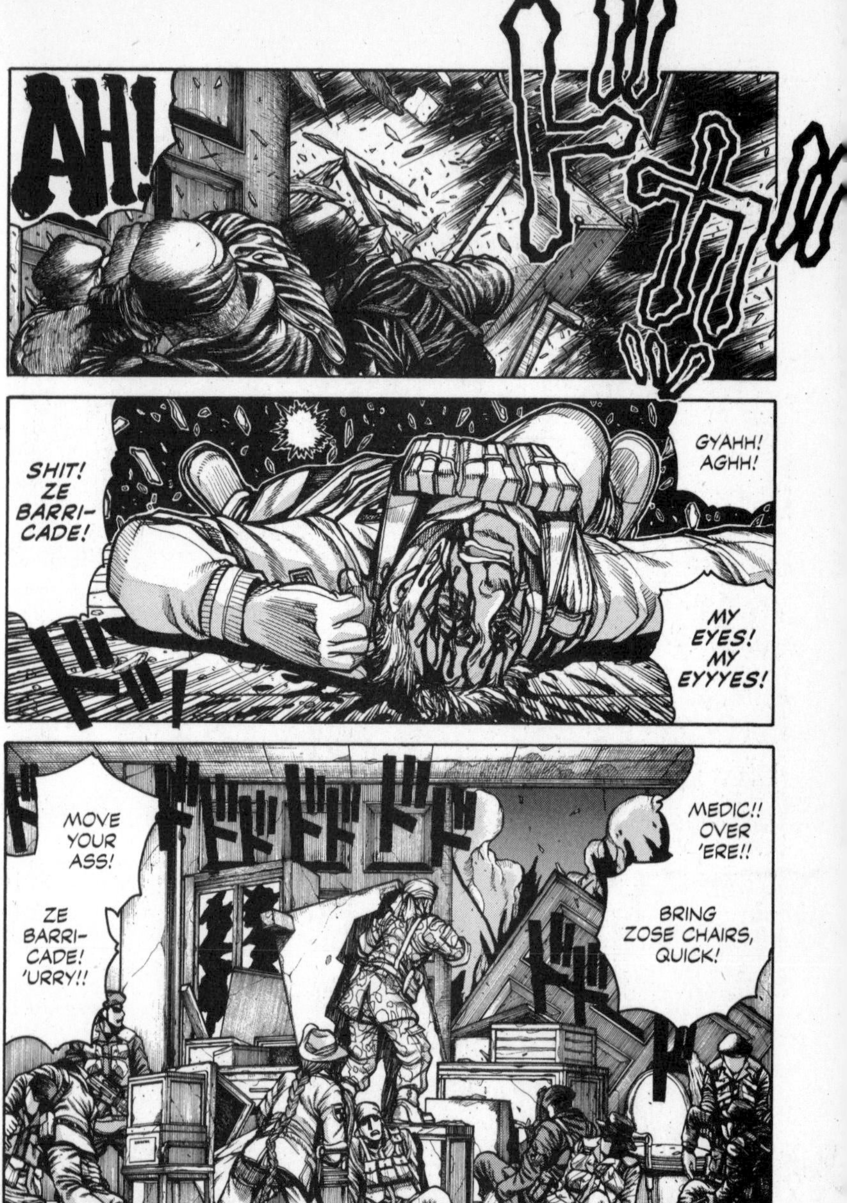
AH!
GYAHH! AGHH!
MY EYES! MY EYYYES!
SHIT! ZE BARRI-CADE!
MEDIC!! OVER 'ERE!!
BRING ZOSE CHAIRS, QUICK!
MOVE YOUR ASS!
ZE BARRI-CADE! 'URRY!!

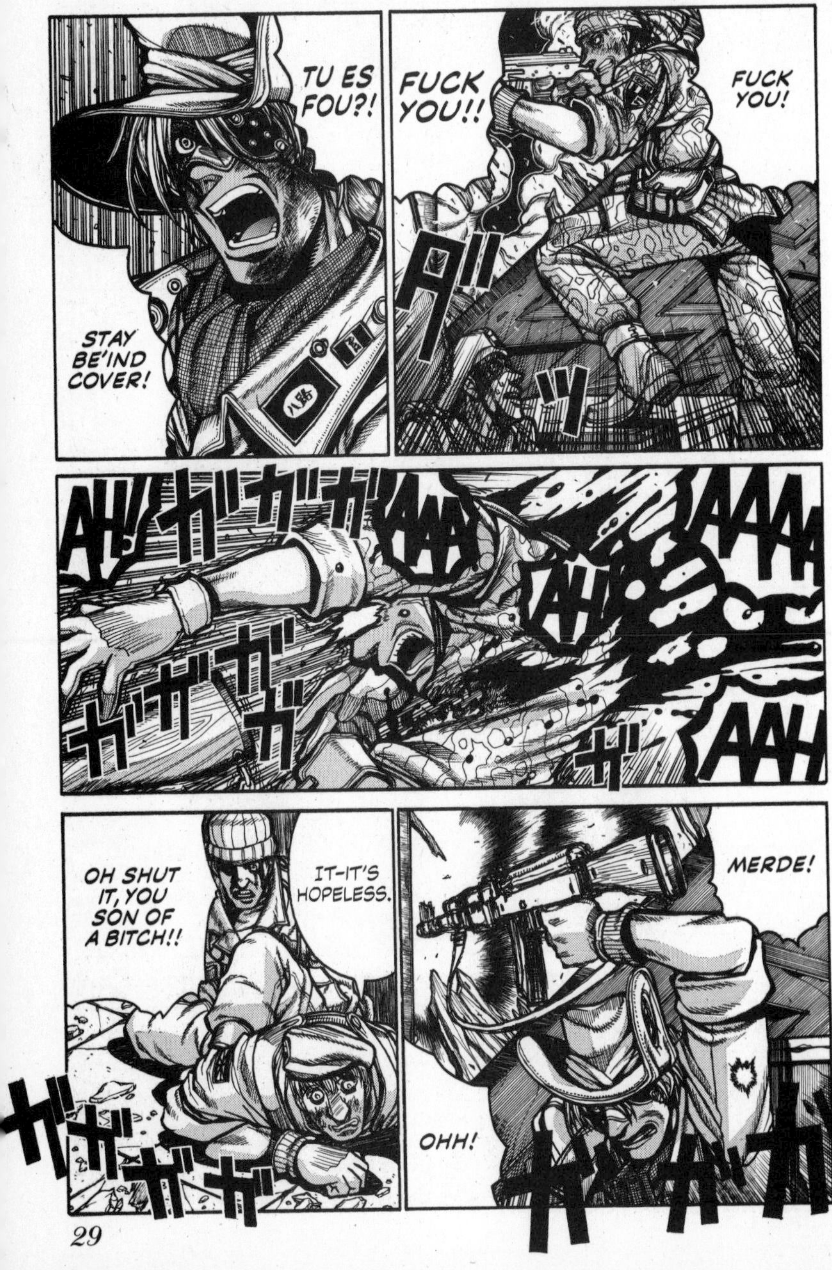
FUCK YOU!
FUCK YOU!!
TU ES FOU?!
STAY BE'IND COVER!
AAAA
AH
AAH
AAA
AH!!
MERDE!
OHH!
IT-IT'S HOPELESS.
OH SHUT IT, YOU SON OF A BITCH!!

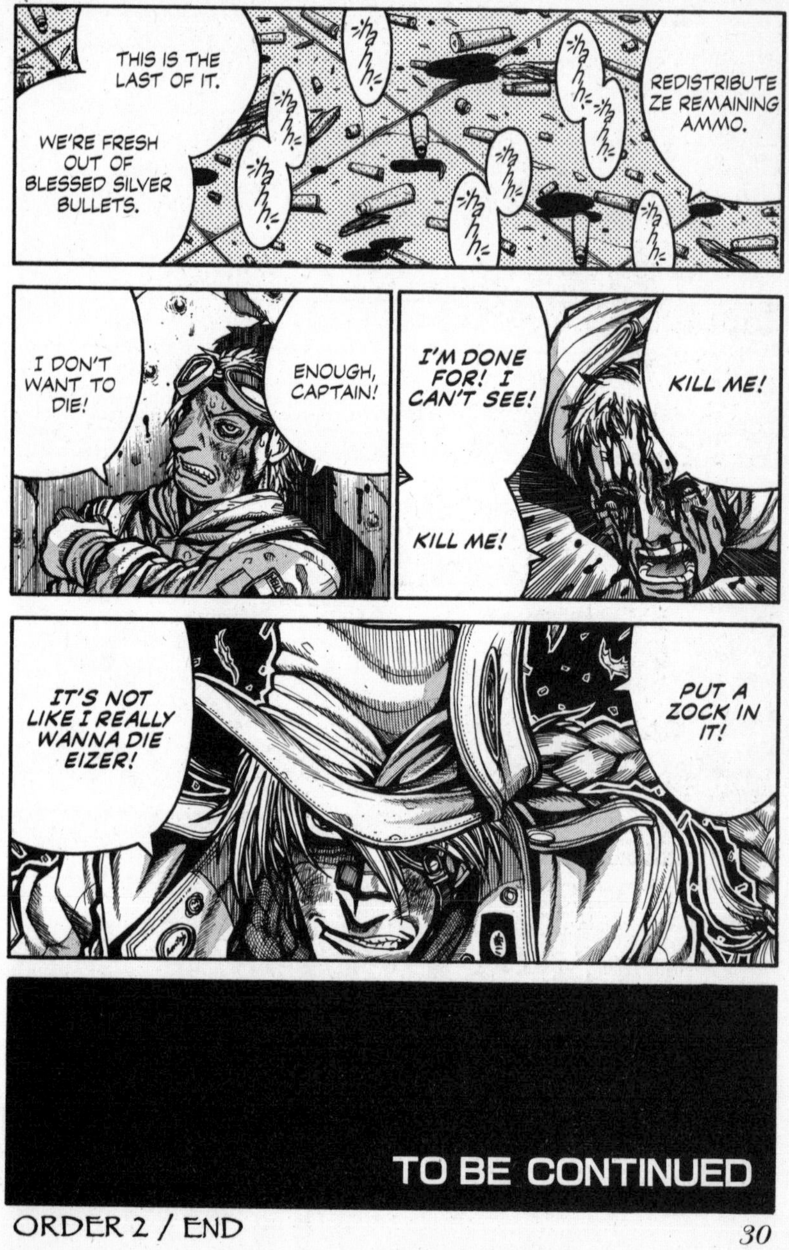
REDISTRIBUTE ZE REMAINING AMMO.
THIS IS THE LAST OF IT.
WE'RE FRESH OUT OF BLESSED SILVER BULLETS.
KILL ME!
I'M DONE FOR! I CAN'T SEE!
KILL ME!
ENOUGH, CAPTAIN!
I DON'T WANT TO DIE!
PUT A ZOCK IN IT!
IT'S NOT LIKE I REALLY WANNA DIE EIZER!

TO BE CONTINUED

ORDER 2 / END

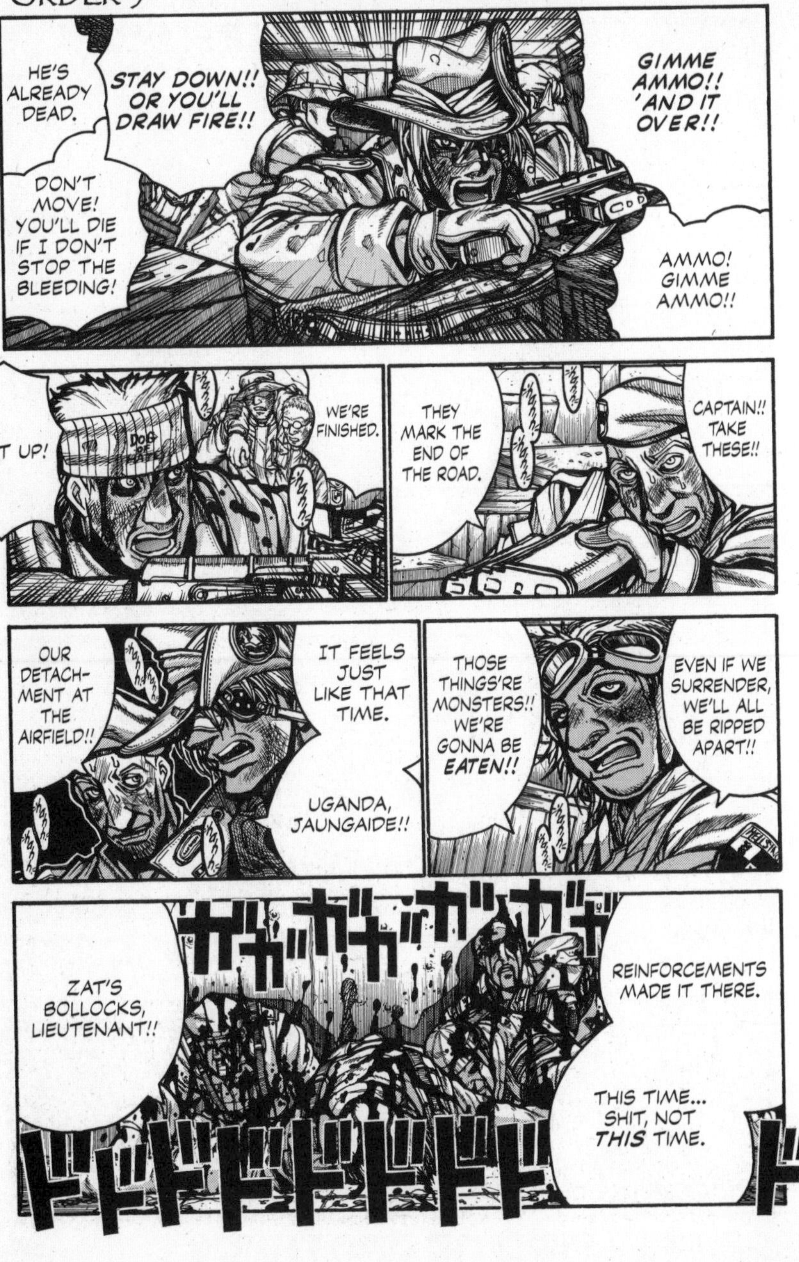
GIMME AMMO!! 'AND IT OVER!!
AMMO! GIMME AMMO!!
STAY DOWN!! OR YOU'LL DRAW FIRE!!
HE'S ALREADY DEAD.
DON'T MOVE! YOU'LL DIE IF I DON'T STOP THE BLEEDING!
CAPTAIN!! TAKE THESE!!
THEY MARK THE END OF THE ROAD.
WE'RE FINISHED.
SHUT UP!
EVEN IF WE SURRENDER, WE'LL ALL BE RIPPED APART!!
THOSE THINGS'RE MONSTERS!! WE'RE GONNA BE EATEN!!
IT FEELS JUST LIKE THAT TIME.
UGANDA, JAUNGAIDE!!
OUR DETACHMENT AT THE AIRFIELD!!
REINFORCEMENTS MADE IT THERE.
THIS TIME... SHIT, NOT THIS TIME.
ZAT'S BOLLOCKS, LIEUTENANT!!

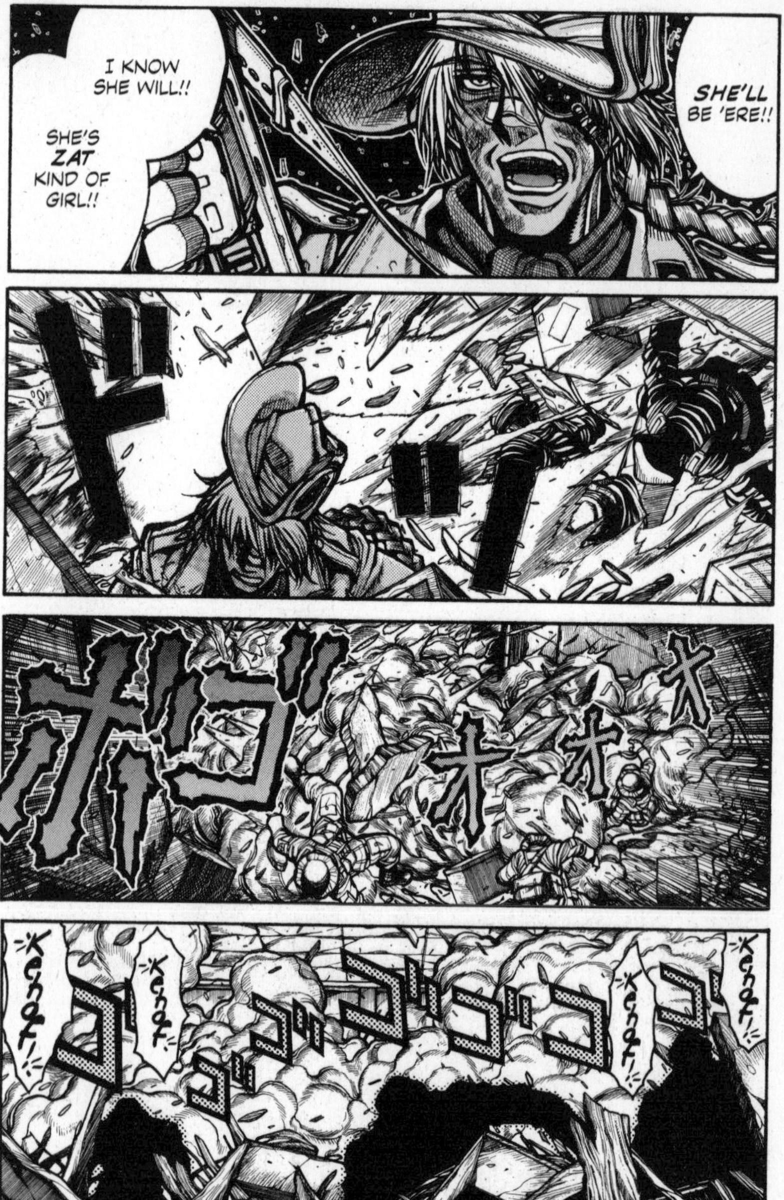
SHE'LL BE 'ERE!!
I KNOW SHE WILL!!
SHE'S ZAT KIND OF GIRL!!
Kenof!!
Kenof!!
Kenof
Kenof!!

ORDER 3 **SOLDIER OF FORTUNE⑥**

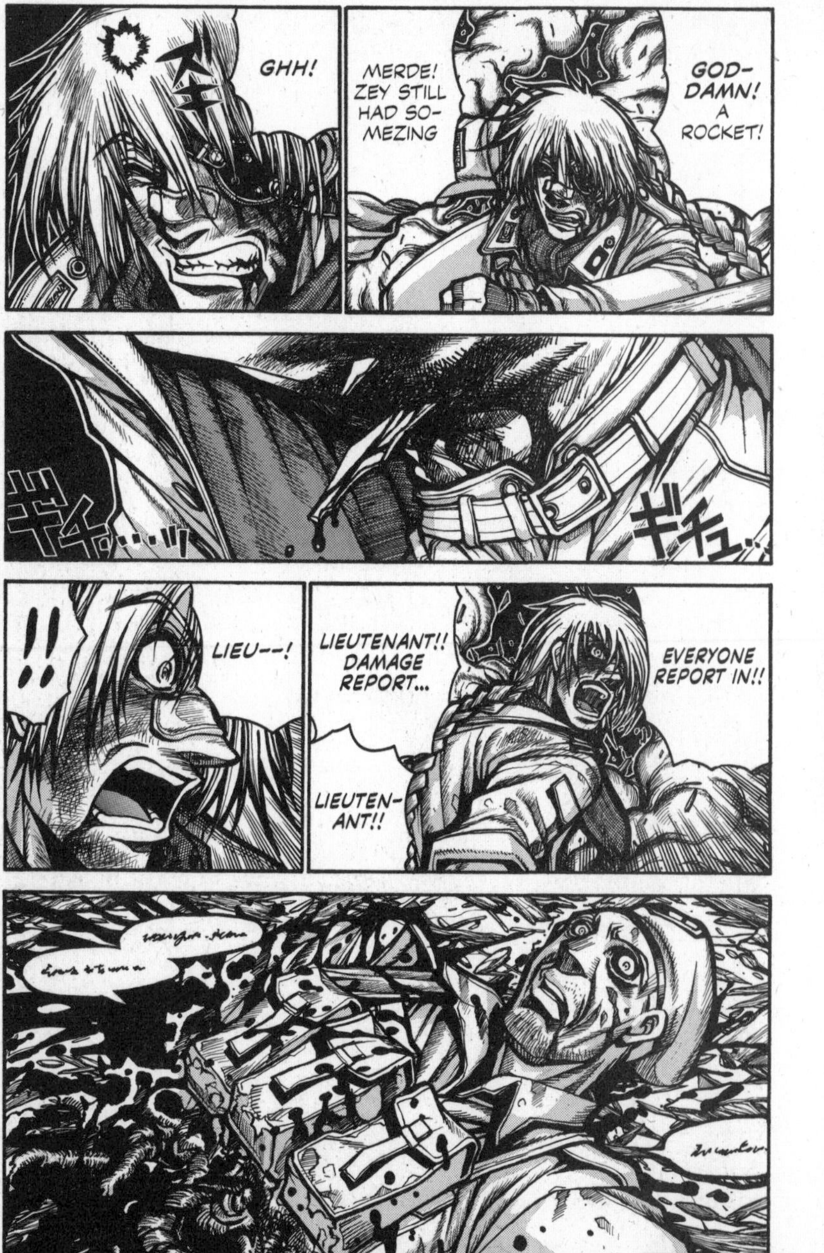
GOD-DAMN! A ROCKET!
MERDE! ZEY STILL HAD SO-MEZING
GHH!
EVERYONE REPORT IN!!
LIEUTENANT!! DAMAGE REPORT...
LIEUTEN-ANT!!
!!
LIEU--!

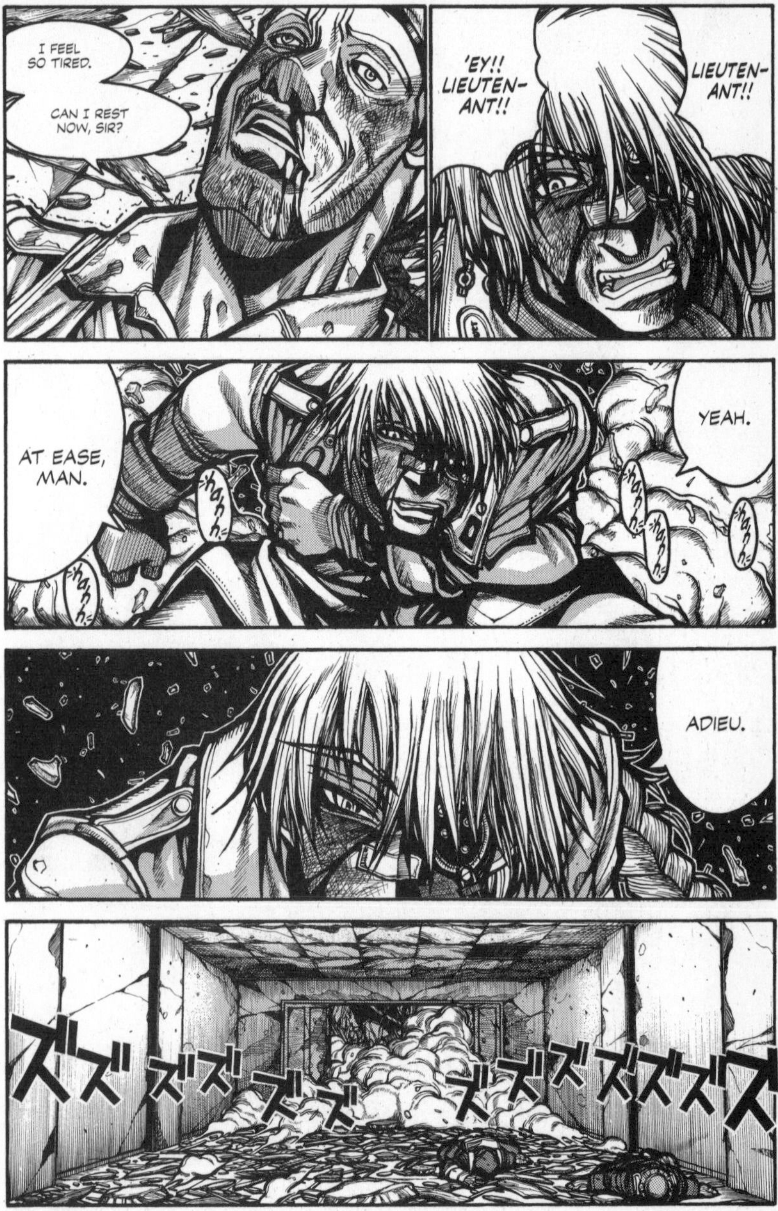
LIEUTEN-ANT!!
'EY!! LIEUTEN-ANT!!
I FEEL SO TIRED.
CAN I REST NOW, SIR?
YEAH.
AT EASE, MAN.
ADIEU.
ズズ ズズ ズズ ズズズ ズズズズ

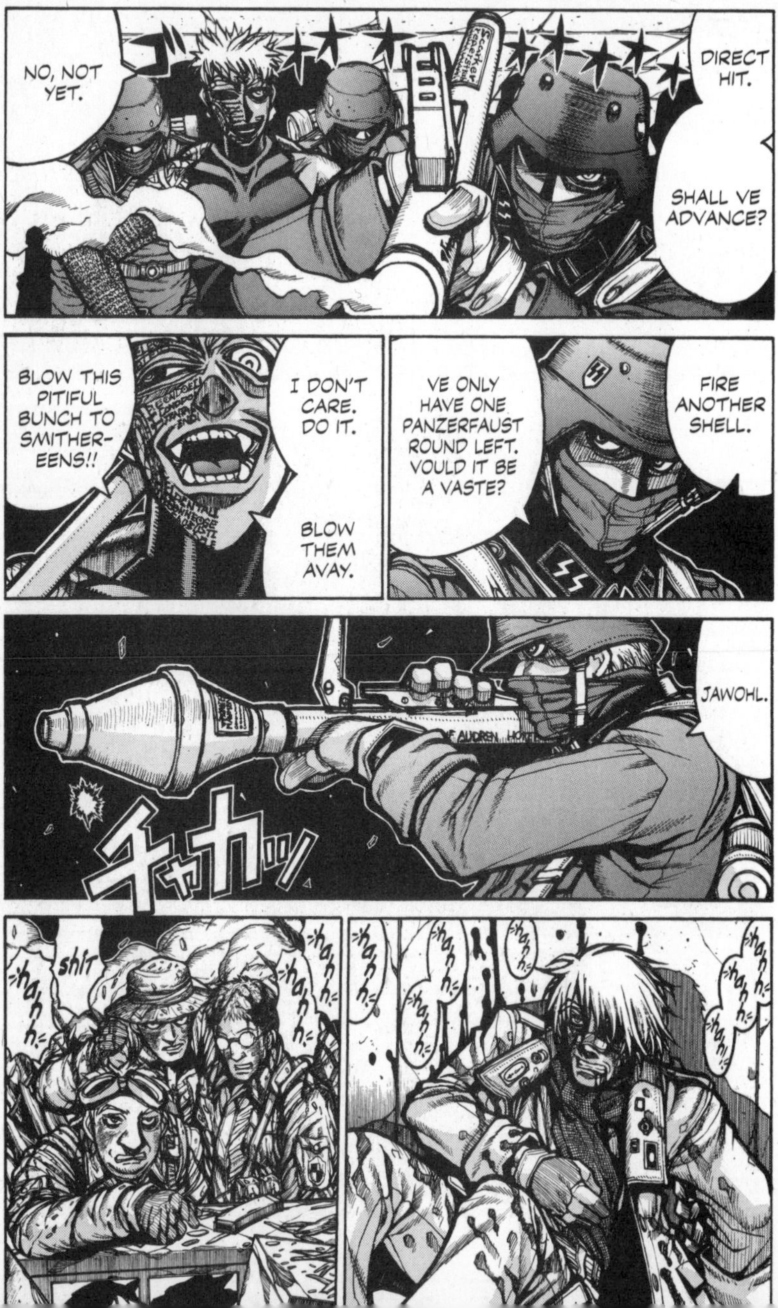
DIRECT HIT.
SHALL VE ADVANCE?
NO, NOT YET.
FIRE ANOTHER SHELL.
VE ONLY HAVE ONE PANZERFAUST ROUND LEFT. VOULD IT BE A VASTE?
I DON'T CARE. DO IT.
BLOW THEM AVAY.
BLOW THIS PITIFUL BUNCH TO SMITHEREENS!!
JAWOHL.
shit

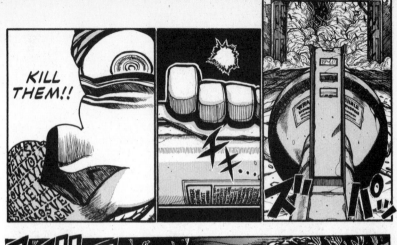

KILL
THEM!!

VHA--?!

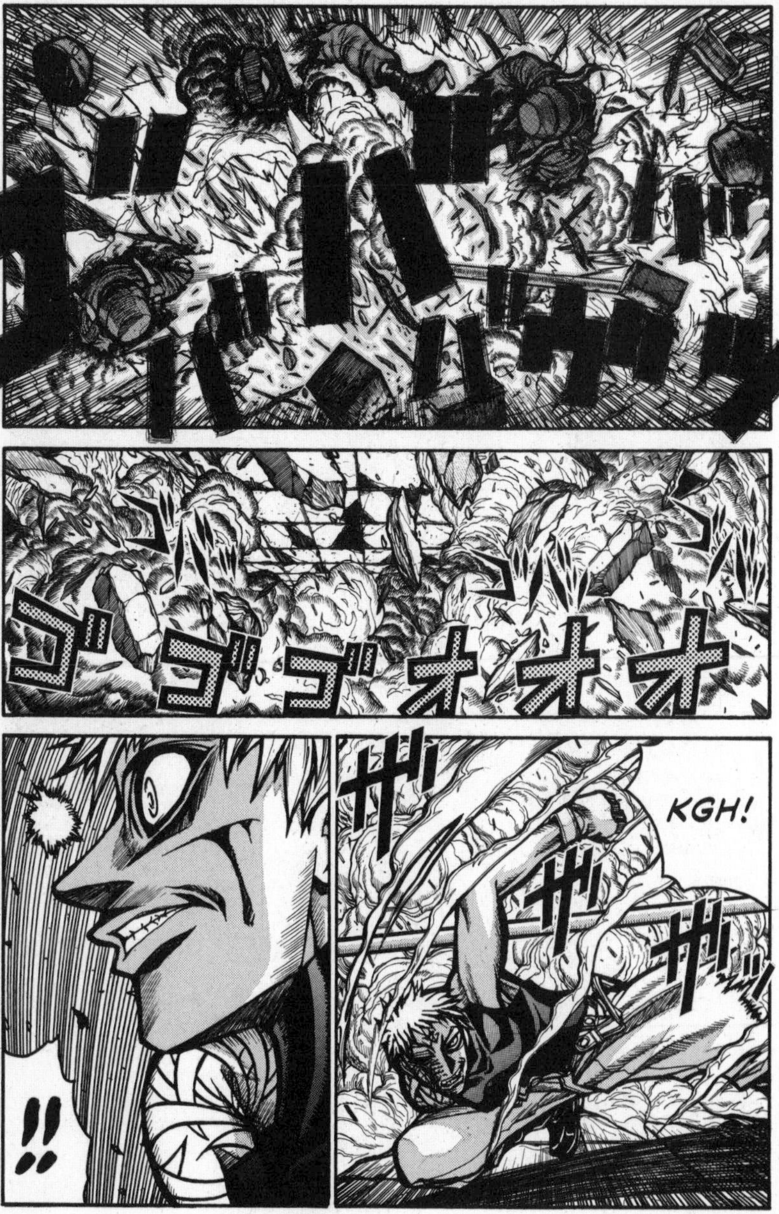
ゴゴゴオオオ
KGH!
!!

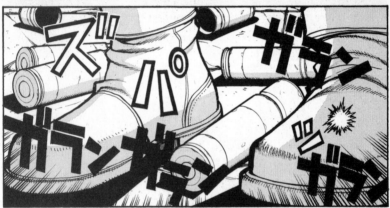

IT'S YOU!!

DIRECT CANNON SUPPORT...!!

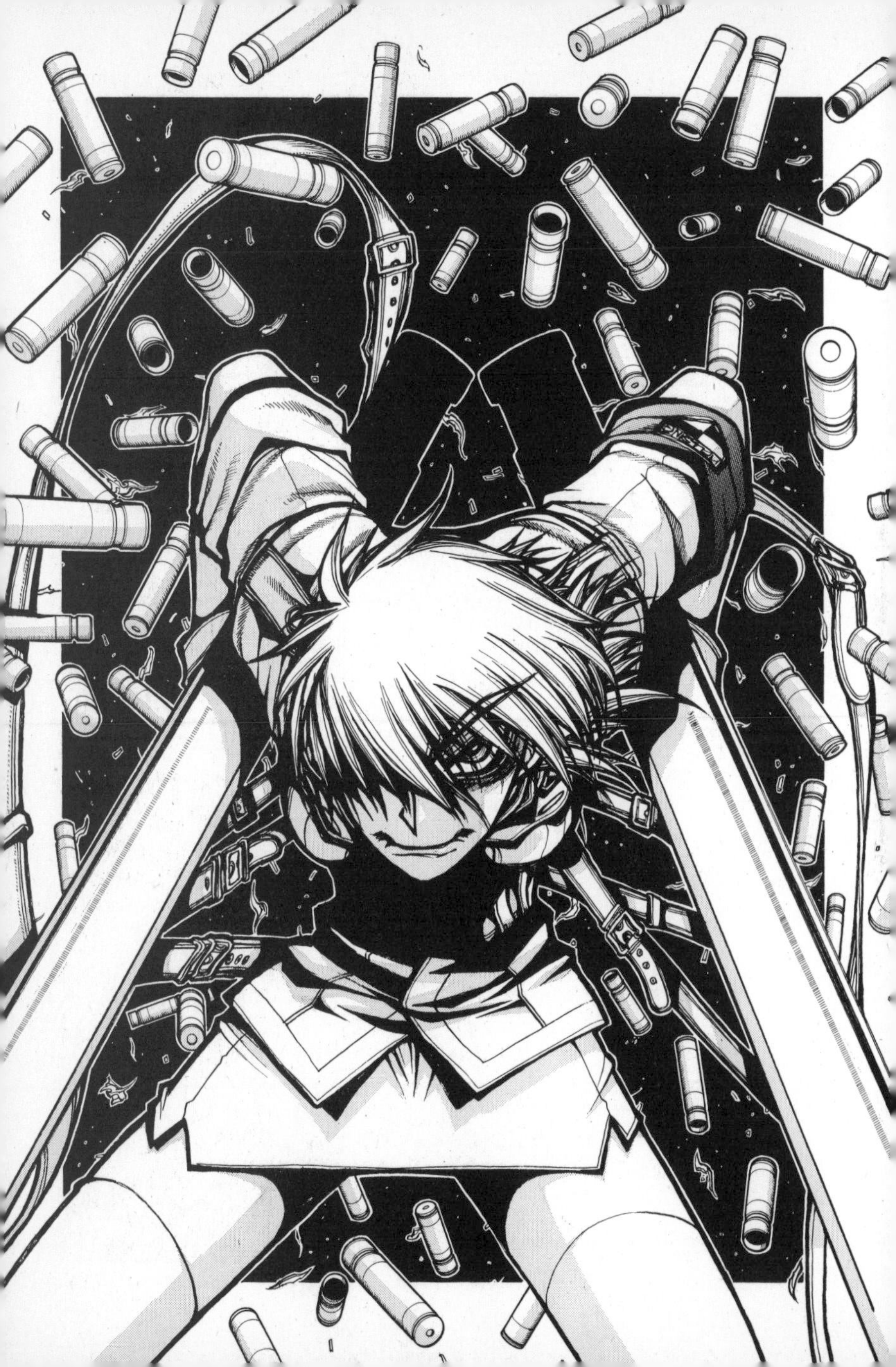

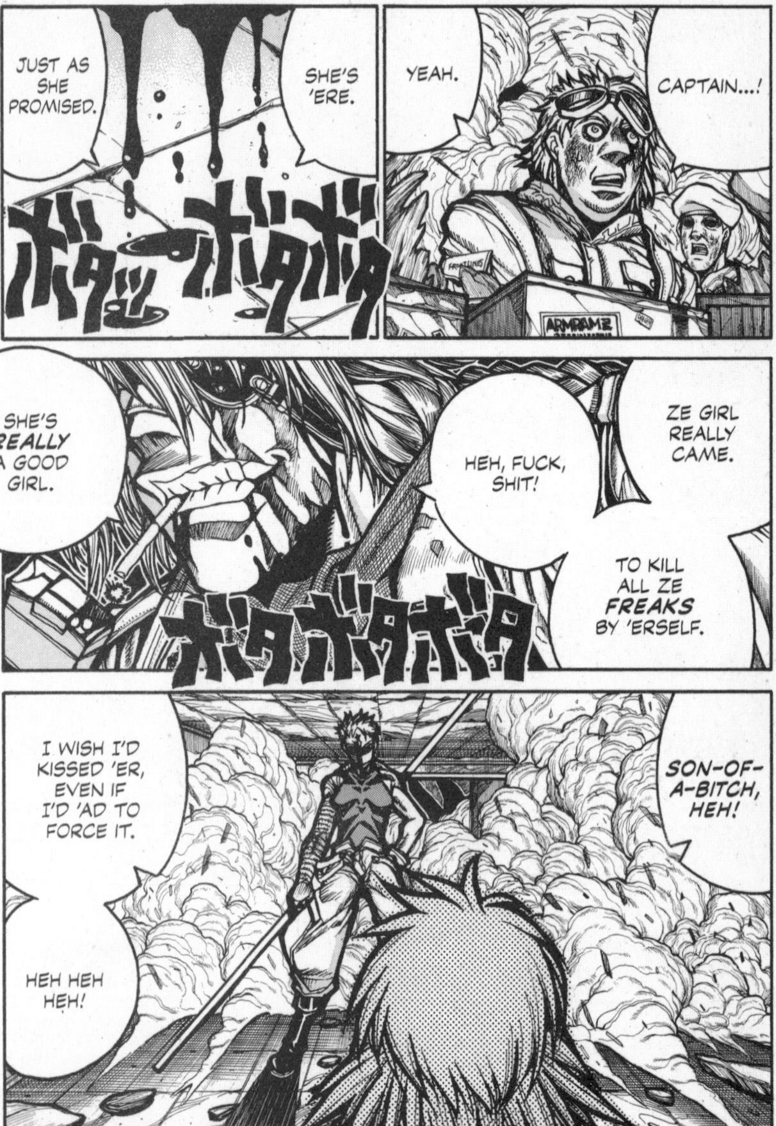
CAPTAIN...!
YEAH.
SHE'S 'ERE.
JUST AS SHE PROMISED.
ボタッ
ボタボタ
ZE GIRL REALLY CAME.
TO KILL ALL ZE **FREAKS** BY 'ERSELF.
HEH, FUCK, SHIT!
SHE'S **REALLY** A GOOD GIRL.
ボタボタボタ
SON-OF-A-BITCH, HEH!
I WISH I'D KISSED 'ER, EVEN IF I'D 'AD TO FORCE IT.
HEH HEH HEH!

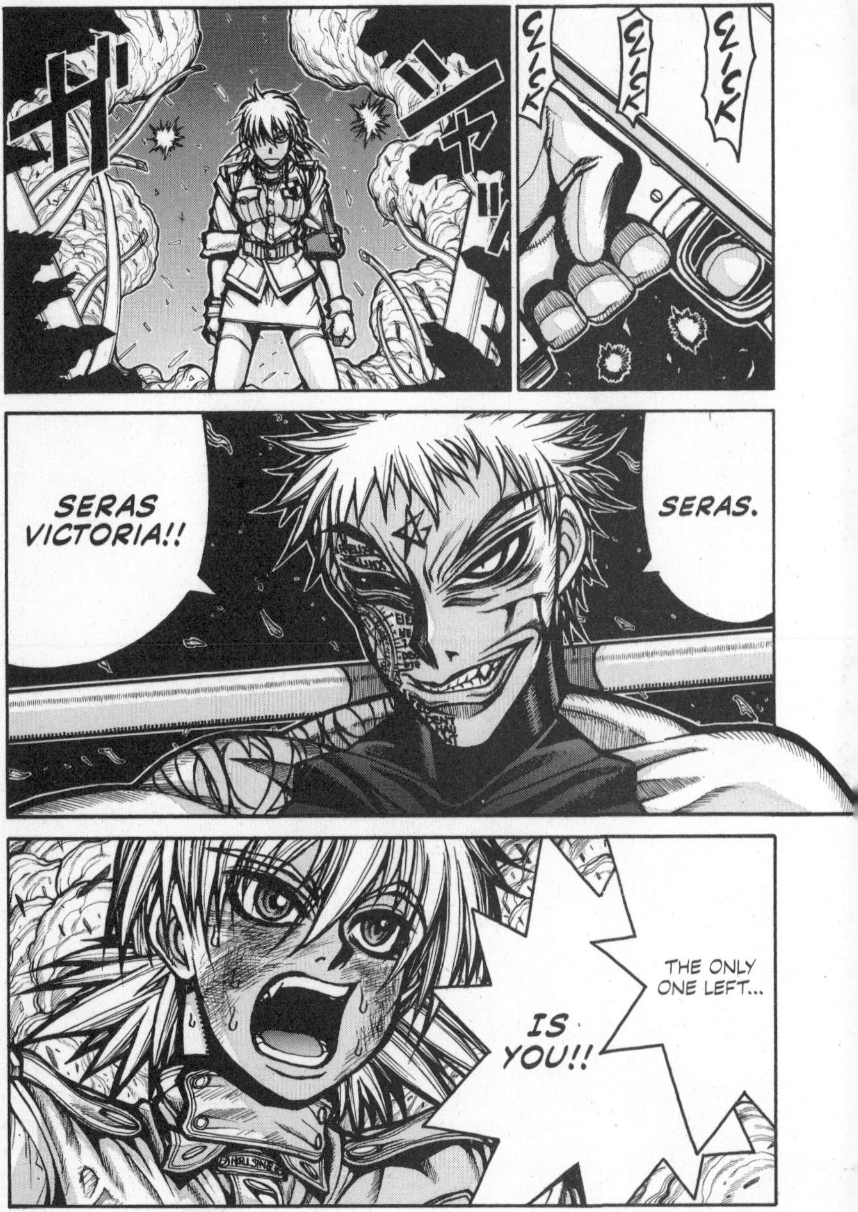
CLICK
CLICK
CLICK
SERAS.
SERAS VICTORIA!!
THE ONLY ONE LEFT...
IS YOU!!

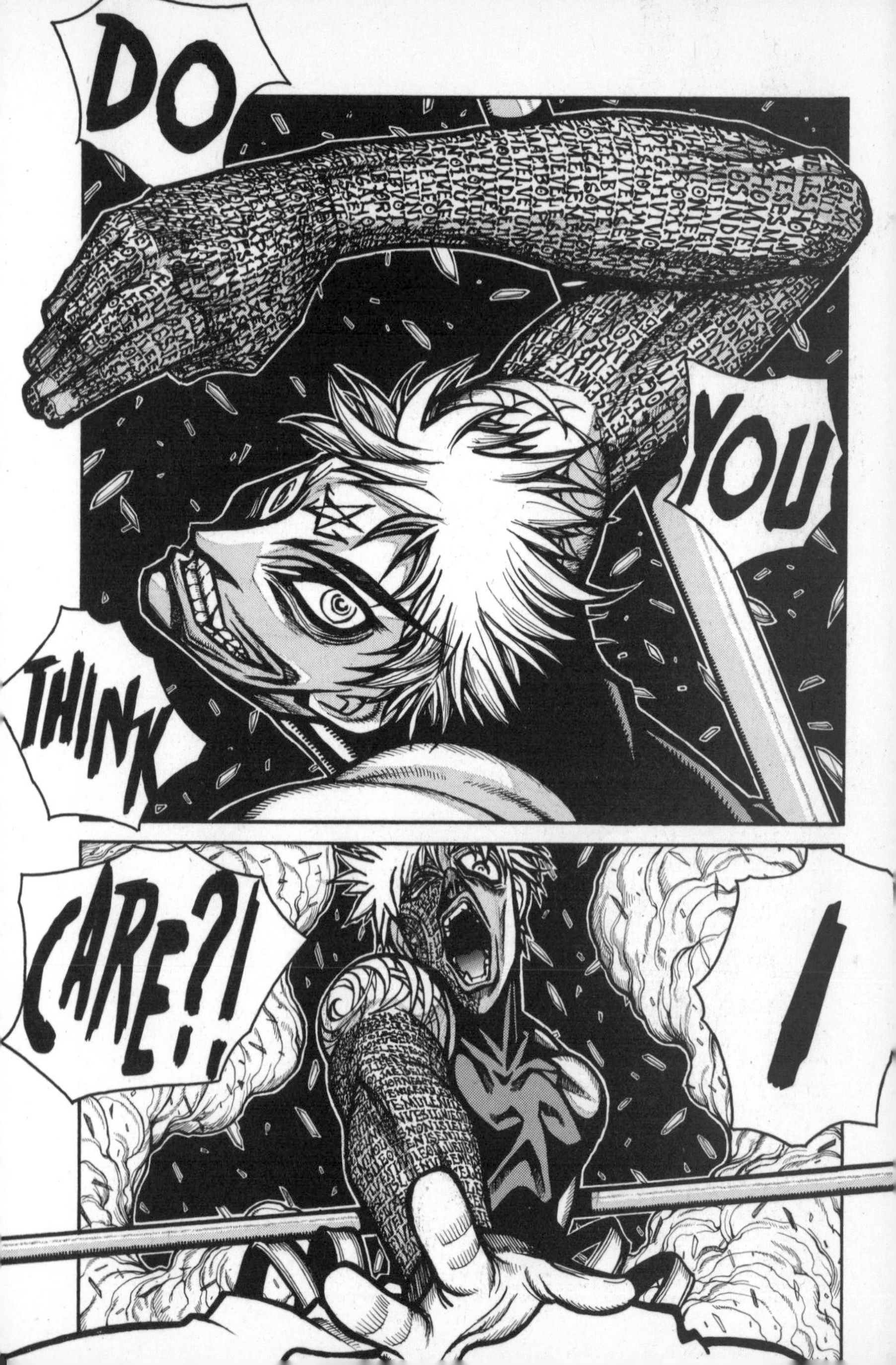
DO
YOU
THINK
I
CARE?!

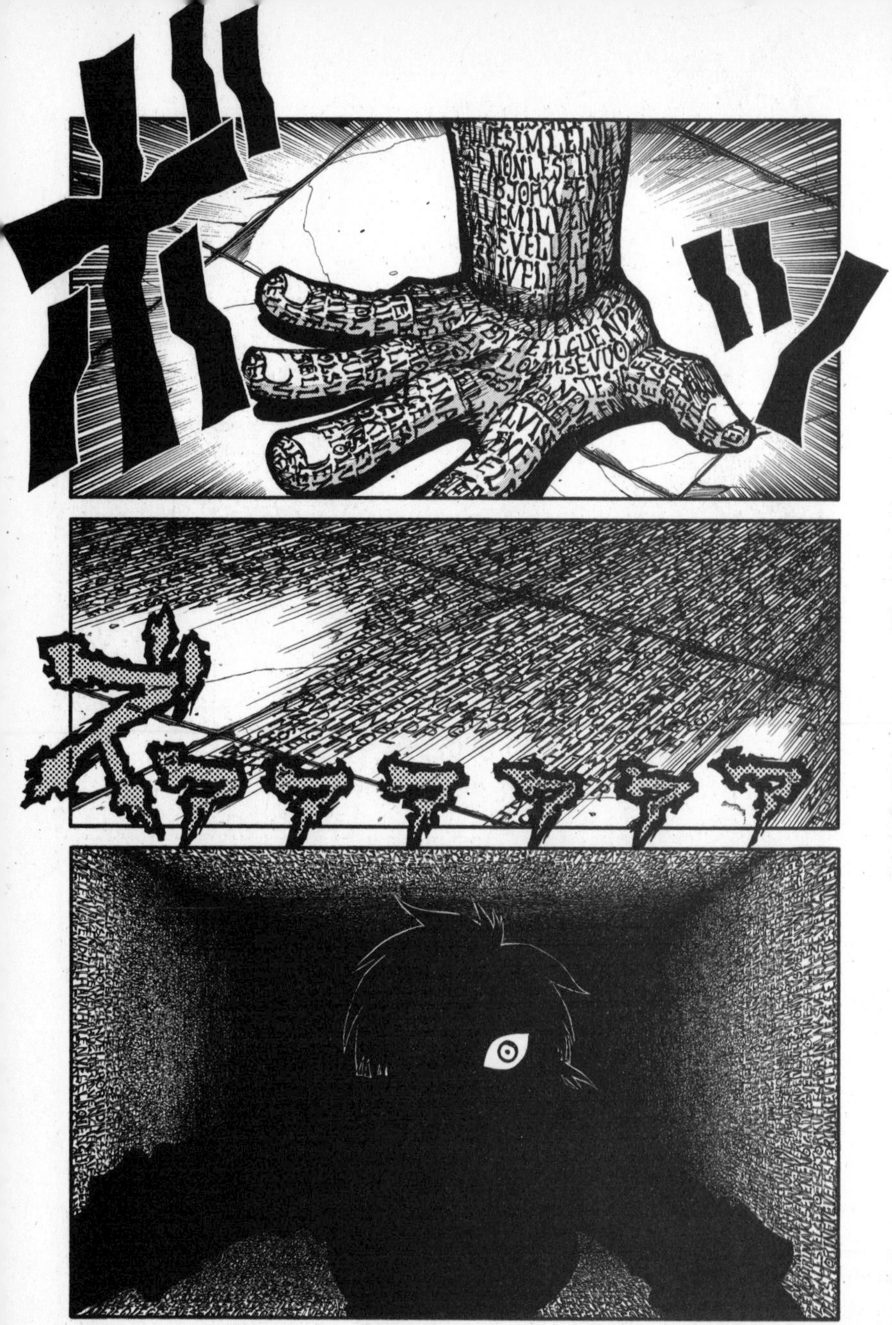
ボッ
ズァァァァァ

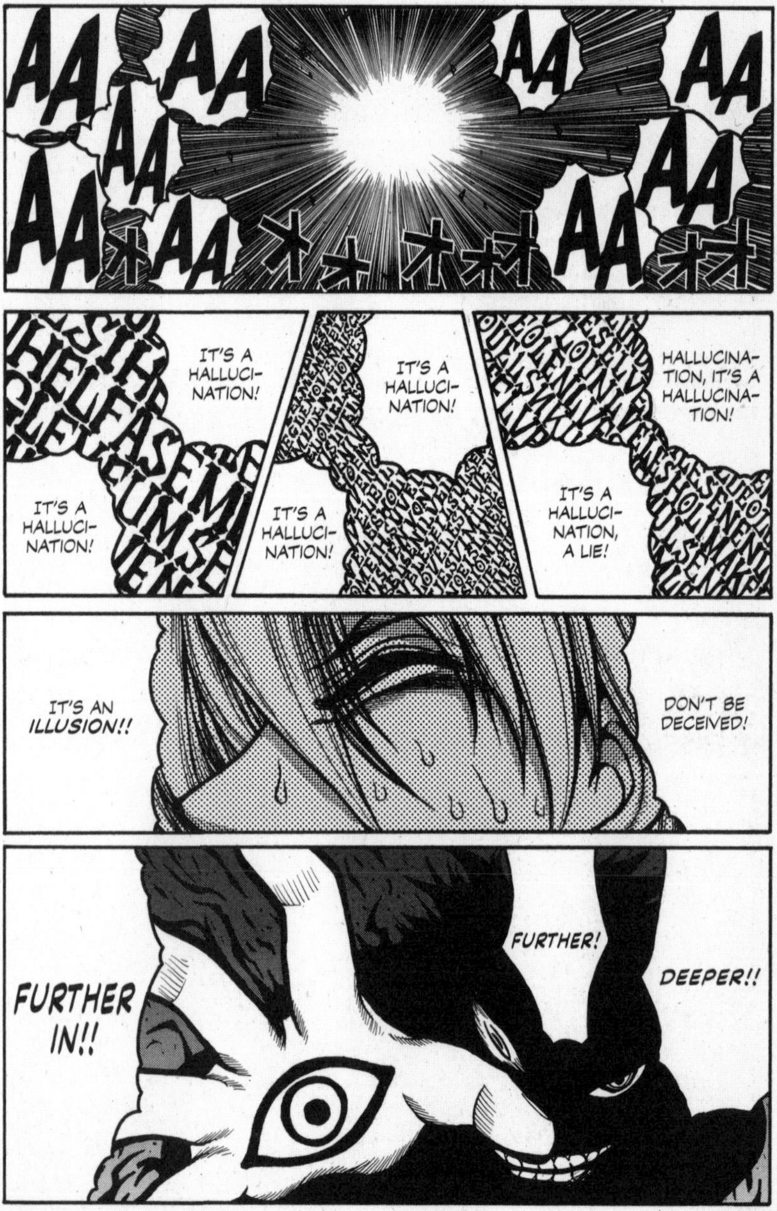
HALLUCINATION, IT'S A HALLUCINATION!
IT'S A HALLUCINATION, A LIE!
IT'S A HALLUCINATION!
IT'S A HALLUCINATION!
IT'S A HALLUCINATION!
IT'S A HALLUCINATION!
DON'T BE DECEIVED!
IT'S AN ILLUSION!!
FURTHER!
DEEPER!!
FURTHER IN!!

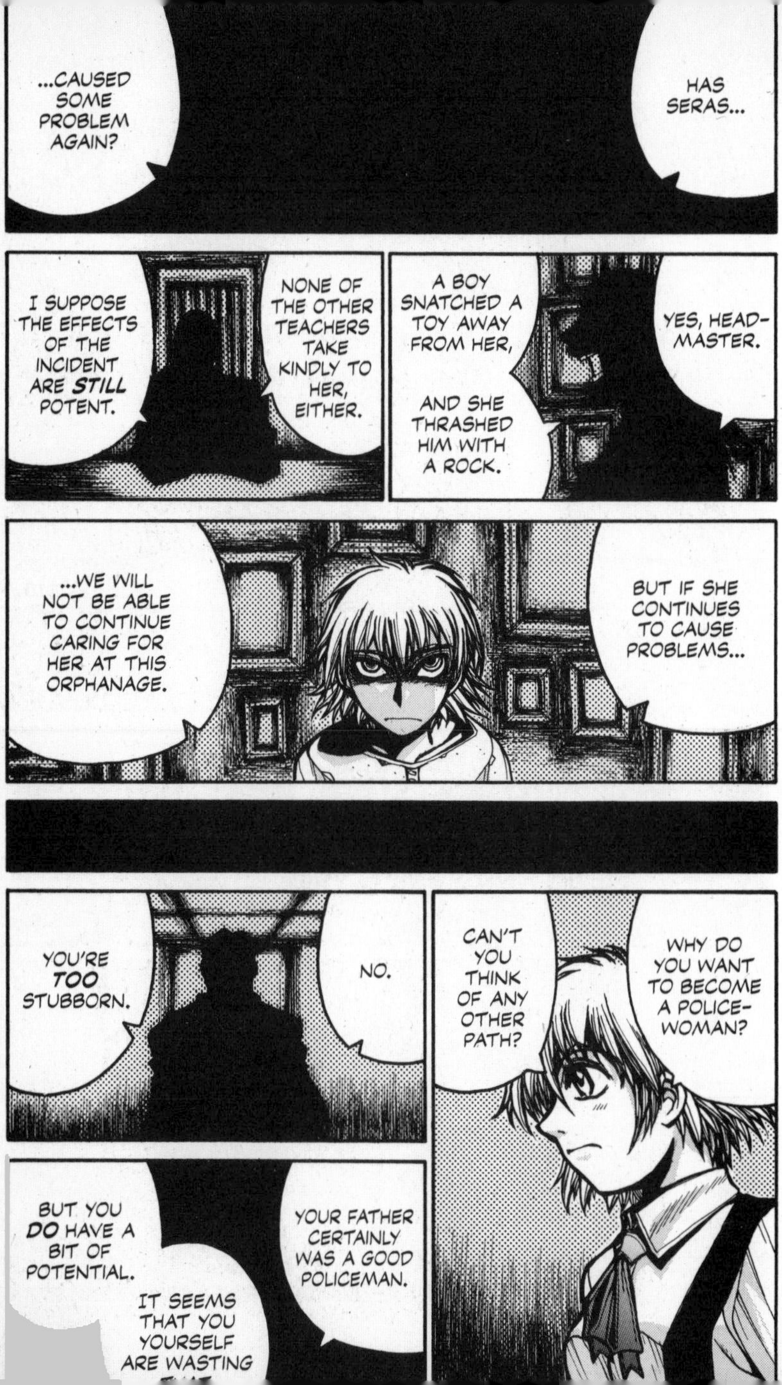
HAS SERAS...
...CAUSED SOME PROBLEM AGAIN?
YES, HEAD-MASTER.
A BOY SNATCHED A TOY AWAY FROM HER,
AND SHE THRASHED HIM WITH A ROCK.
NONE OF THE OTHER TEACHERS TAKE KINDLY TO HER, EITHER.
I SUPPOSE THE EFFECTS OF THE INCIDENT ARE *STILL* POTENT.
BUT IF SHE CONTINUES TO CAUSE PROBLEMS...
...WE WILL NOT BE ABLE TO CONTINUE CARING FOR HER AT THIS ORPHANAGE.
WHY DO YOU WANT TO BECOME A POLICE-WOMAN?
CAN'T YOU THINK OF ANY OTHER PATH?
NO.
YOU'RE *TOO* STUBBORN.
YOUR FATHER CERTAINLY WAS A GOOD POLICEMAN.
BUT YOU *DO* HAVE A BIT OF POTENTIAL.
IT SEEMS THAT YOU YOURSELF ARE WASTING

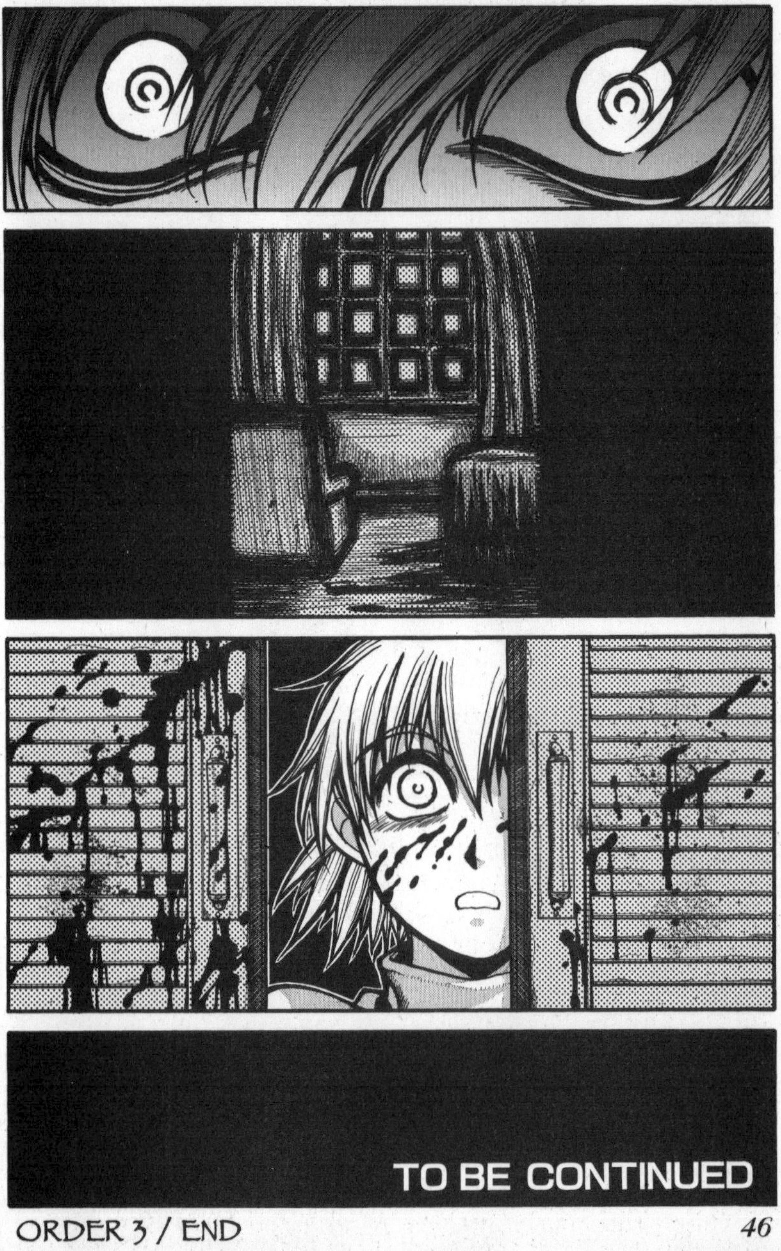
TO BE CONTINUED

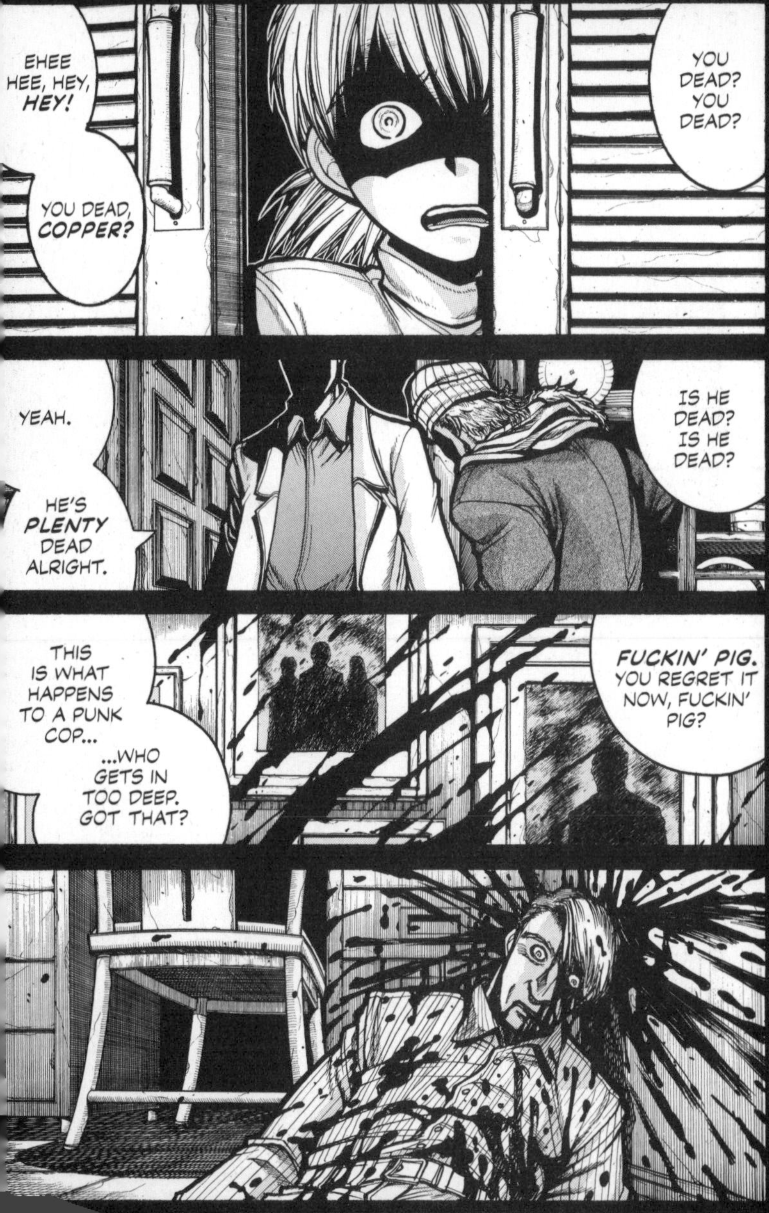
YOU DEAD? YOU DEAD?
EHEE HEE, HEY, *HEY!*
YOU DEAD, *COPPER?*
IS HE DEAD? IS HE DEAD?
YEAH.
HE'S *PLENTY* DEAD ALRIGHT.
FUCKIN' PIG. YOU REGRET IT NOW, FUCKIN' PIG?
THIS IS WHAT HAPPENS TO A PUNK COP...
...WHO GETS IN TOO DEEP. GOT THAT?

✤ ORDER 4
LAST MISSION

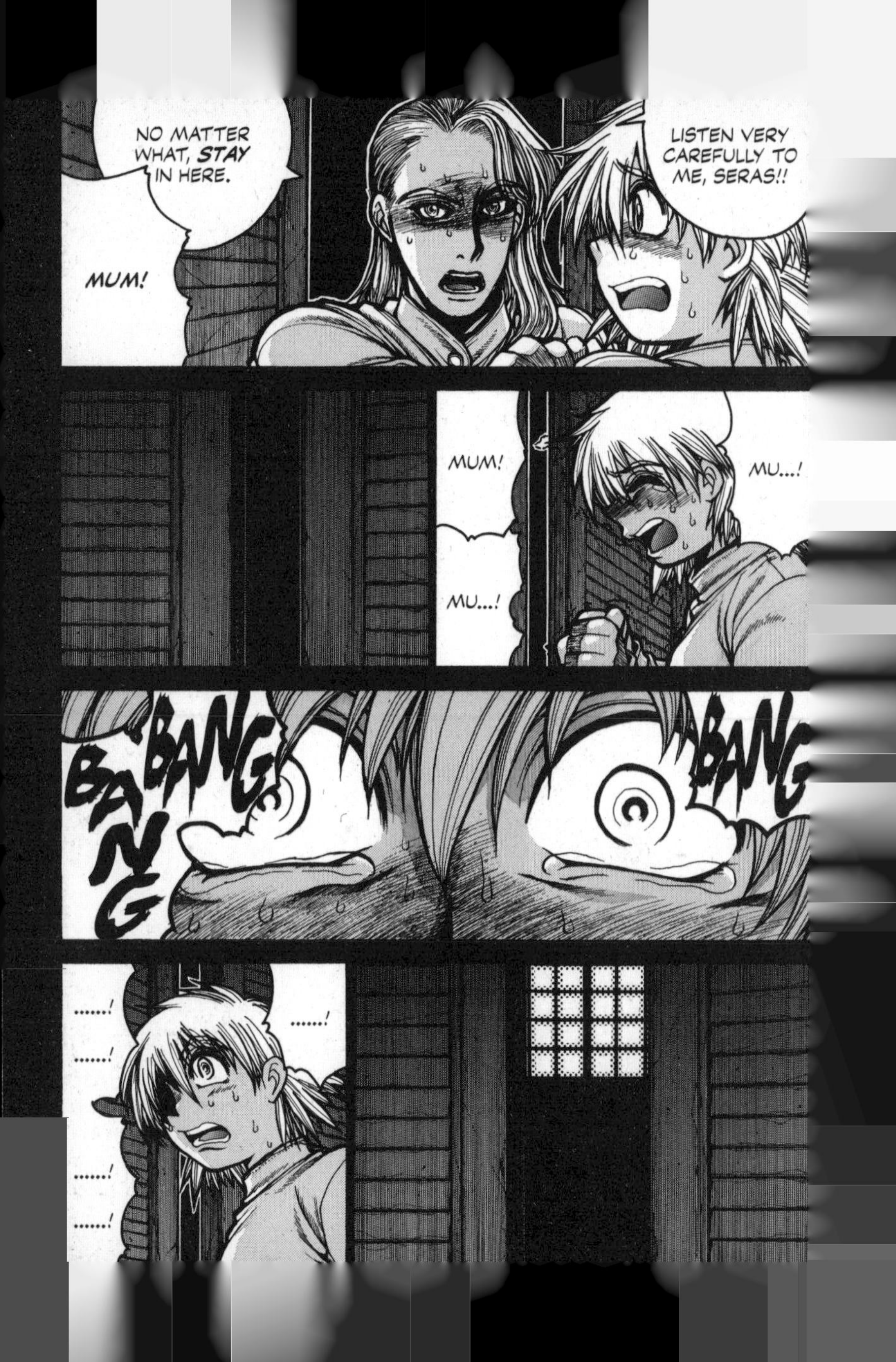

LISTEN VERY CAREFULLY TO ME, SERAS!!
NO MATTER WHAT, STAY IN HERE.
MUM!
MU...!
MUM!
MU...!
BANG
BANG
BANG
......!
......!
......!
......!
......!

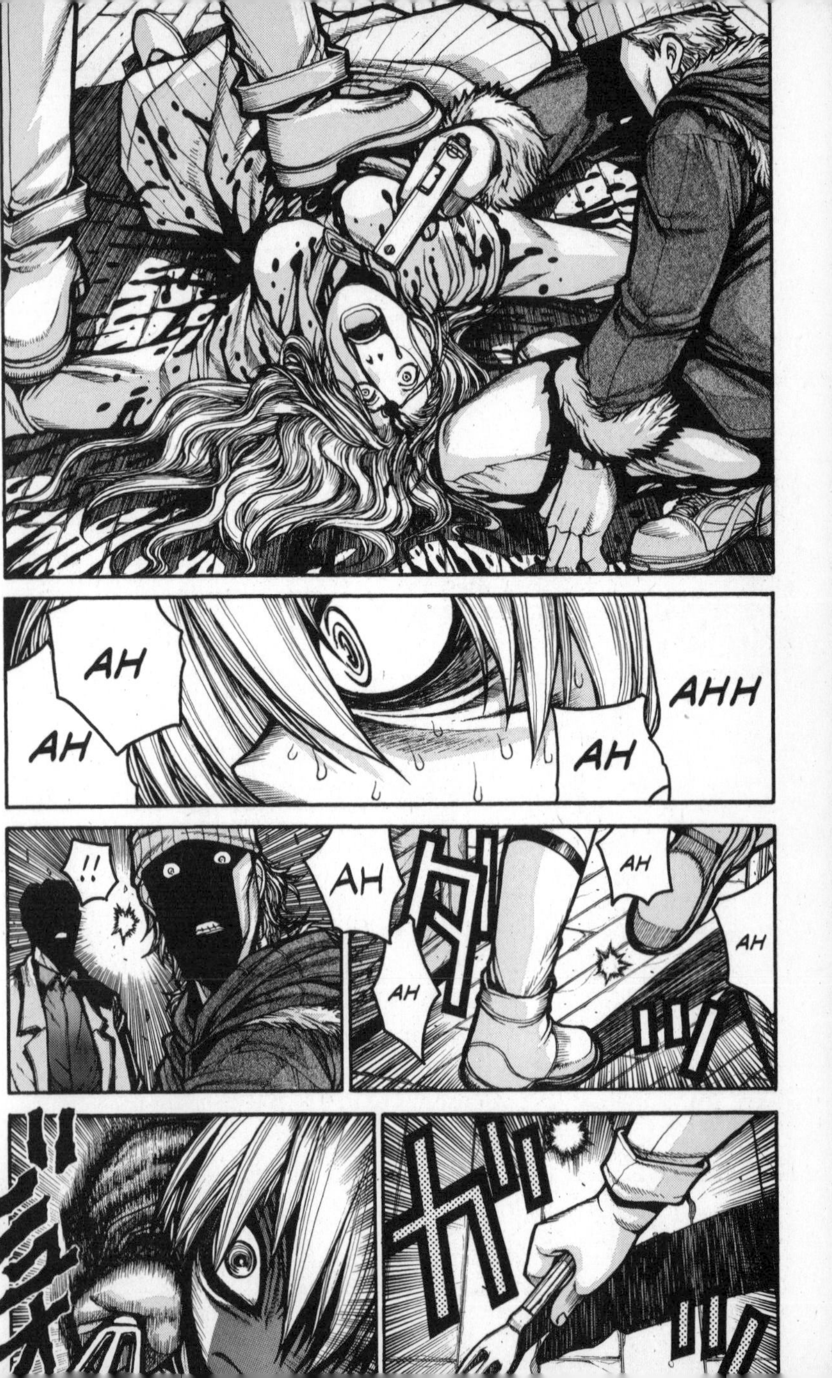
AHH
AH
AH
AH
AH
AH
AH
AH
!!

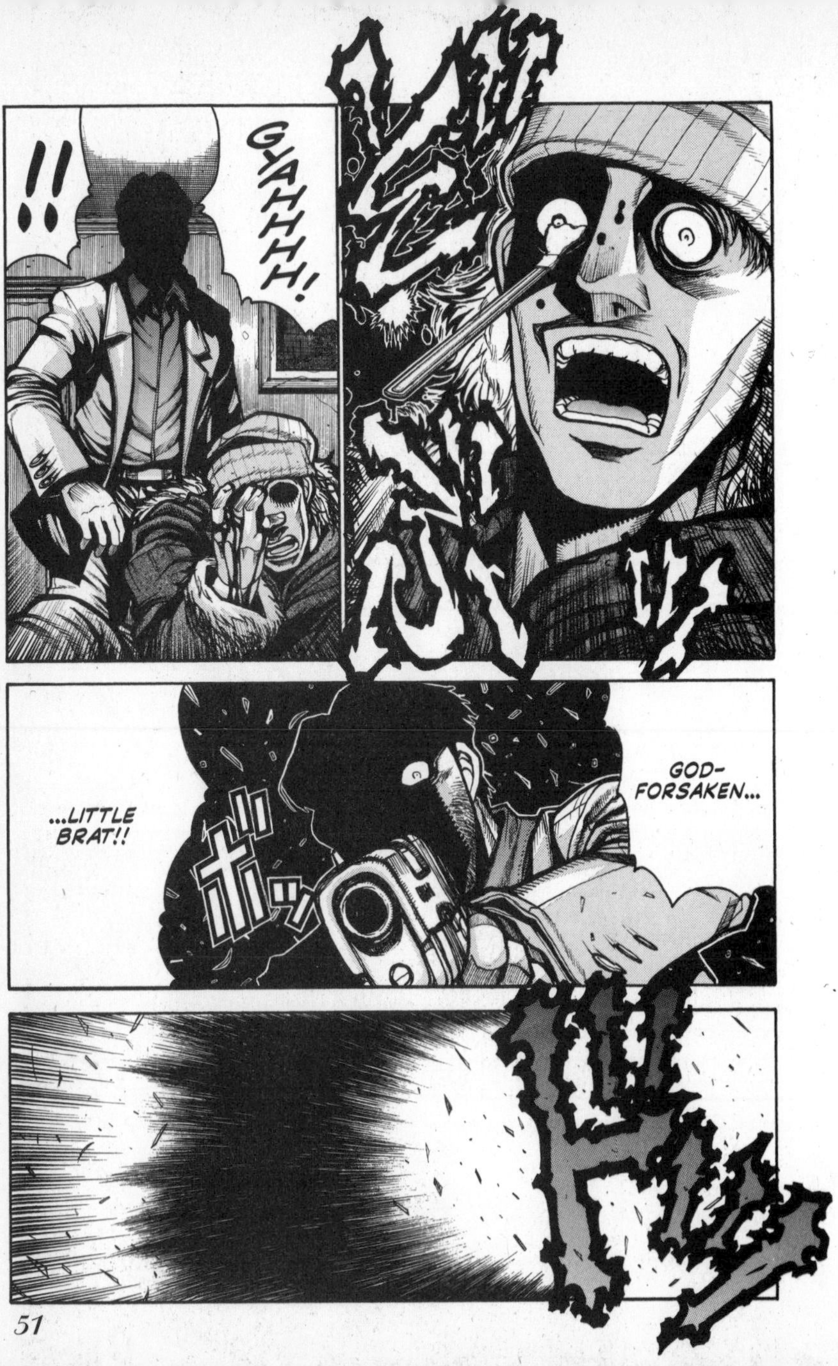
GYAHHHH!
!!
GOD-FORSAKEN...
...LITTLE BRAT!!

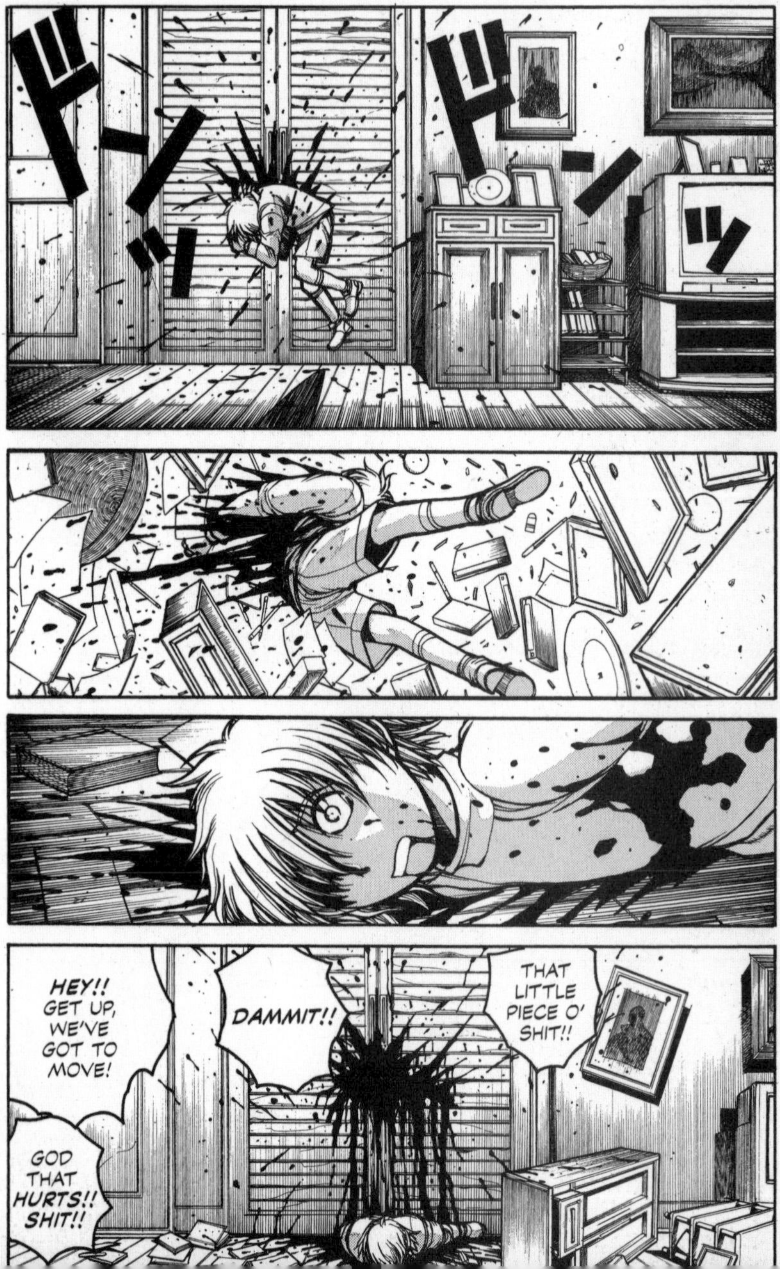
THAT LITTLE PIECE O' SHIT!!
DAMMIT!!
HEY!! GET UP, WE'VE GOT TO MOVE!
GOD THAT HURTS!! SHIT!!

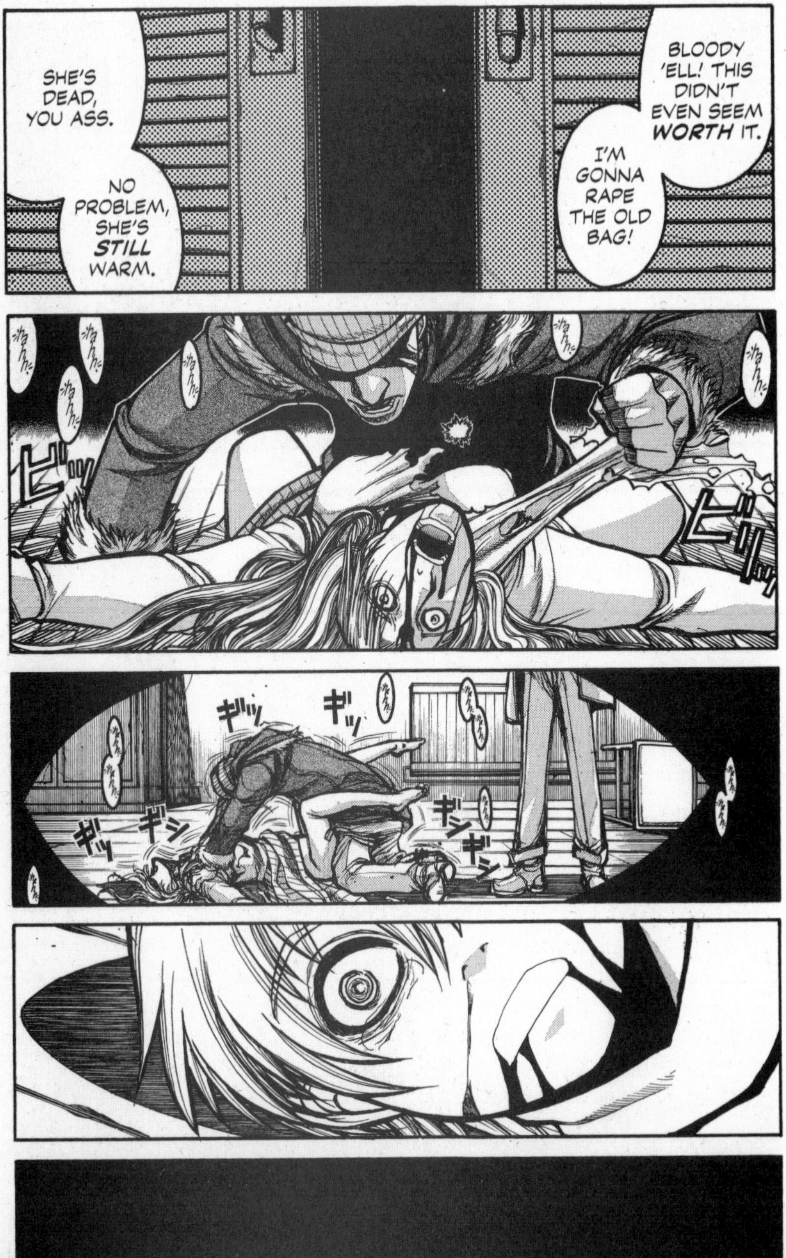
BLOODY 'ELL! THIS DIDN'T EVEN SEEM WORTH IT.
I'M GONNA RAPE THE OLD BAG!
SHE'S DEAD, YOU ASS.
NO PROBLEM, SHE'S STILL WARM.
ビリッ
ビッ
ギッ
ギッ
ギシ
ギシ
ギシ
ギッ

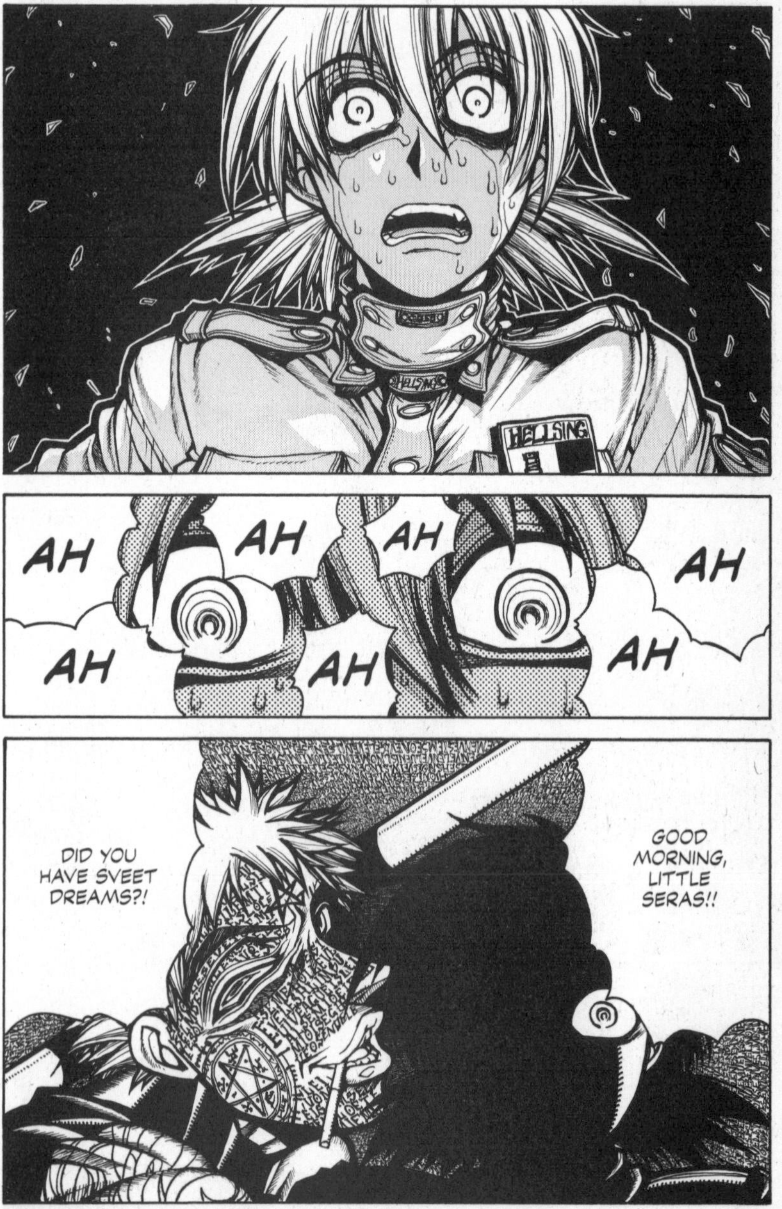
HELLSING
AH
AH
AH
AH
AH
AH
AH
GOOD MORNING, LITTLE SERAS!!
DID YOU HAVE SVEET DREAMS?!

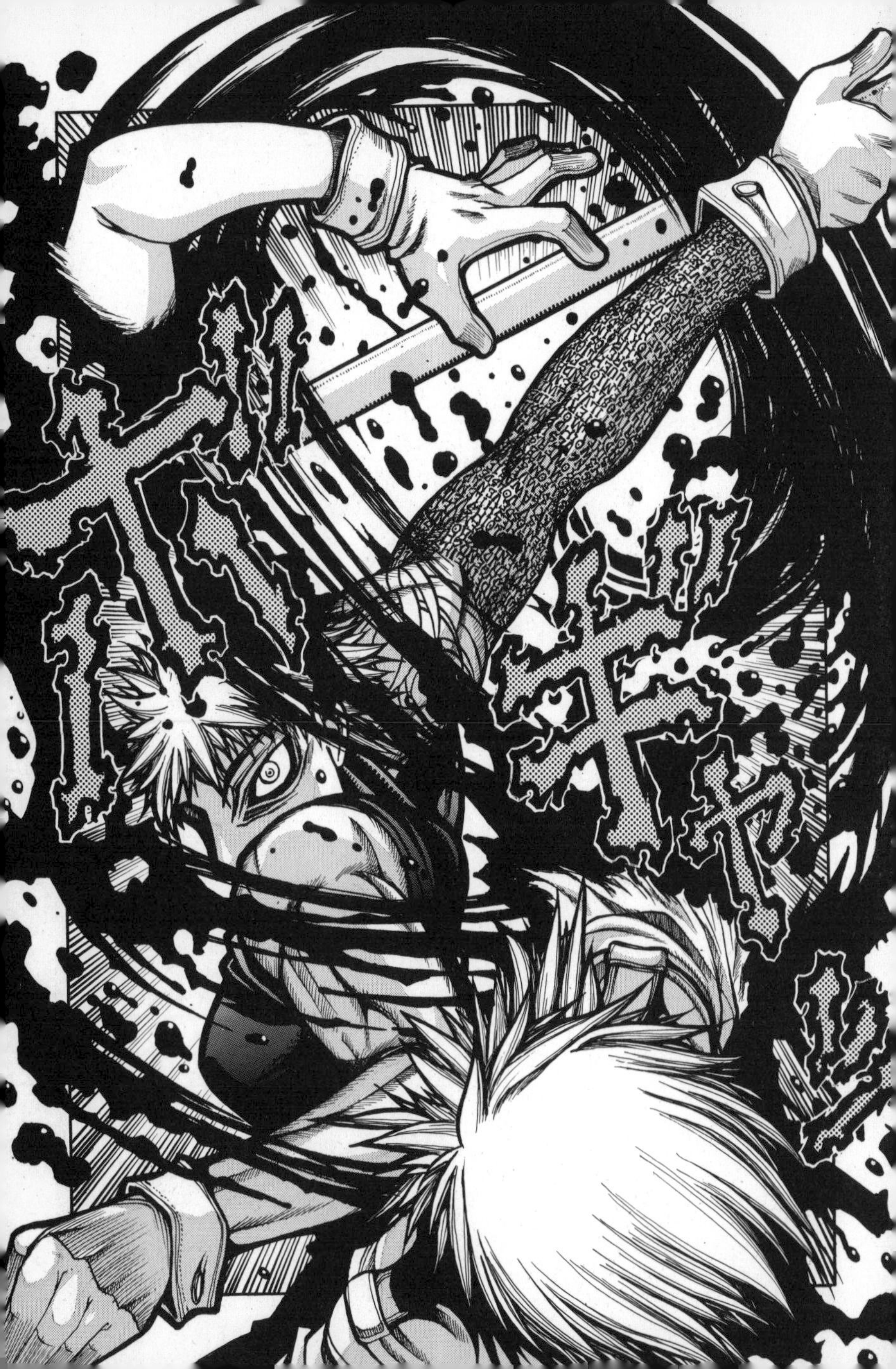

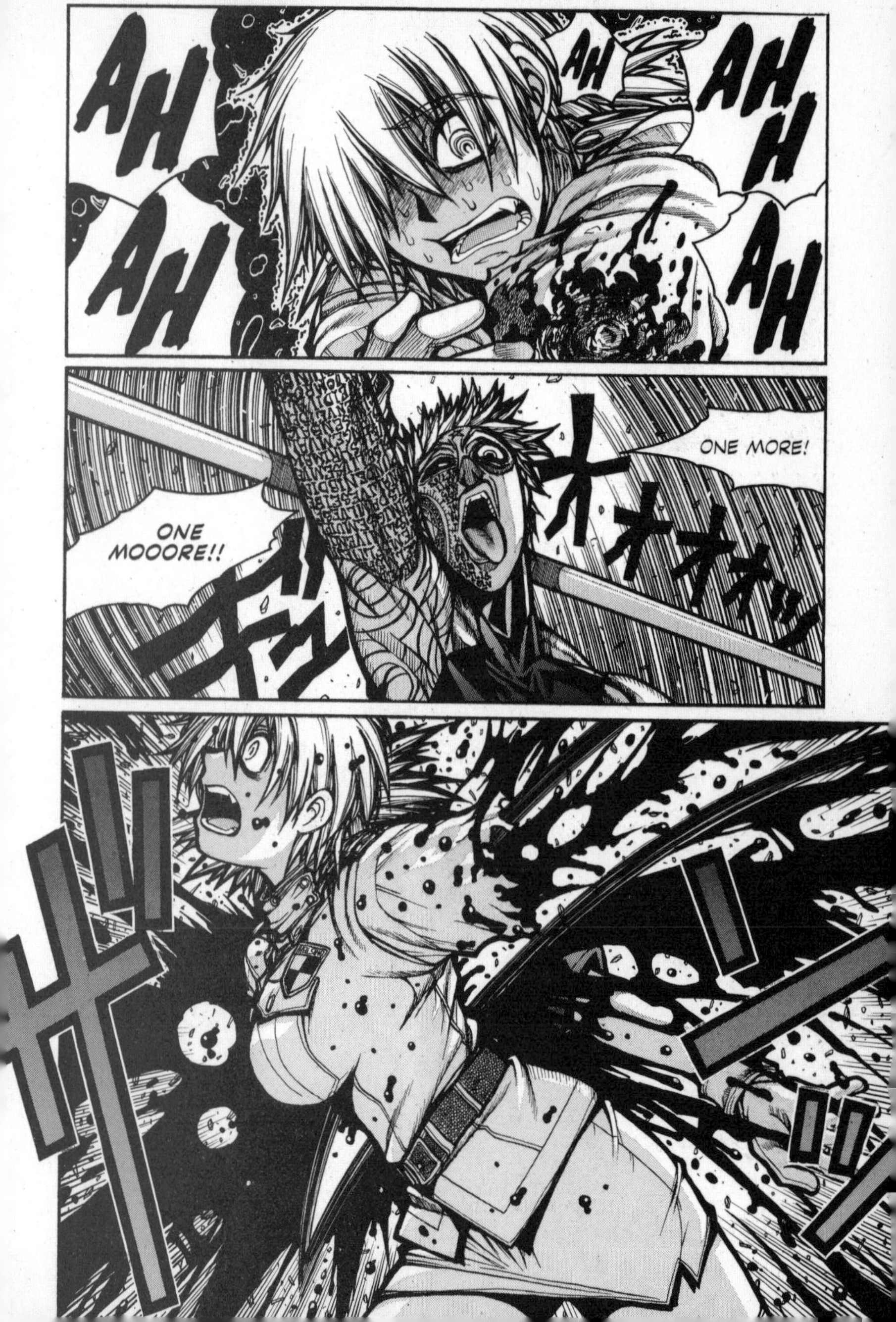
AH AH AH
AHHAH AH
ONE MORE!
ONE MOOORE!!

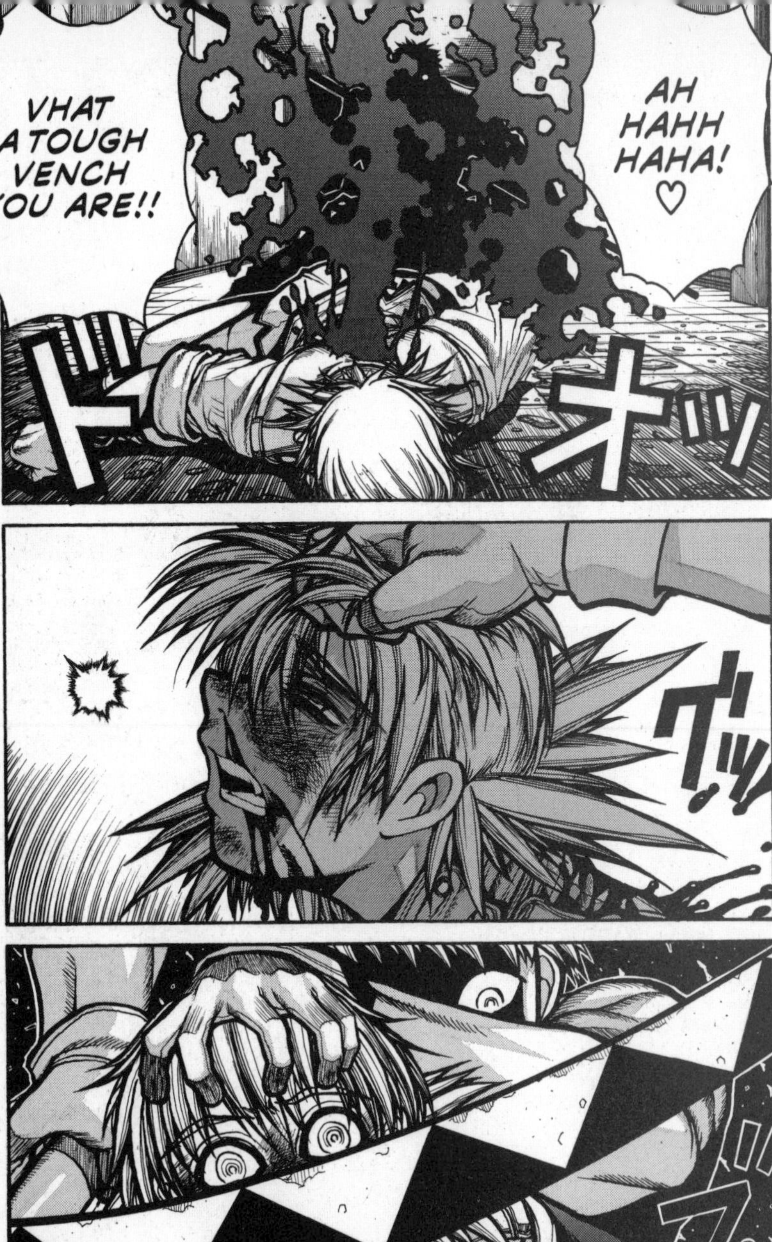
AH HAHH HAHA! ♡
VHAT A TOUGH VENCH YOU ARE!!

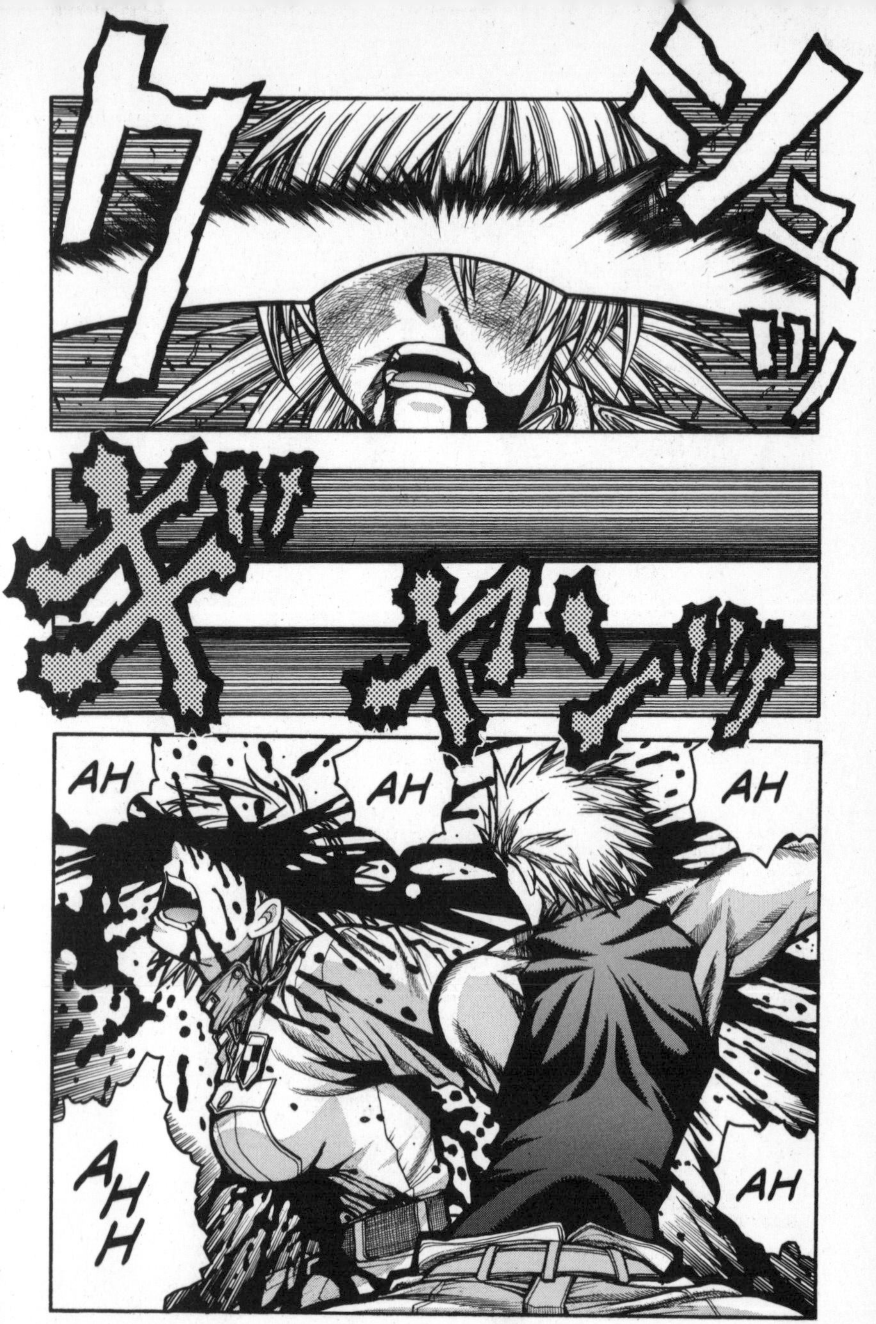
AH
AH
AH
AH
AHH

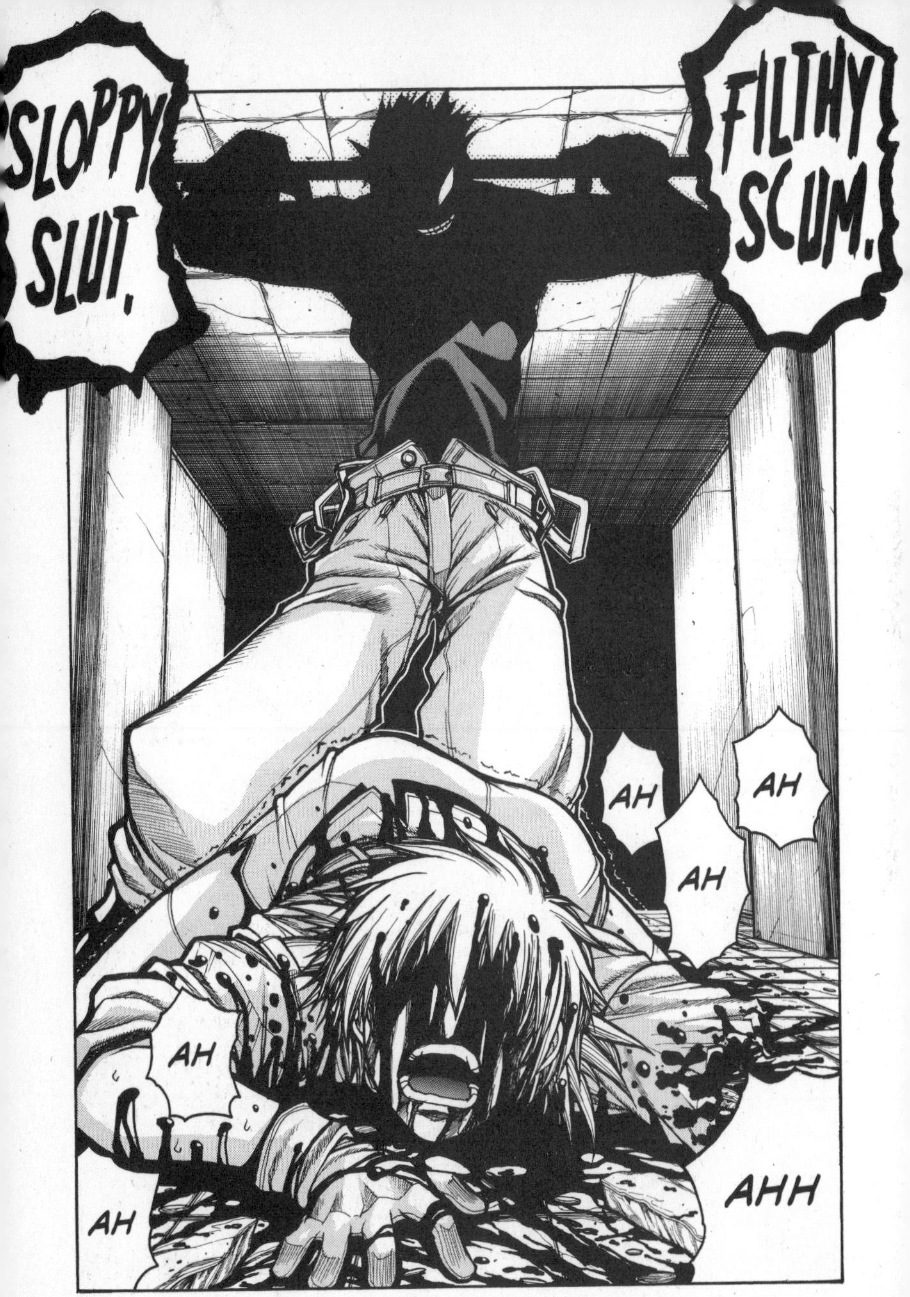
FILTHY SCUM.
SLOPPY SLUT.
AH
AH
AH
AH
AHH
AH

MAYBE, JUST MAYBE...

NOW, THENNN.

...I FINISH YOU OFF NOW.

SHOVE OFF, 'AG.

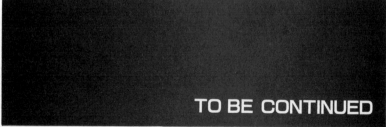

TO BE CONTINUED

ORDER 4 / END

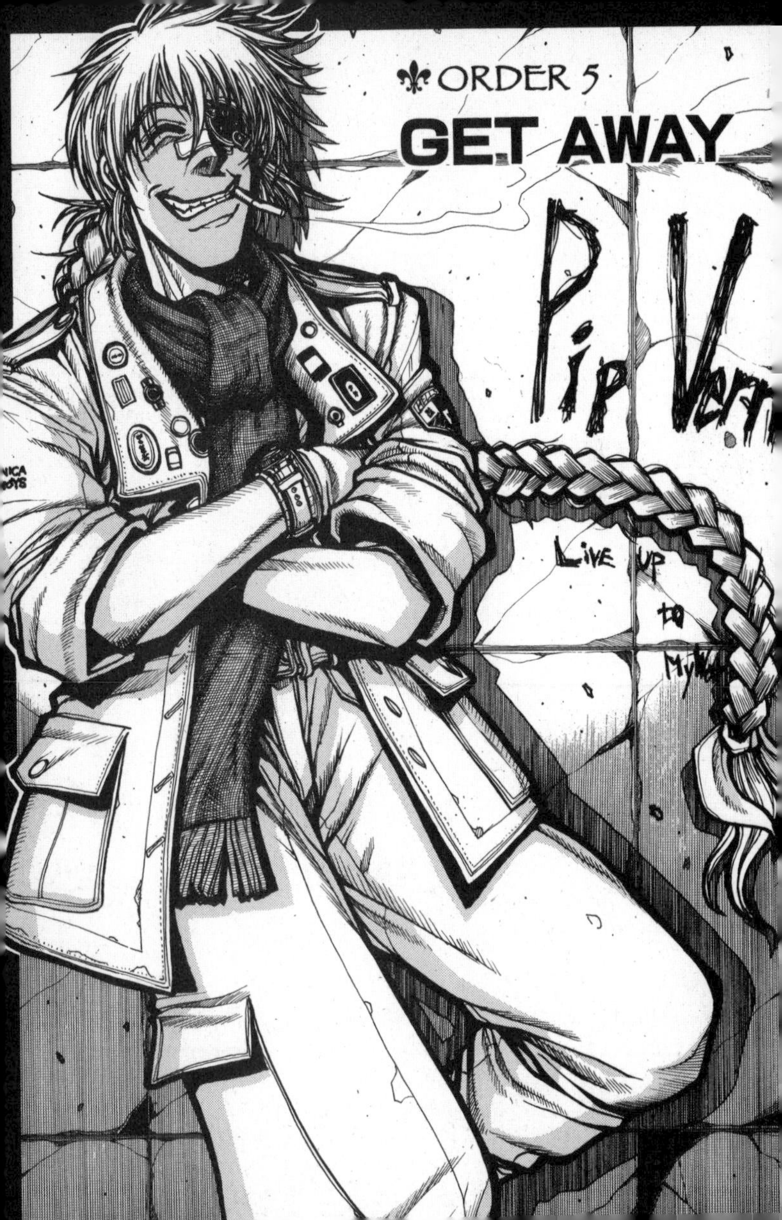
ORDER 5
GET AWAY
Live up to

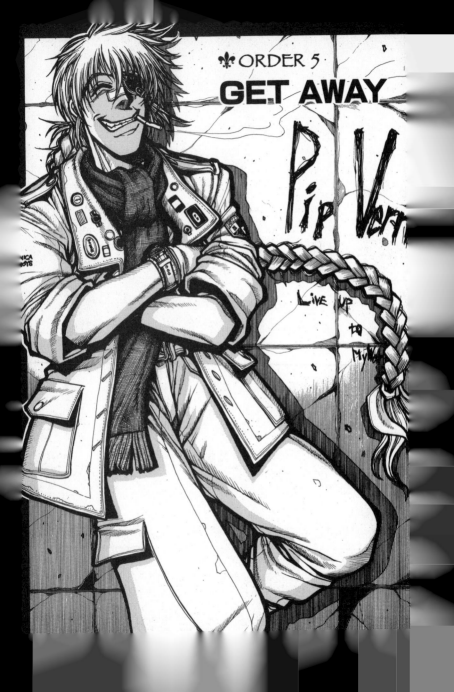

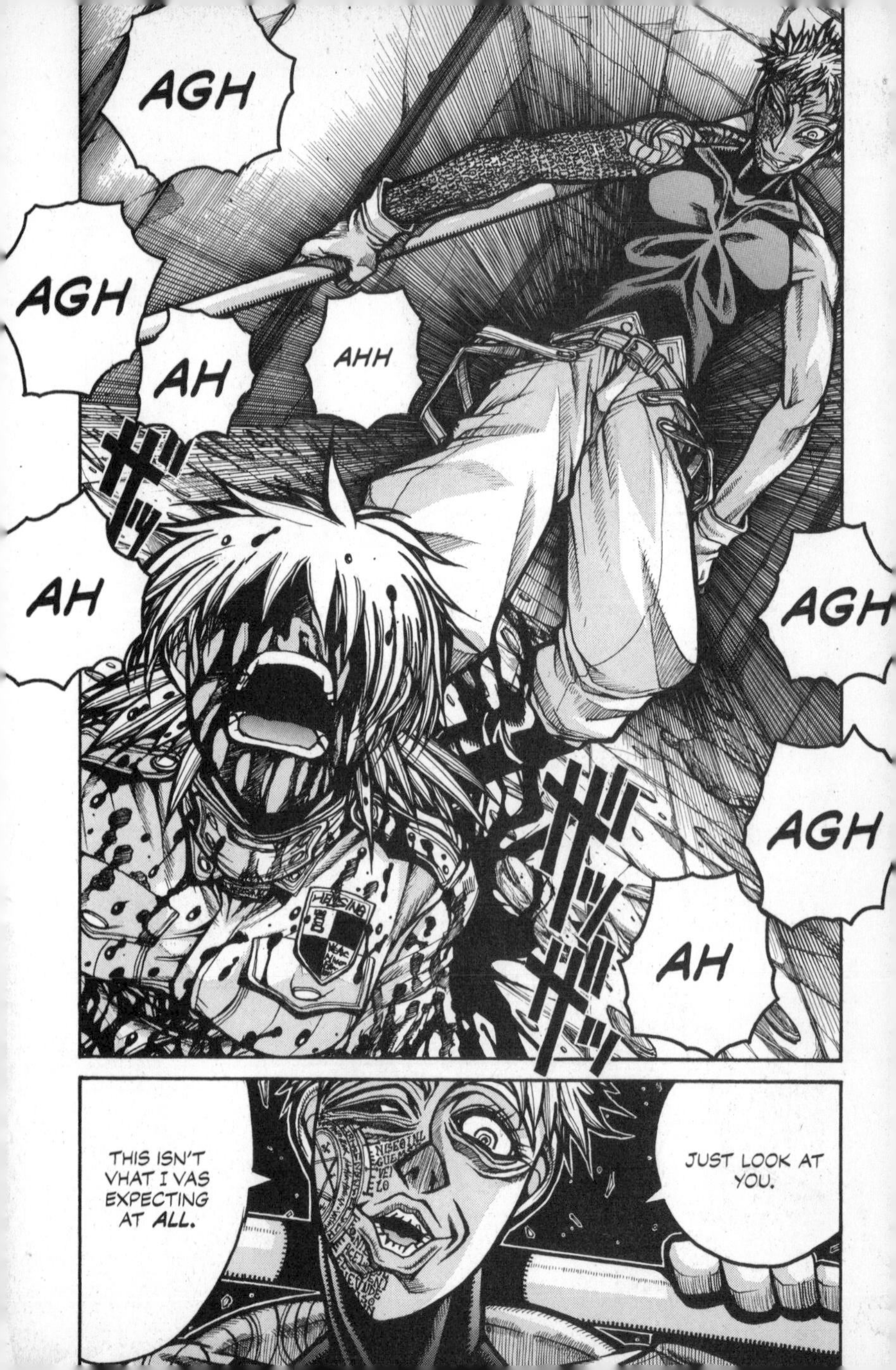
AGH
AGH
AHH
AH
AGH
AH
AGH
AH
JUST LOOK AT YOU.
THIS ISN'T VHAT I VAS EXPECTING AT ALL.

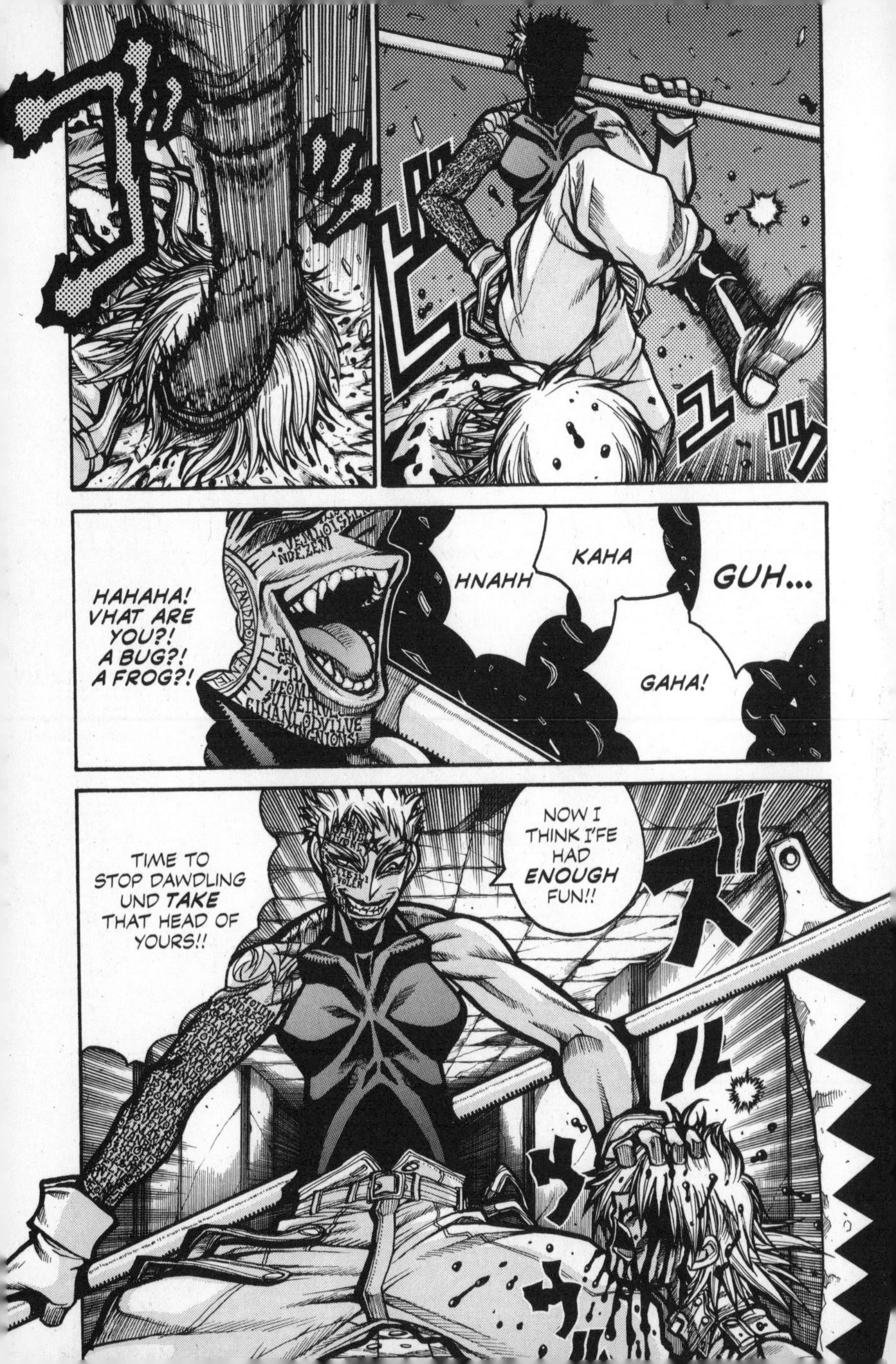
GUH...
KAHA
GAHA!
HNAHH
HAHAHA! VHAT ARE YOU?! A BUG?! A FROG?!
NOW I THINK I'FE HAD ENOUGH FUN!!
TIME TO STOP DAWDLING UND TAKE THAT HEAD OF YOURS!!

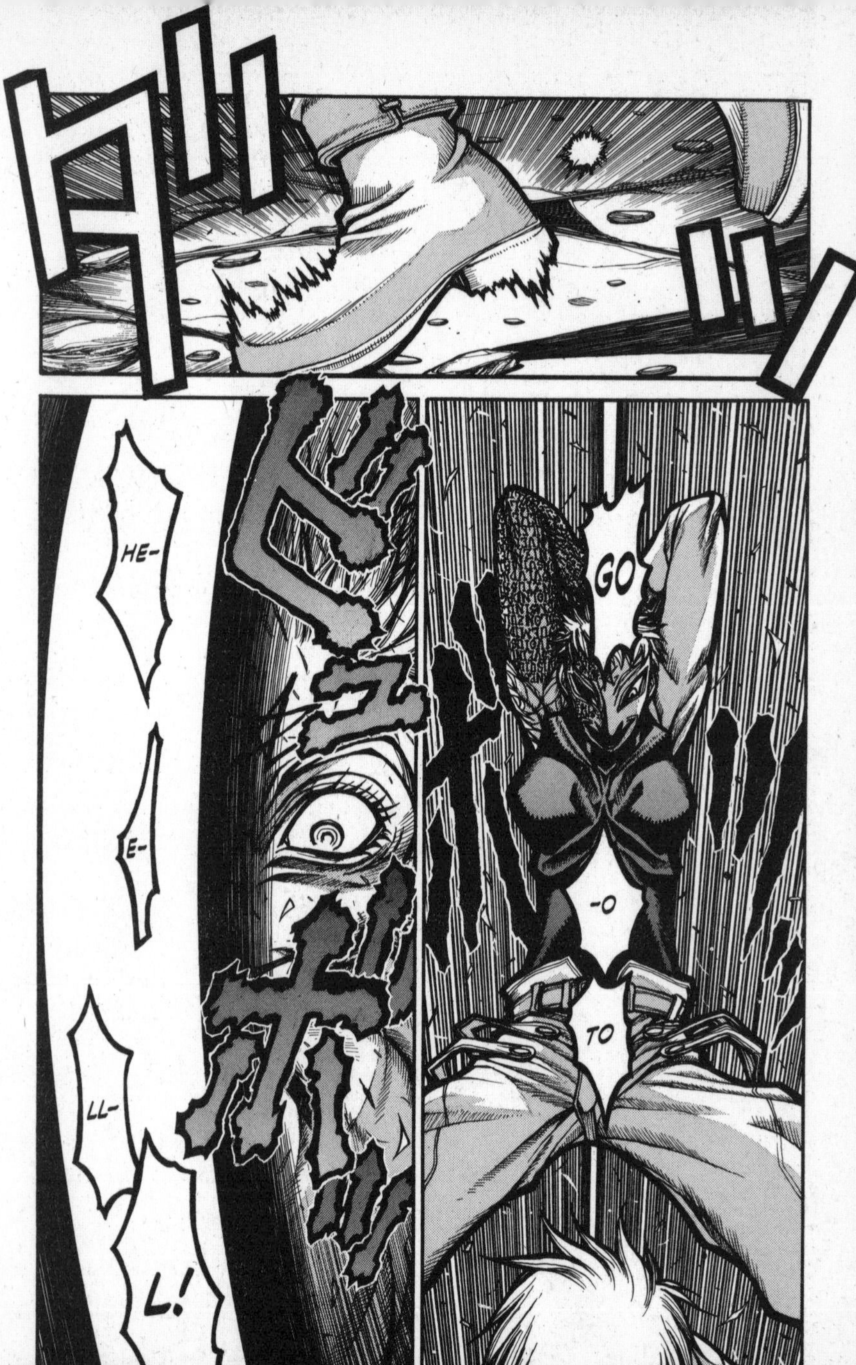
GO
-O
TO
HE-
E-
LL-
L!

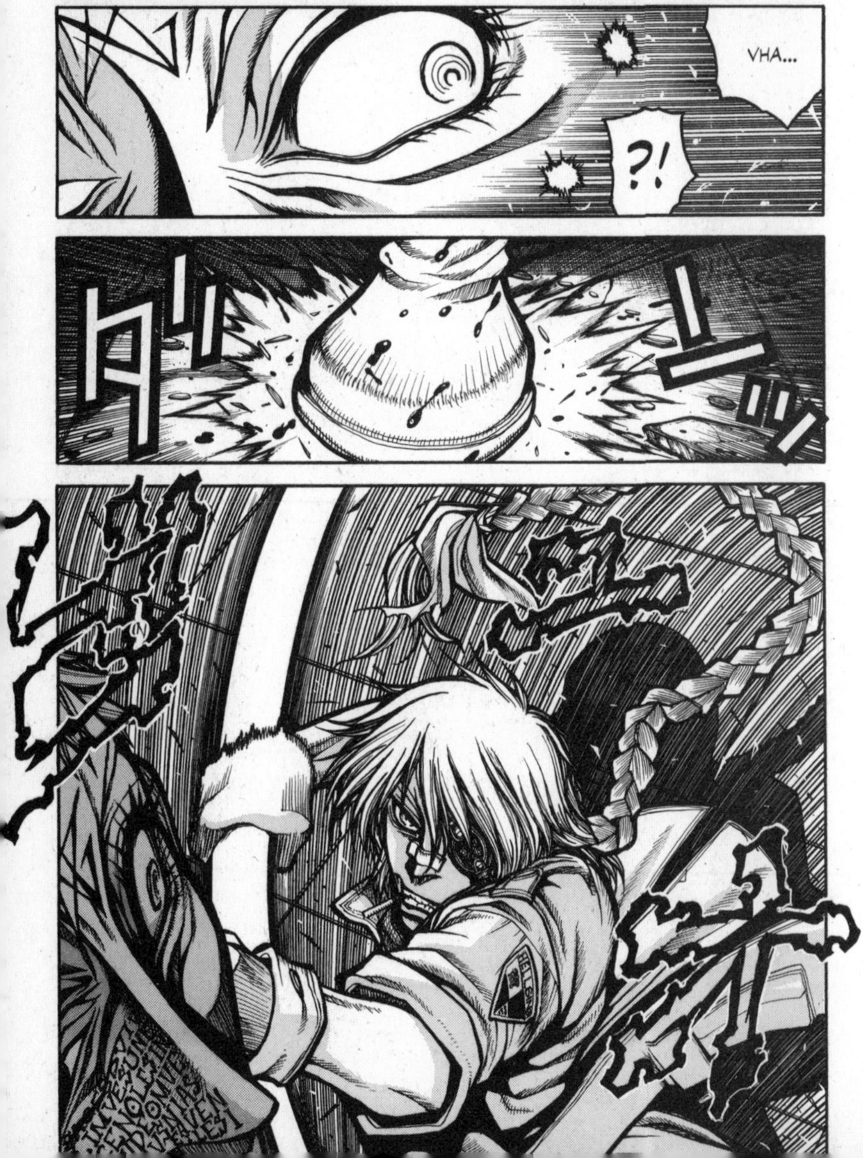
VHA...
?!

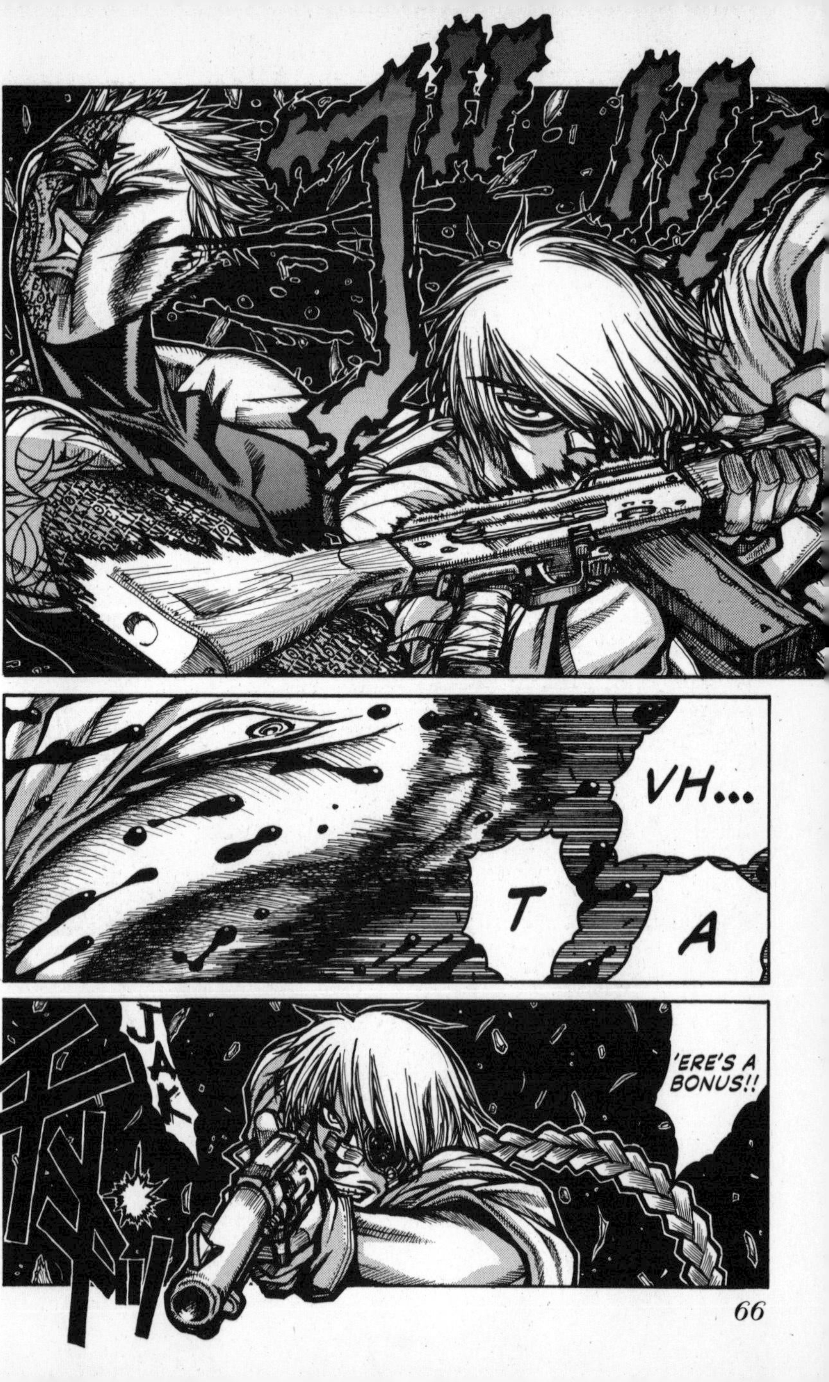
VH...
T
A
'ERE'S A BONUS!!
JAK

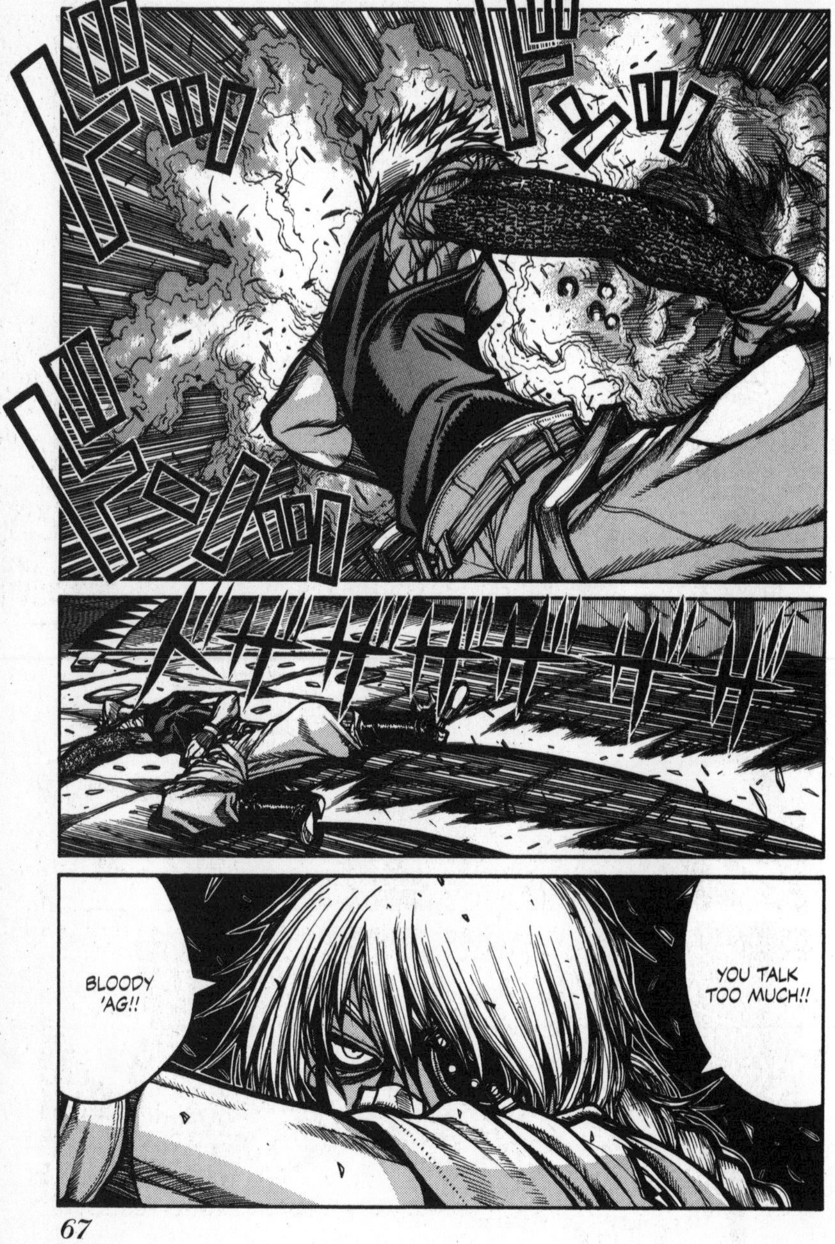
YOU TALK TOO MUCH!!
BLOODY 'AG!!

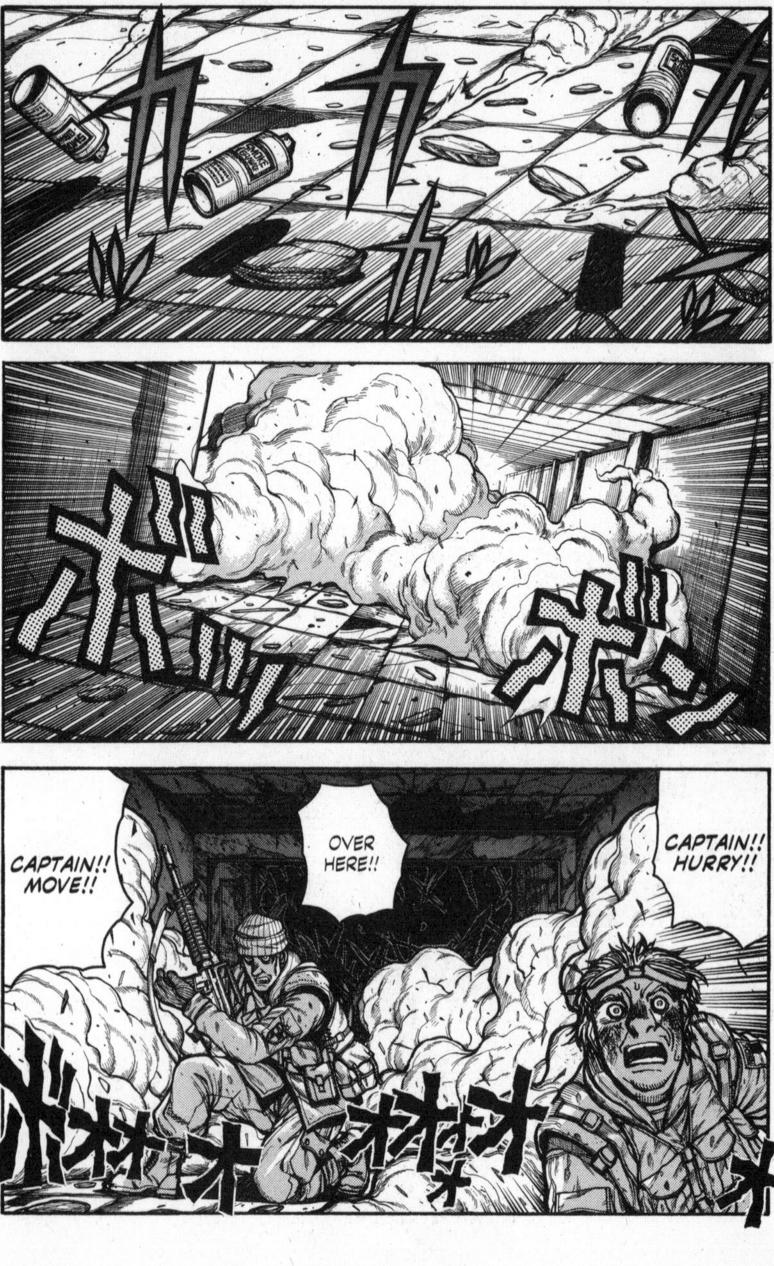
CAPTAIN!! HURRY!!
OVER HERE!!
CAPTAIN!! MOVE!!

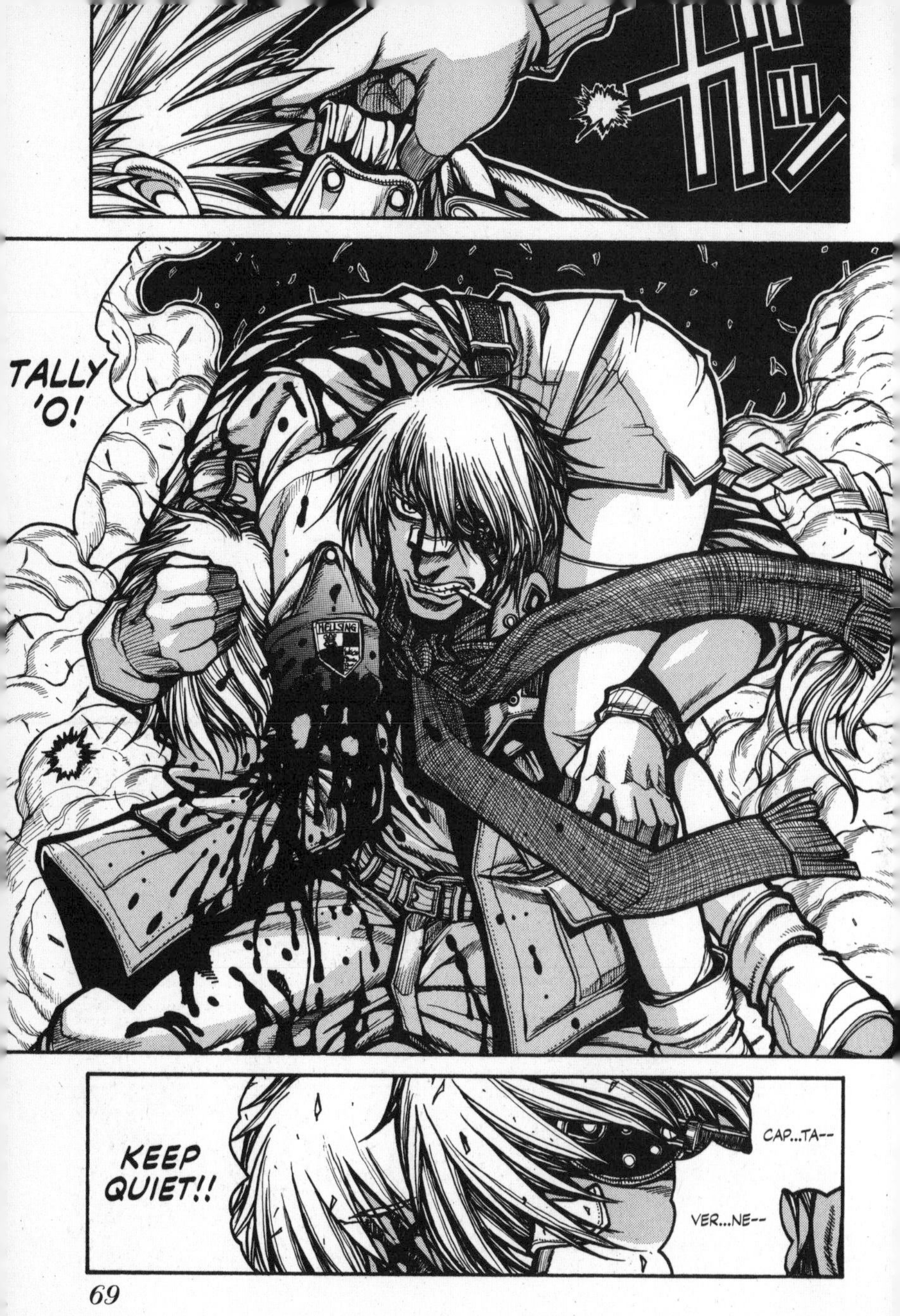
ガッ
TALLY 'O!
CAP...TA--
VER...NE--
KEEP QUIET!!

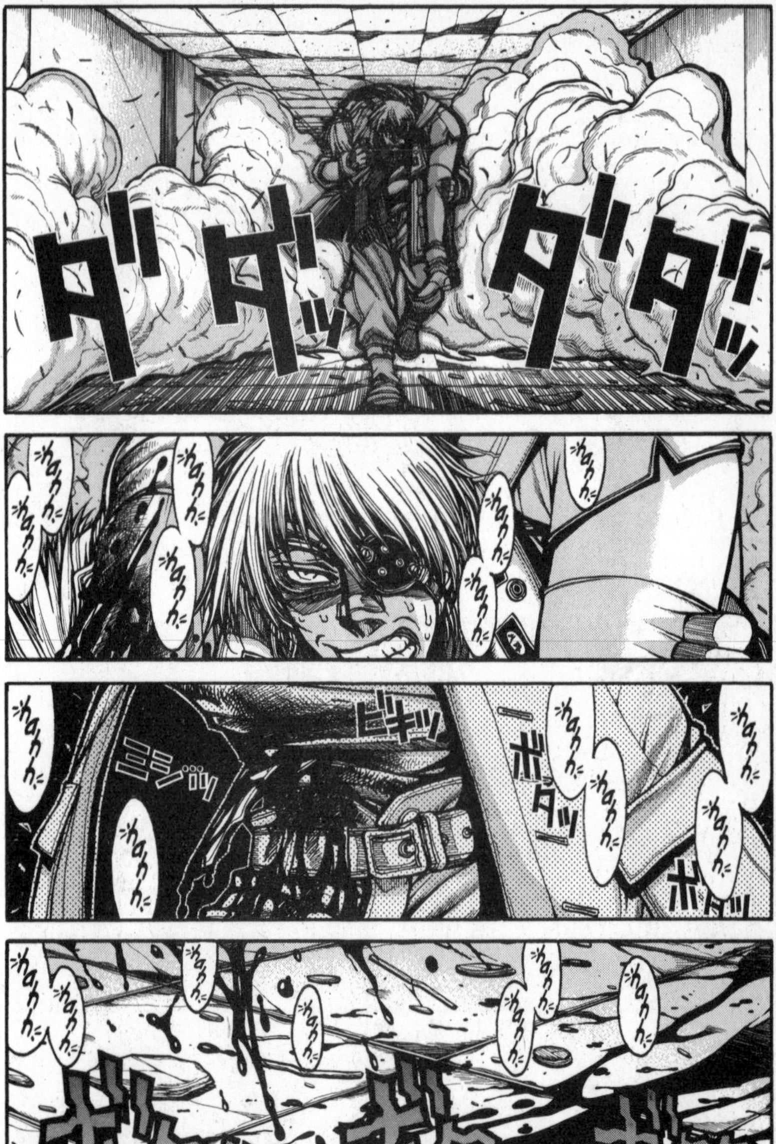
ダダダッ
ダダッ
ビキッ
ミシッ
ボタッ
ボタッ
ボタッ ボタッ ボタタッ

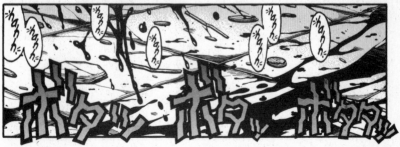

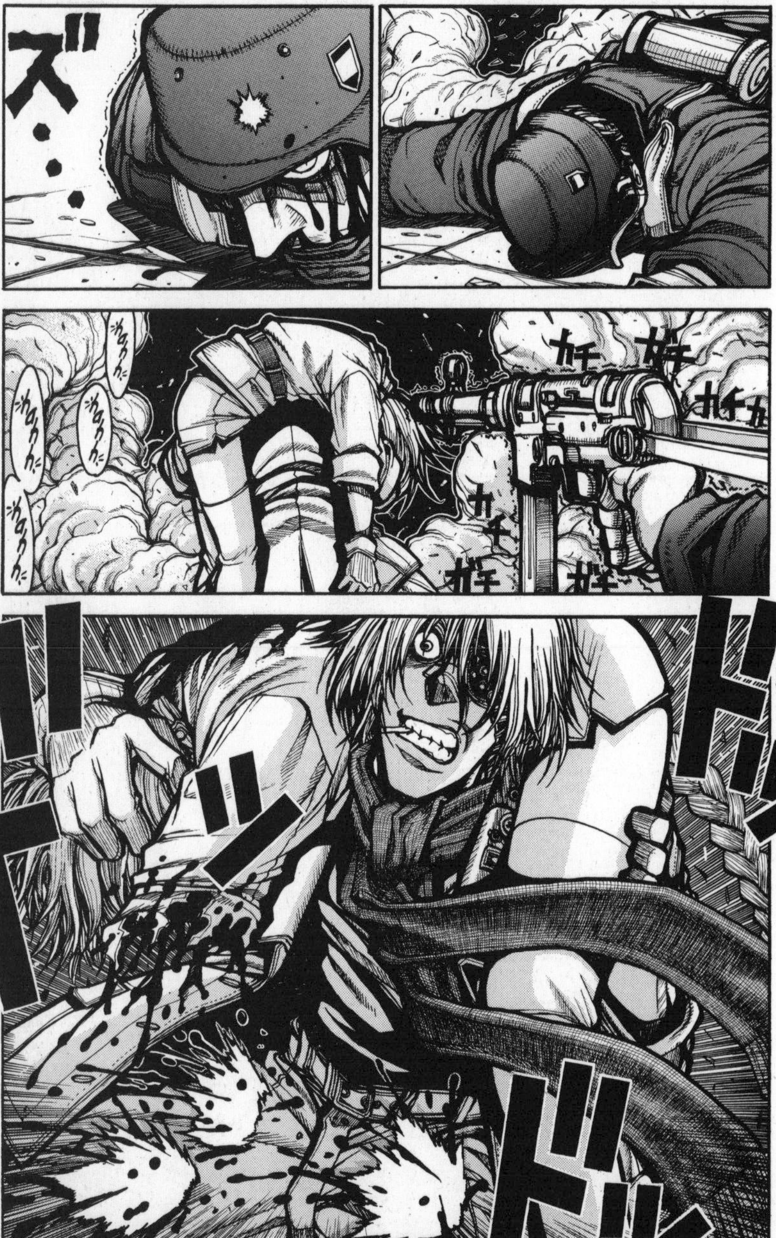
ズ…
ガチ
ガチ
ガチガ
わあんん
わあんん
わあんん
わあんん
ガチ
ガチ
ガチ
ガチ
ドドド
ドドッ
ドドド

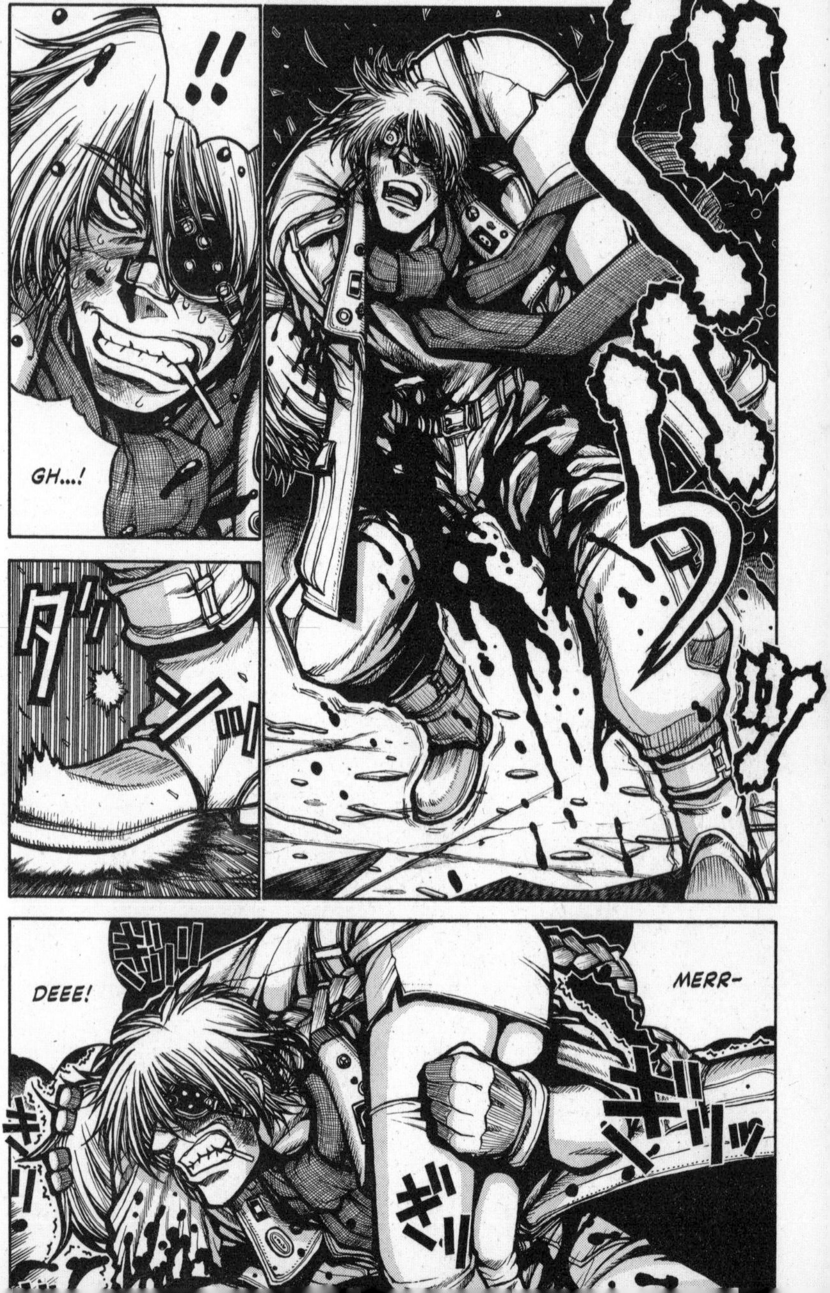
!!
GH...!
MERR-
DEEE!

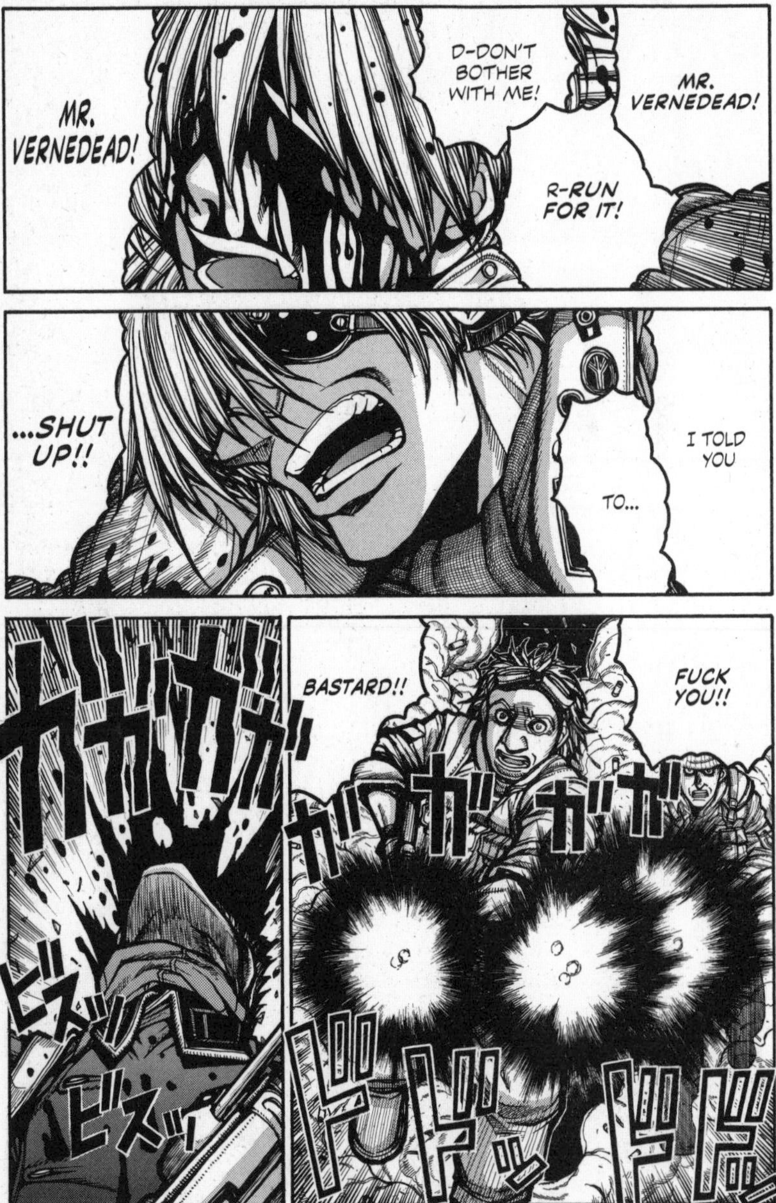
MR. VERNEDEAD!
D-DON'T BOTHER WITH ME!
R-RUN FOR IT!
MR. VERNEDEAD!
I TOLD YOU
TO...
...SHUT UP!!
FUCK YOU!!
BASTARD!!
ビズッ
ビズッ

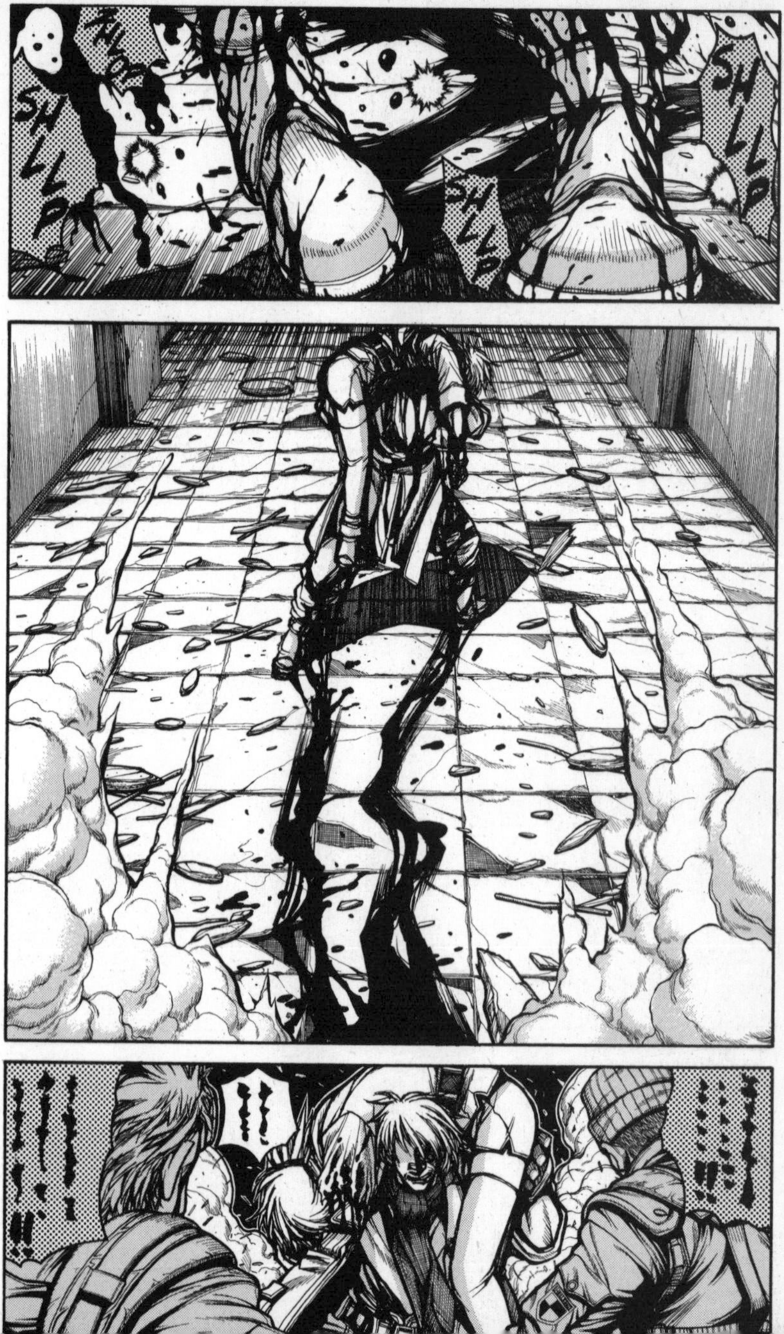
SHLLLP
SHLLP
SHLLLP

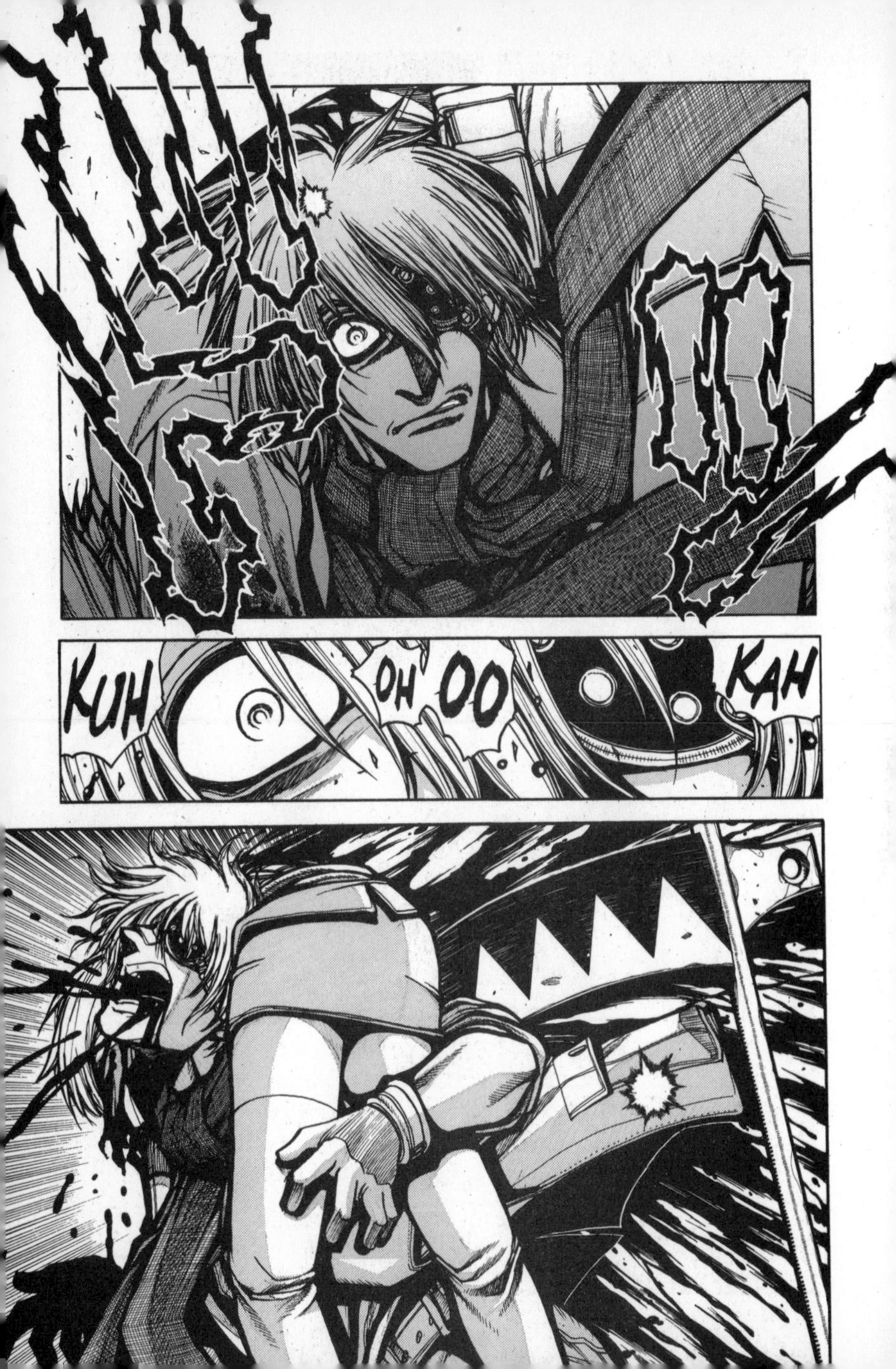
KUH OH OO KAH

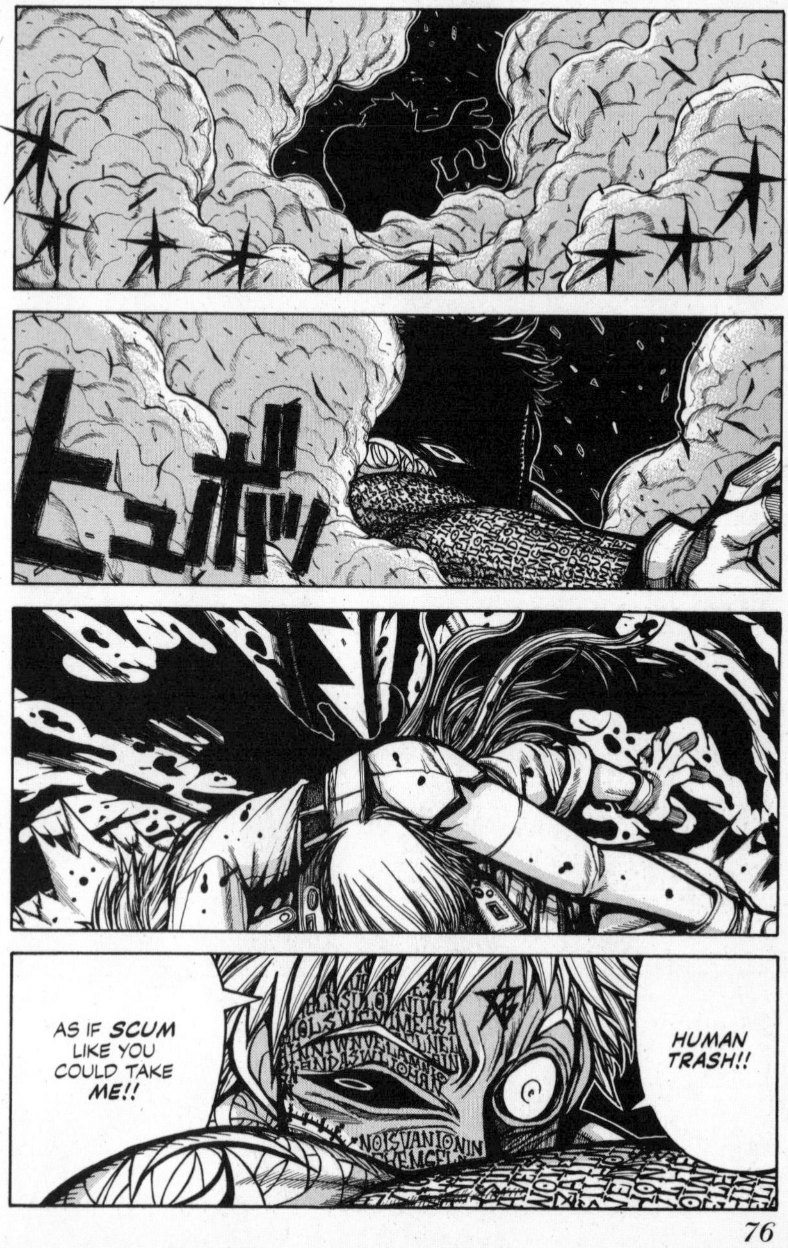
ヒュボッ
HUMAN TRASH!!
AS IF SCUM LIKE YOU COULD TAKE ME!!

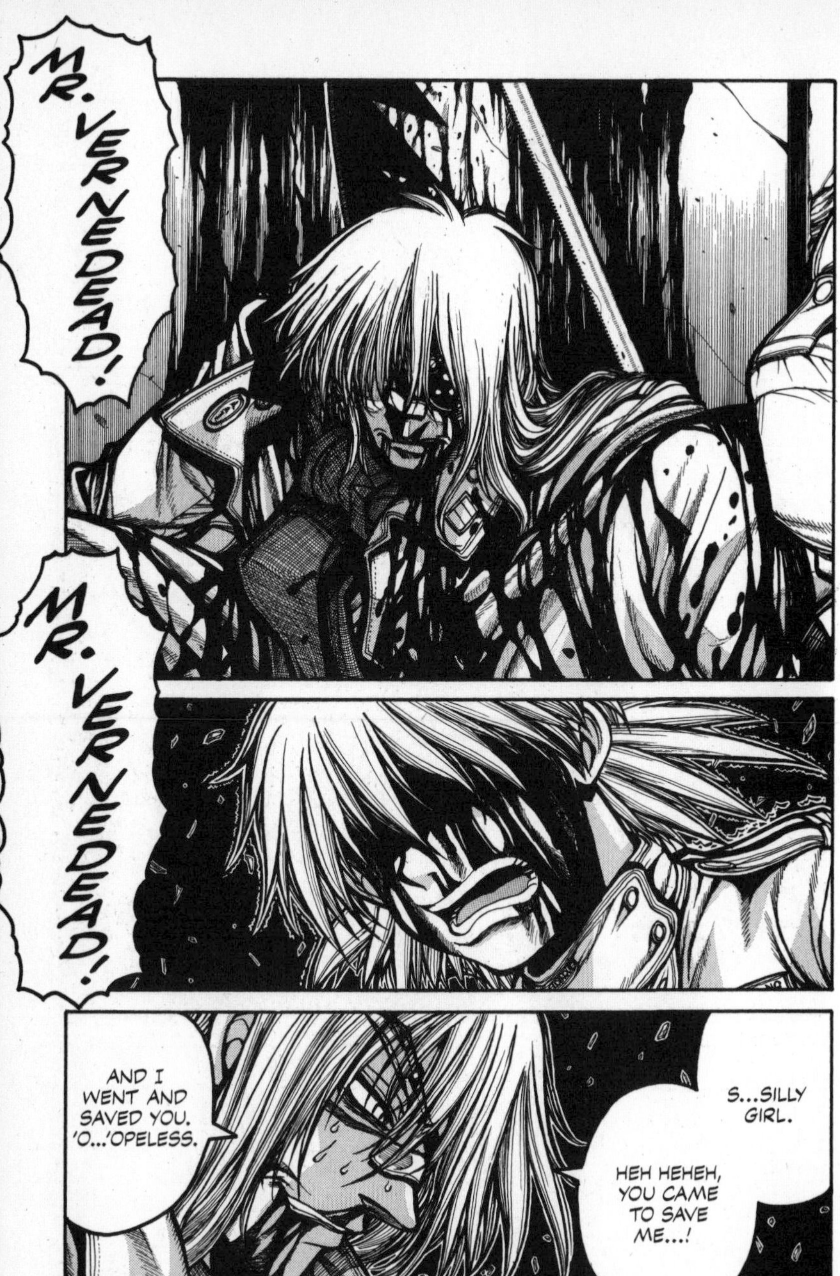
MR. VERNEDEAD!
MR. VERNEDEAD!
S...SILLY GIRL.
HEH HEHEH, YOU CAME TO SAVE ME...!
AND I WENT AND SAVED YOU. 'O...'OPELESS.

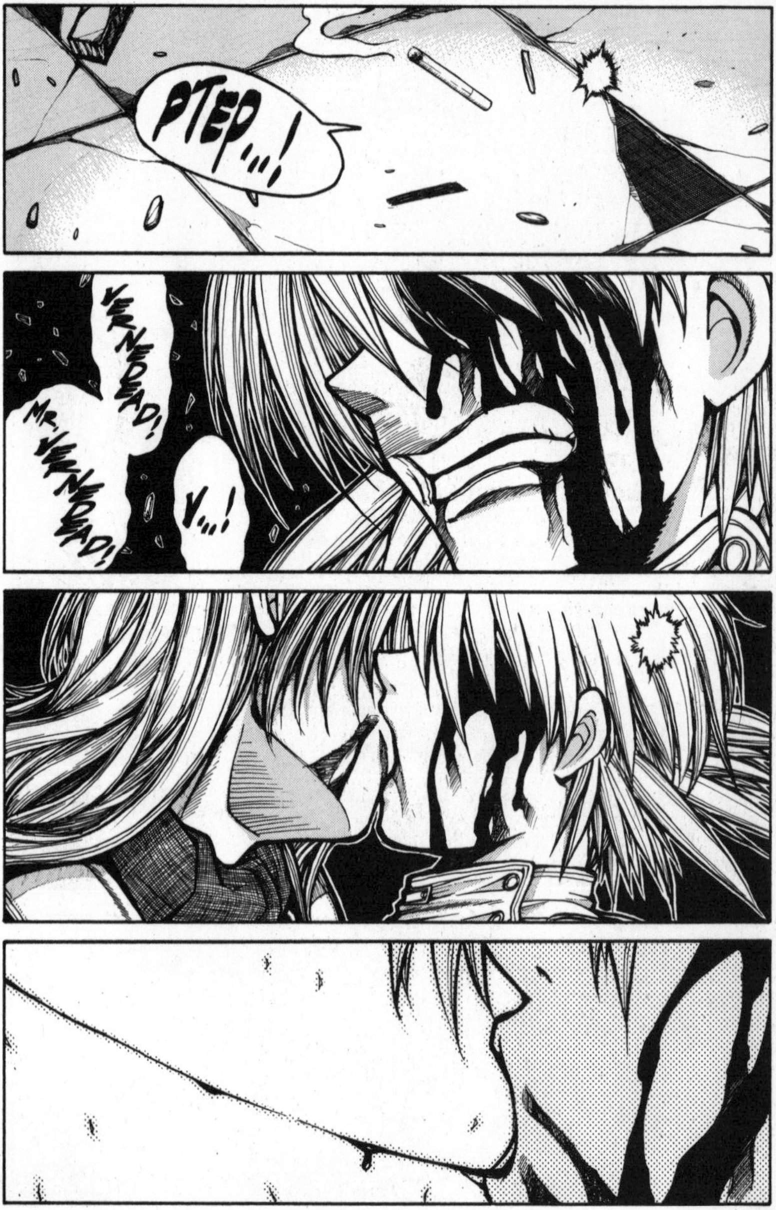
PTEP...!
V...!
MR. VERNEDEAD!
VERNEDEAD!

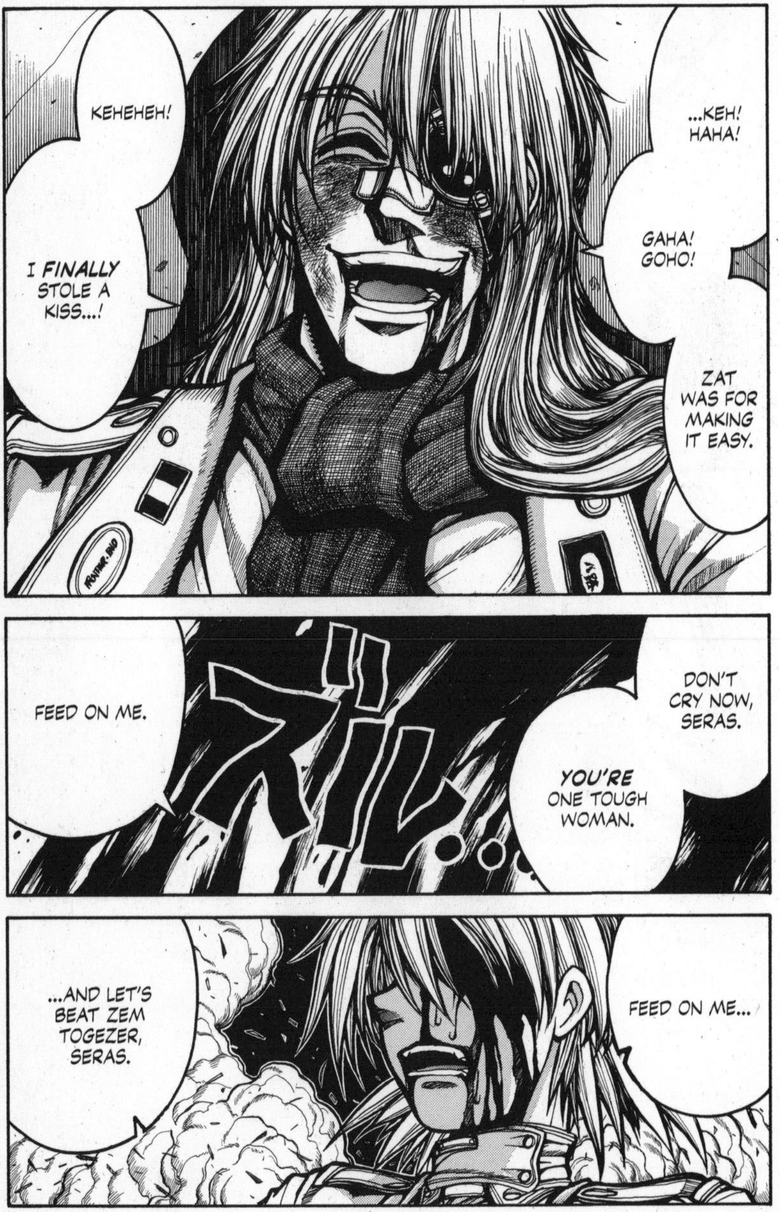
...KEH! HAHA!
GAHA! GOHO!
ZAT WAS FOR MAKING IT EASY.
KEHEHEH!
I FINALLY STOLE A KISS...!
DON'T CRY NOW, SERAS.
YOU'RE ONE TOUGH WOMAN.
ズル...
FEED ON ME.
FEED ON ME...
...AND LET'S BEAT ZEM TOGEZER, SERAS.

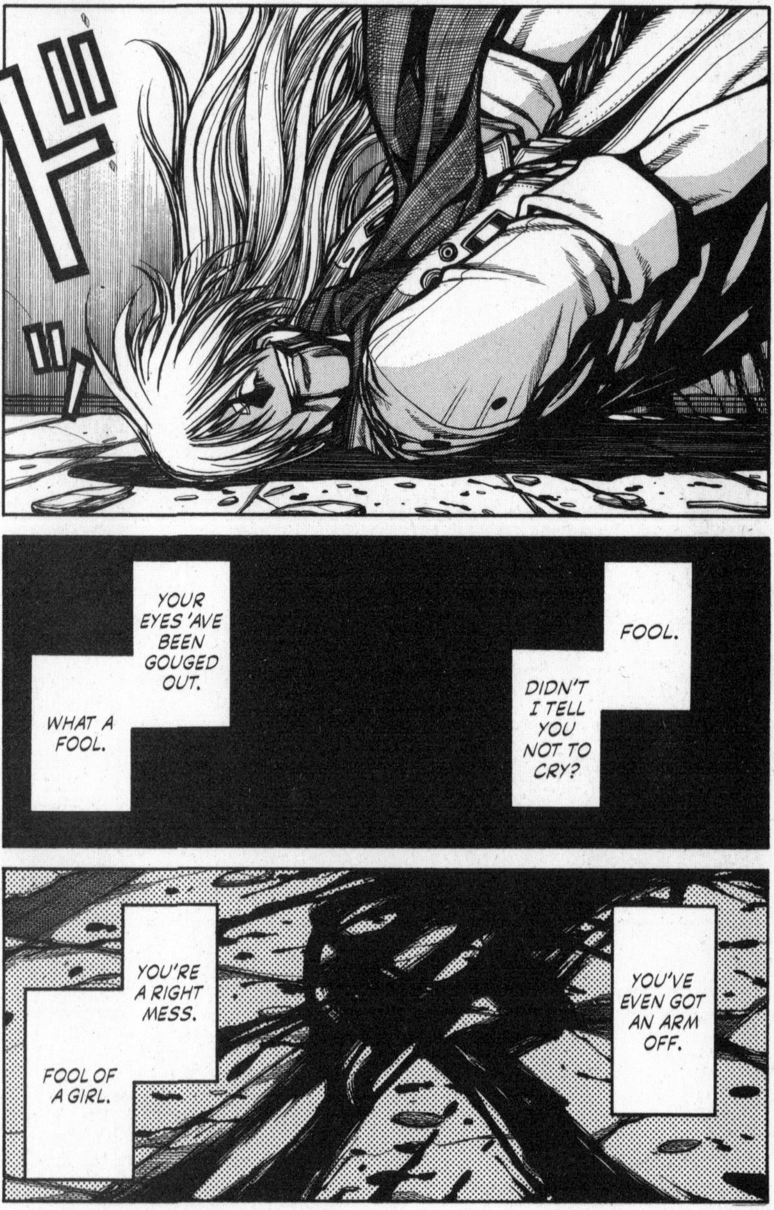
ドッ
FOOL.
DIDN'T I TELL YOU NOT TO CRY?
YOUR EYES 'AVE BEEN GOUGED OUT.
WHAT A FOOL.
YOU'VE EVEN GOT AN ARM OFF.
YOU'RE A RIGHT MESS.
FOOL OF A GIRL.

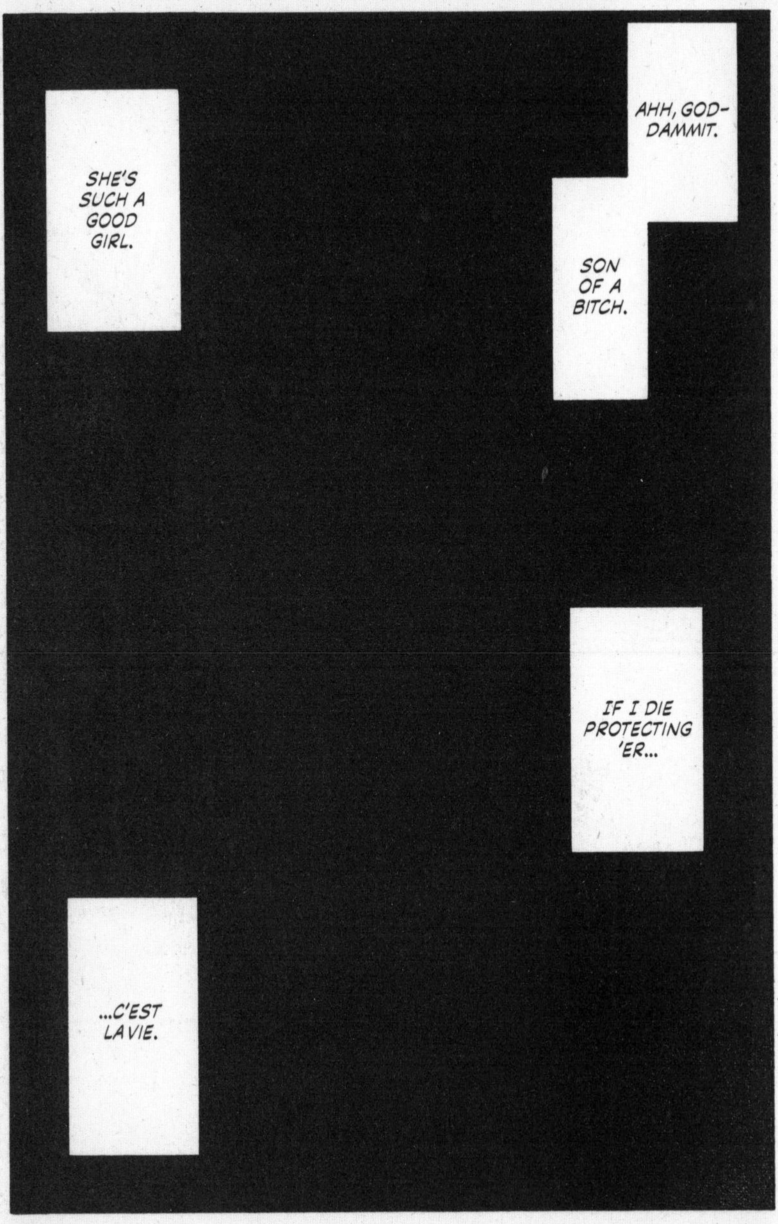
AHH, GOD-DAMMIT.
SON OF A BITCH.
SHE'S SUCH A GOOD GIRL.
IF I DIE PROTECTING 'ER...
...C'EST LA VIE.

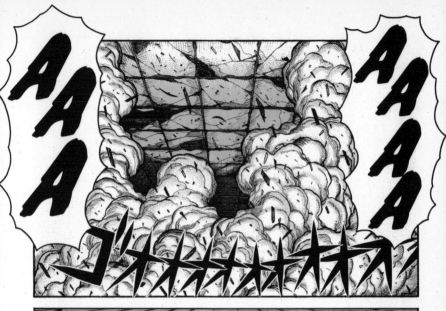

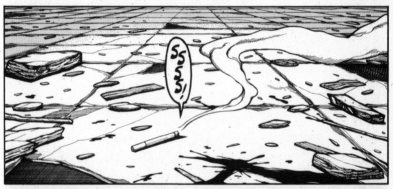

TO BE CONTINUED

ORDER 5 / END

82

ORDER 6

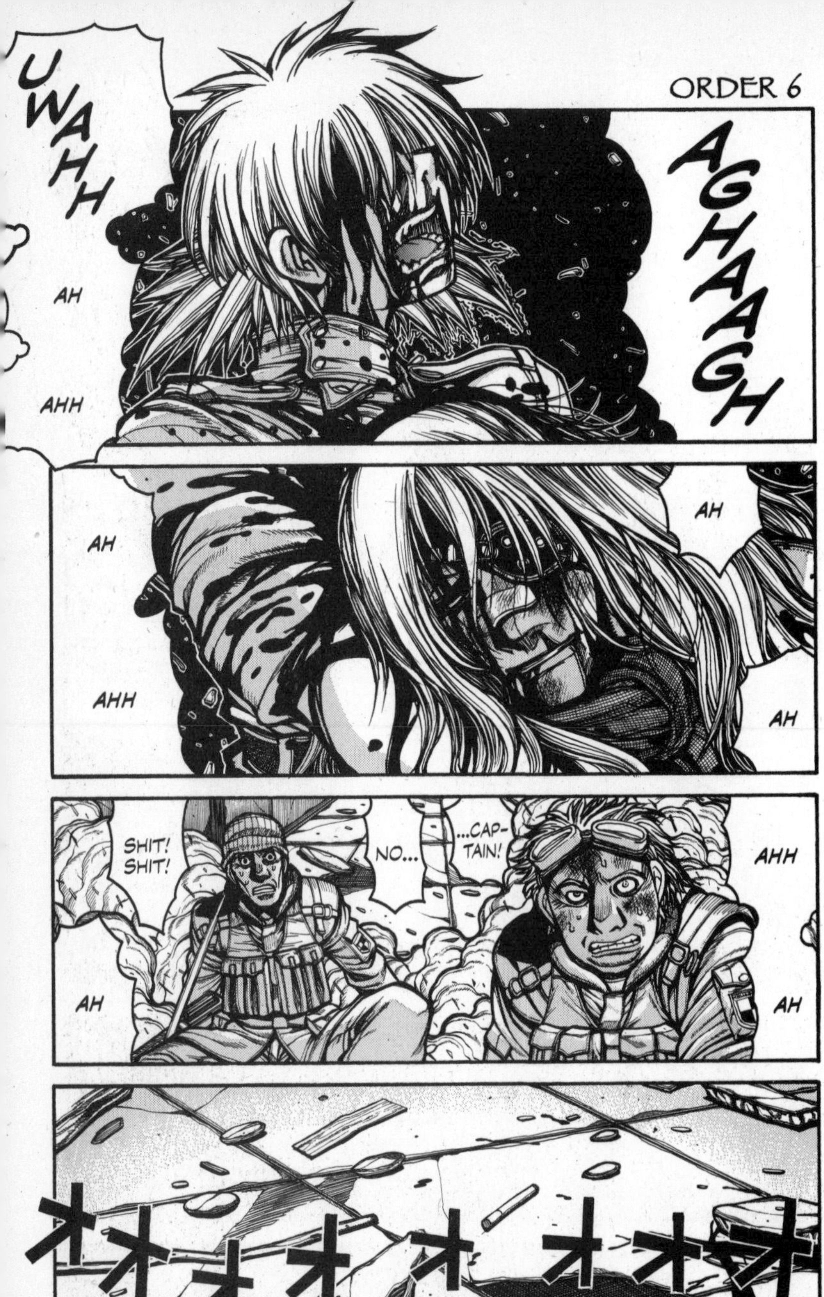
AGHAAAGH
UWAHH
AH
AHH
AH
AH
AH
AHH
AHH
AH
...CAP-TAIN!
NO...
SHIT! SHIT!
AH
オオオオオオオオ

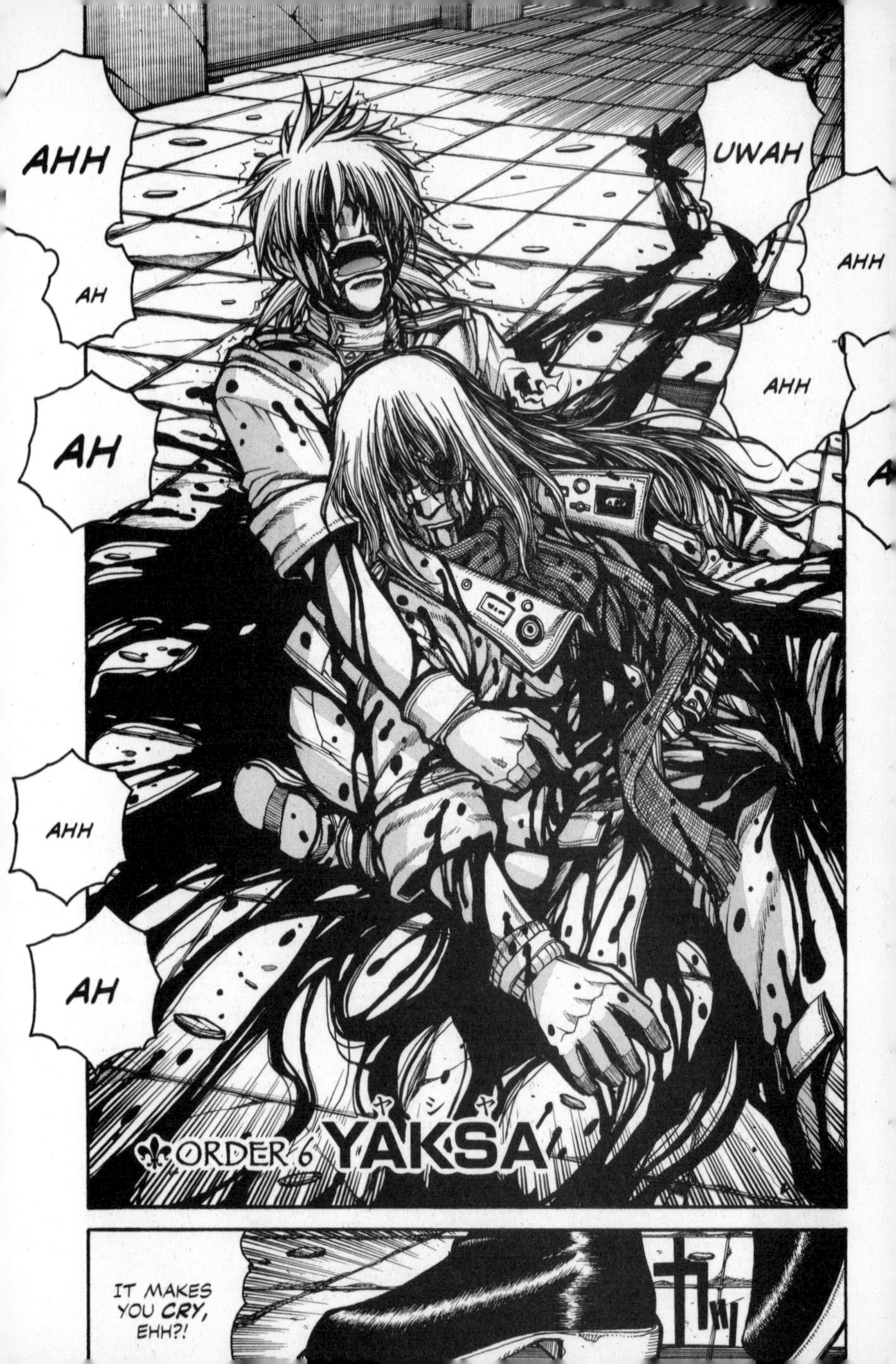
UWAH
AHH
AHH
AHH
AH
AH
AHH
AH
ヤシャ
ORDER 6 YAKSA
カッ
IT MAKES YOU CRY, EHH?!

...IT IST BECAUSE HE FLITS ABOUT...

...LIKE SOME ANNOYING *INSECT*...

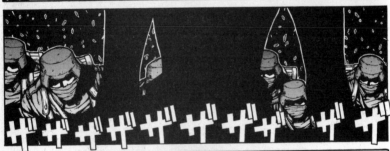

...THAT HE IST DEAD!!

NOW YOU'VE *REALLY* SUCCEEDED IN *PISSING* ME OFF!!

VHAT SHALL I DO VITH YOU THEN, EH?!

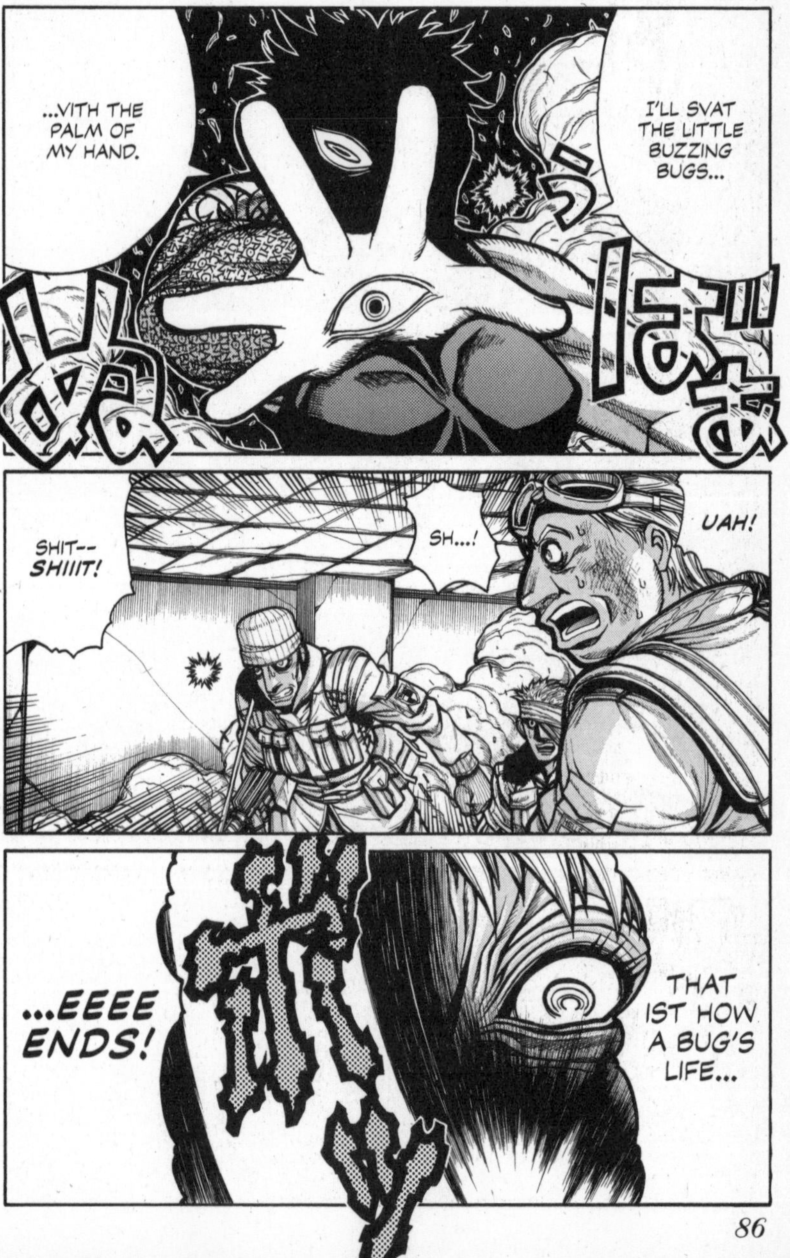
I'LL SVAT THE LITTLE BUZZING BUGS...
...VITH THE PALM OF MY HAND.
UAH!
SH...!
SHIT-- SHIIIT!
THAT IST HOW A BUG'S LIFE...
...EEEE ENDS!

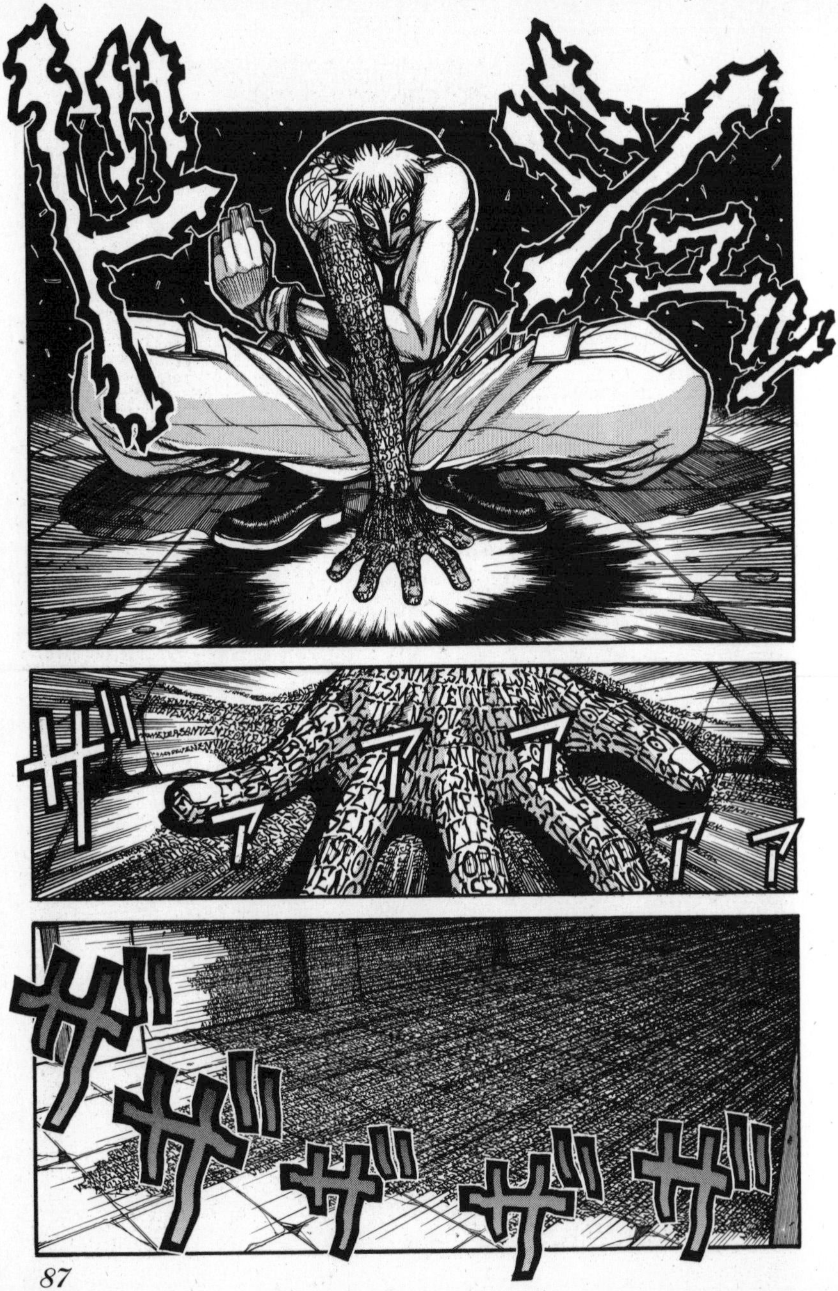
ザァァァァァ
ザザザザザ

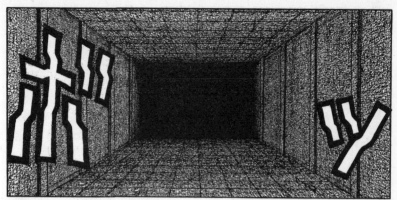

AGAIN, DAMMIT?!

AGAIN?!

AHH!

OO

AH!

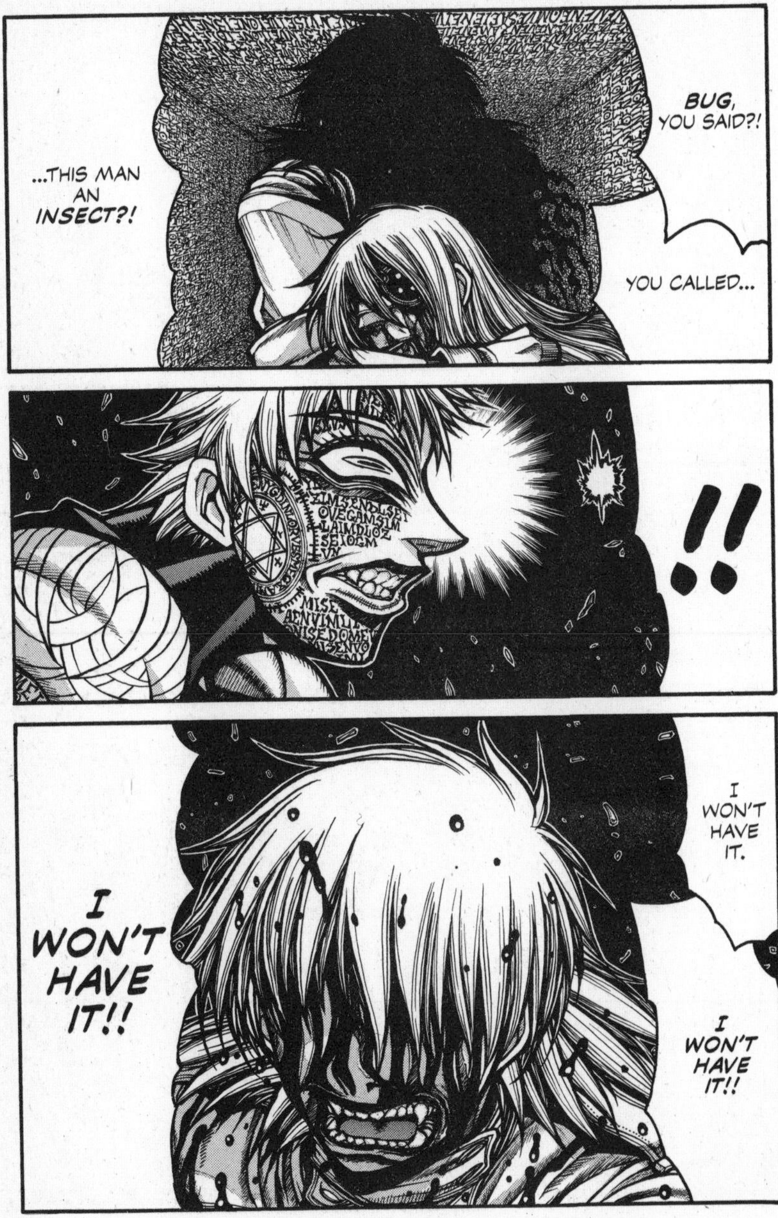
BUG, YOU SAID?!
YOU CALLED...
...THIS MAN AN INSECT?!
!!
I WON'T HAVE IT.
I WON'T HAVE IT!!
I WON'T HAVE IT!!

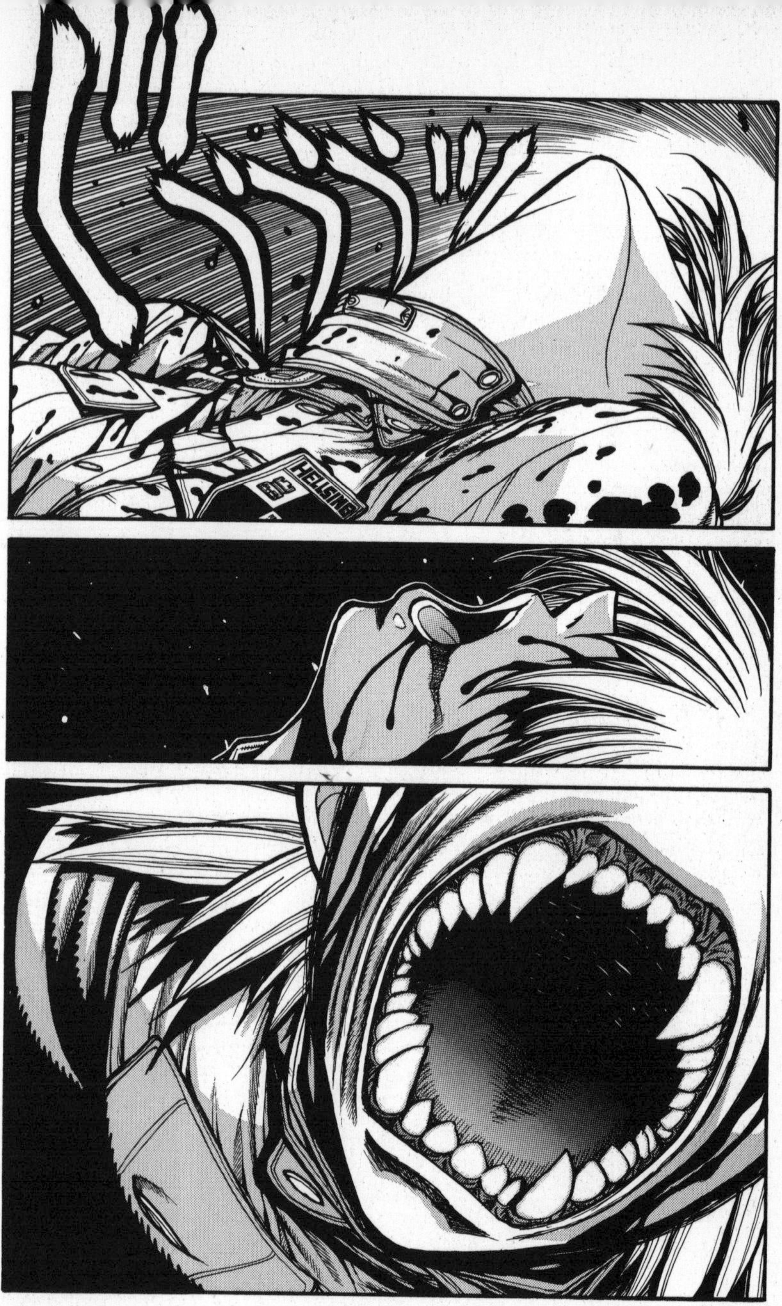
HELLSING

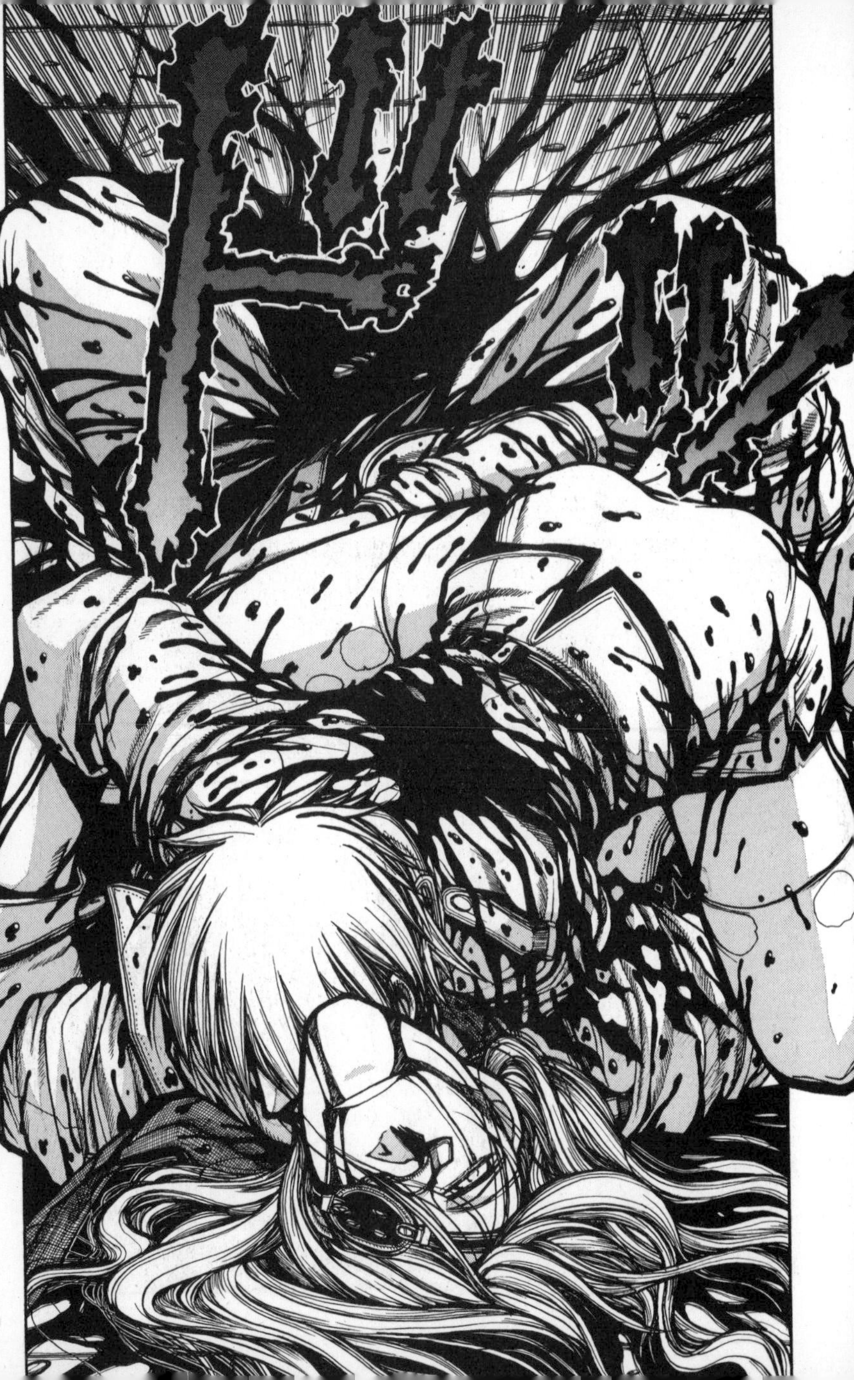

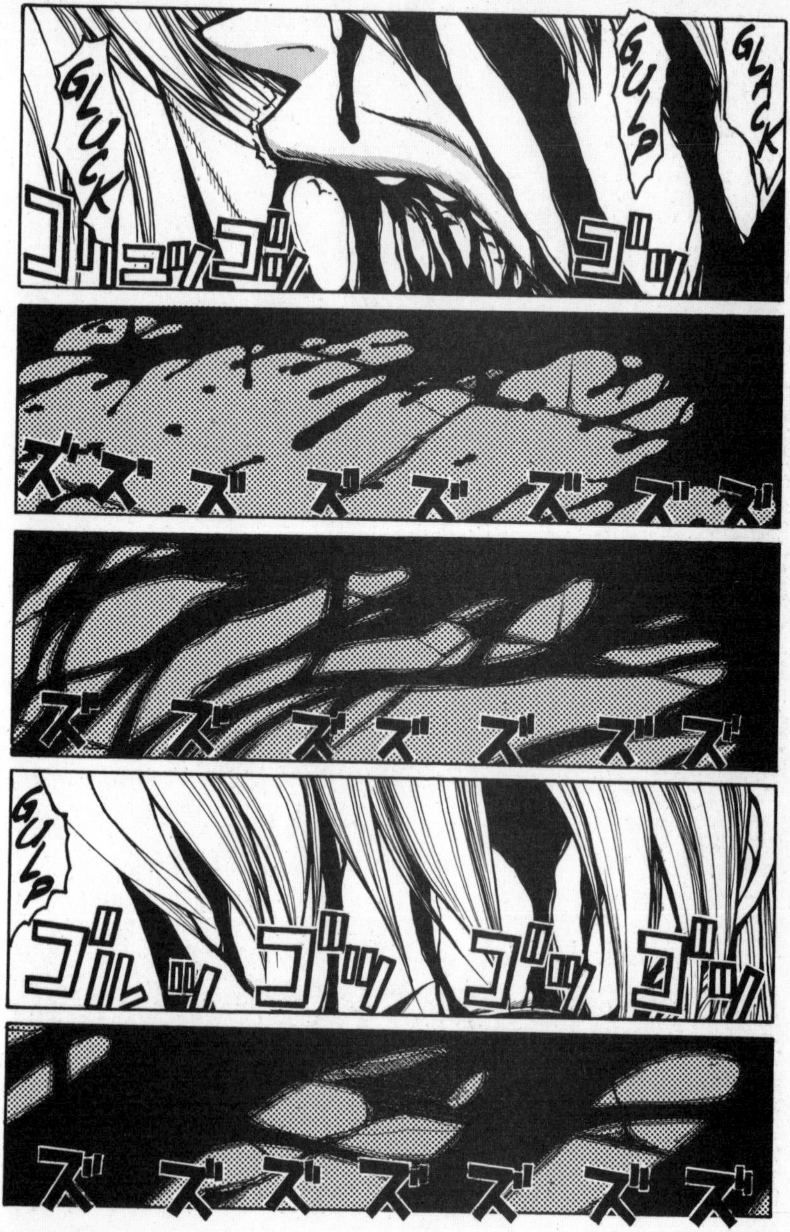
GLACK
GULP
ゴッ
ゴッ
ゴリュッ
GLUCK
ズズズズズズズズ
ズズズズズズズ
ゴクッ
ゴッ
ゴッ
ゴルッ
GULP
ズズズズズズズ

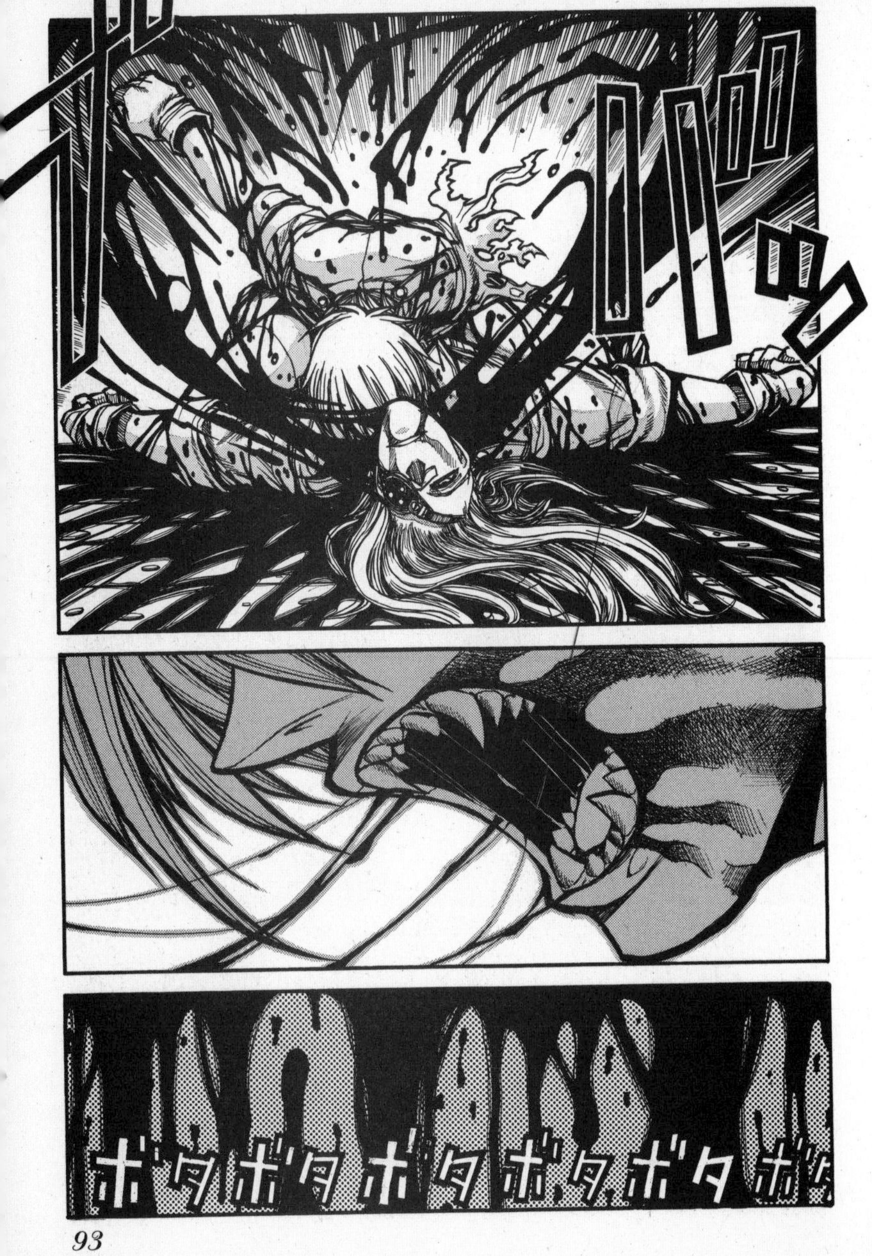
ボタボタボタボタボタボタ

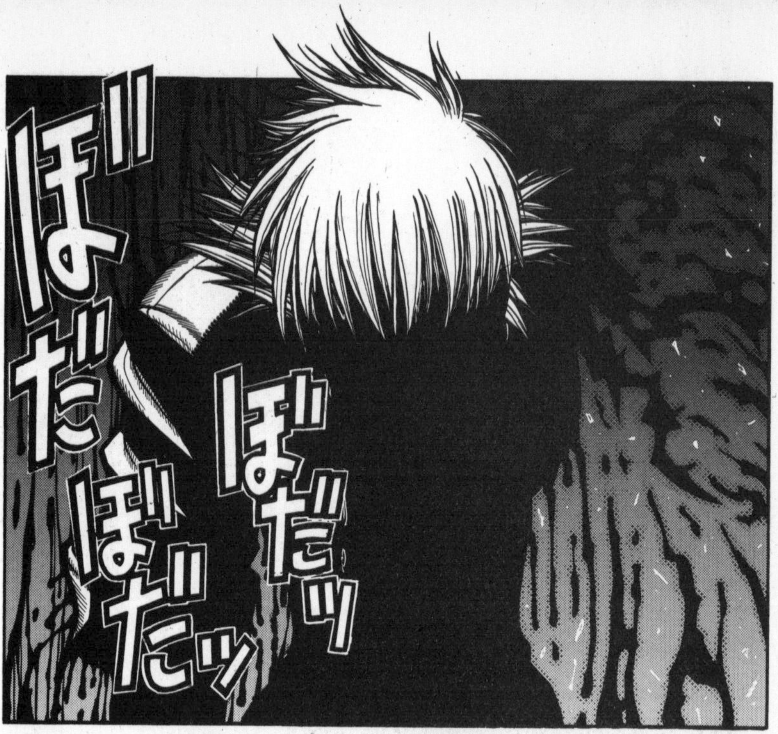
ぼたッ
ぼたぼたッ
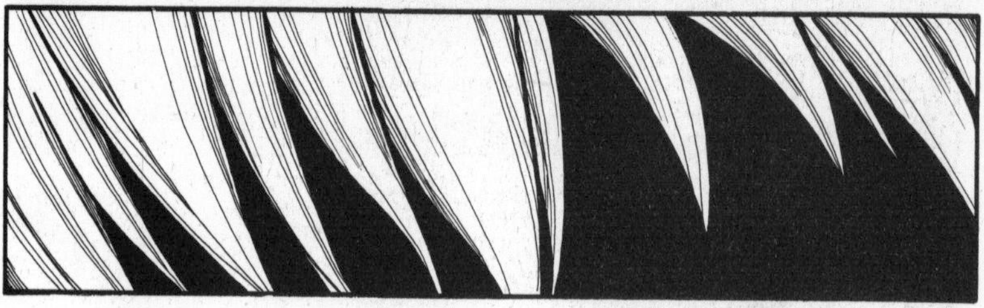
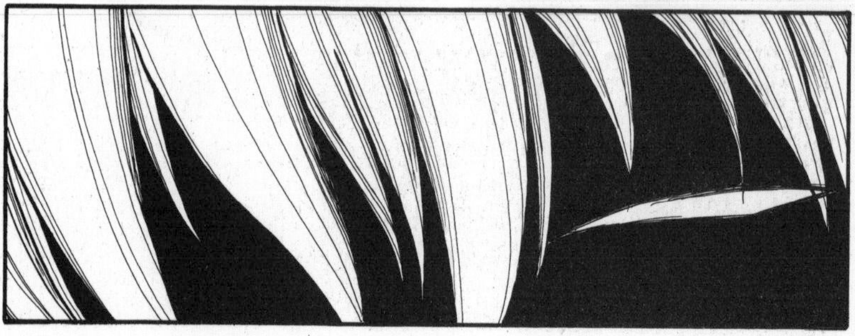

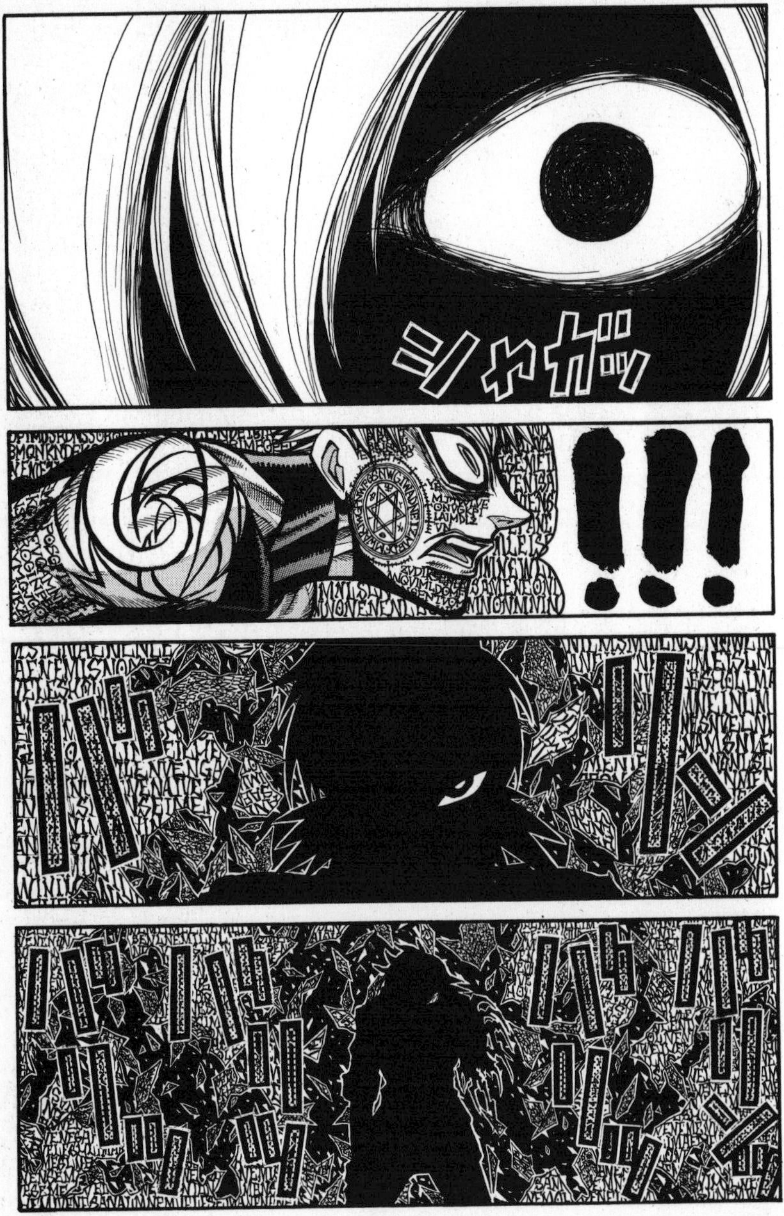
シャガッ
!!!

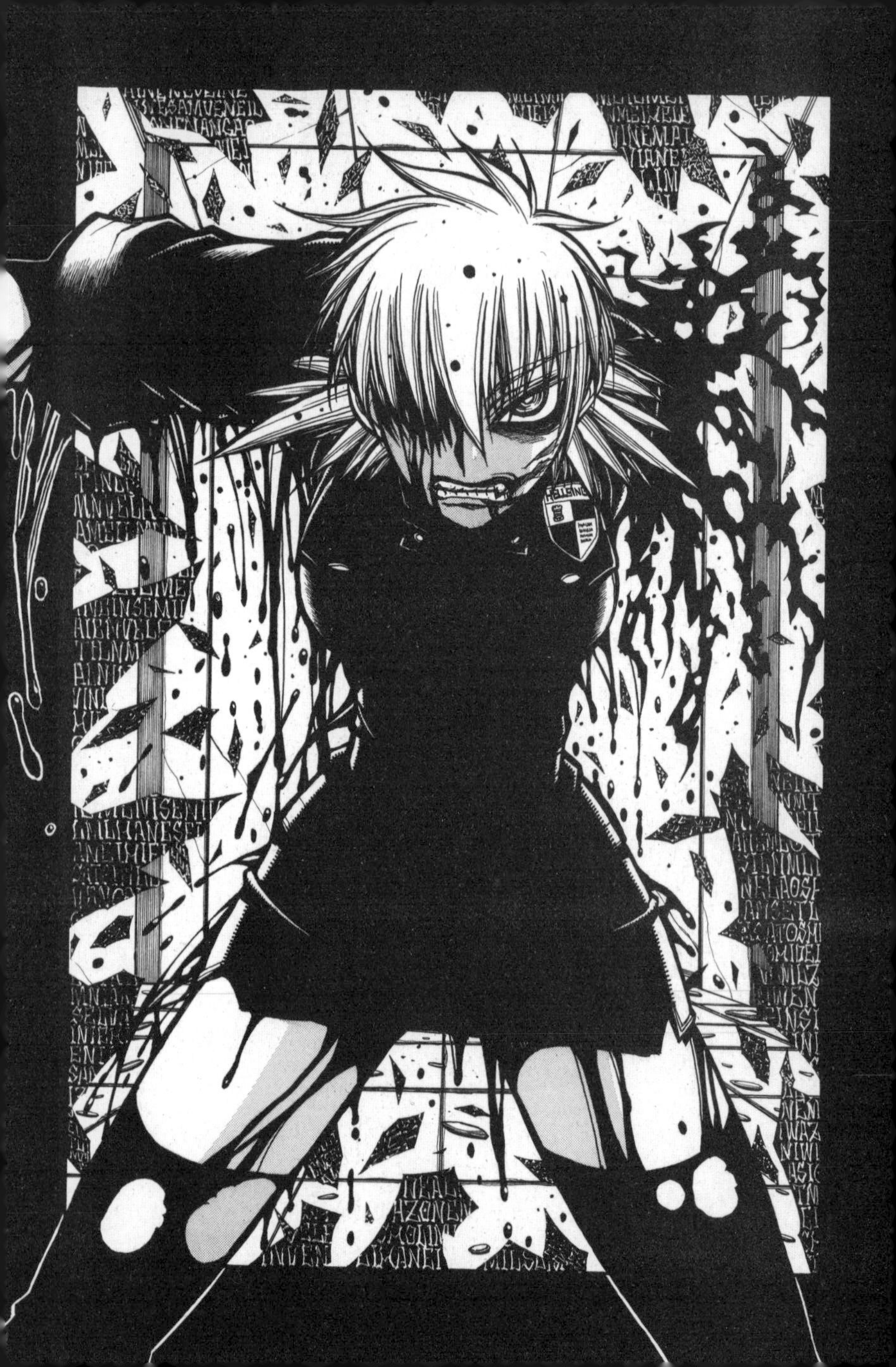
HELLSING

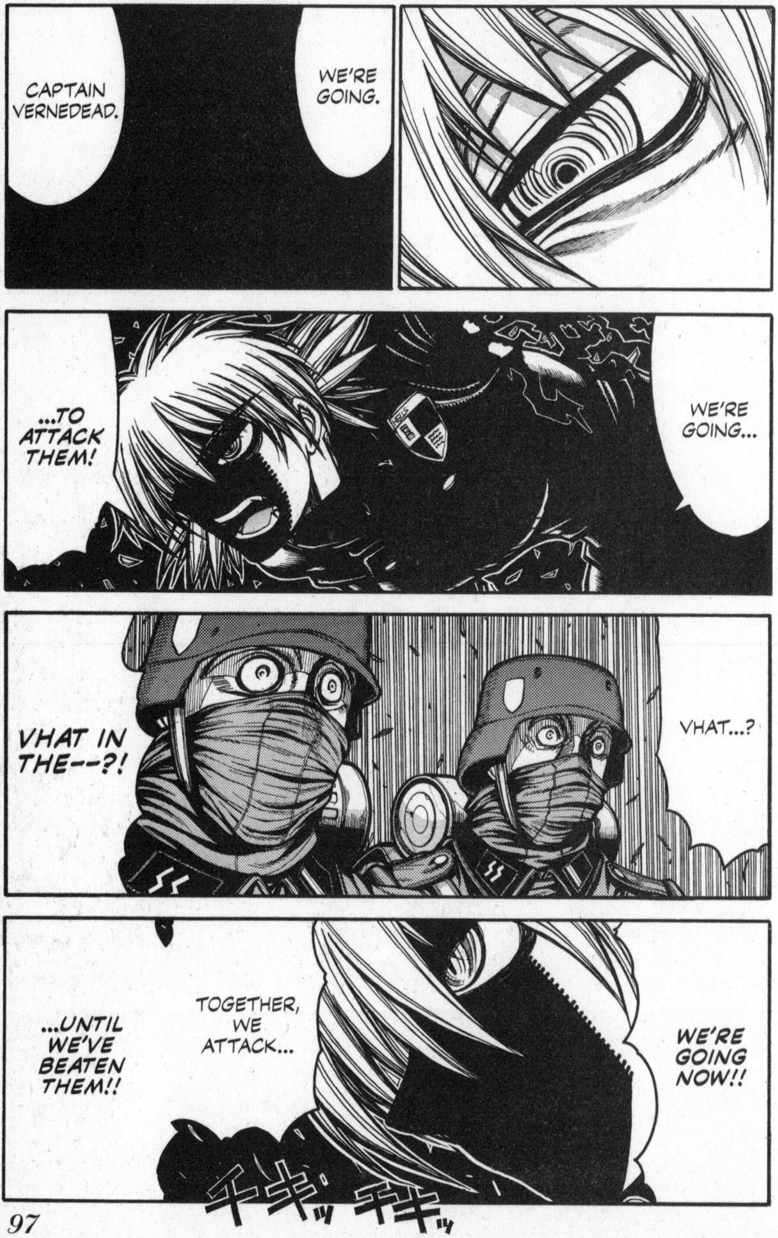
WE'RE GOING.
CAPTAIN VERNEDEAD.
WE'RE GOING...
...TO ATTACK THEM!
VHAT...?
VHAT IN THE--?!
WE'RE GOING NOW!!
TOGETHER, WE ATTACK...
...UNTIL WE'VE BEATEN THEM!!
チギッ チギッ

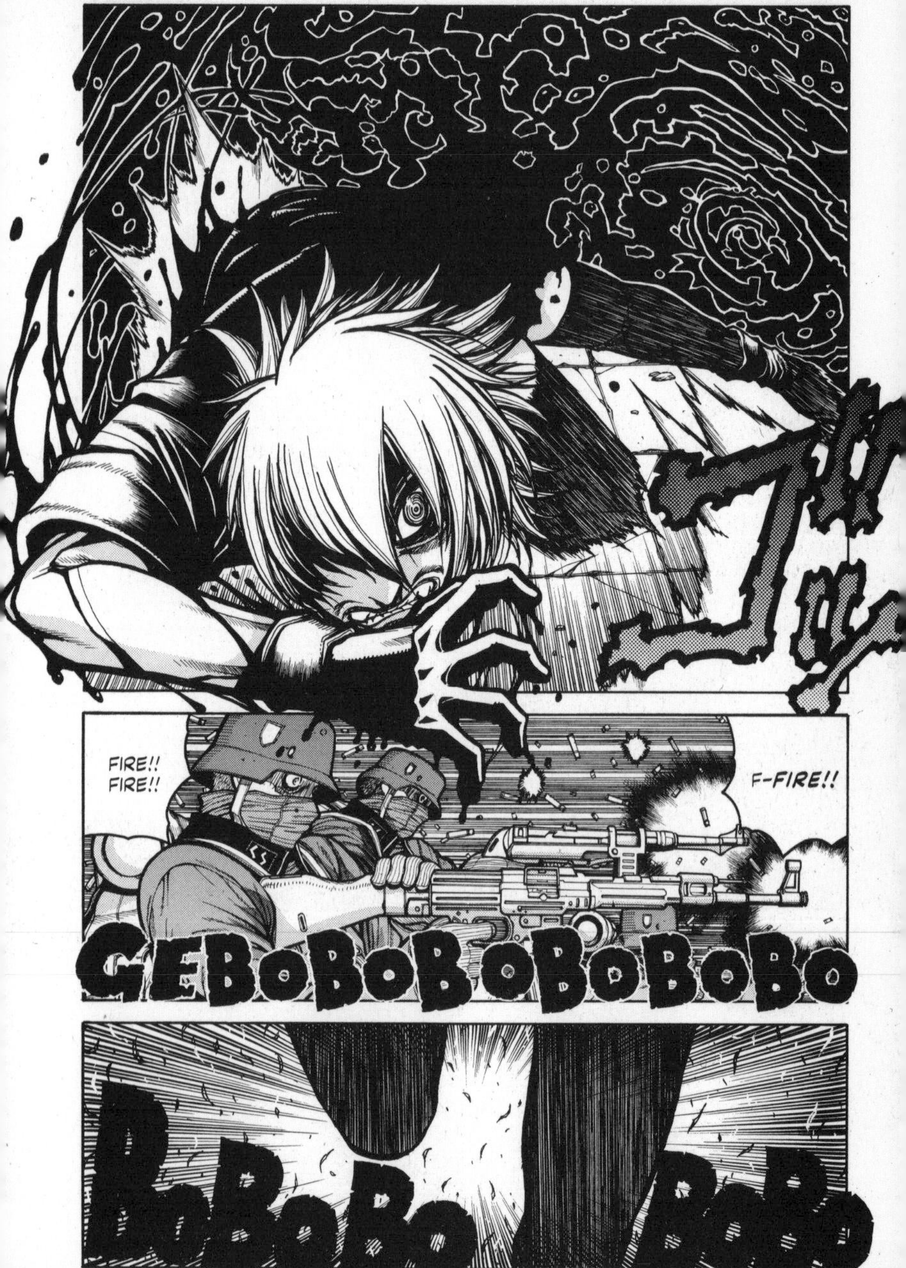
F-FIRE!!
FIRE!! FIRE!!
GEBOBOBOBOBOBO

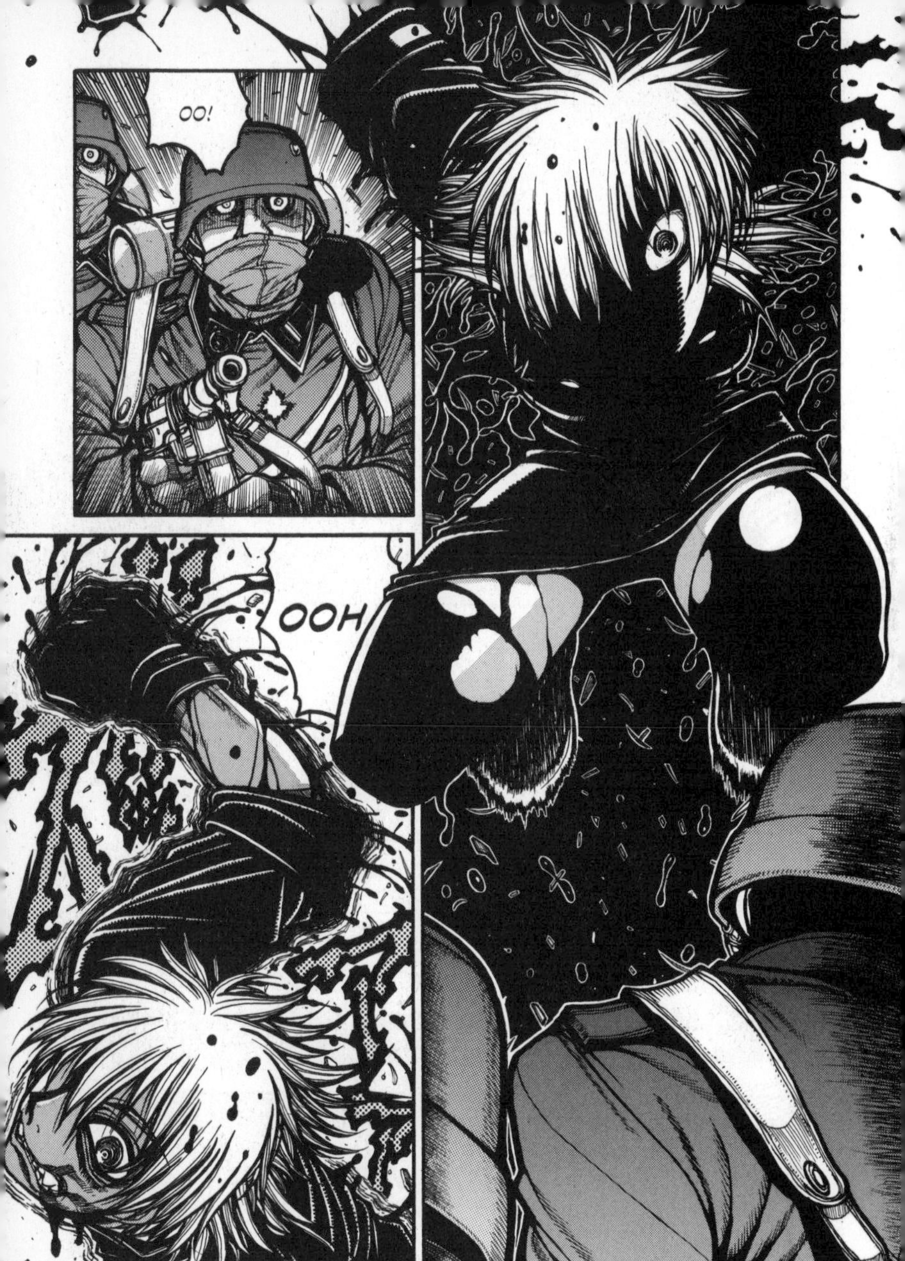
OO!
OOH

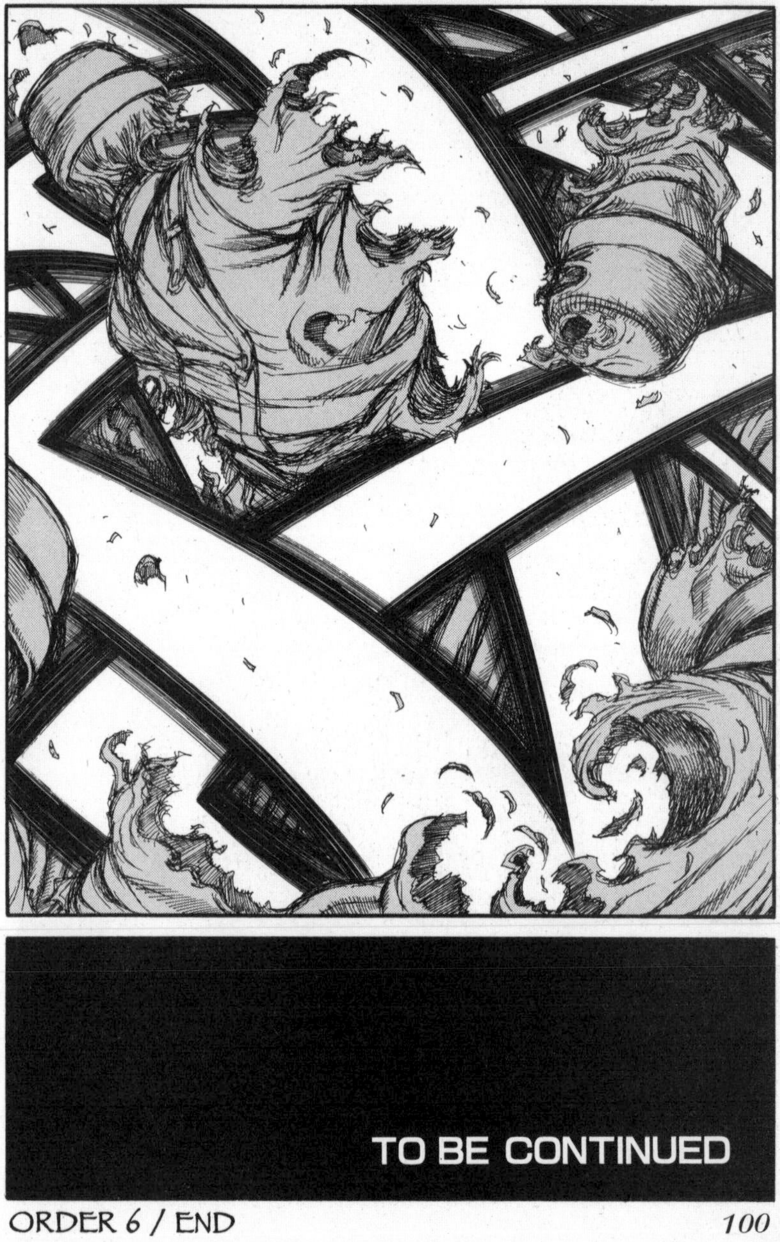

TO BE CONTINUED

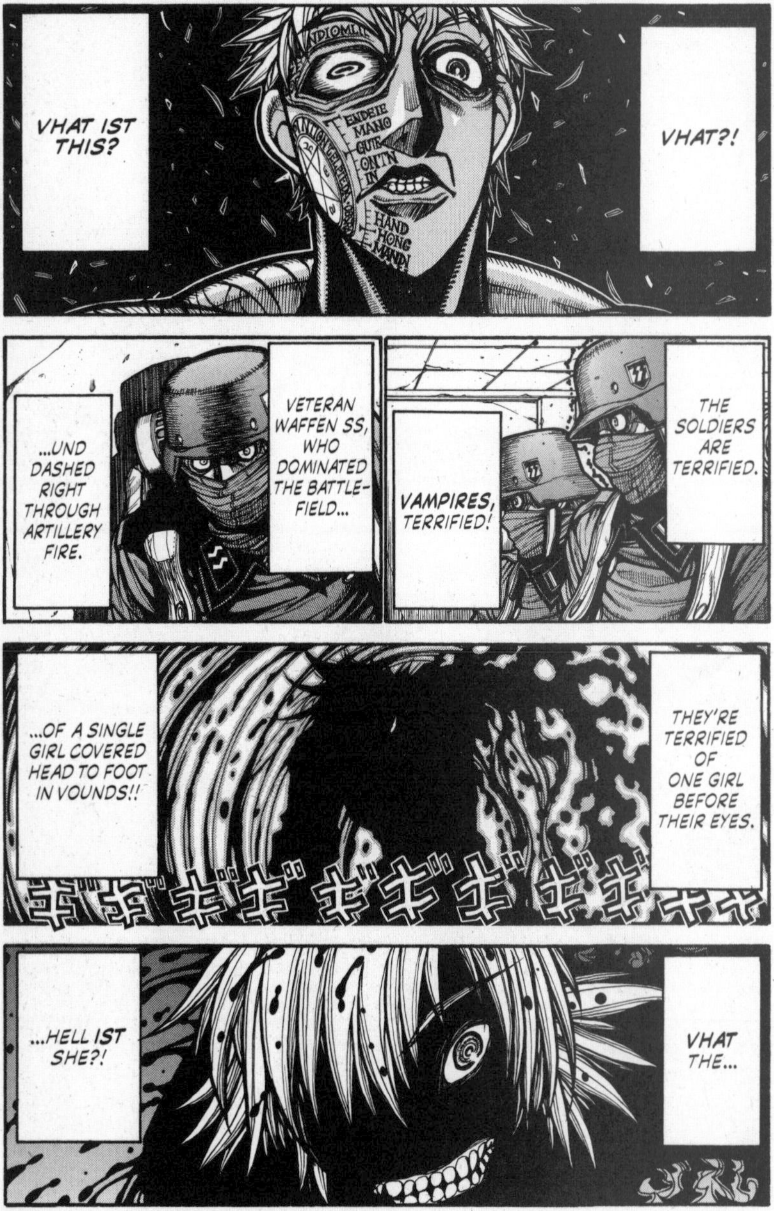
VHAT?!
VHAT IST THIS?
THE SOLDIERS ARE TERRIFIED.
VAMPIRES, TERRIFIED!
VETERAN WAFFEN SS, WHO DOMINATED THE BATTLE-FIELD...
...UND DASHED RIGHT THROUGH ARTILLERY FIRE.
THEY'RE TERRIFIED OF ONE GIRL BEFORE THEIR EYES.
...OF A SINGLE GIRL COVERED HEAD TO FOOT IN VOUNDS!!
VHAT THE...
...HELL IST SHE?!

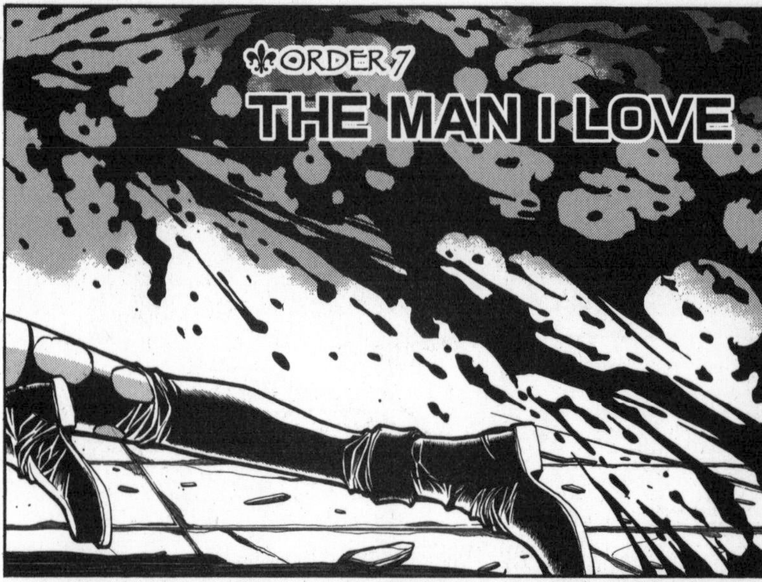
ORDER 7
THE MAN I LOVE

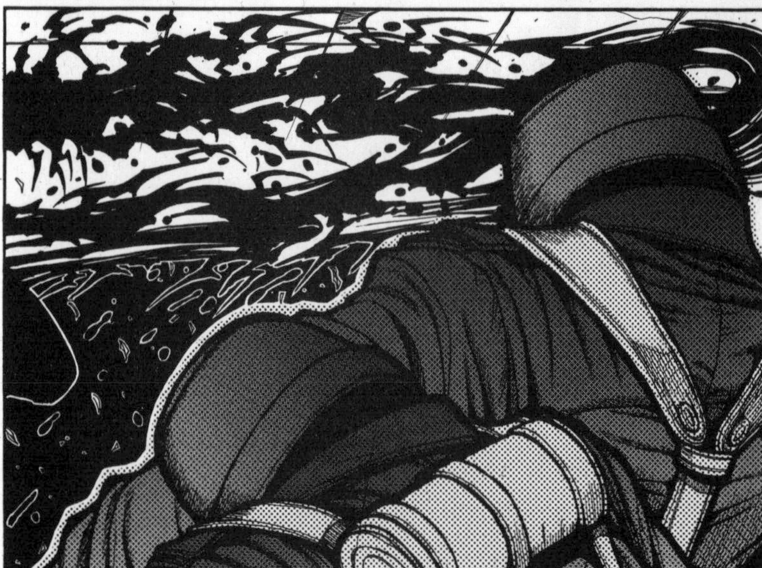

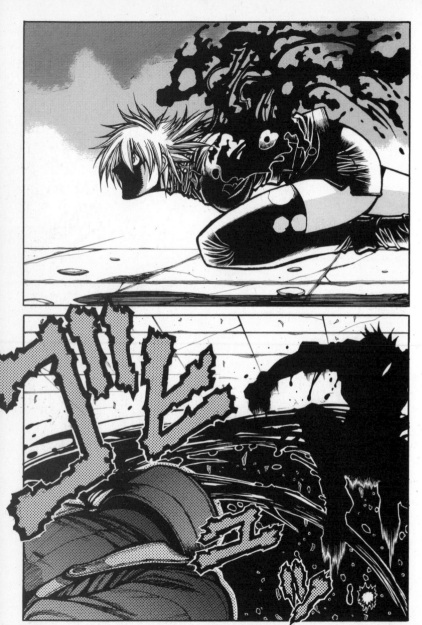

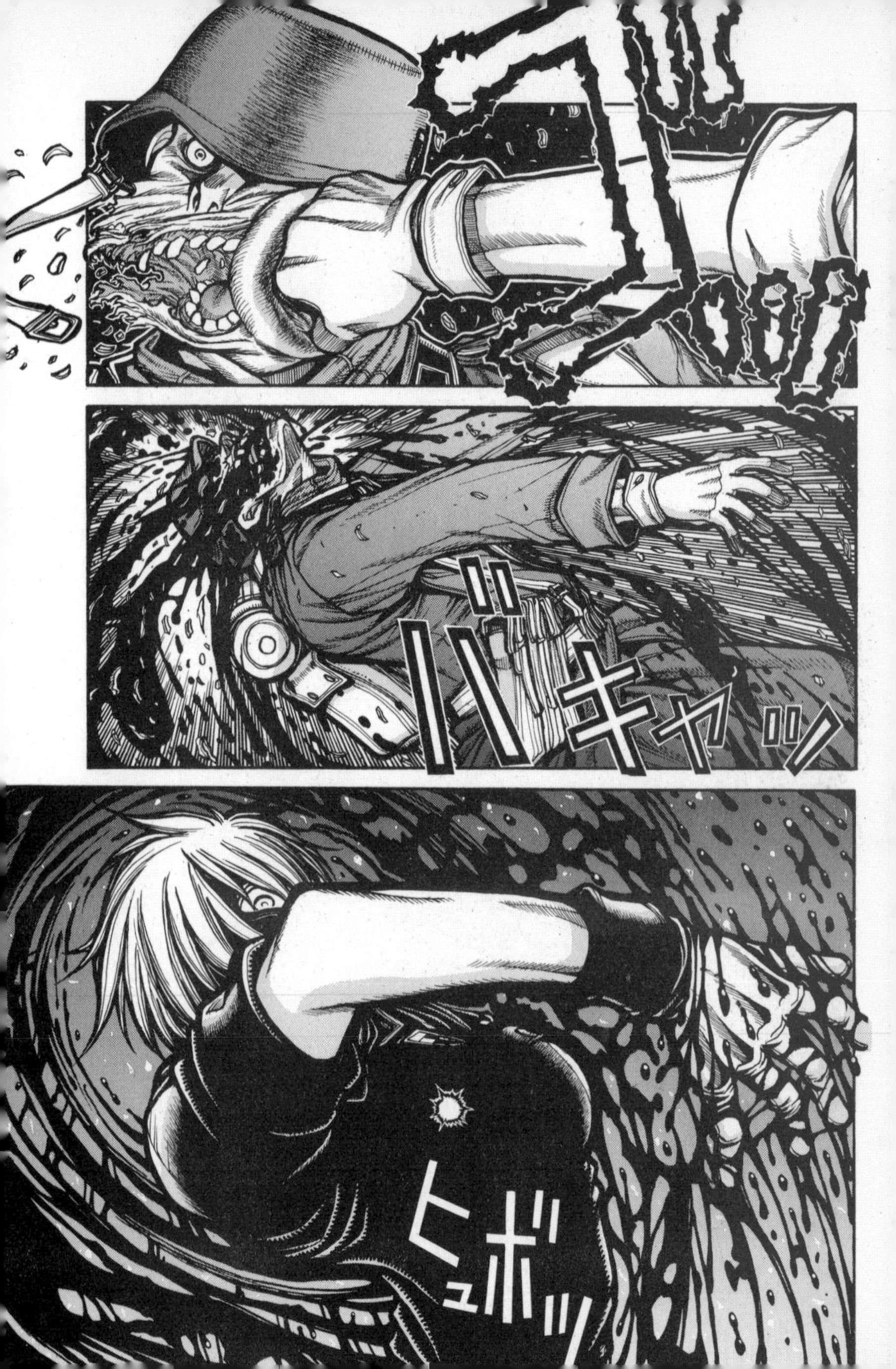

バキャッ
ヒュボッ

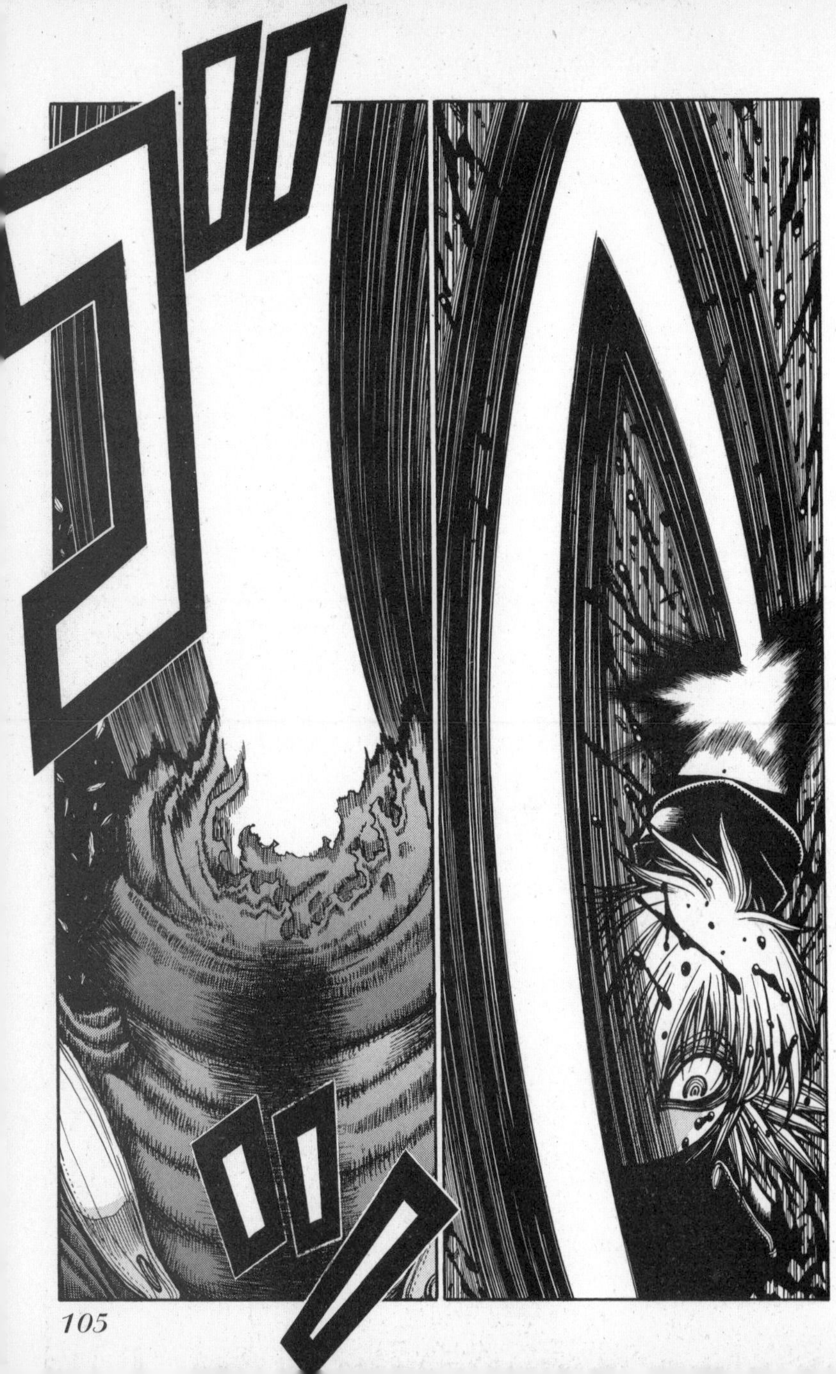

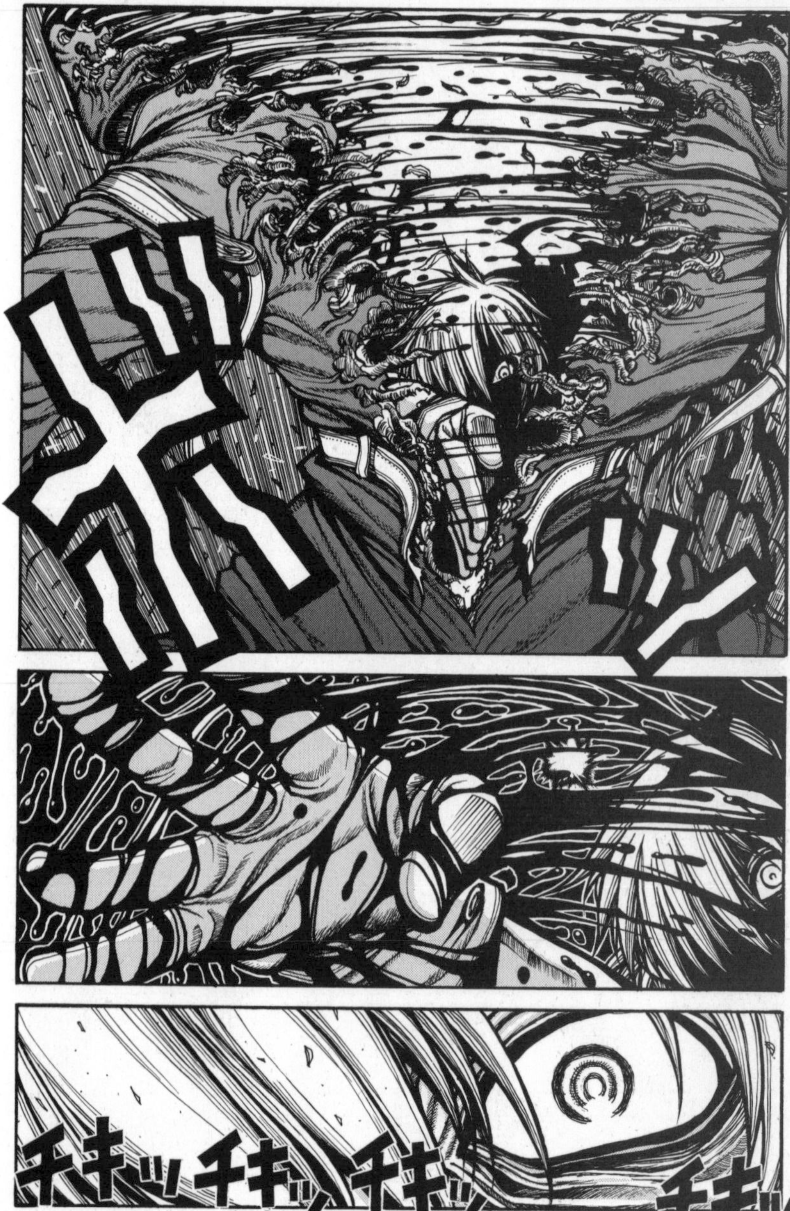
チキッ
チキッ
チギッ
チギッ

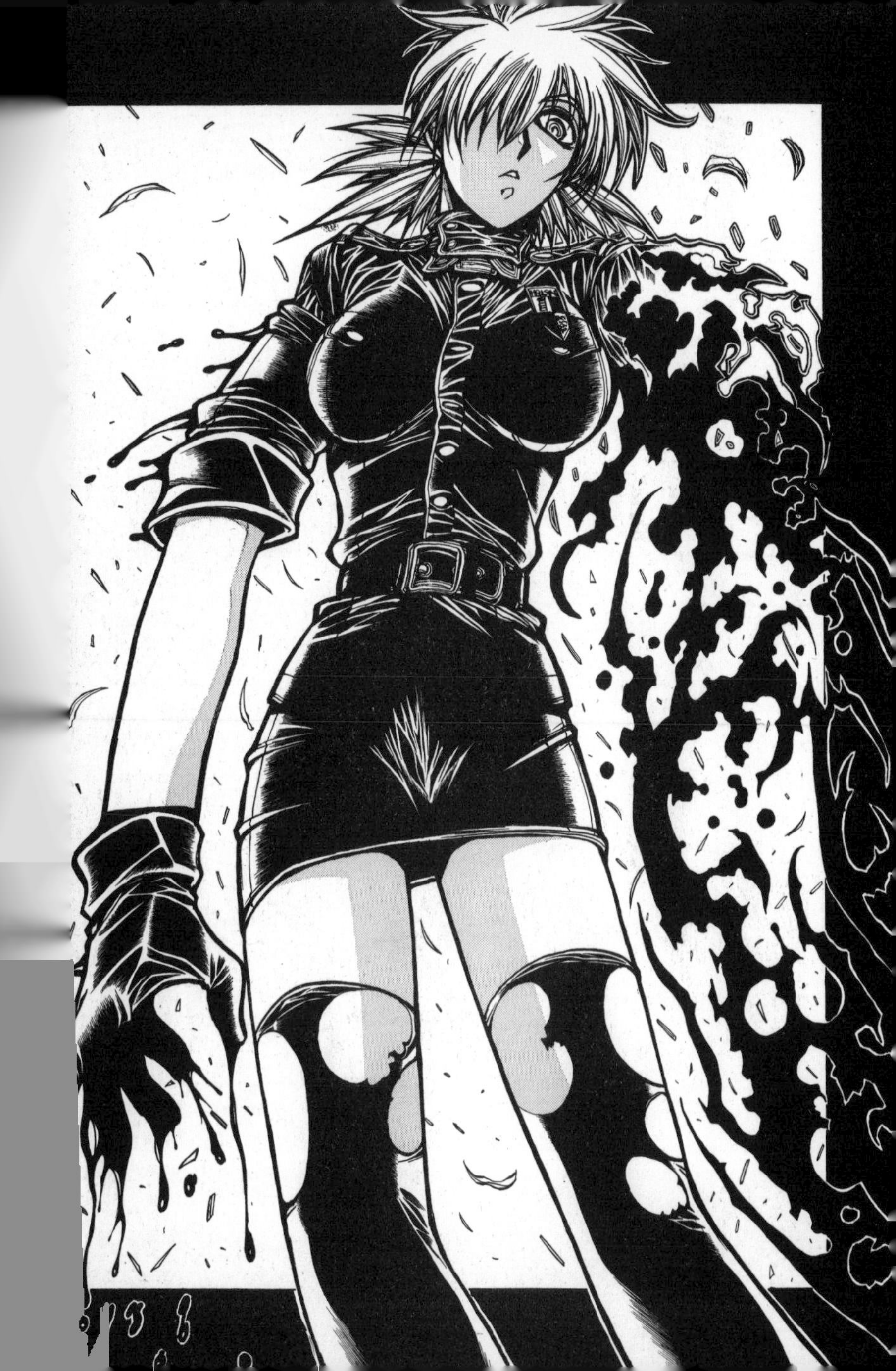

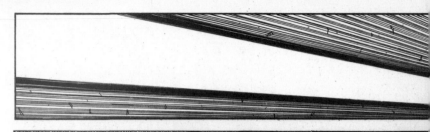

TO BE CONTINUED

ORDER 7/ END

ORDER 8

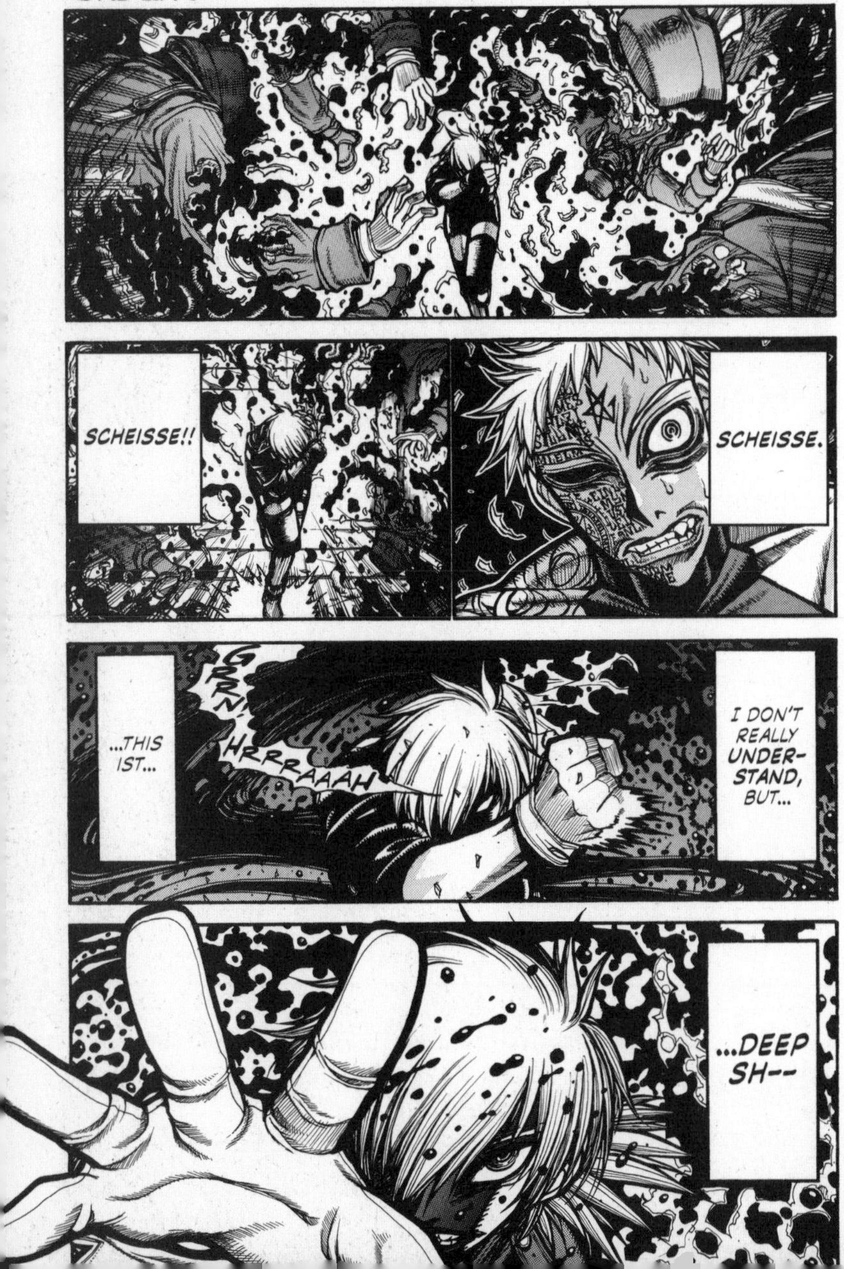
SCHEISSE.
SCHEISSE!!
I DON'T REALLY UNDERSTAND, BUT...
GRRN
HRRRAAAH
...THIS IST...
...DEEP SH--

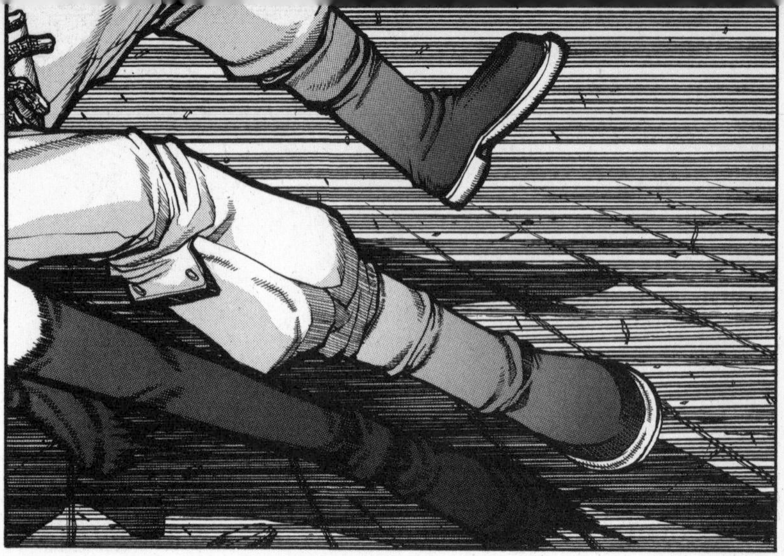

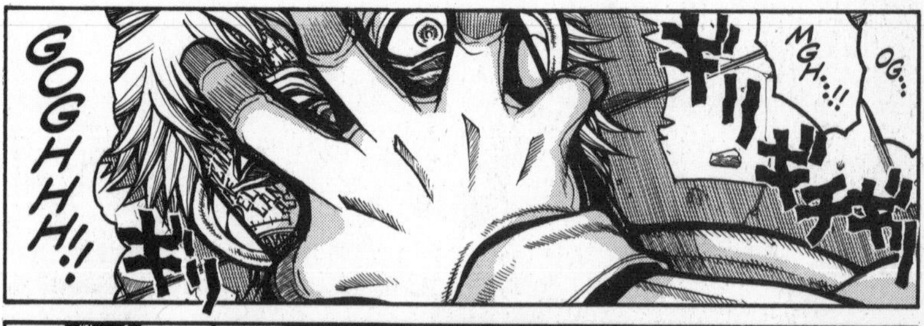
OG...
MGH...!!
ギリ
ギギギリ
GOGHHH!!
ギリ

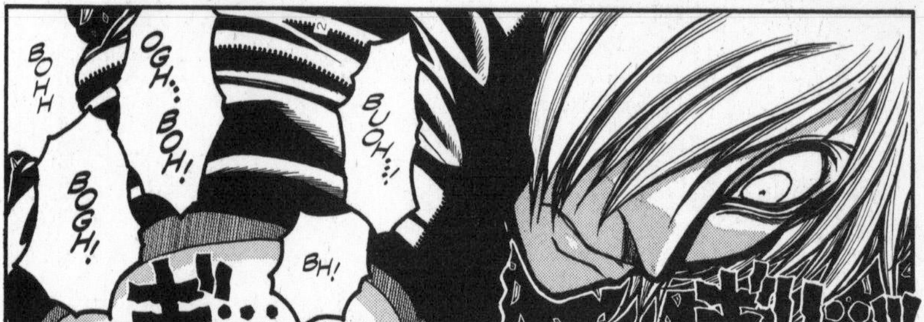
ギリ…ッ
BUOH...!
OGH... BOH!
BOHH
BOGH!
BH!
ギリ...ギ

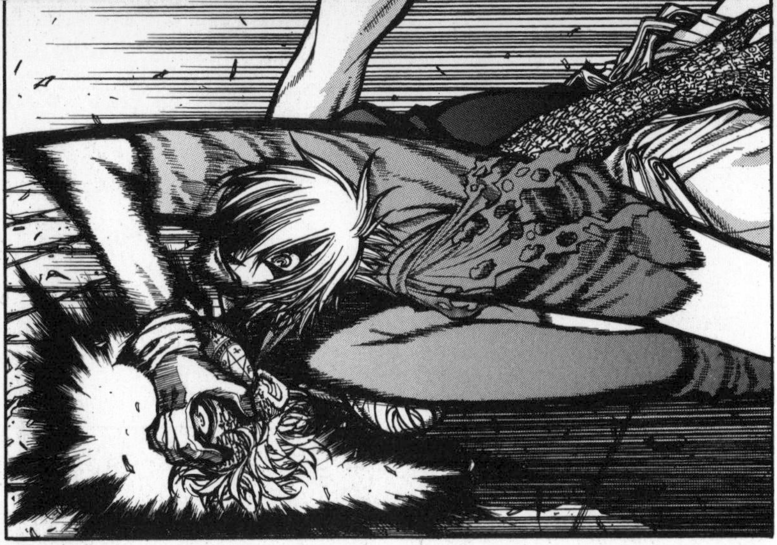

⚜ORDER 8

OGRE BATTLE

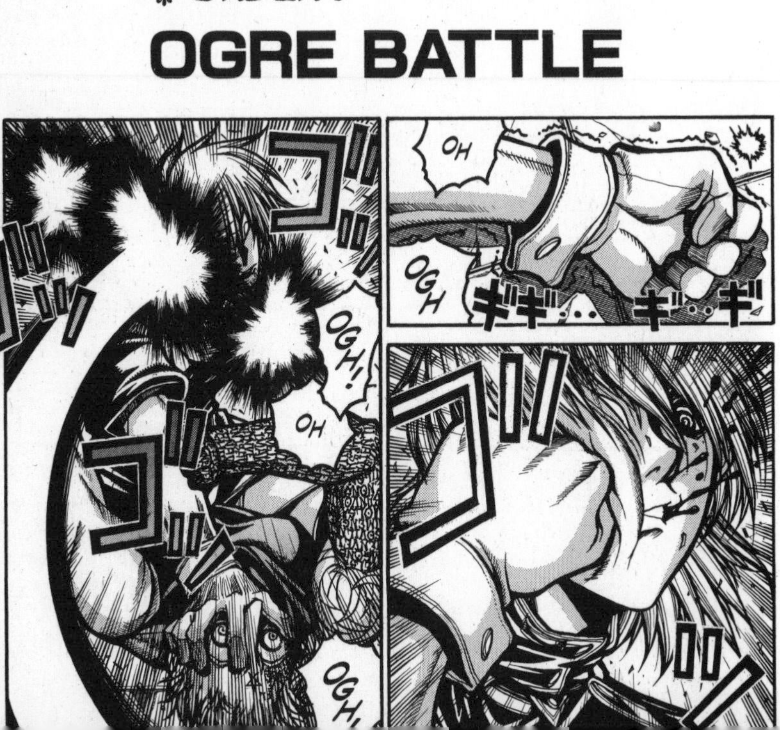
OH
OGH
ギギ… ギ・ギ
OGH!
OH
OGH

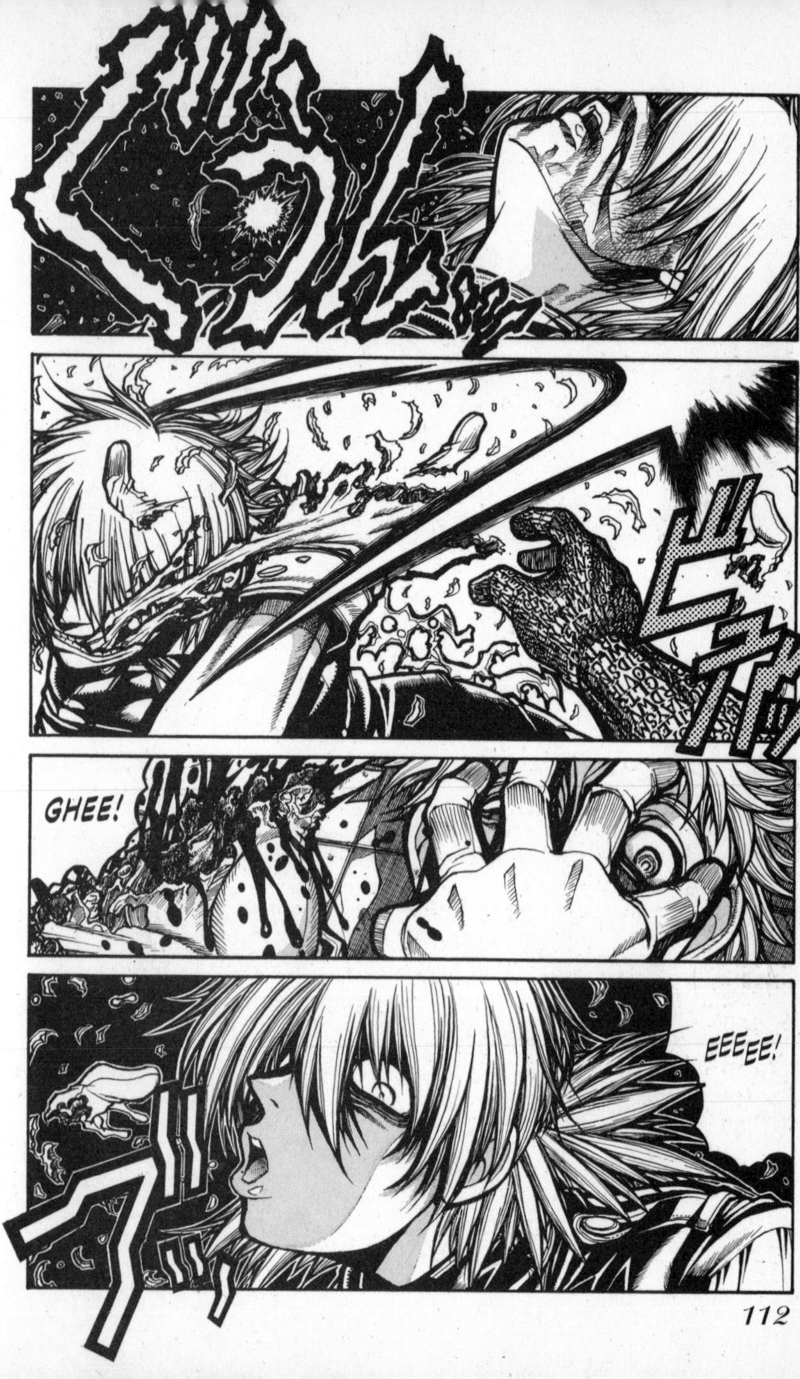
GHEE!
EEEEE!

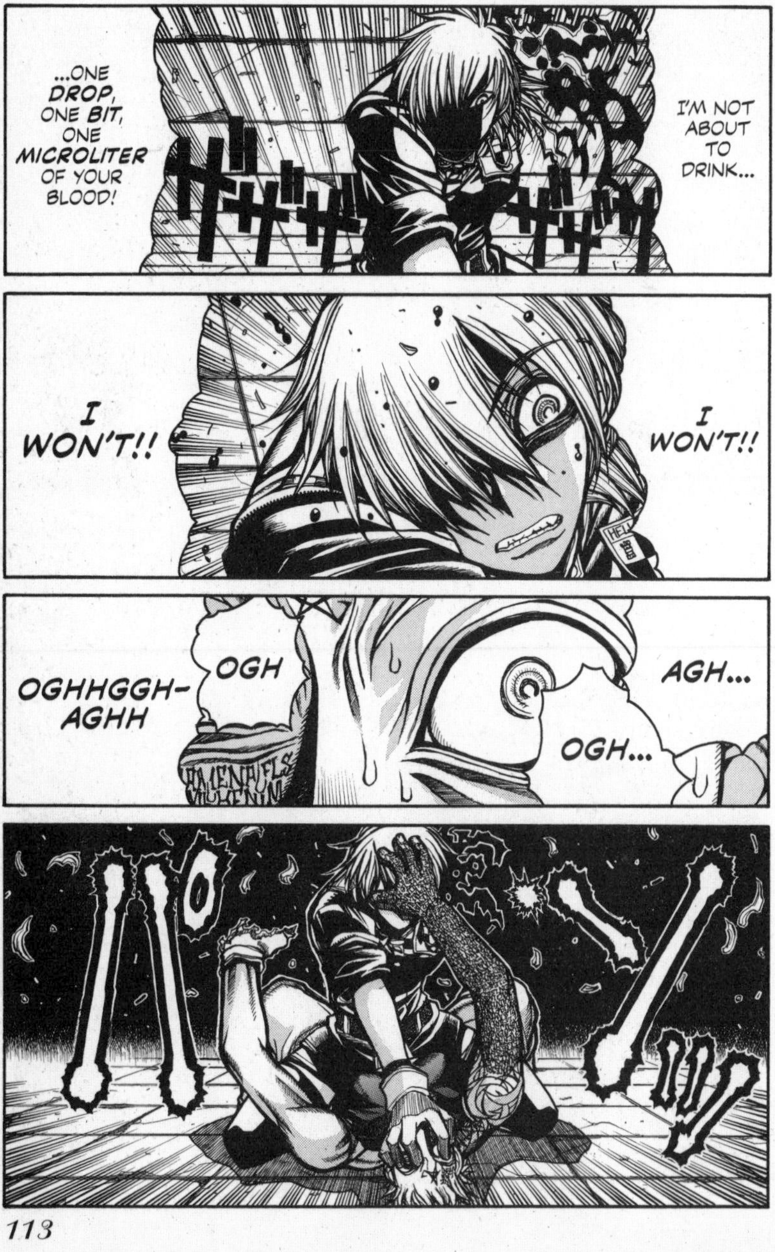
I'M NOT ABOUT TO DRINK...
...ONE DROP, ONE BIT, ONE MICROLITER OF YOUR BLOOD!
I WON'T!!
I WON'T!!
AGH...
OGH...
OGH
OGHHGGH-AGHH

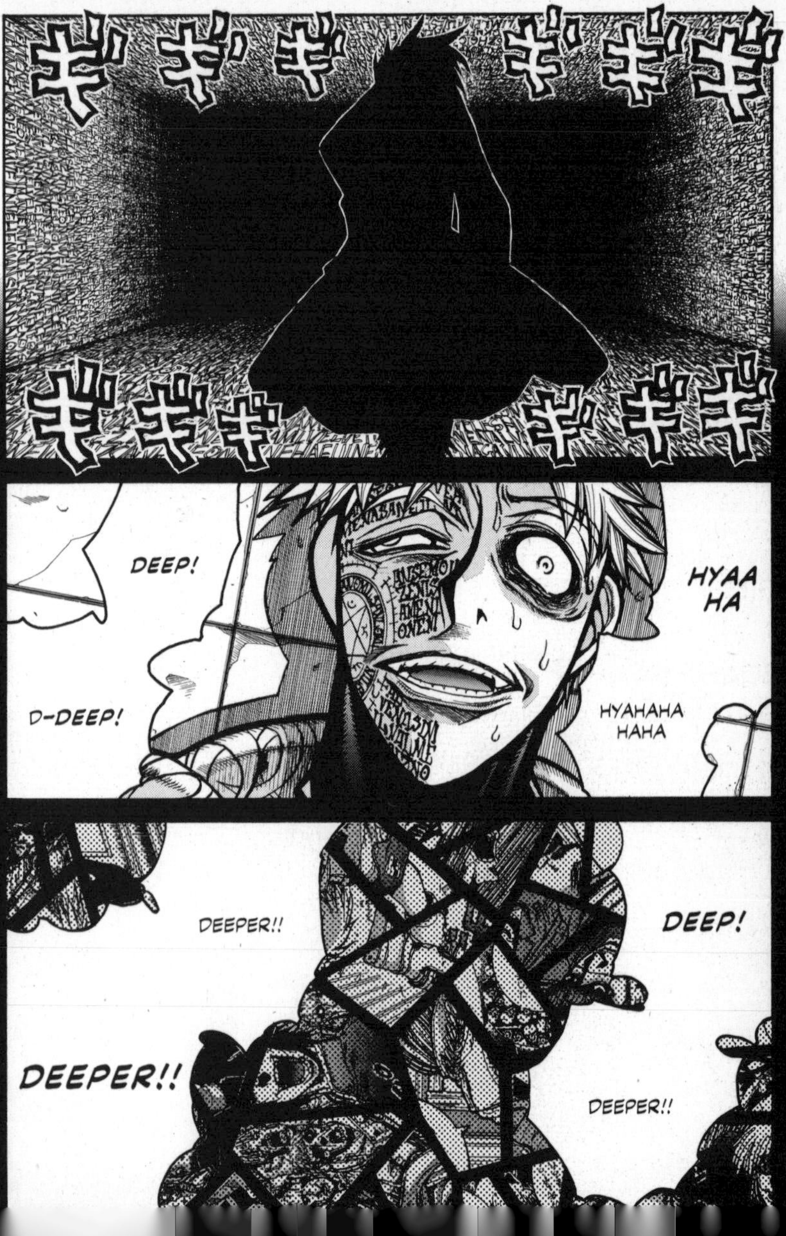
ギギギ
ギギギ
ギギギ
ギギギ
HYAA HA
HYAHAHA HAHA
DEEP!
D-DEEP!
DEEP!
DEEPER!!
DEEPER!!
DEEPER!!

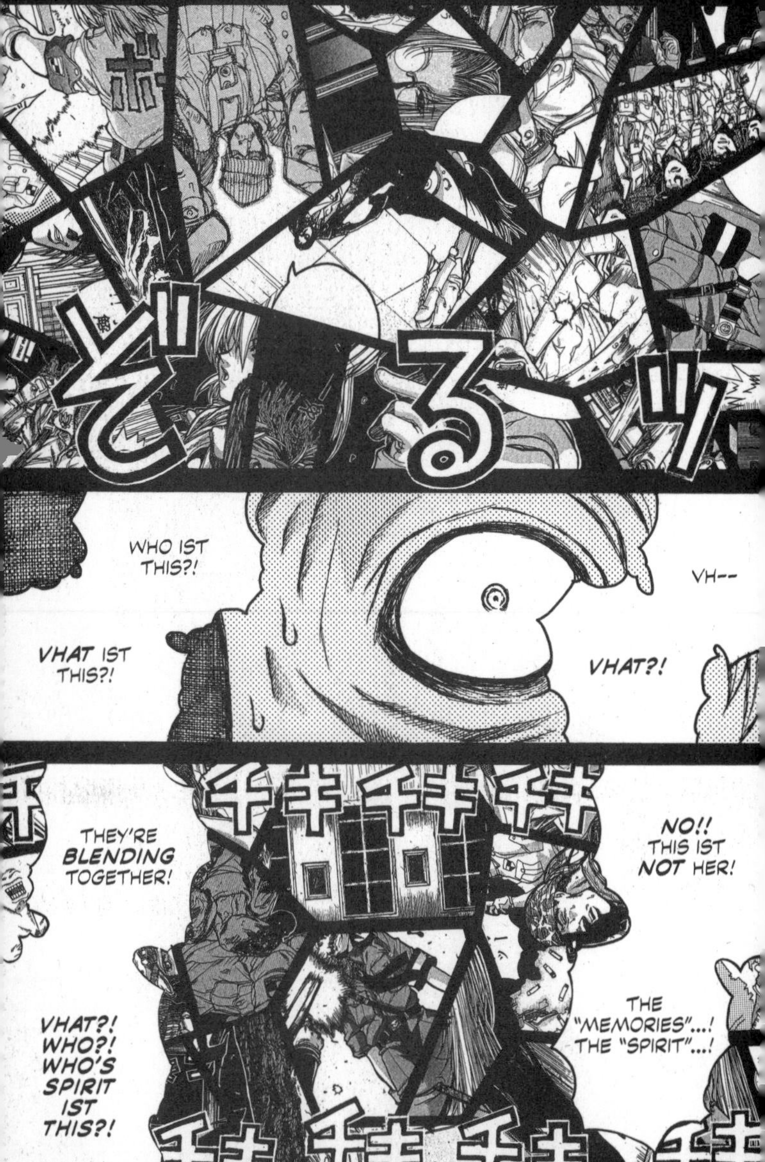
ぞるッ
VH--
VHAT?!
WHO IST THIS?!
VHAT IST THIS?!
チキチキチキチキ
NO!! THIS IST NOT HER!
THEY'RE BLENDING TOGETHER!
THE "MEMORIES"...! THE "SPIRIT"...!
VHAT?! WHO?! WHO'S SPIRIT IST THIS?!
チキチキチキチキ

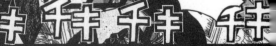

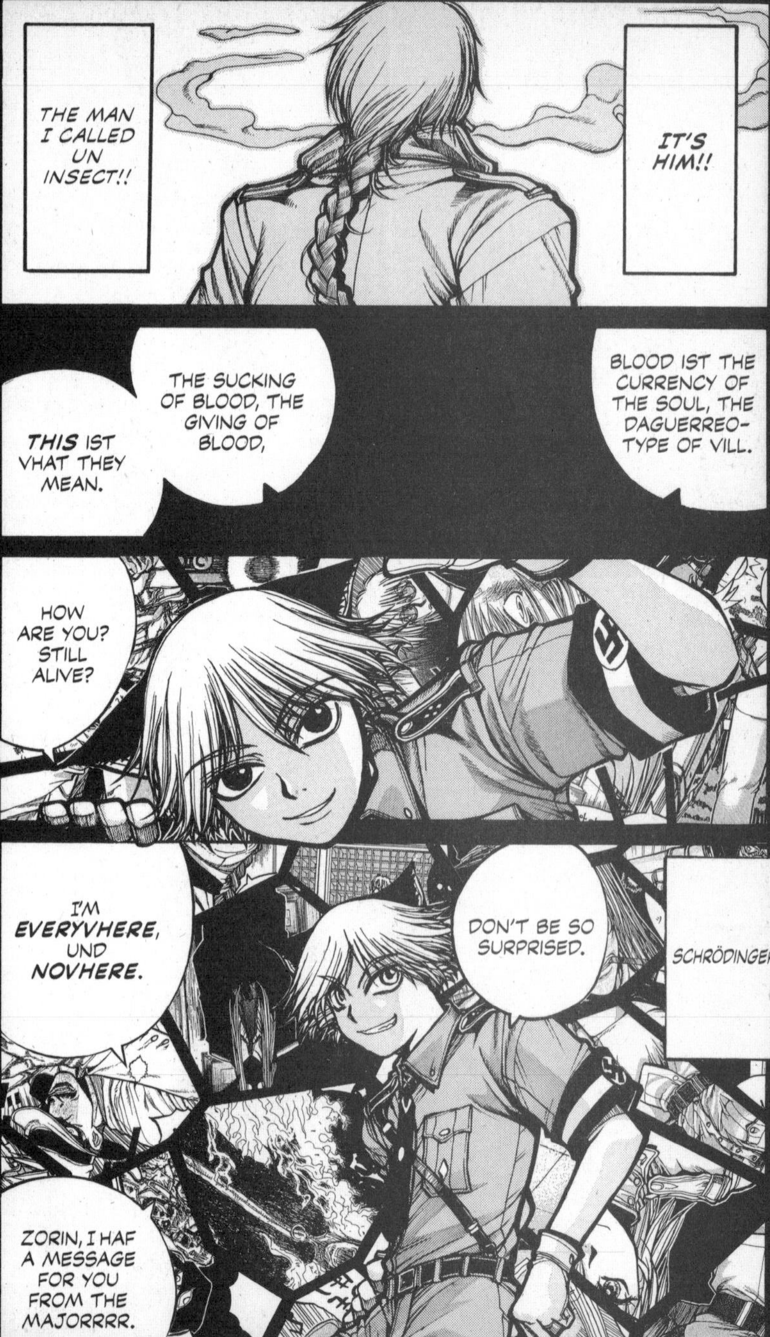
IT'S HIM!!
THE MAN I CALLED UN INSECT!!
BLOOD IST THE CURRENCY OF THE SOUL, THE DAGUERREO-TYPE OF VILL.
THE SUCKING OF BLOOD, THE GIVING OF BLOOD,
THIS IST VHAT THEY MEAN.
HOW ARE YOU? STILL ALIVE?
SCHRÖDINGER!!
DON'T BE SO SURPRISED.
I'M EVERYVHERE, UND NOVHERE.
ZORIN, I HAF A MESSAGE FOR YOU FROM THE MAJORRRR.

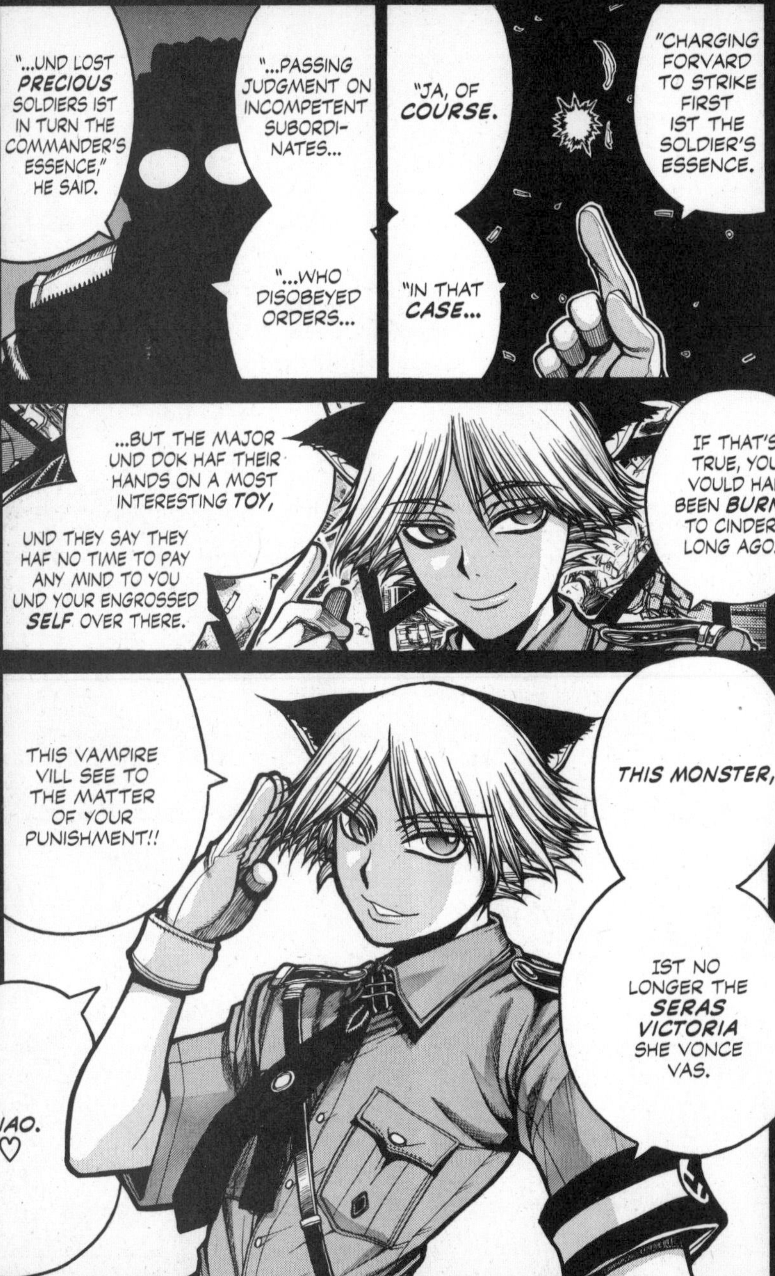
"CHARGING FORVARD TO STRIKE FIRST IST THE SOLDIER'S ESSENCE.
"JA, OF COURSE.
"IN THAT CASE...
"...PASSING JUDGMENT ON INCOMPETENT SUBORDINATES...
"...WHO DISOBEYED ORDERS...
"...UND LOST PRECIOUS SOLDIERS IST IN TURN THE COMMANDER'S ESSENCE," HE SAID.
IF THAT'S TRUE, YOU VOULD HAF BEEN BURNT TO CINDERS LONG AGO...
...BUT THE MAJOR UND DOK HAF THEIR HANDS ON A MOST INTERESTING TOY,
UND THEY SAY THEY HAF NO TIME TO PAY ANY MIND TO YOU UND YOUR ENGROSSED SELF OVER THERE.
THIS MONSTER,
IST NO LONGER THE SERAS VICTORIA SHE VONCE VAS.
THIS VAMPIRE VILL SEE TO THE MATTER OF YOUR PUNISHMENT!!
CIAO. ♡

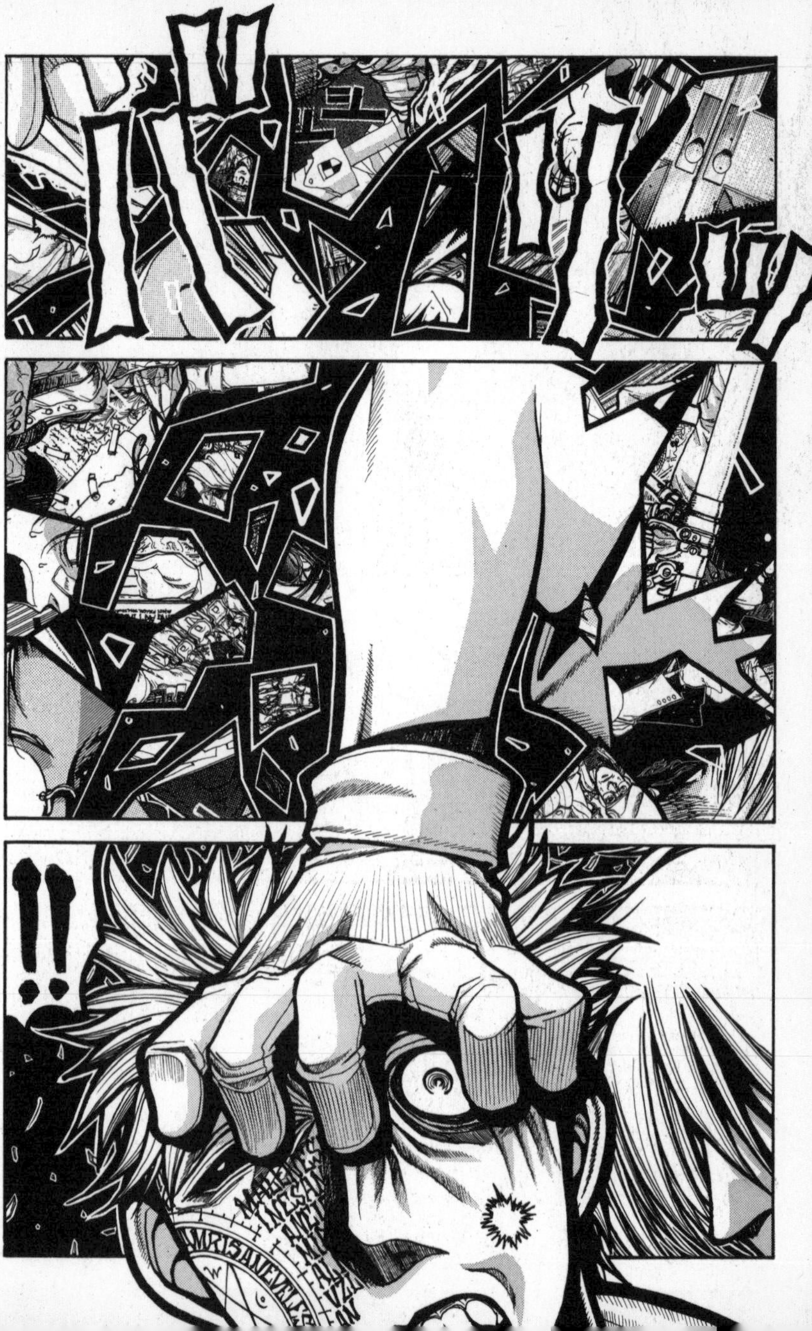
!!

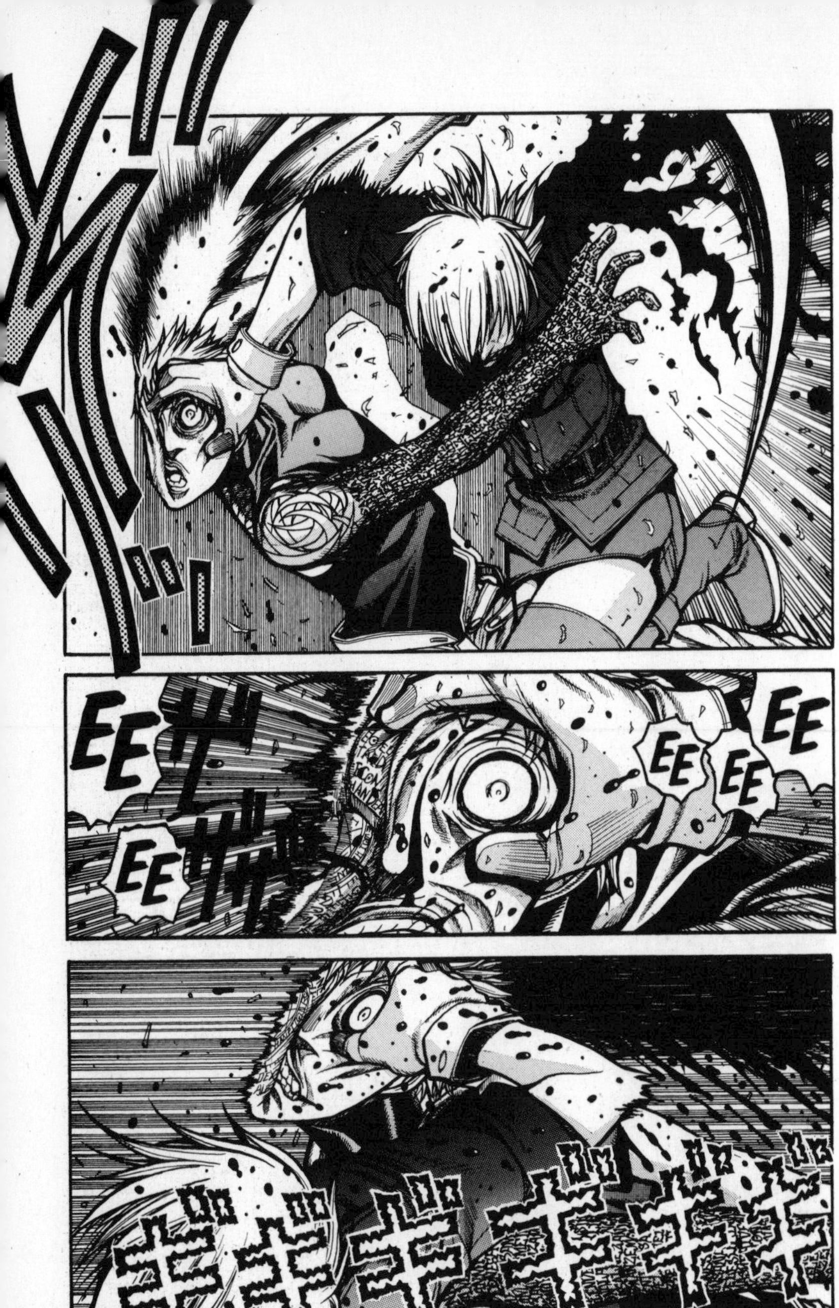
EE
EE
EE
EE
EE

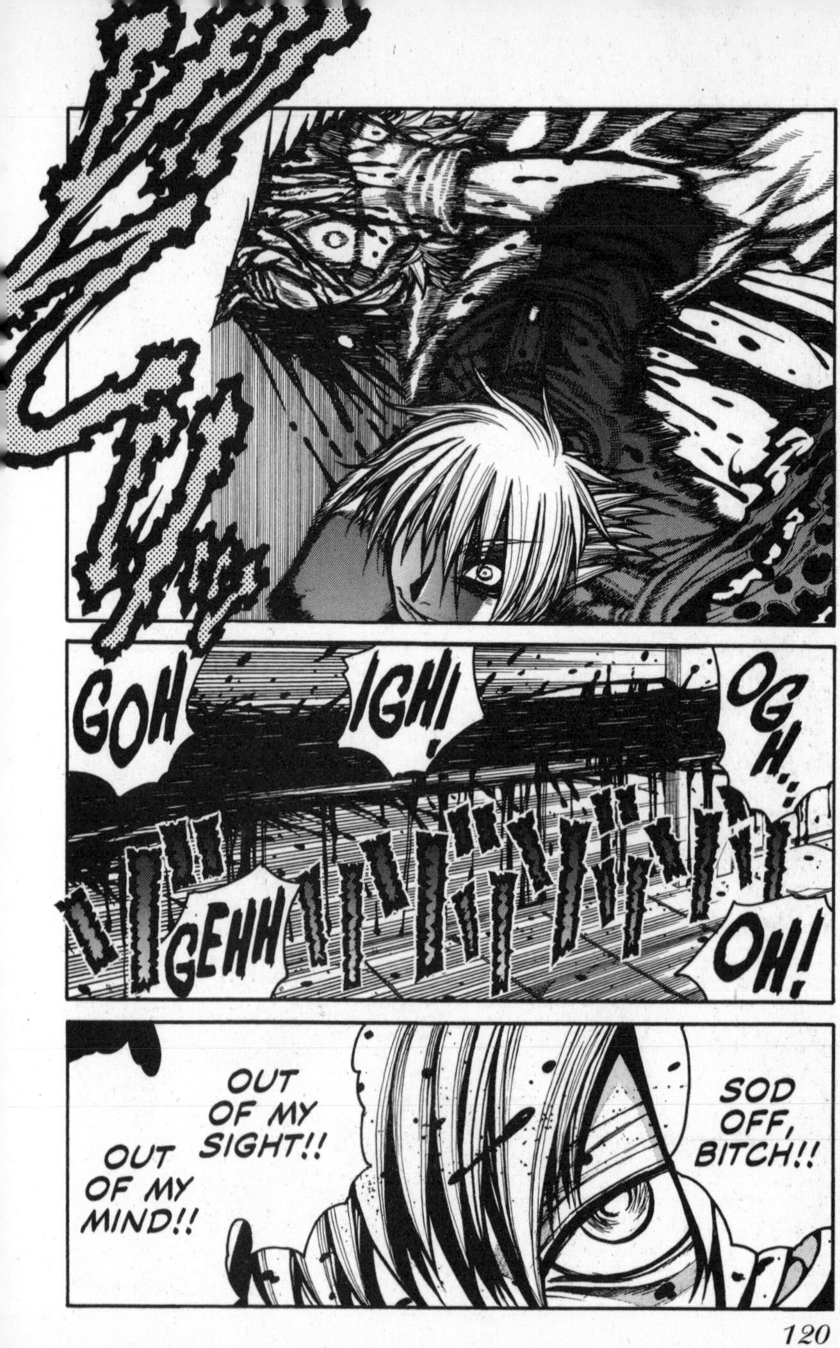
OGH...
IGH!
GOH
OH!
GEHH
SOD OFF, BITCH!!
OUT OF MY SIGHT!!
OUT OF MY MIND!!

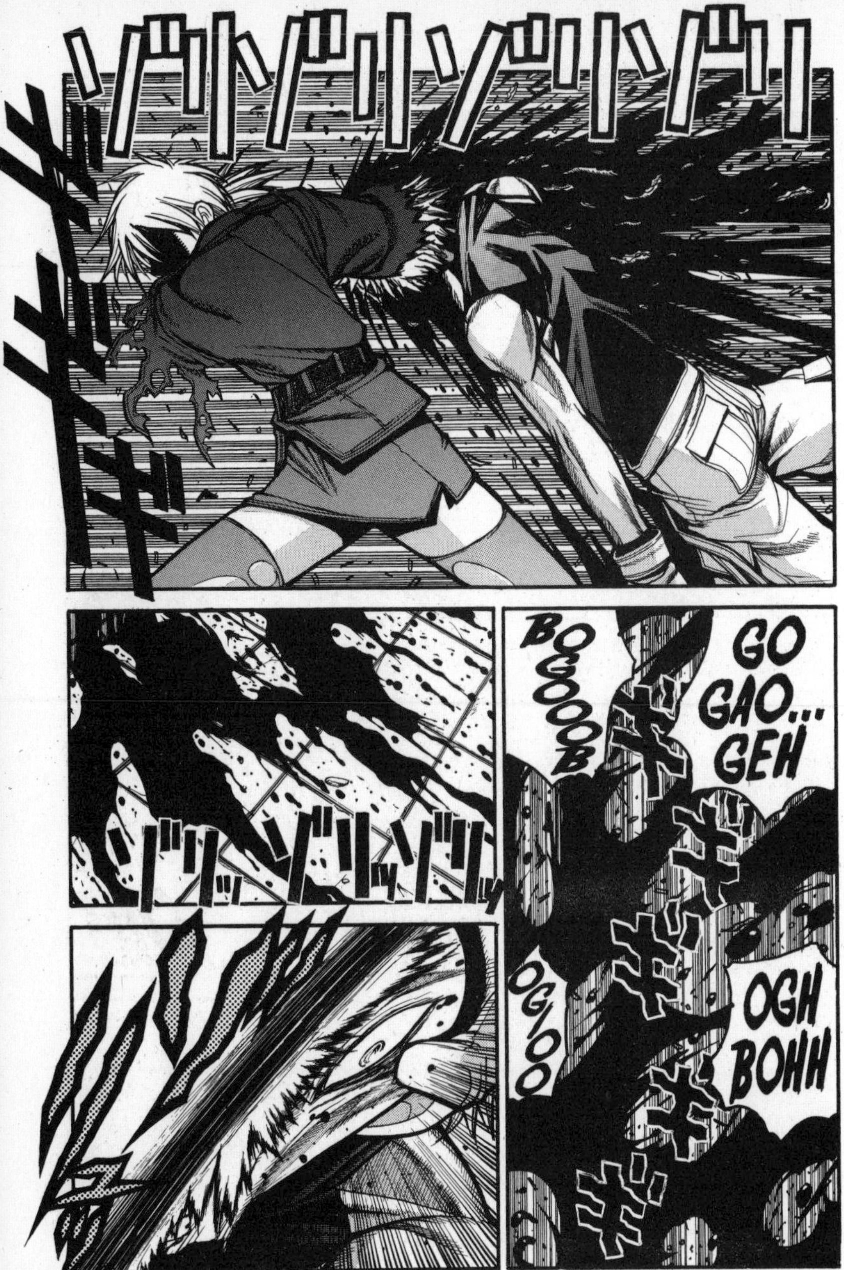
GO GAO... GEH
BOGOOOOB
OGH BOHH
OGOO

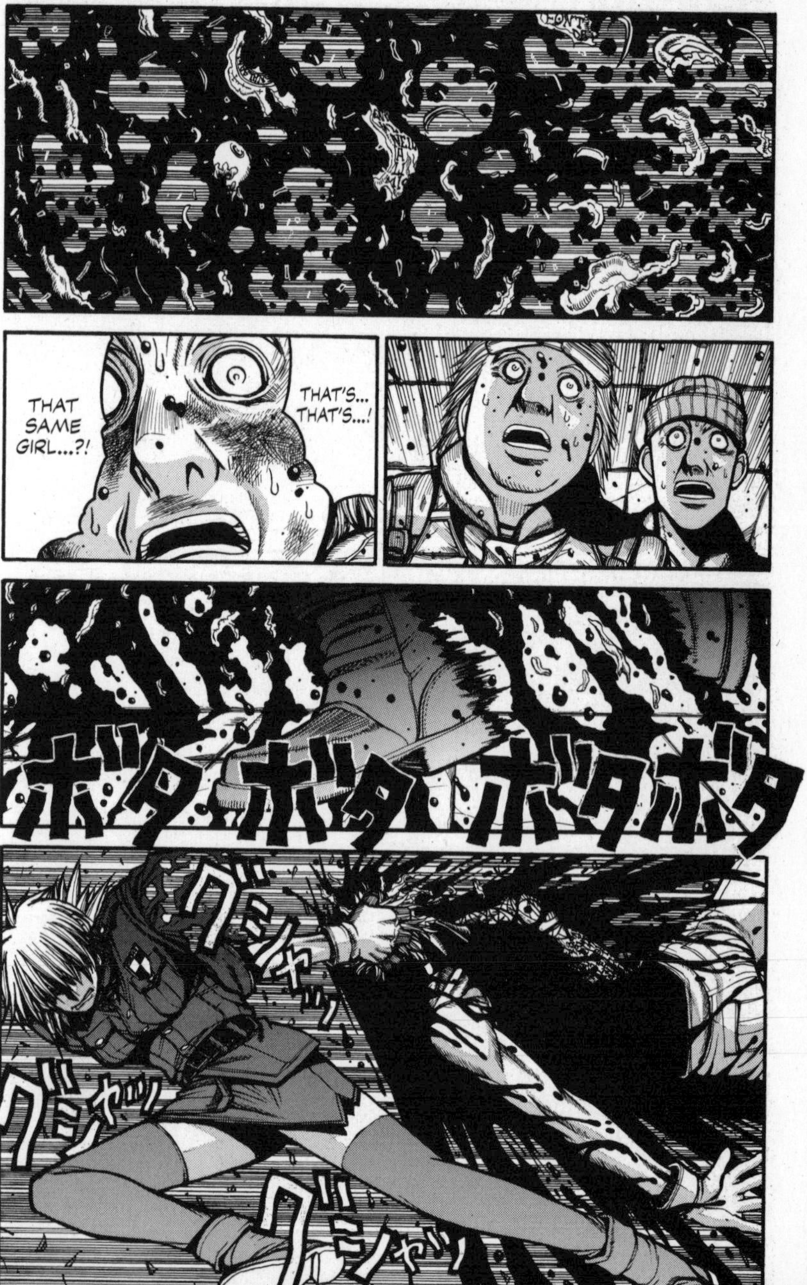
THAT'S... THAT'S...!
THAT SAME GIRL...?!

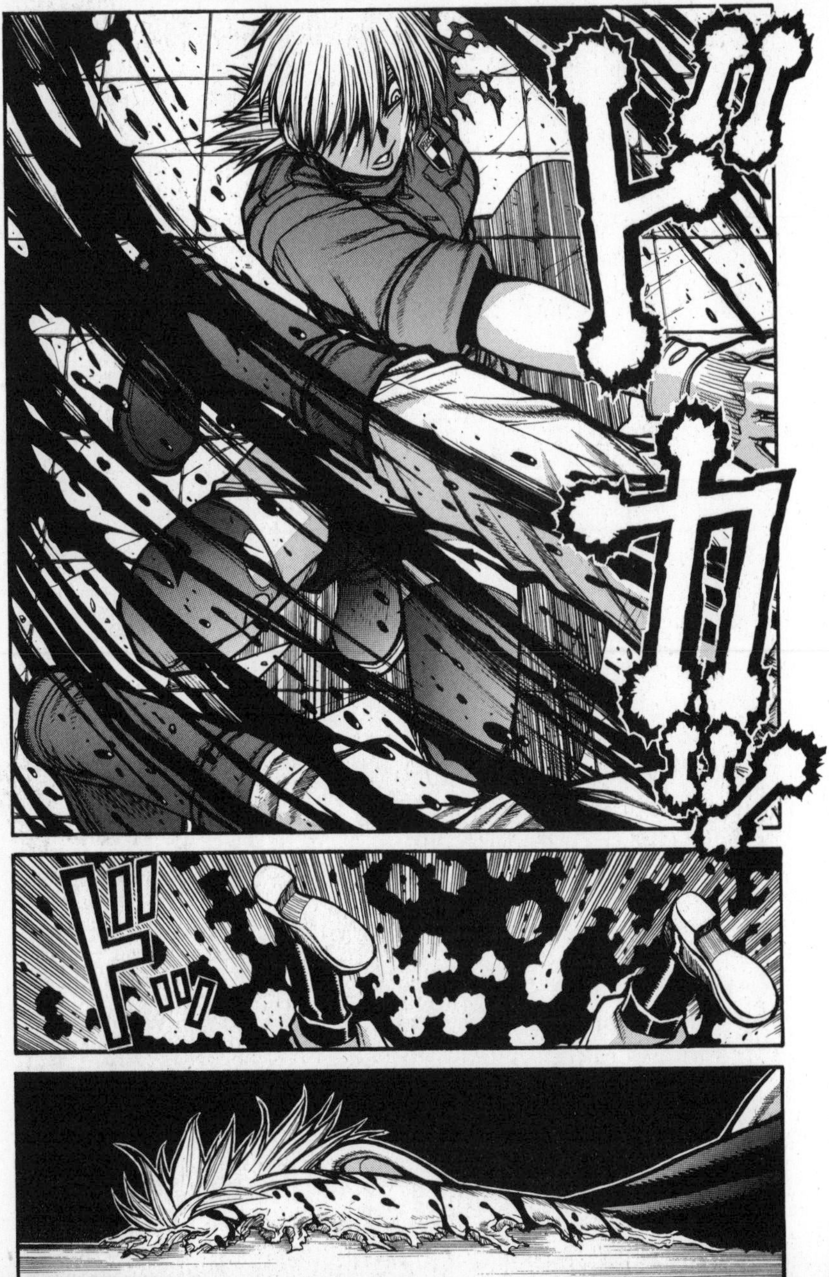
ドガッ
ドッ

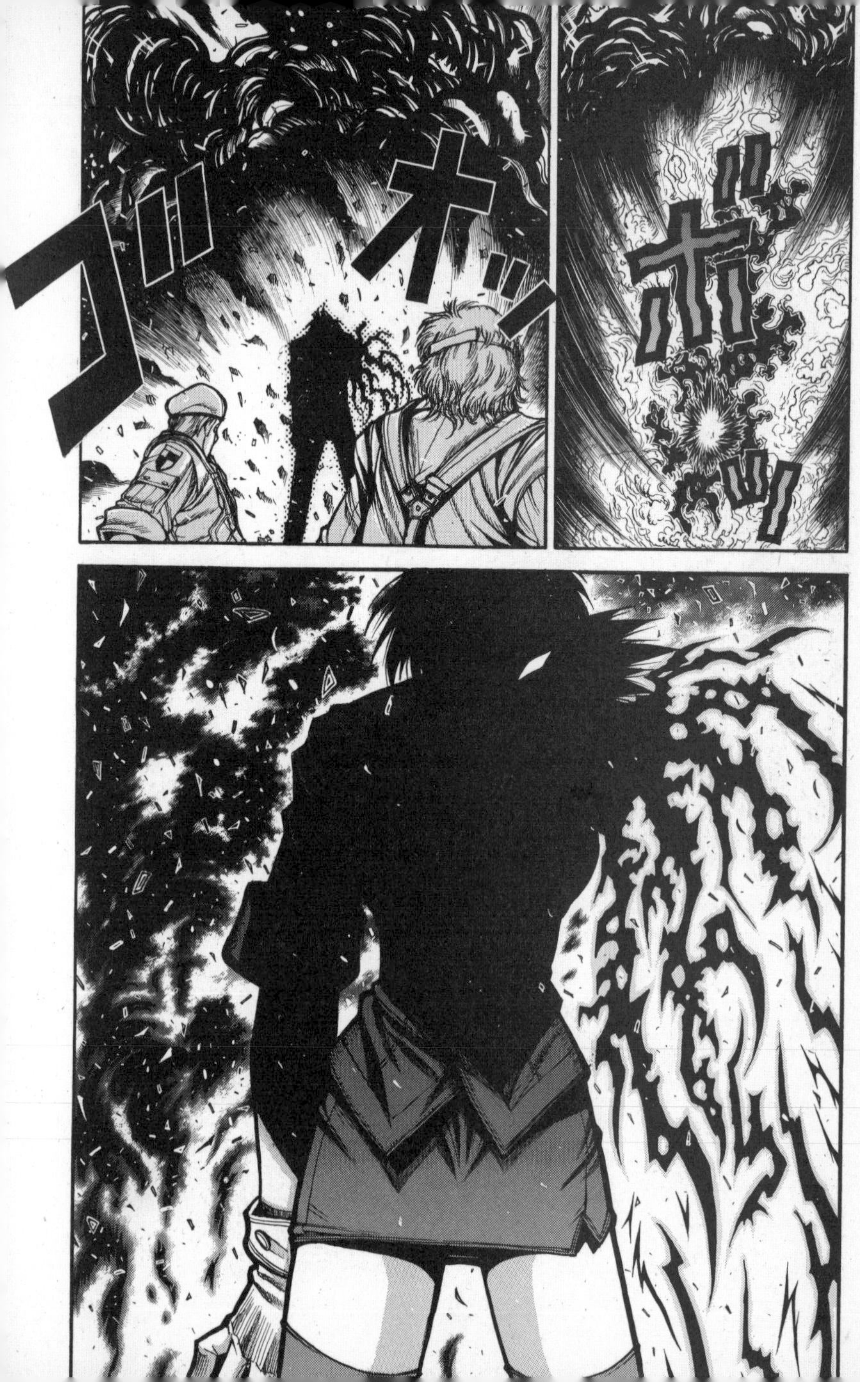
ボッ
ッ
ゴッ
オッ

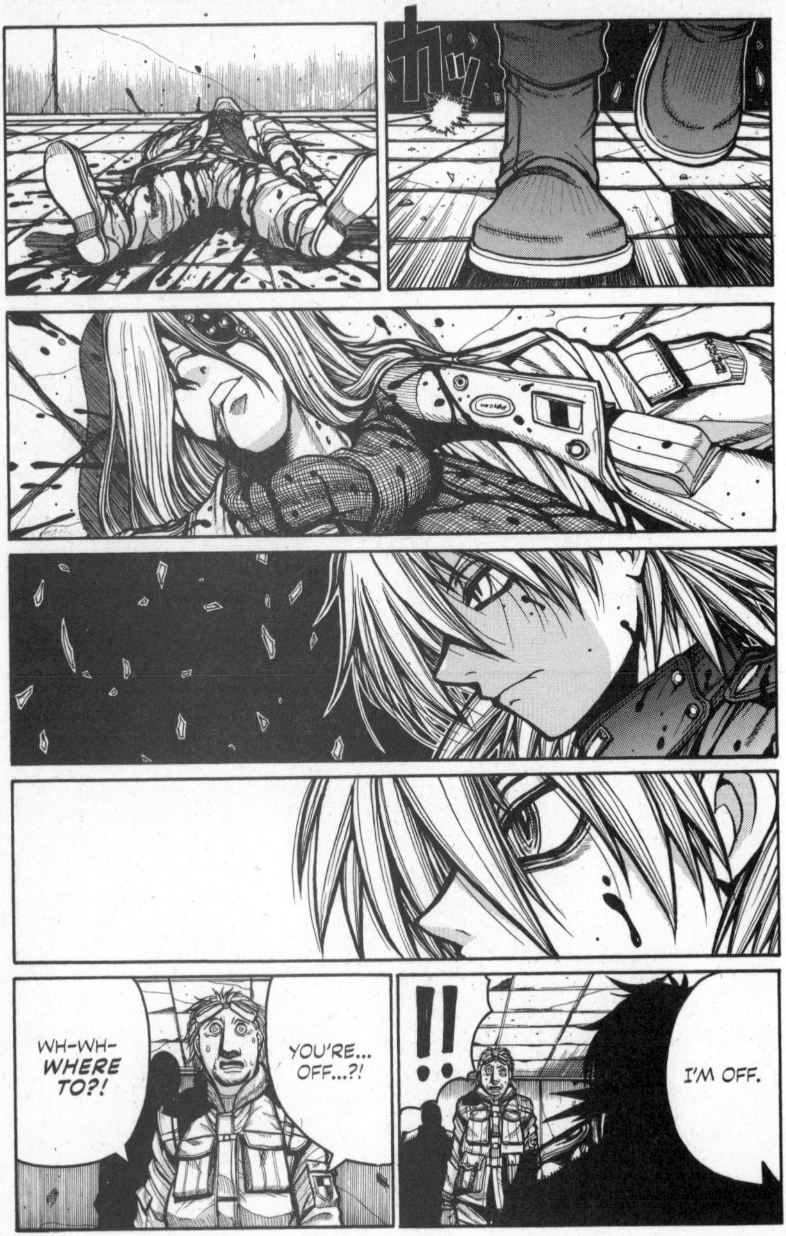
カッ
!!
I'M OFF.
YOU'RE... OFF...?!
WH-WH- *WHERE TO?!*

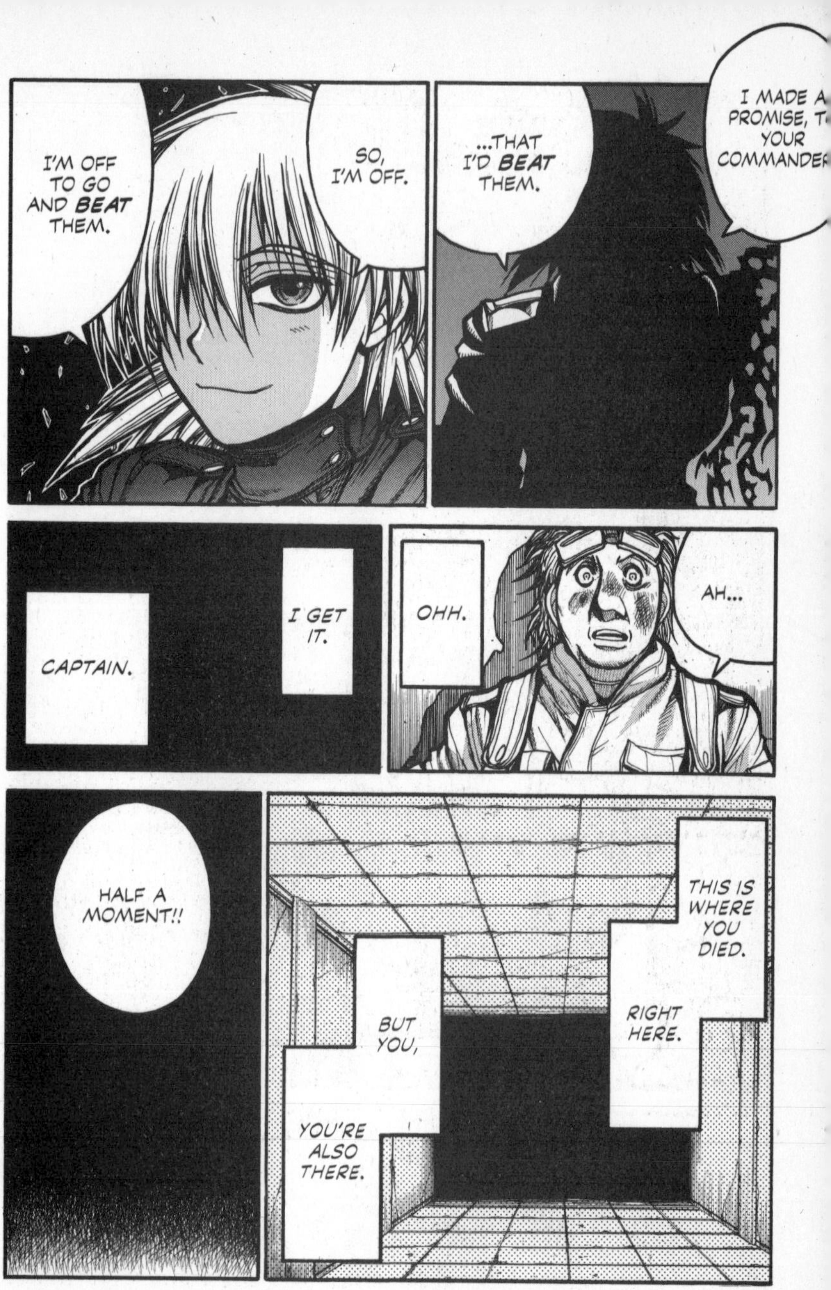
I MADE A PROMISE, T YOUR COMMANDE
...THAT I'D BEAT THEM.
SO, I'M OFF.
I'M OFF TO GO AND BEAT THEM.
AH...
OHH.
I GET IT.
CAPTAIN.
THIS IS WHERE YOU DIED.
RIGHT HERE.
BUT YOU,
YOU'RE ALSO THERE.
HALF A MOMENT!!

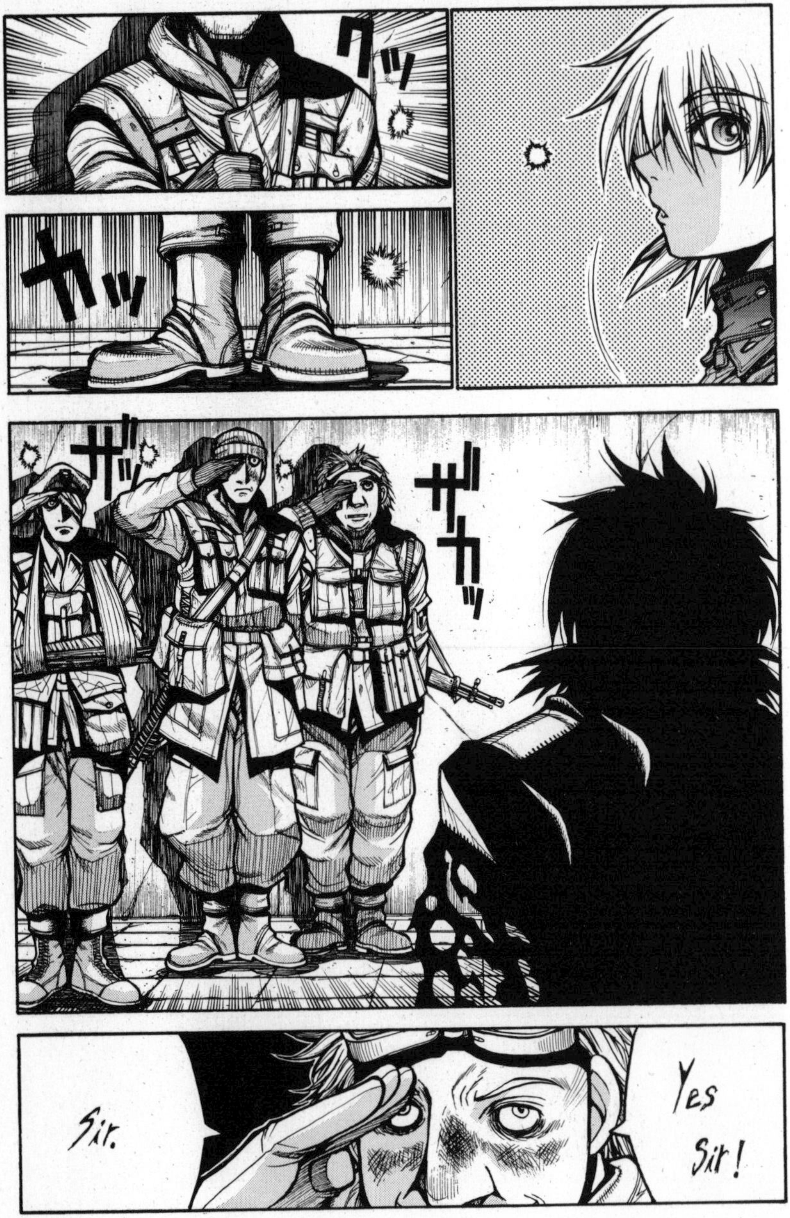
クッ
カッ
ザッ
ザカッ
Yes Sir!
Sir.

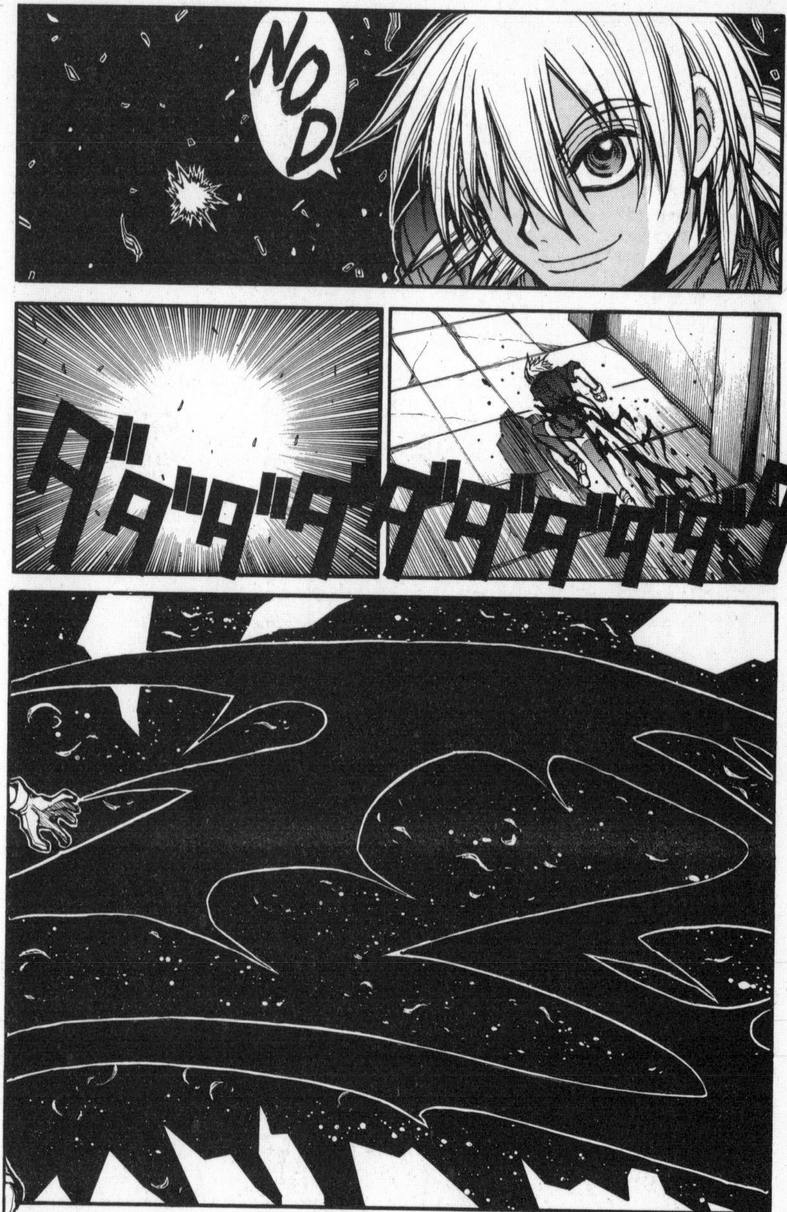
NOD
ダダダダダダダダダダダ

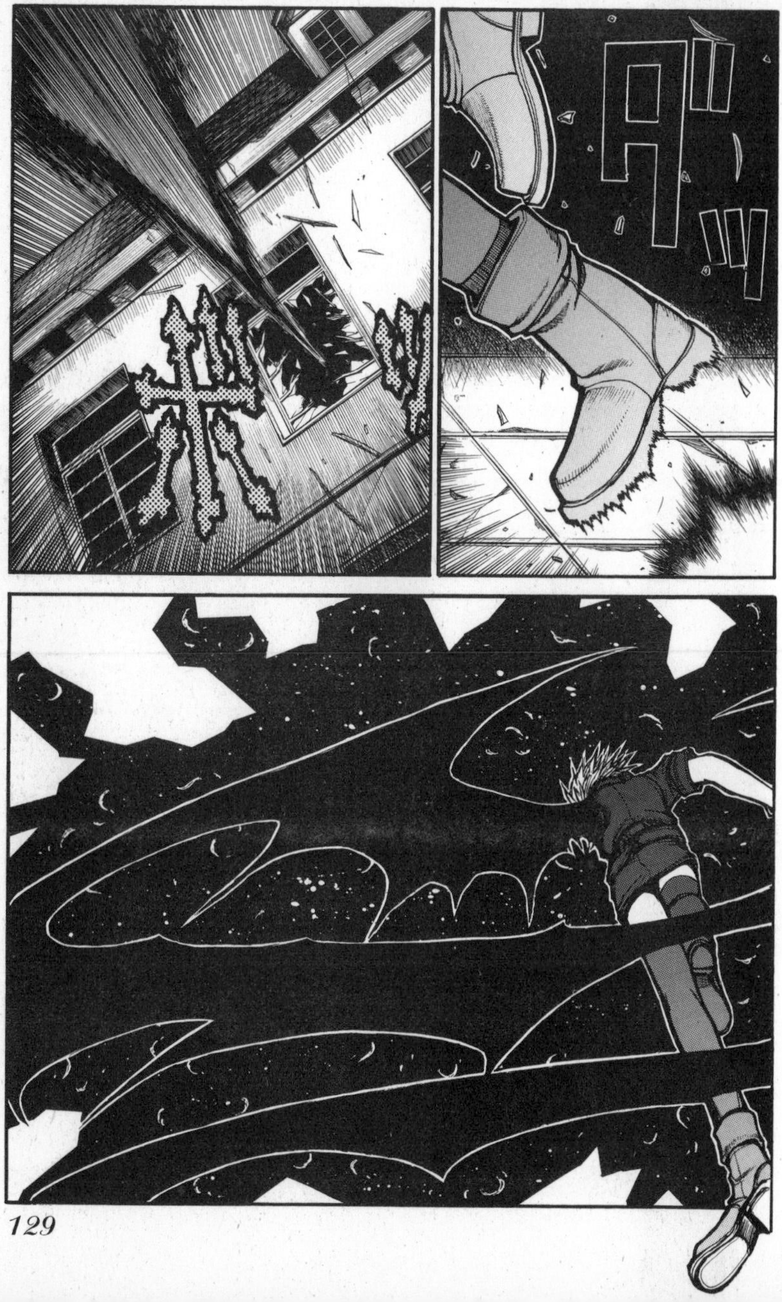
ダッ!!
ボッ

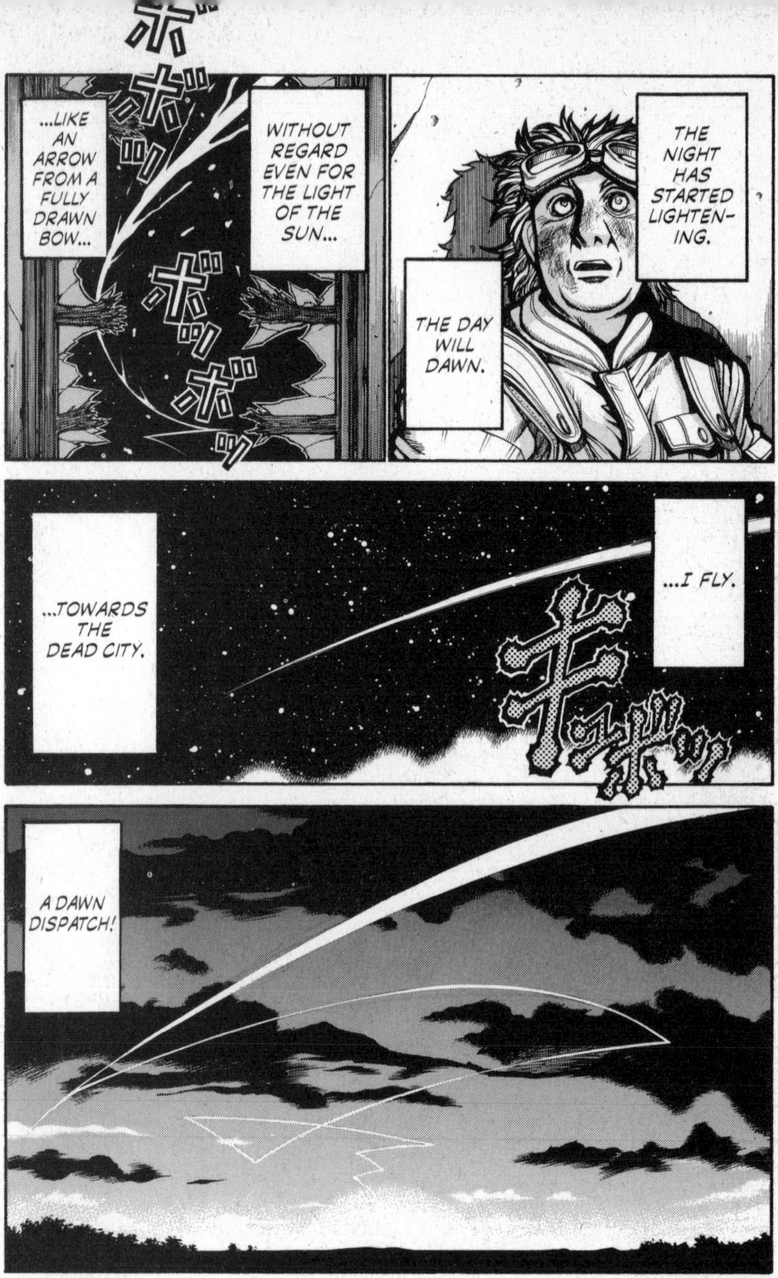
THE NIGHT HAS STARTED LIGHTEN-ING.
THE DAY WILL DAWN.
WITHOUT REGARD EVEN FOR THE LIGHT OF THE SUN...
...LIKE AN ARROW FROM A FULLY DRAWN BOW...
...I FLY.
...TOWARDS THE DEAD CITY.
A DAWN DISPATCH!

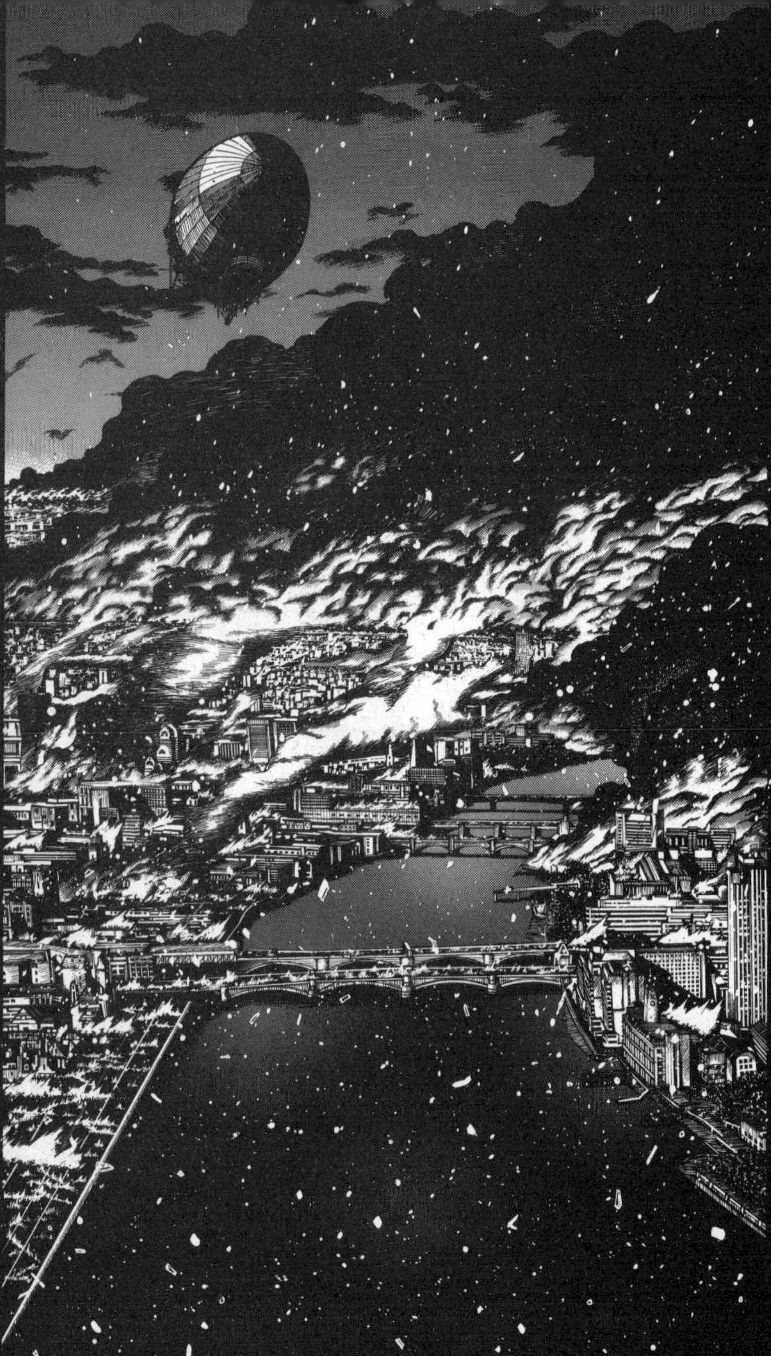

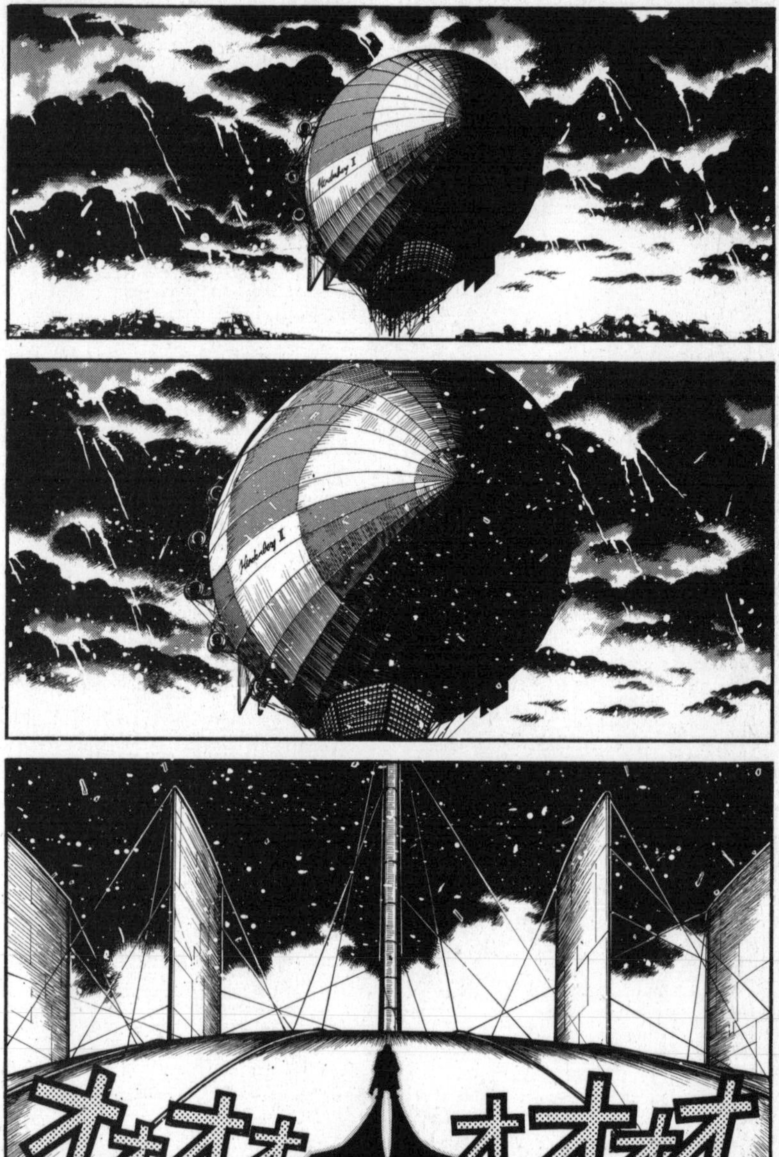
オォオォ
ォオォオ

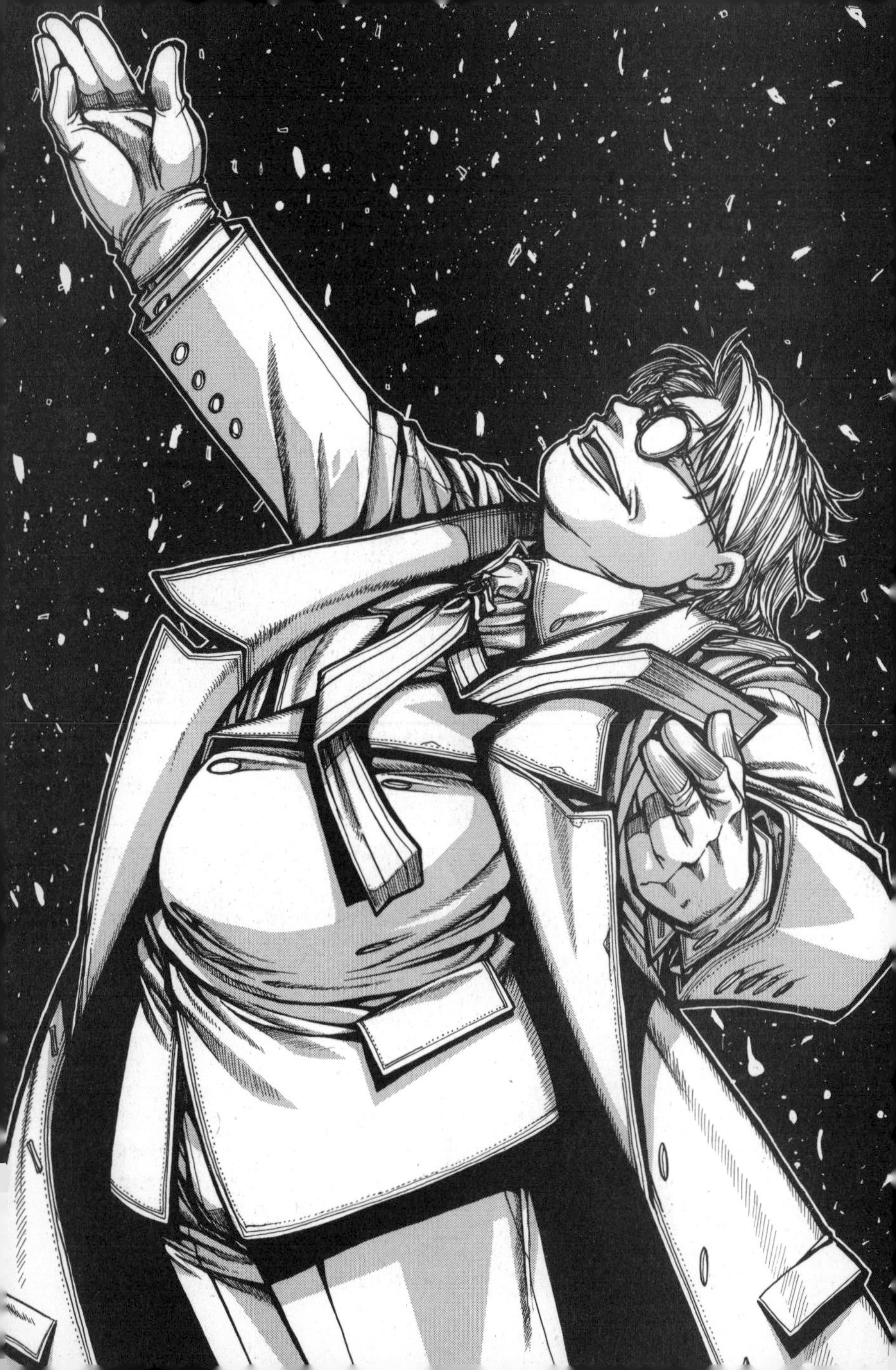

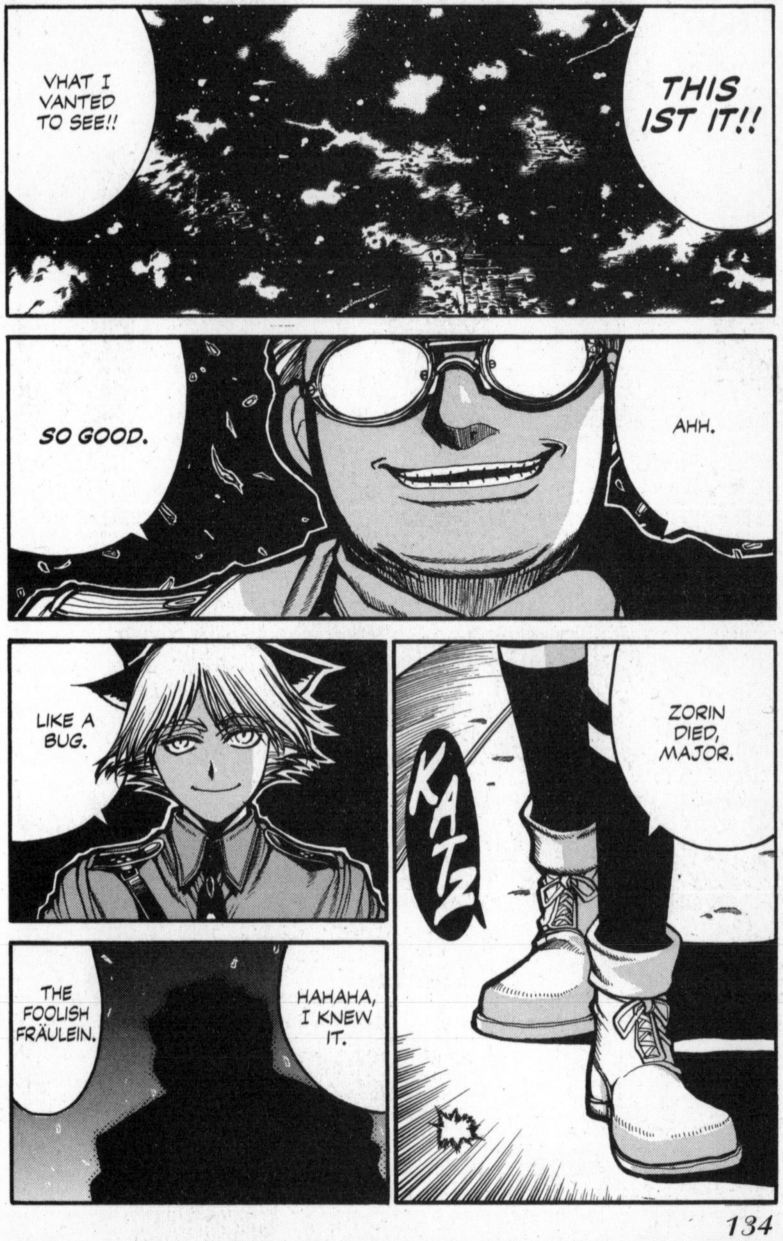
THIS IST IT!!
VHAT I VANTED TO SEE!!
AHH.
SO GOOD.
ZORIN DIED, MAJOR.
KATZ
LIKE A BUG.
HAHAHA, I KNEW IT.
THE FOOLISH FRÄULEIN.

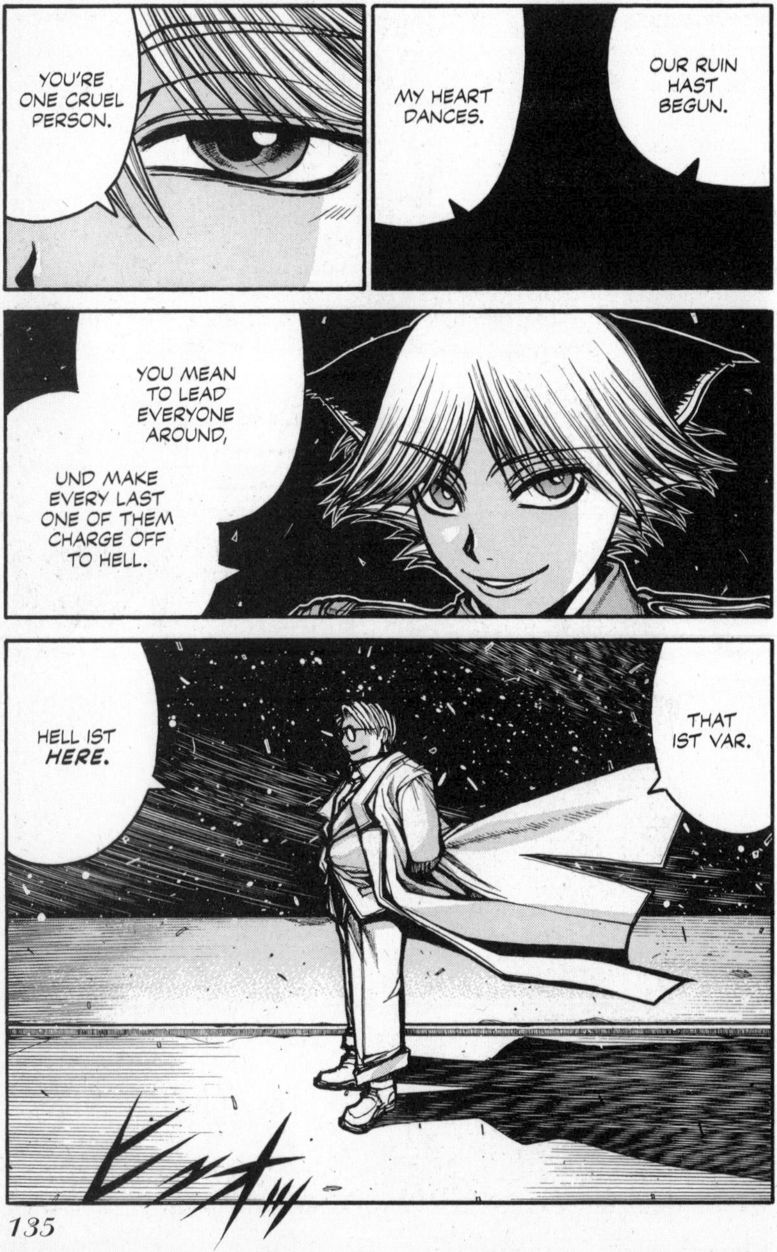
OUR RUIN HAST BEGUN.
MY HEART DANCES.
YOU'RE ONE CRUEL PERSON.
YOU MEAN TO LEAD EVERYONE AROUND,
UND MAKE EVERY LAST ONE OF THEM CHARGE OFF TO HELL.
THAT IST VAR.
HELL IST *HERE*.

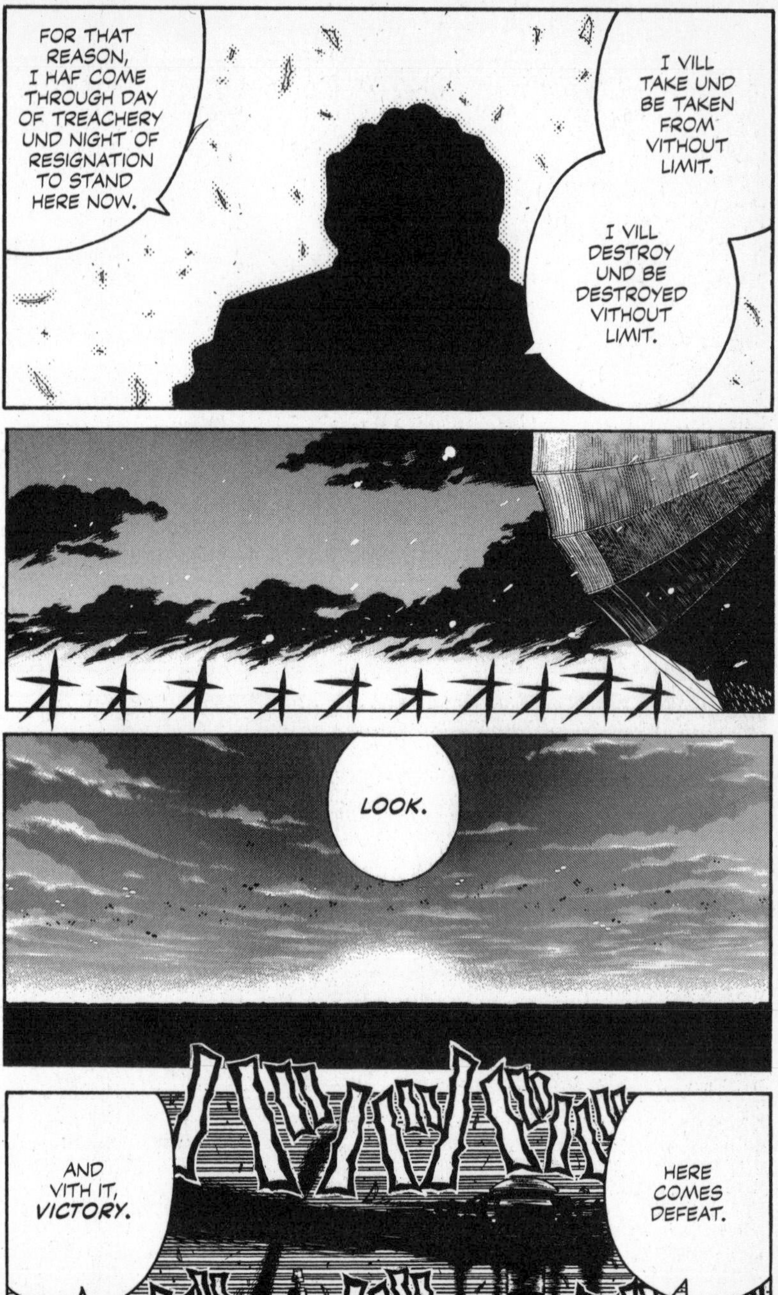
I VILL TAKE UND BE TAKEN FROM VITHOUT LIMIT.
I VILL DESTROY UND BE DESTROYED VITHOUT LIMIT.
FOR THAT REASON, I HAF COME THROUGH DAY OF TREACHERY UND NIGHT OF RESIGNATION TO STAND HERE NOW.
LOOK.
HERE COMES DEFEAT.
AND VITH IT, VICTORY.

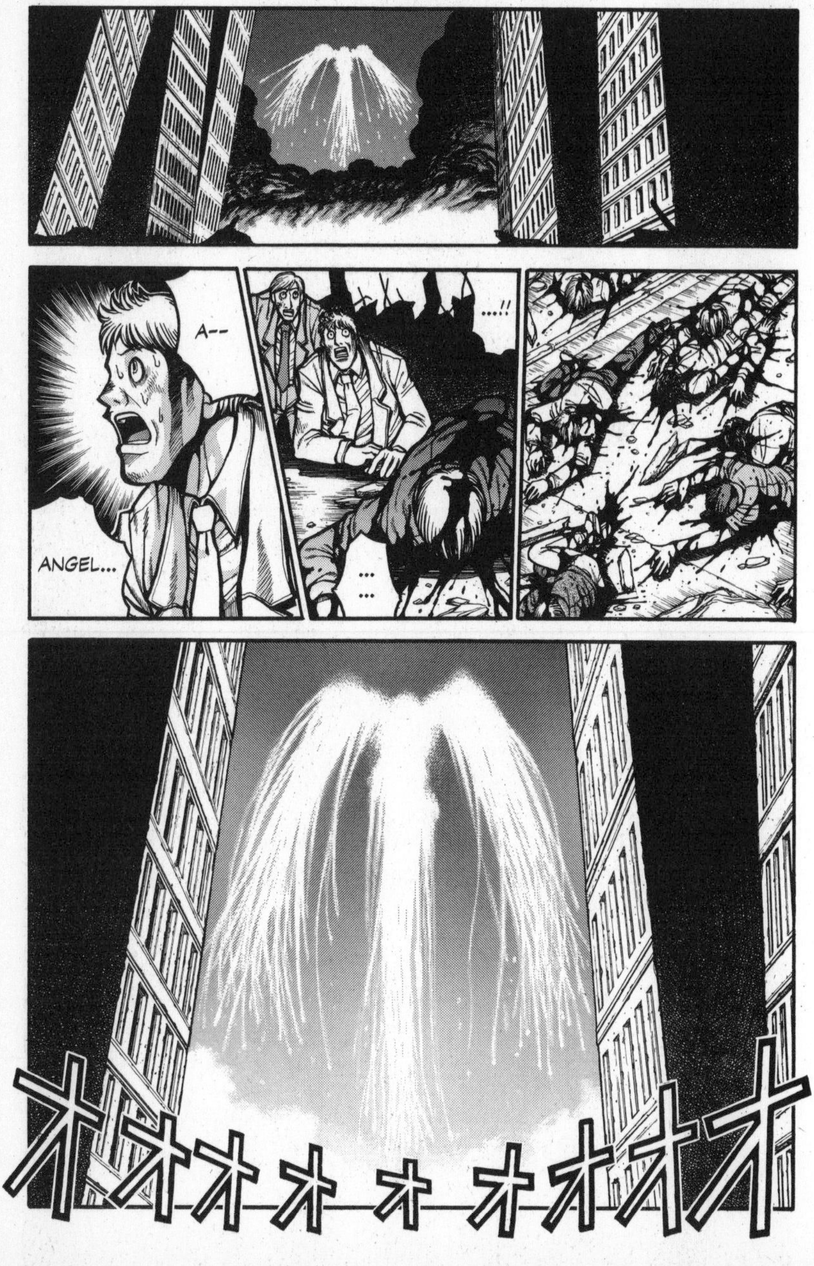
...!!
...
...
A--
ANGEL...
オオオオォオオオオ

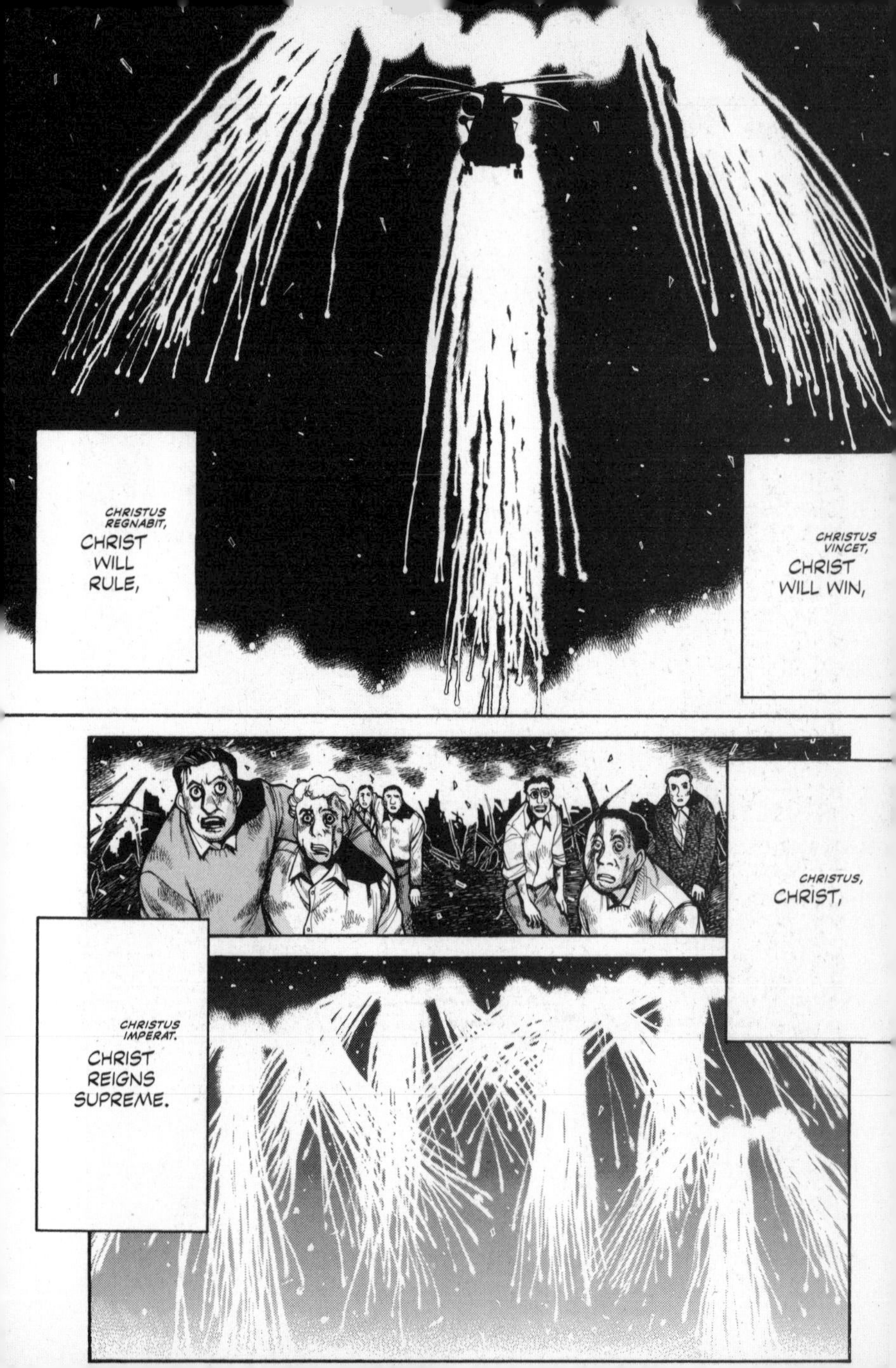
CHRISTUS VINCET,
CHRIST WILL WIN,
CHRISTUS REGNABIT,
CHRIST WILL RULE,
CHRISTUS,
CHRIST,
CHRISTUS IMPERAT.
CHRIST REIGNS SUPREME.

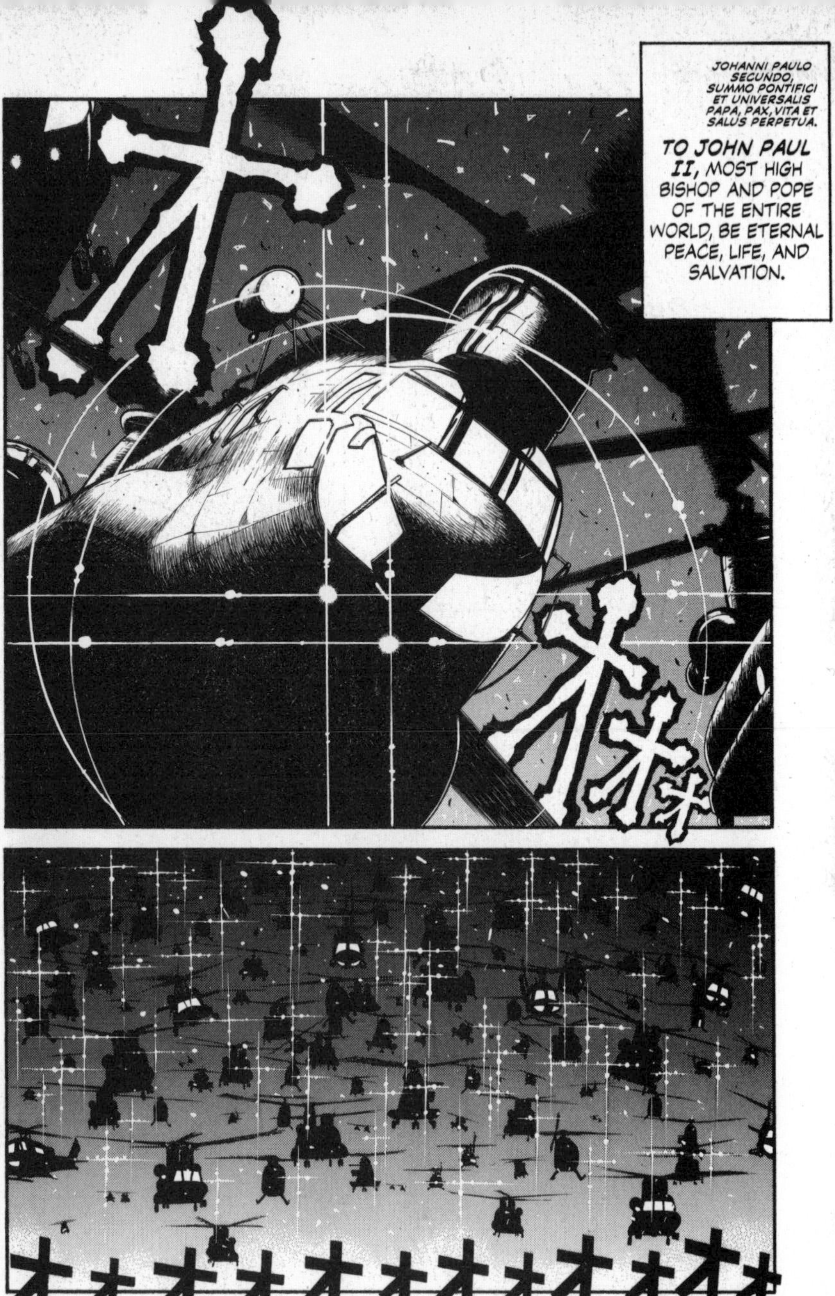
JOHANNI PAULO SECUNDO, SUMMO PONTIFICI ET UNIVERSALIS PAPA, PAX, VITA ET SALUS PERPETUA.
TO JOHN PAUL II, MOST HIGH BISHOP AND POPE OF THE ENTIRE WORLD, BE ETERNAL PEACE, LIFE, AND SALVATION.

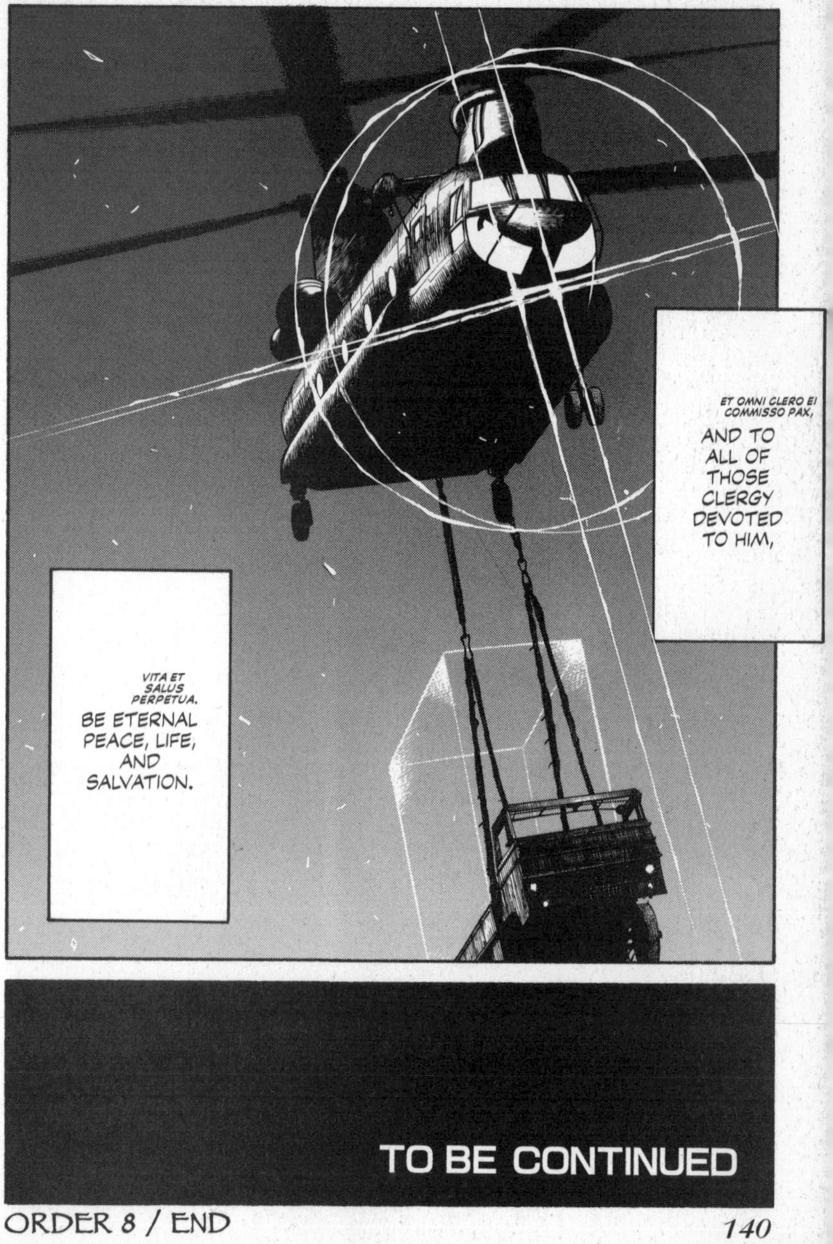
ET OMNI CLERO EI COMMISSO PAX,
AND TO ALL OF THOSE CLERGY DEVOTED TO HIM,
VITA ET SALUS PERPETUA.
BE ETERNAL PEACE, LIFE, AND SALVATION.

TO BE CONTINUED

ORDER 9

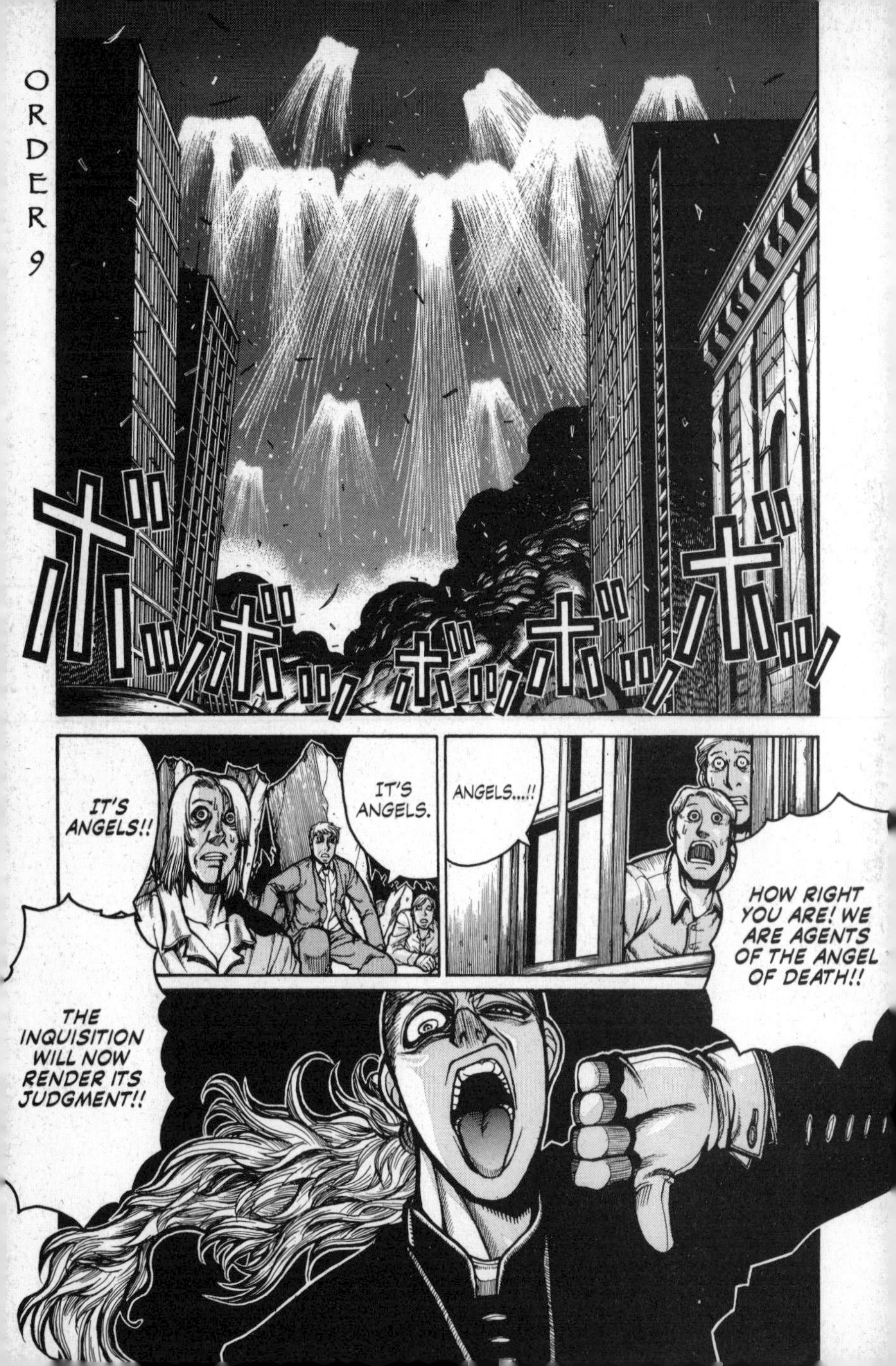
ボッ
ボッ
ボッ
ボッ
ボッ
ANGELS...!!
IT'S ANGELS.
IT'S ANGELS!!
HOW RIGHT YOU ARE! WE ARE AGENTS OF THE ANGEL OF DEATH!!
THE INQUISITION WILL NOW RENDER ITS JUDGMENT!!

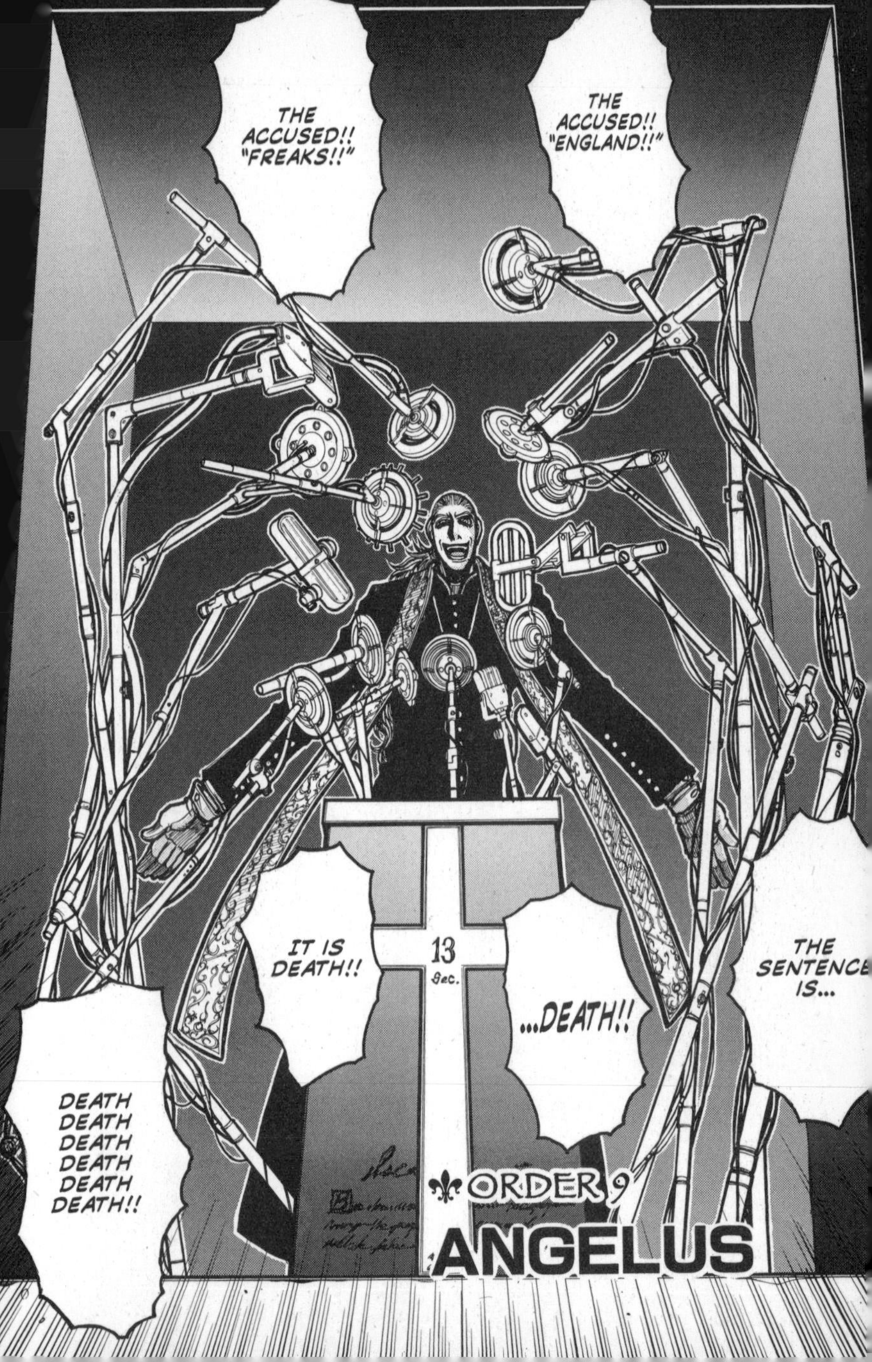
THE ACCUSED!! "ENGLAND!!"
THE ACCUSED!! "FREAKS!!"
THE SENTENCE IS...
...DEATH!!
IT IS DEATH!!
DEATH DEATH DEATH DEATH DEATH DEATH!!
13 Sec.
ORDER 9
ANGELUS

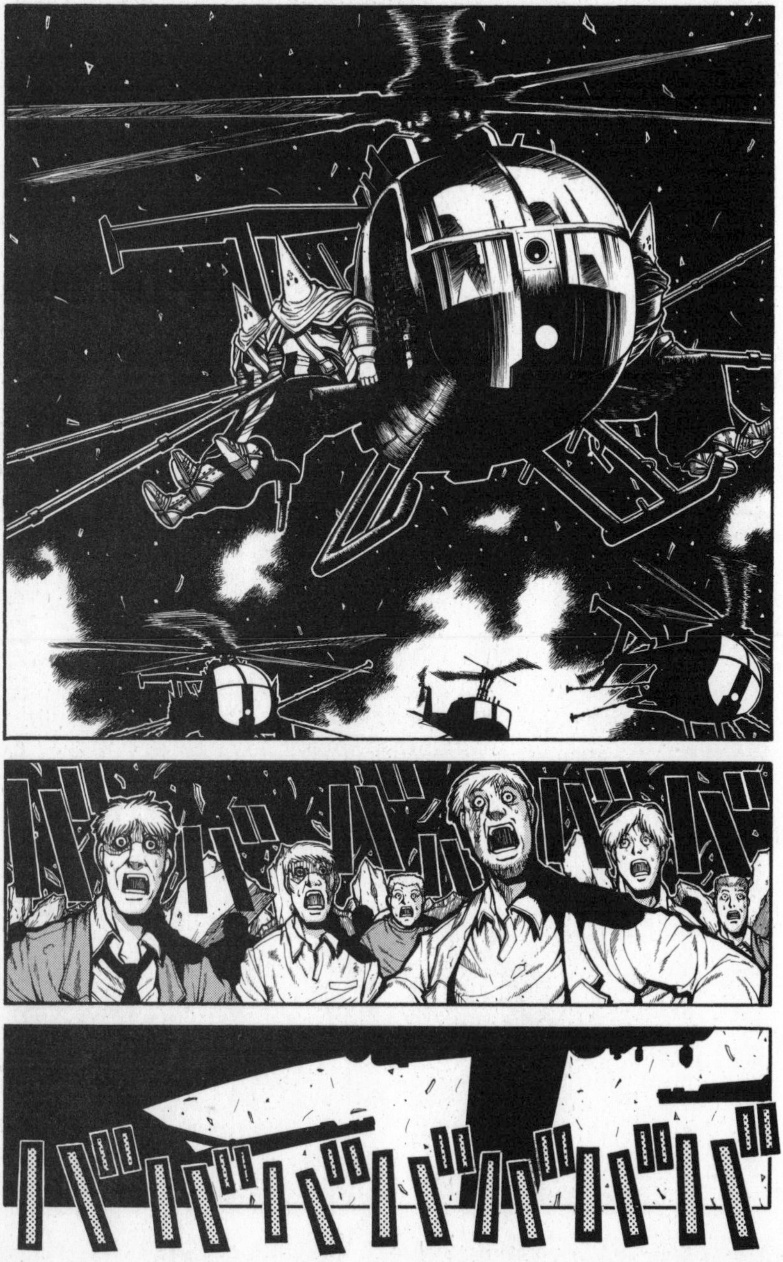

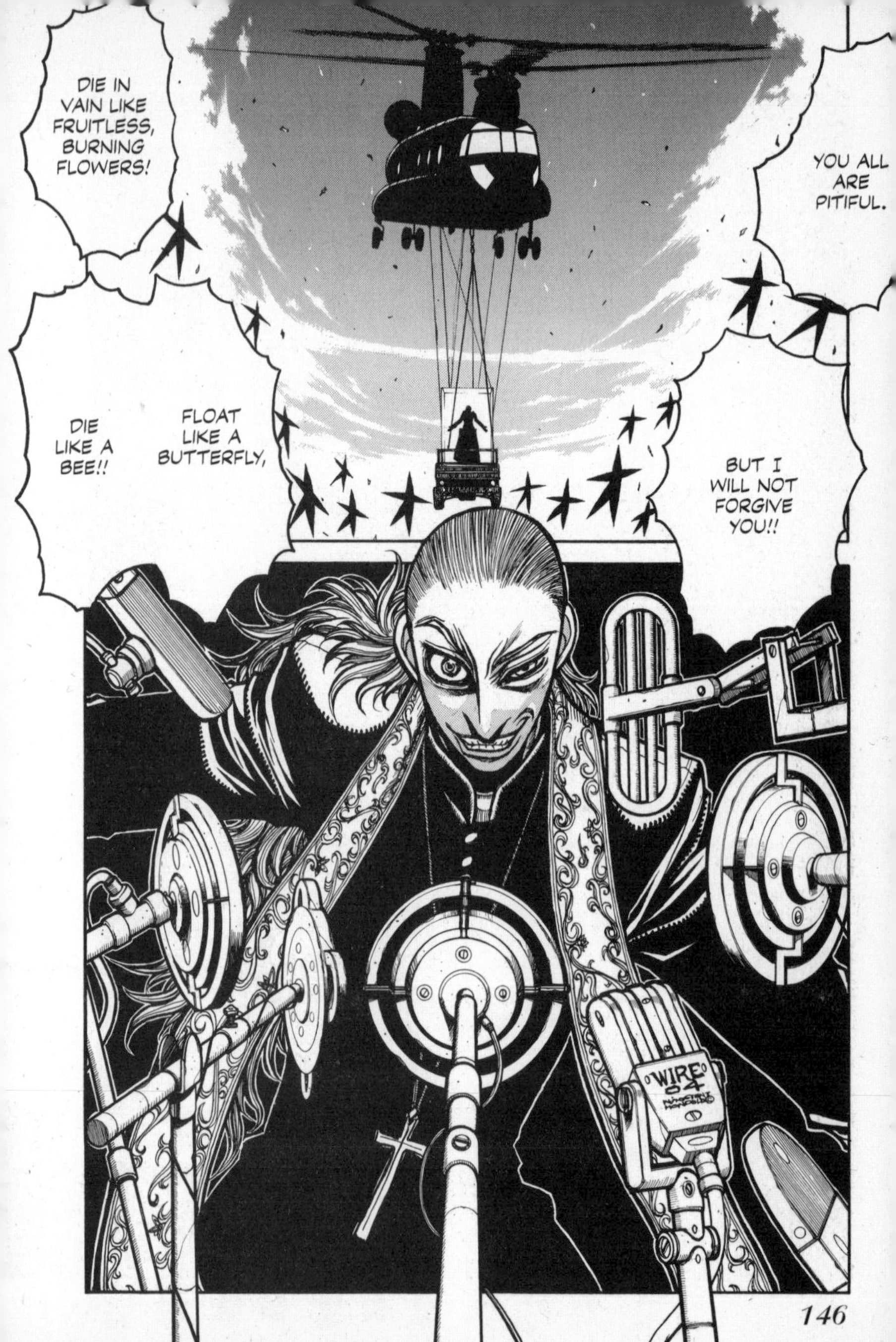
YOU ALL ARE PITIFUL.
BUT I WILL NOT FORGIVE YOU!!
FLOAT LIKE A BUTTERFLY,
DIE LIKE A BEE!!
DIE IN VAIN LIKE FRUITLESS, BURNING FLOWERS!
WIRE 04

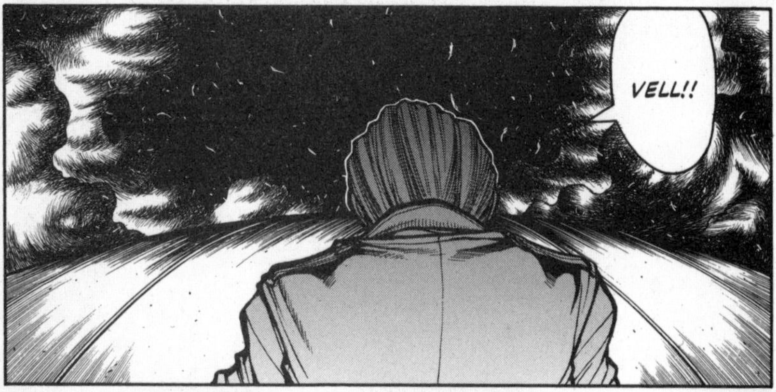
VELL!!

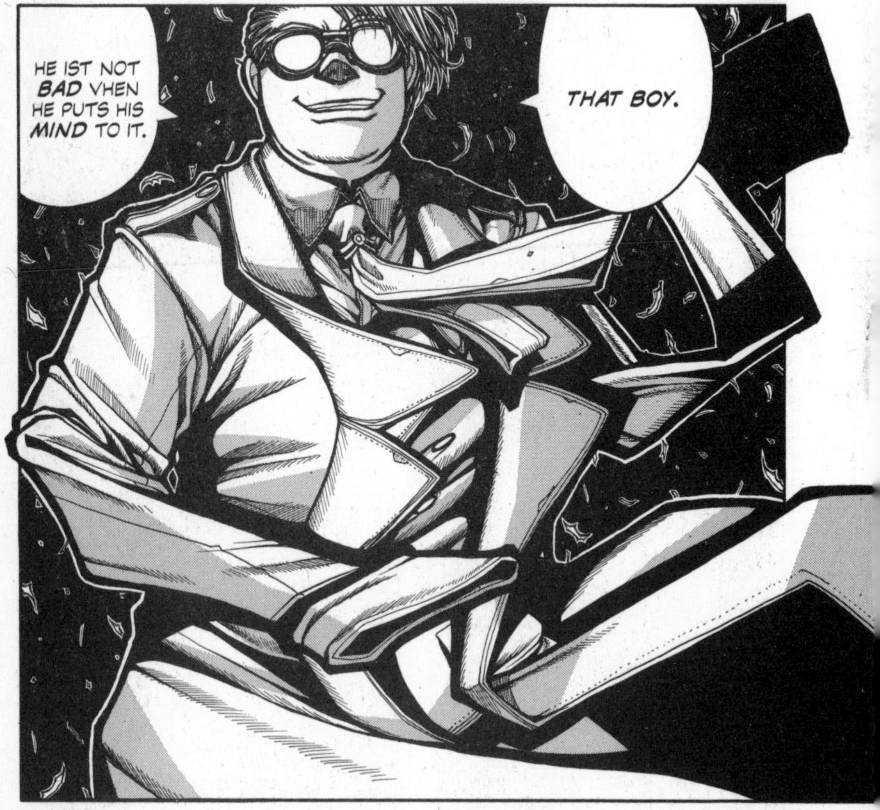
THAT BOY.
HE IST NOT BAD VHEN HE PUTS HIS MIND TO IT.

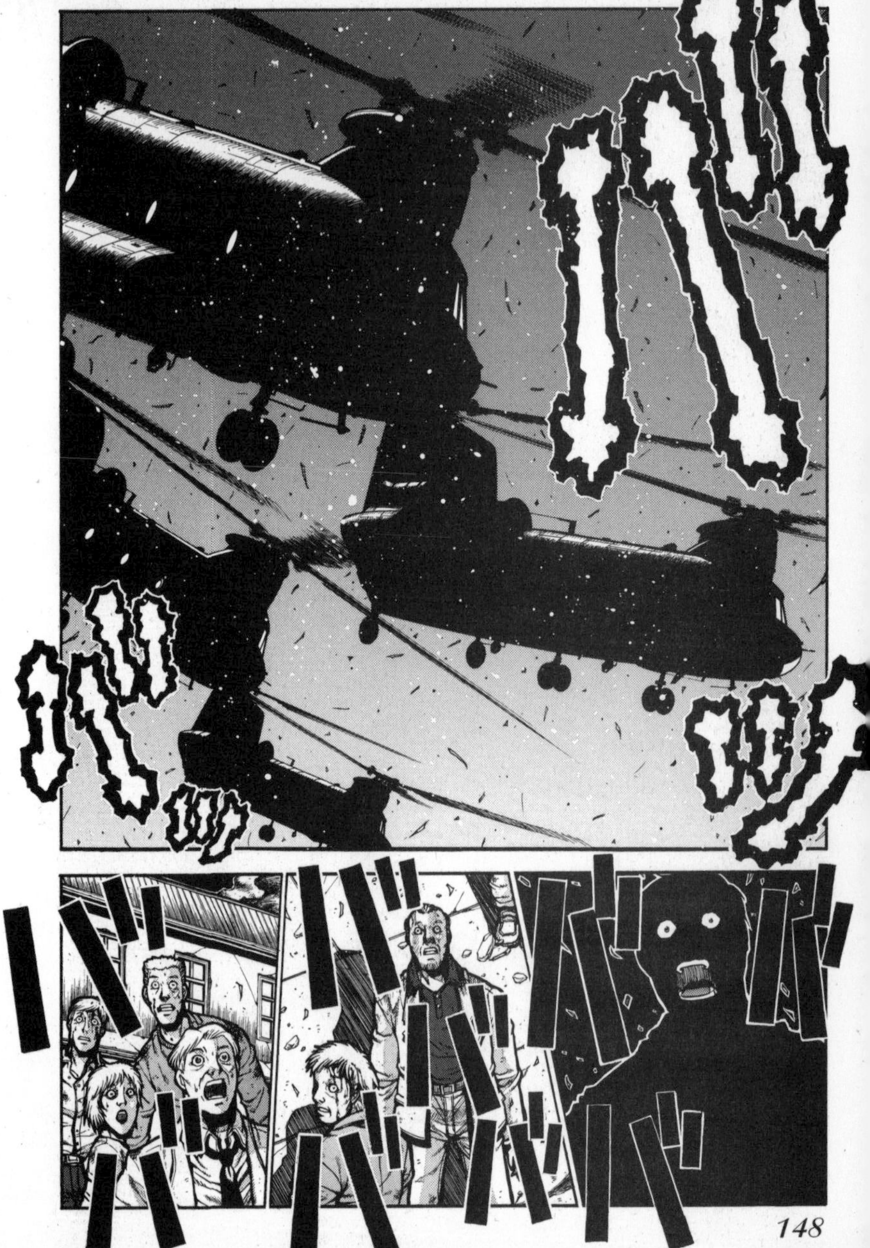

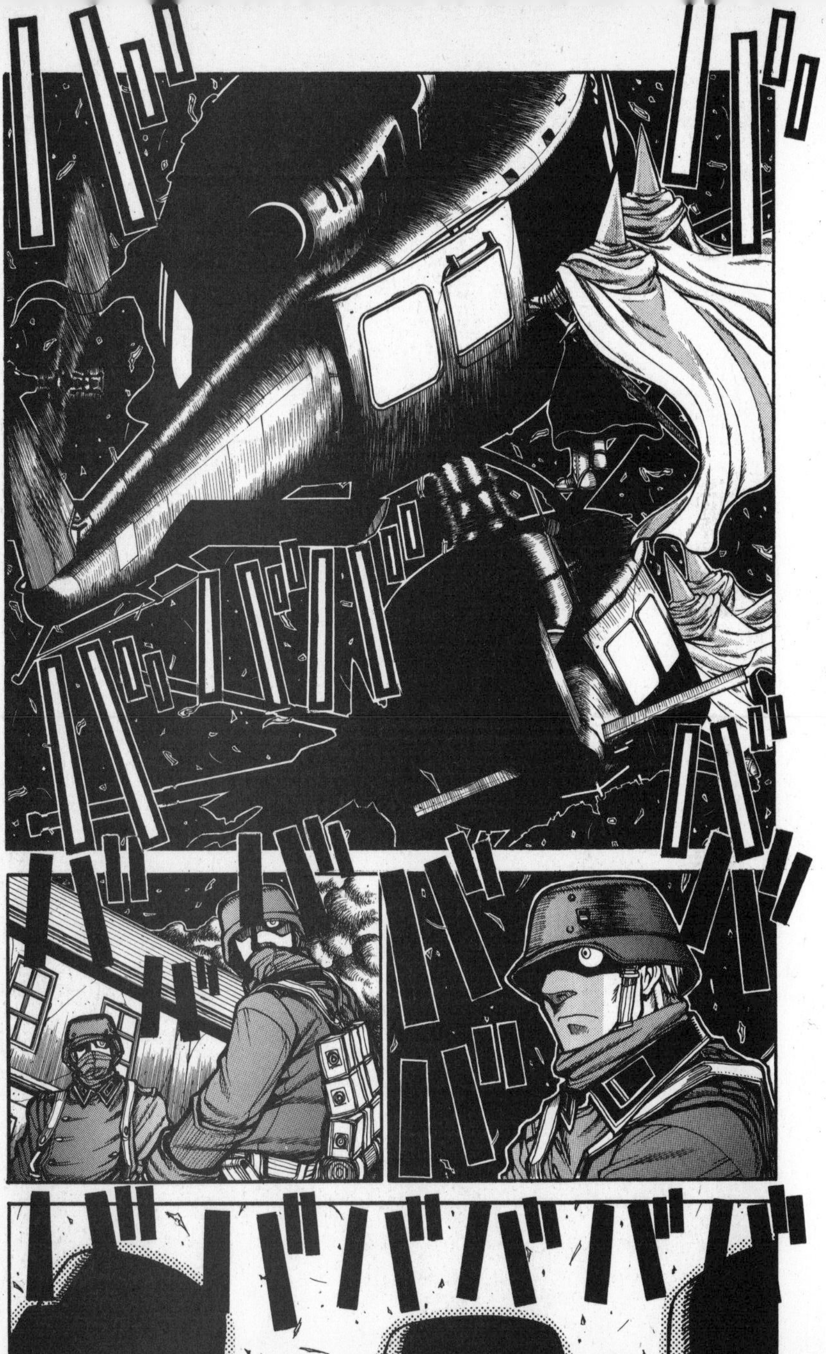

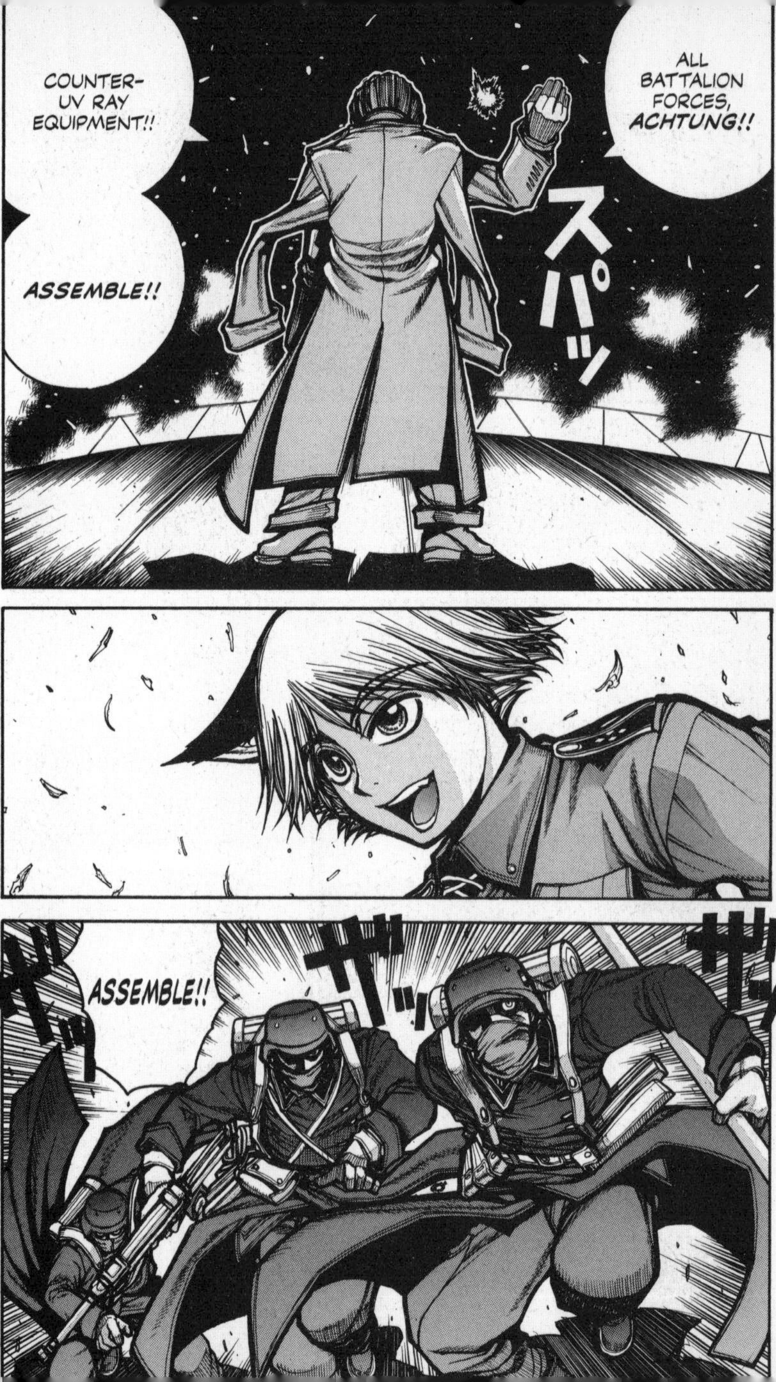
ALL BATTALION FORCES, ACHTUNG!!
COUNTER-UV RAY EQUIPMENT!!
ASSEMBLE!!
スパッ
ザッ
ザッ
ASSEMBLE!!
ザッ

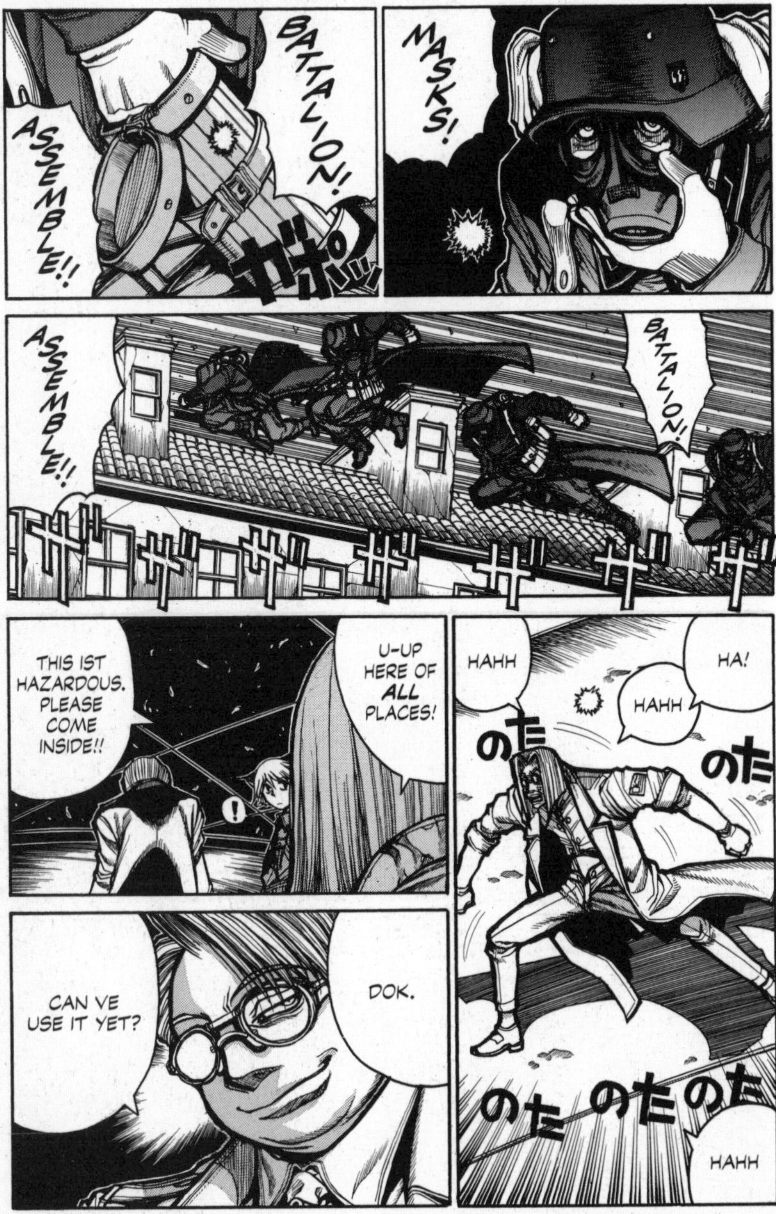
MASKS!
BATTALION!
ASSEMBLE!!
BATTALION!
ASSEMBLE!!
HA!
HAHH
HAHH
のた
のた
のた のたのた
HAHH
U-UP HERE OF ALL PLACES!
THIS IST HAZARDOUS. PLEASE COME INSIDE!!
!
DOK.
CAN VE USE IT YET?

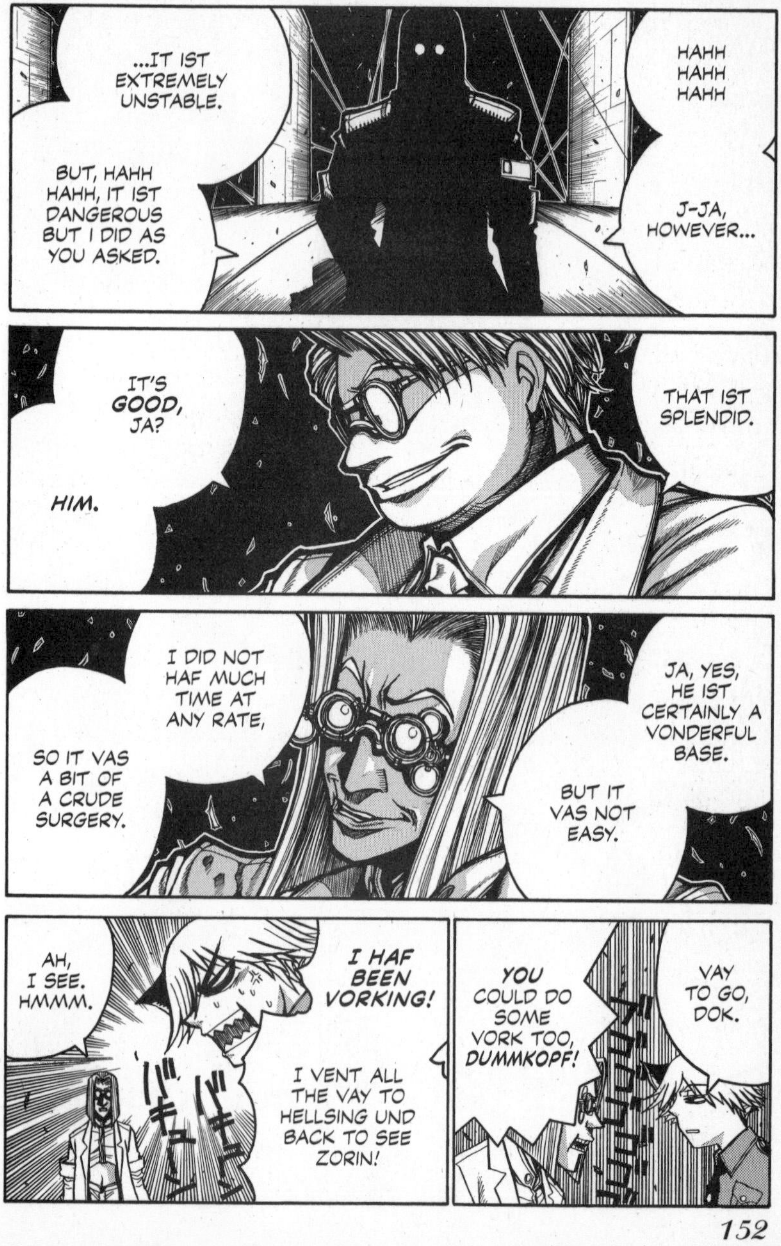
HAHH HAHH HAHH
J-JA, HOWEVER...
...IT IST EXTREMELY UNSTABLE.
BUT, HAHH HAHH, IT IST DANGEROUS BUT I DID AS YOU ASKED.
THAT IST SPLENDID.
IT'S *GOOD*, JA?
HIM.
JA, YES, HE IST CERTAINLY A VONDERFUL BASE.
BUT IT VAS NOT EASY.
I DID NOT HAF MUCH TIME AT ANY RATE,
SO IT VAS A BIT OF A CRUDE SURGERY.
VAY TO GO, DOK.
YOU COULD DO SOME VORK TOO, *DUMMKOPF!*
I HAF BEEN VORKING!
I VENT ALL THE VAY TO HELLSING UND BACK TO SEE ZORIN!
AH, I SEE. HMMM.

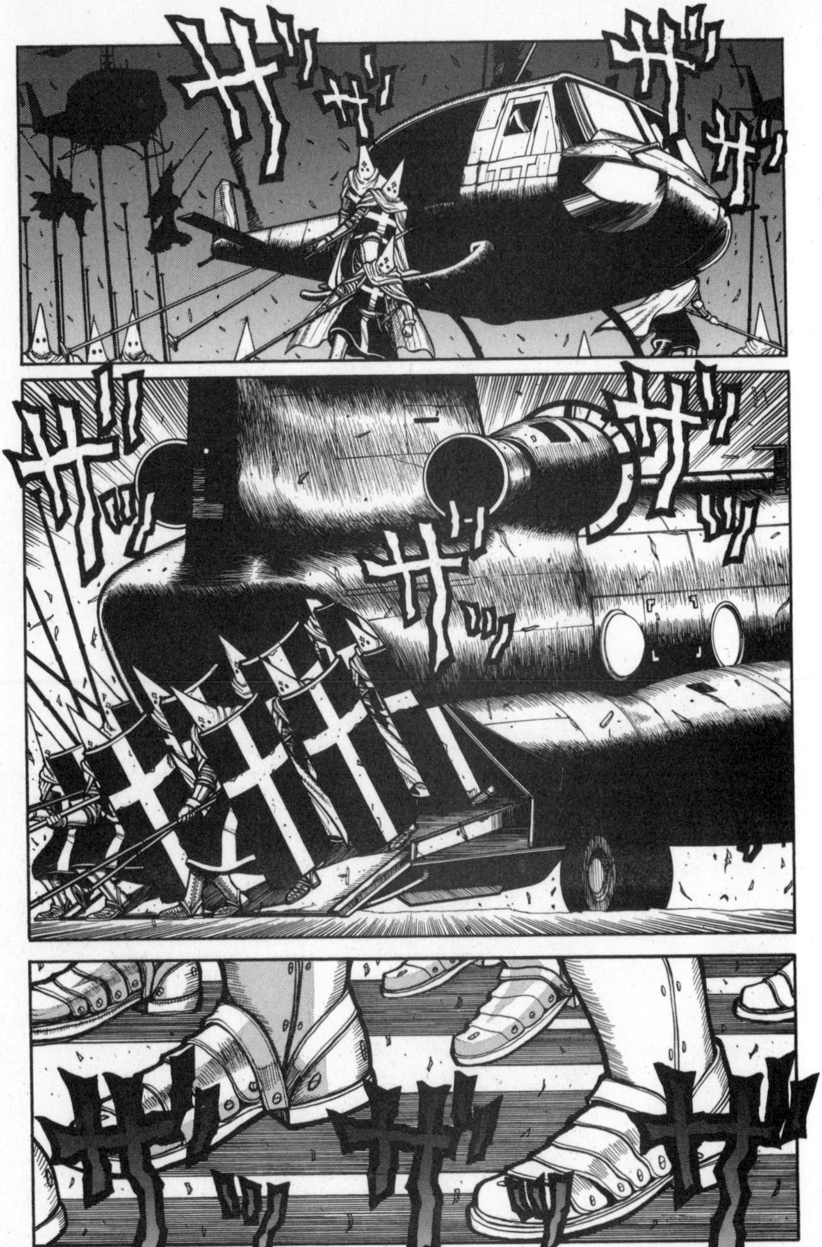
ザッ
ザッ
ザッ
ザッ
ザッ
ザッ
ザッ
ザッ
ザッ
ザッ

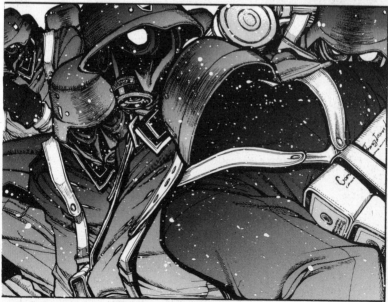

154

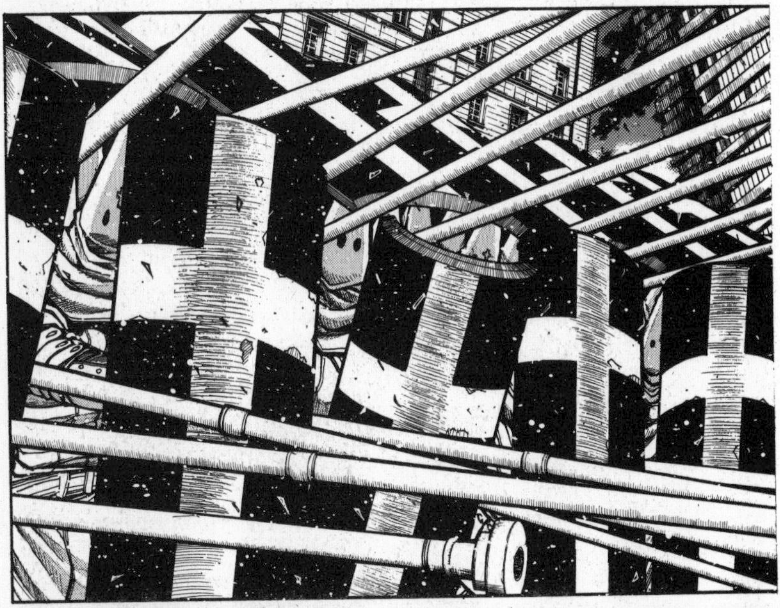

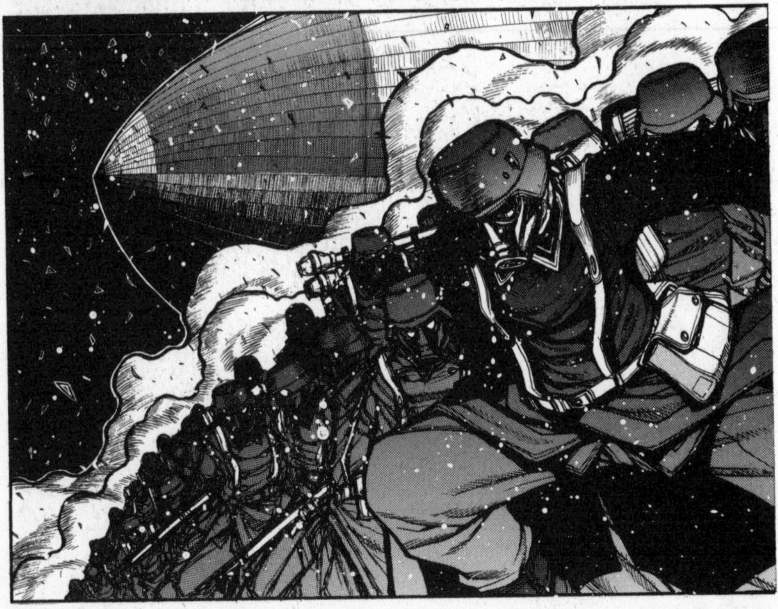

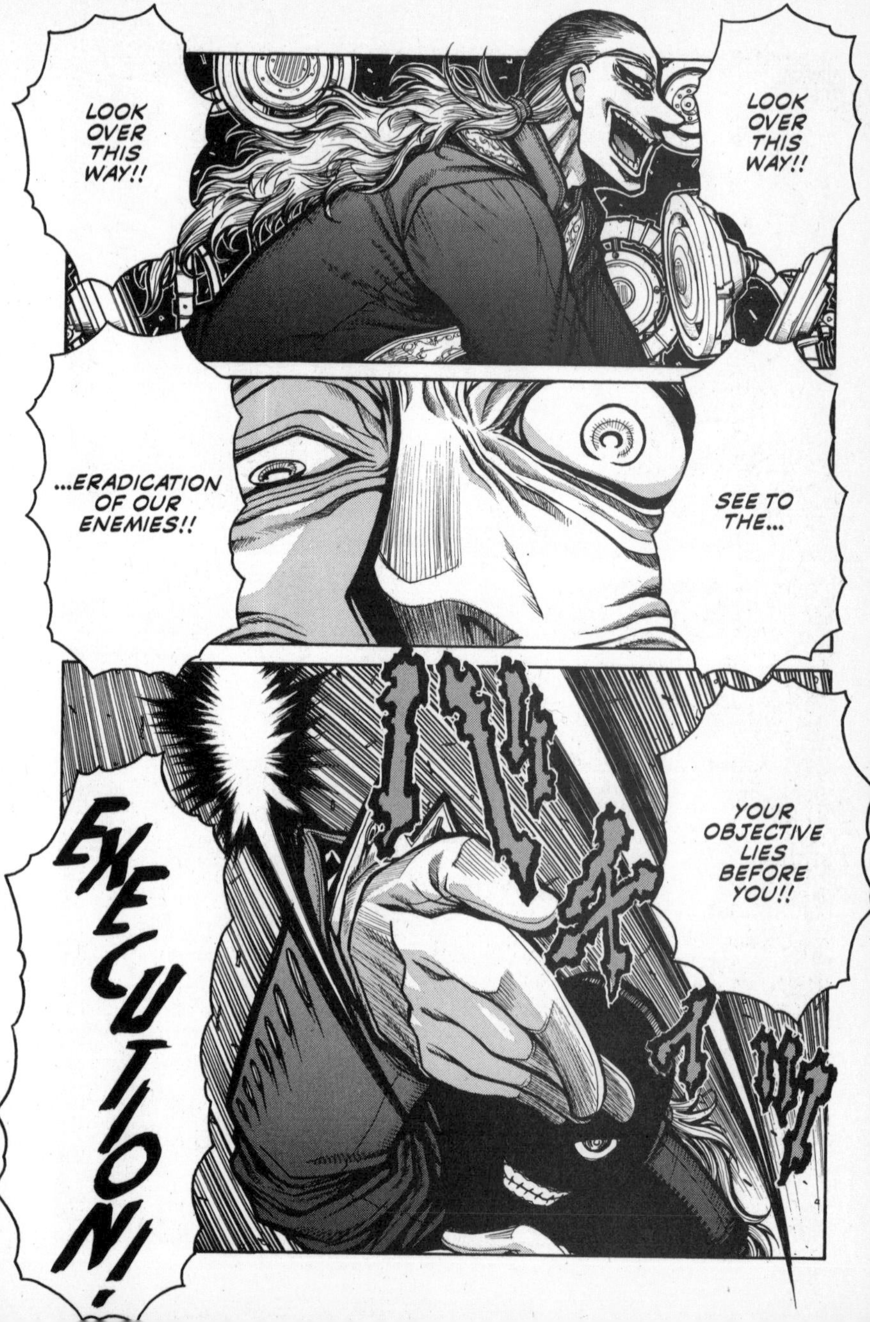
LOOK OVER THIS WAY!!
LOOK OVER THIS WAY!!
SEE TO THE...
...ERADICATION OF OUR ENEMIES!!
YOUR OBJECTIVE LIES BEFORE YOU!!
EXECUTION!

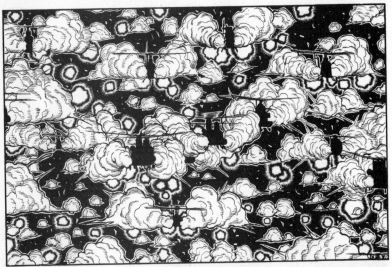

ボッ ボッ ボッ ボッ ボッ ボッ ボッ ボッ

キュワッ キュワッ キュワッ

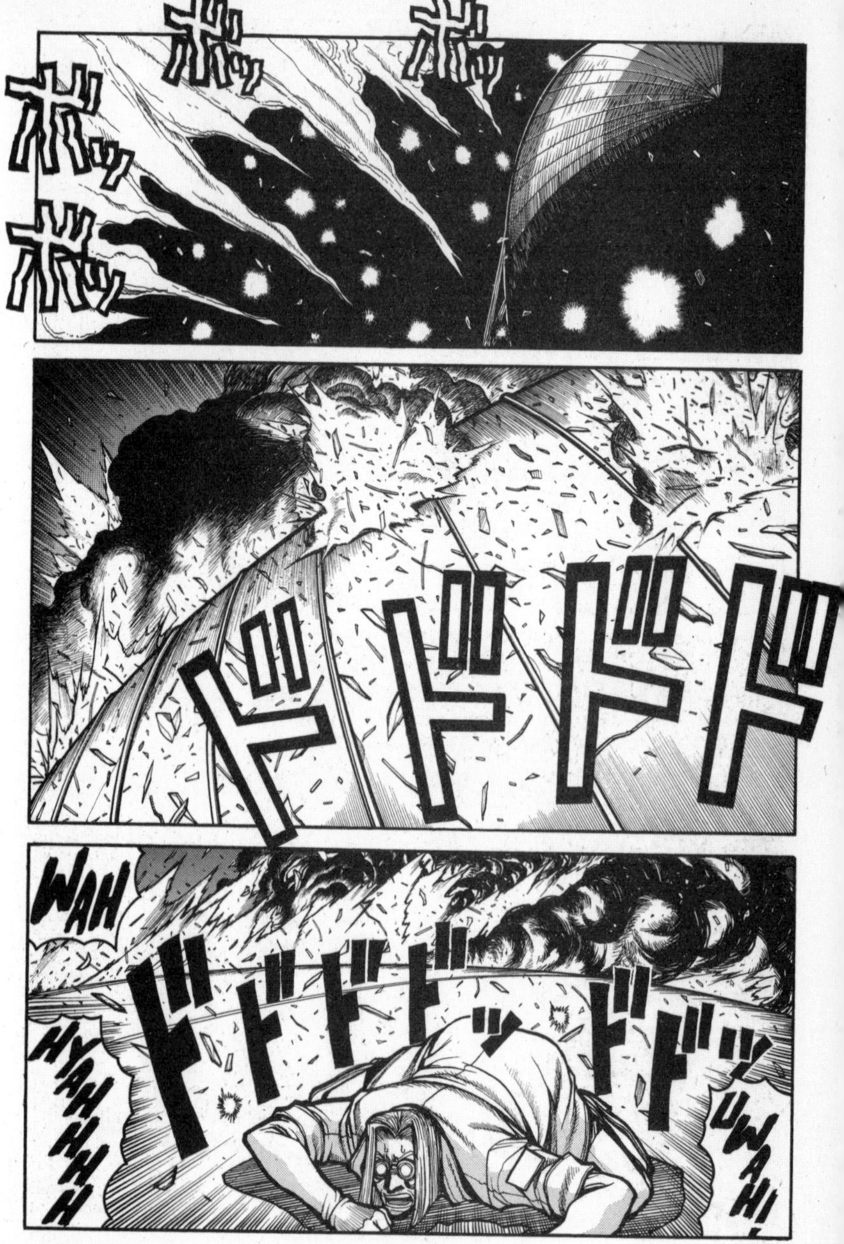
ボッ
ボッ
ボッ
ボッ
ドドドド
UWAH!
ドドドドッ
ドドッ
WAH
HYAHHHHH

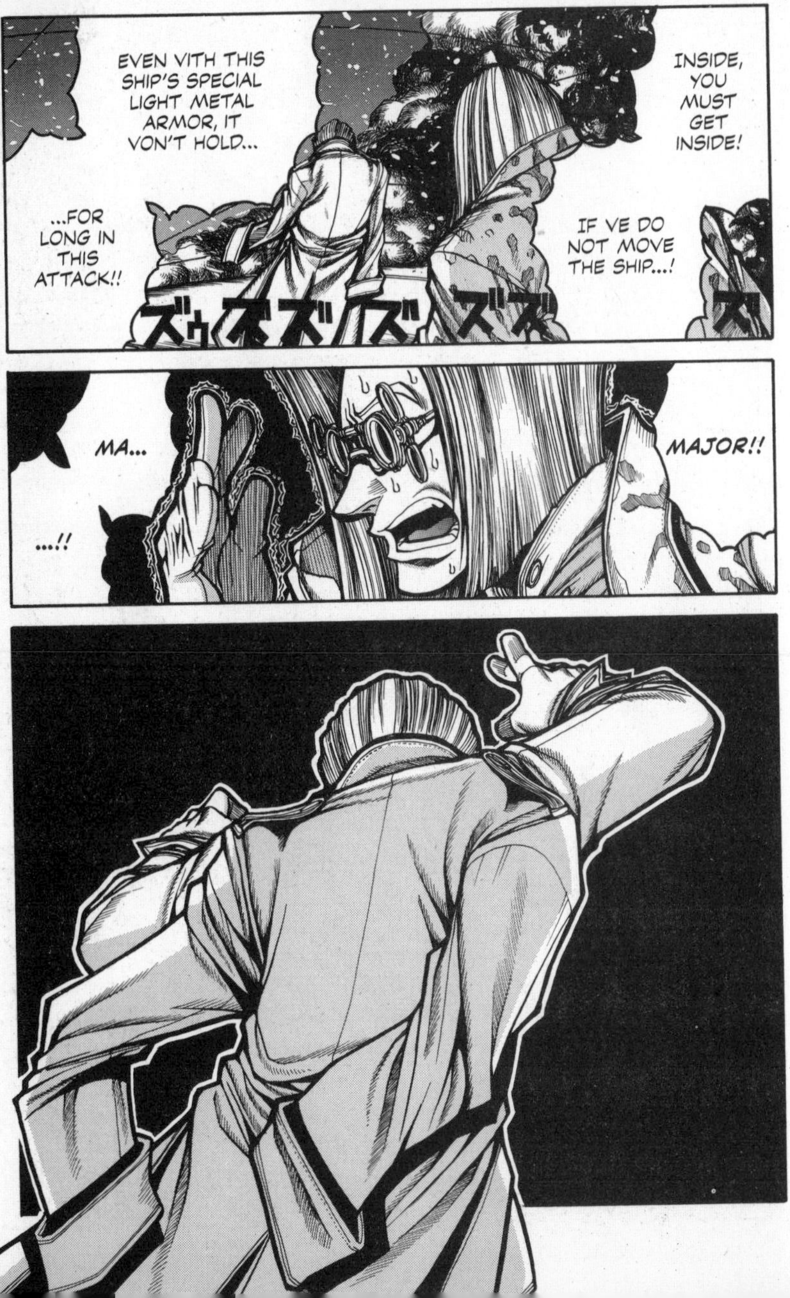
INSIDE, YOU MUST GET INSIDE!
IF VE DO NOT MOVE THE SHIP...!
EVEN VITH THIS SHIP'S SPECIAL LIGHT METAL ARMOR, IT VON'T HOLD...
...FOR LONG IN THIS ATTACK!!
ズ
ズズ
ズゥズズズ
MAJOR!!
MA...
...!!

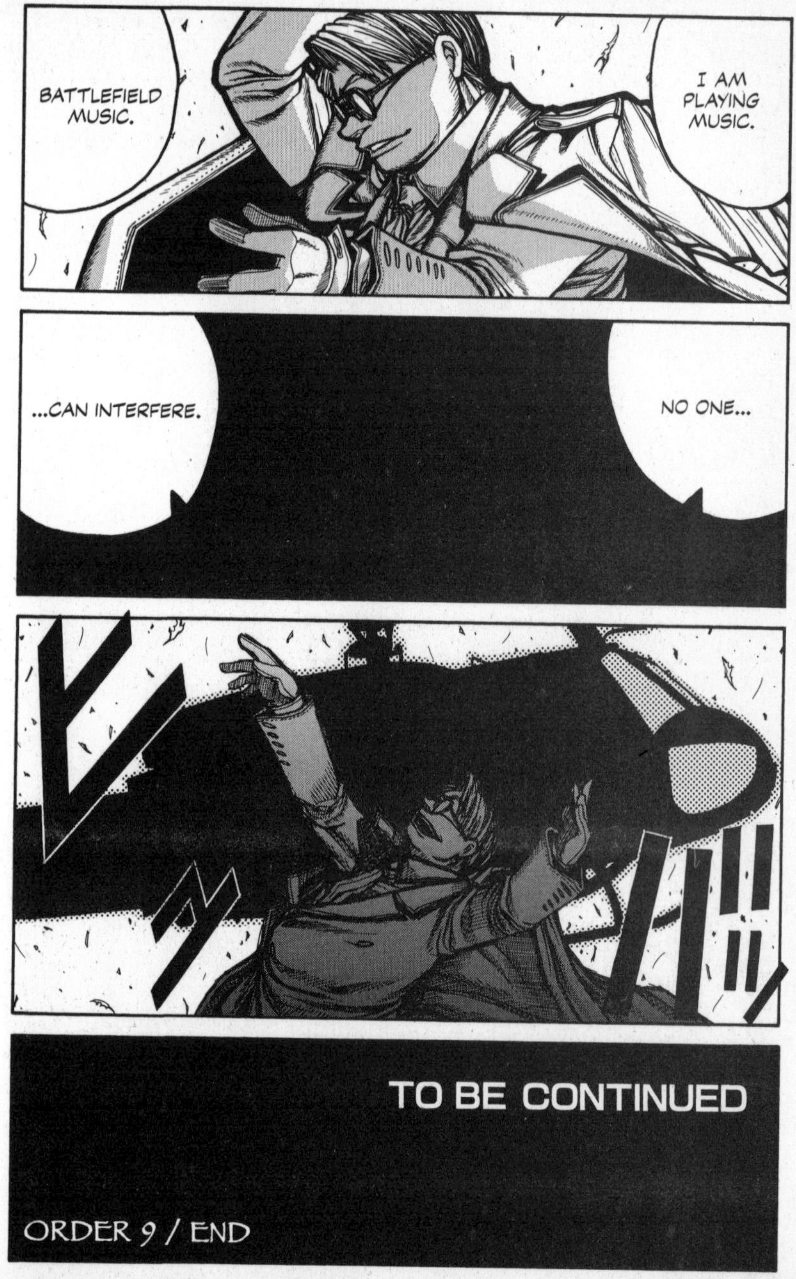
I AM PLAYING MUSIC.
BATTLEFIELD MUSIC.
NO ONE...
...CAN INTERFERE.

TO BE CONTINUED

ORDER 9 / END

ORDER 10

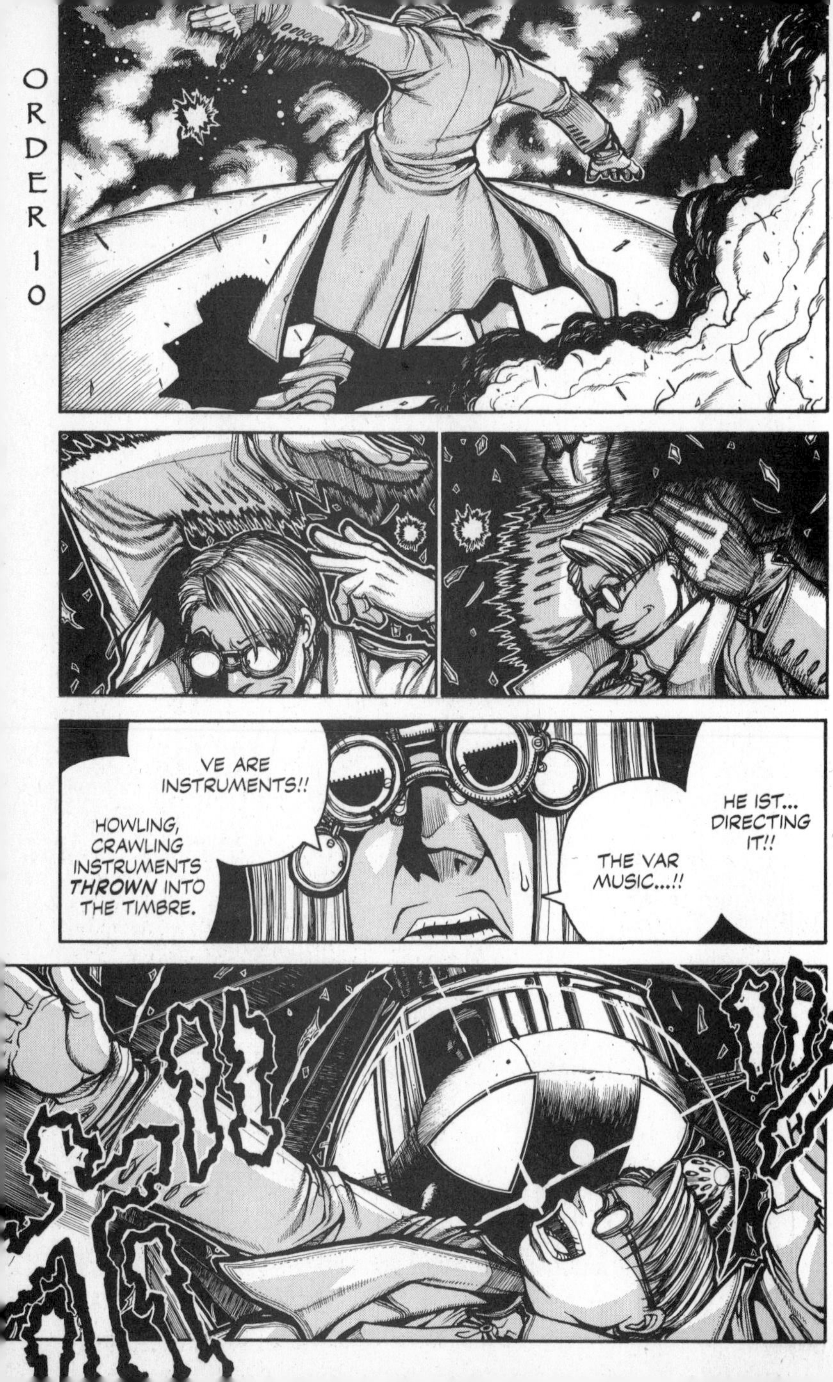
HE IST... DIRECTING IT!!
THE VAR MUSIC...!!
VE ARE INSTRUMENTS!!
HOWLING, CRAWLING INSTRUMENTS *THROWN* INTO THE TIMBRE.

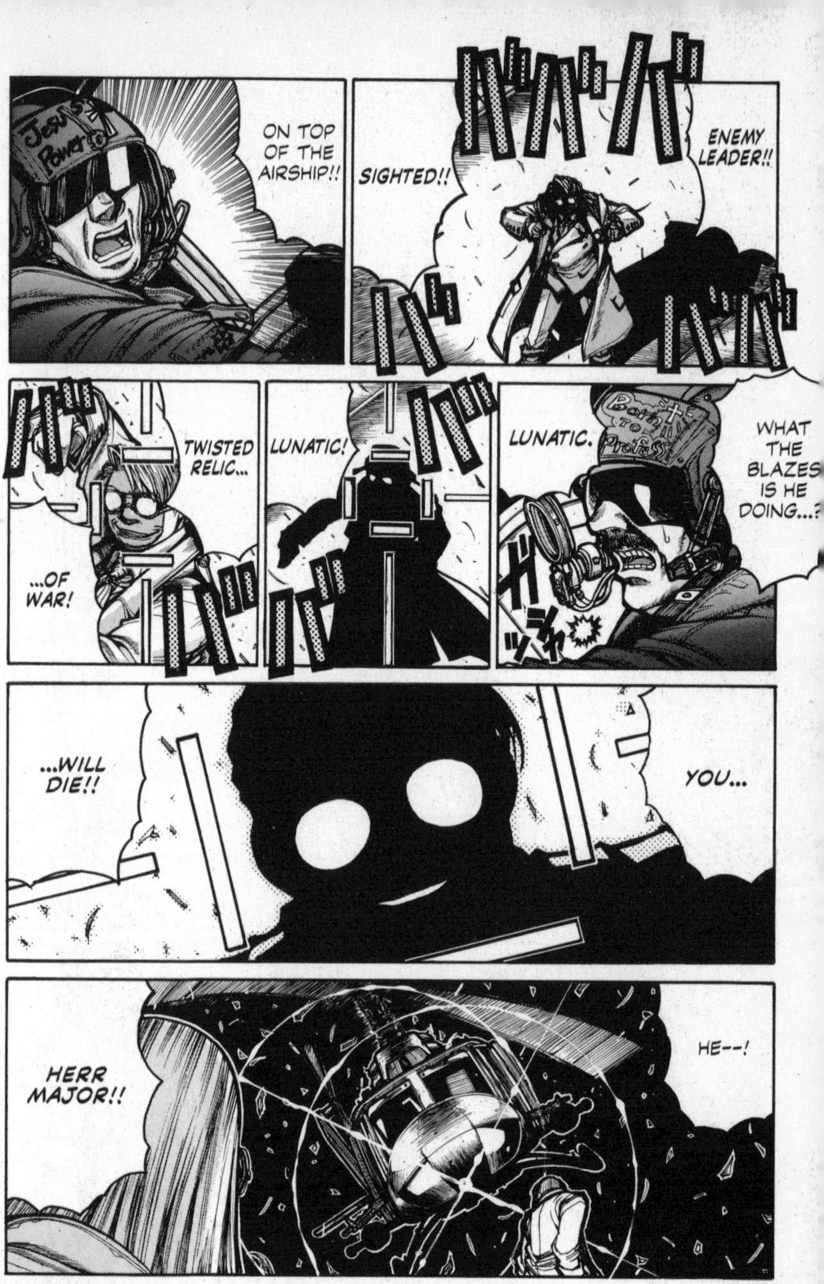
ENEMY LEADER!!
SIGHTED!!
ON TOP OF THE AIRSHIP!!
WHAT THE BLAZES IS HE DOING...?
LUNATIC.
LUNATIC!
TWISTED RELIC...
...OF WAR!
YOU...
...WILL DIE!!
HE--!
HERR MAJOR!!

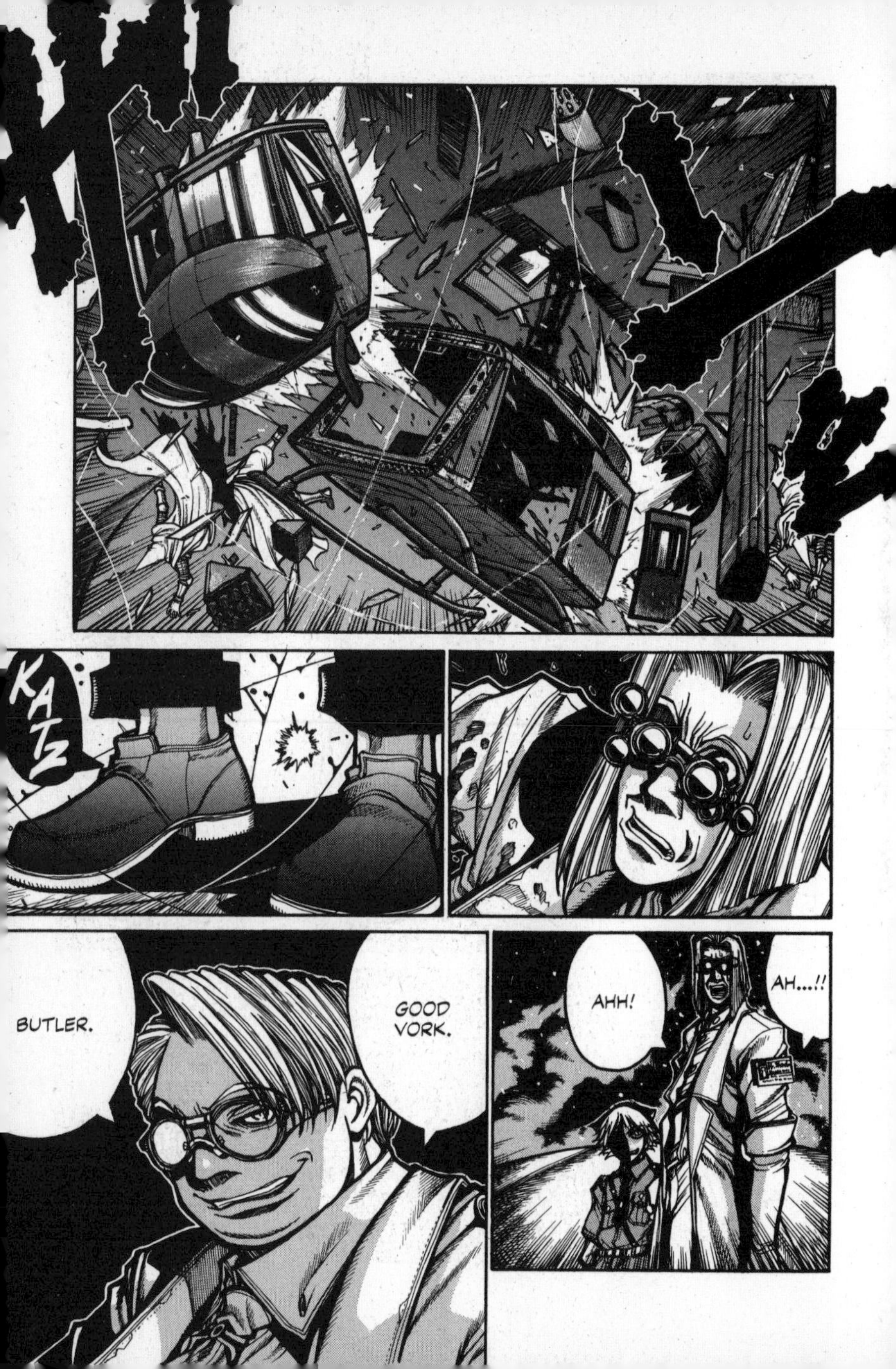

KATZ
AH...!!
AHH!
GOOD VORK.
BUTLER.

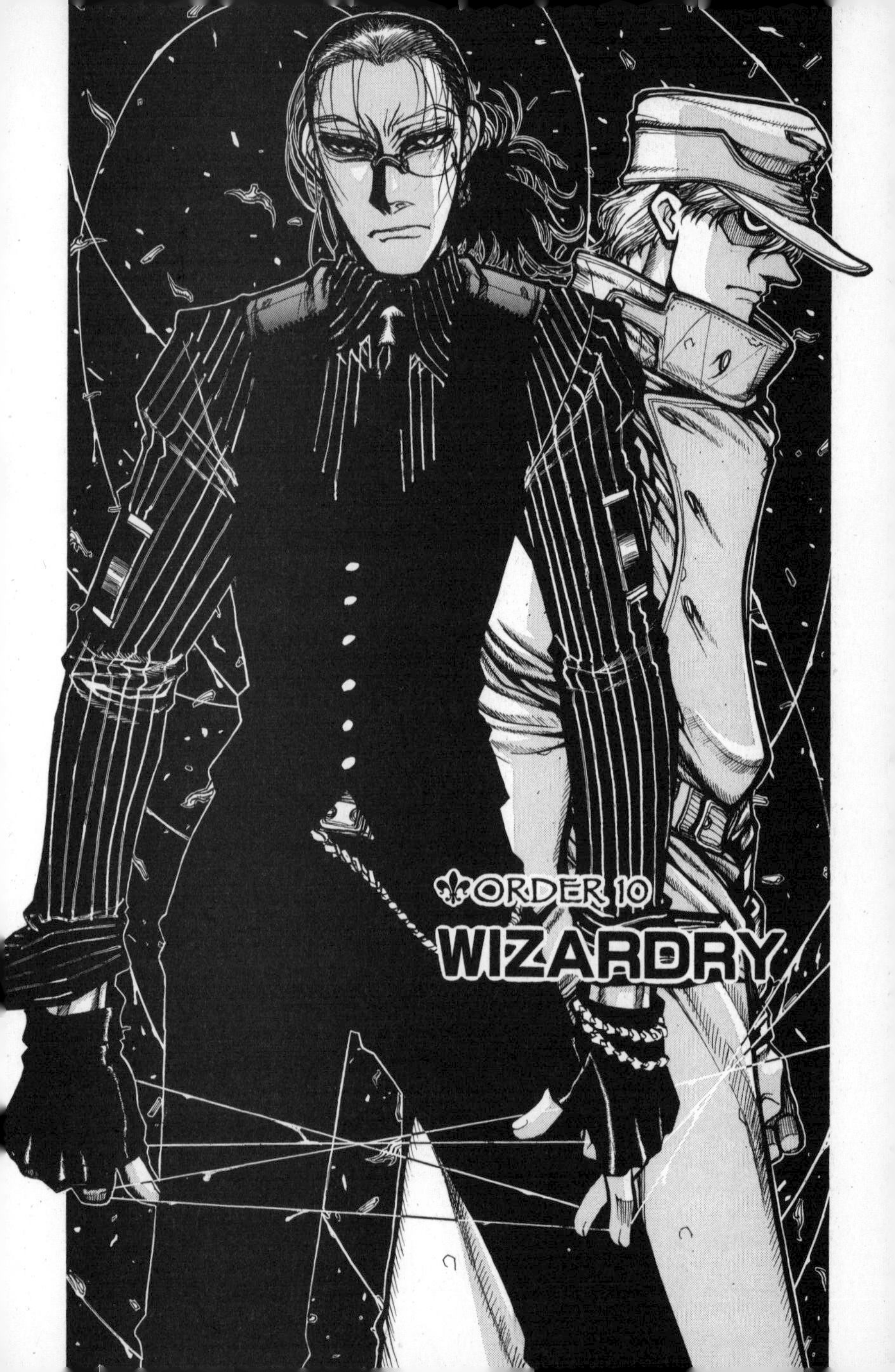
ORDER 10
WIZARDRY

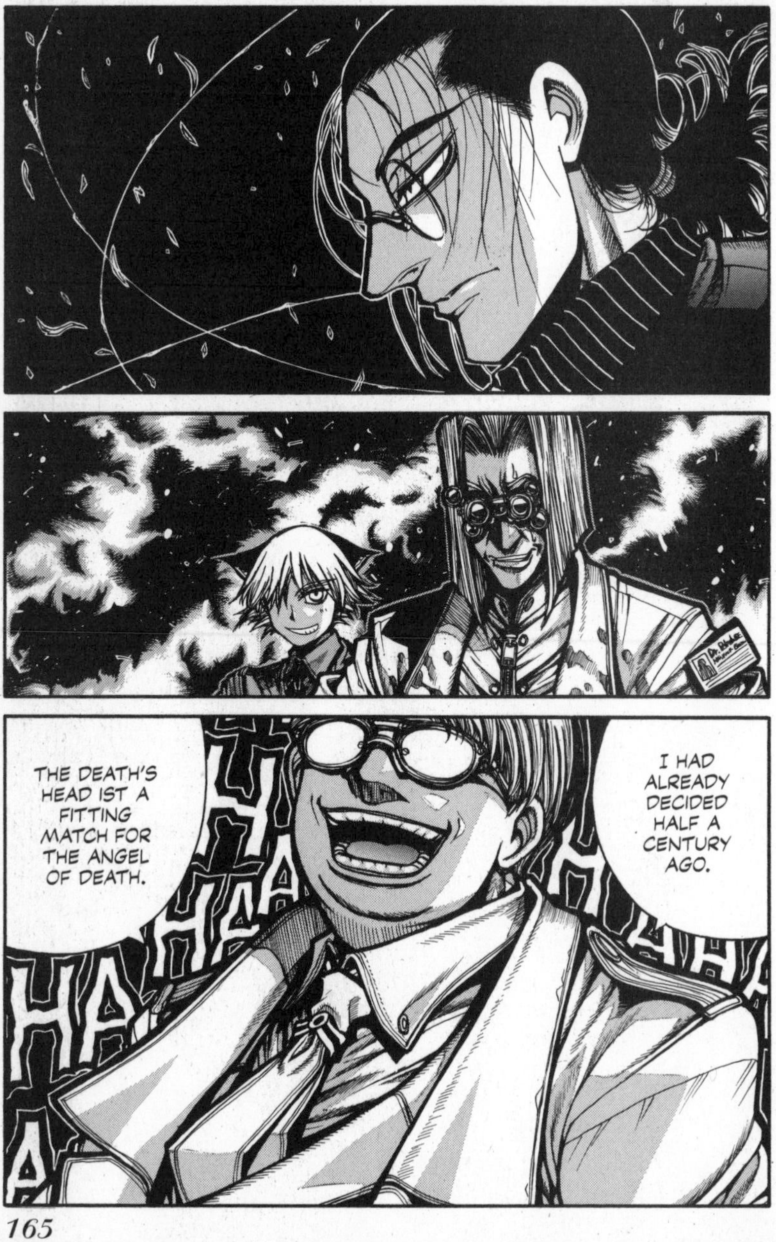
I HAD ALREADY DECIDED HALF A CENTURY AGO.
THE DEATH'S HEAD IST A FITTING MATCH FOR THE ANGEL OF DEATH.
HAHAHAHA

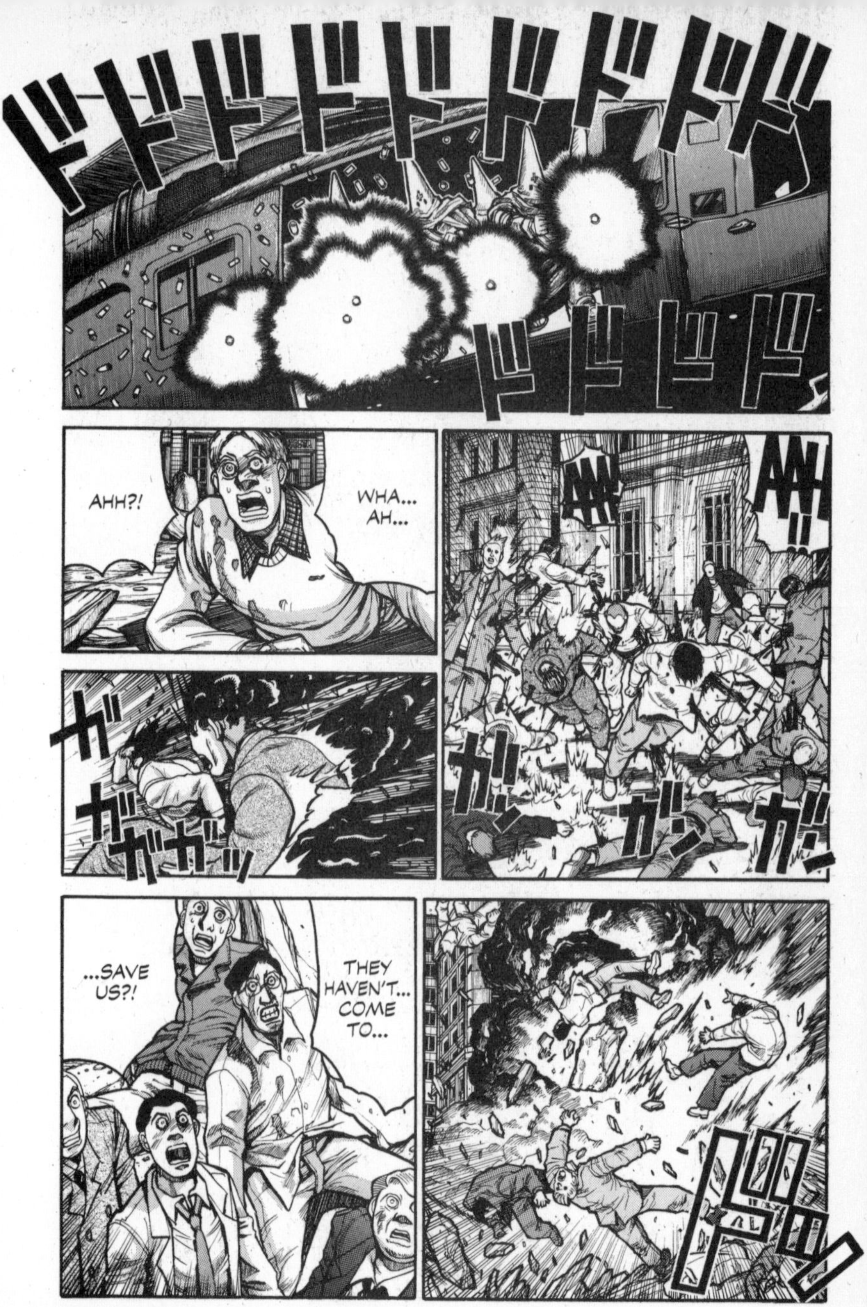
AAH!!
AA
WHA... AH...
AHH?!
THEY HAVEN'T... COME TO...
...SAVE US?!

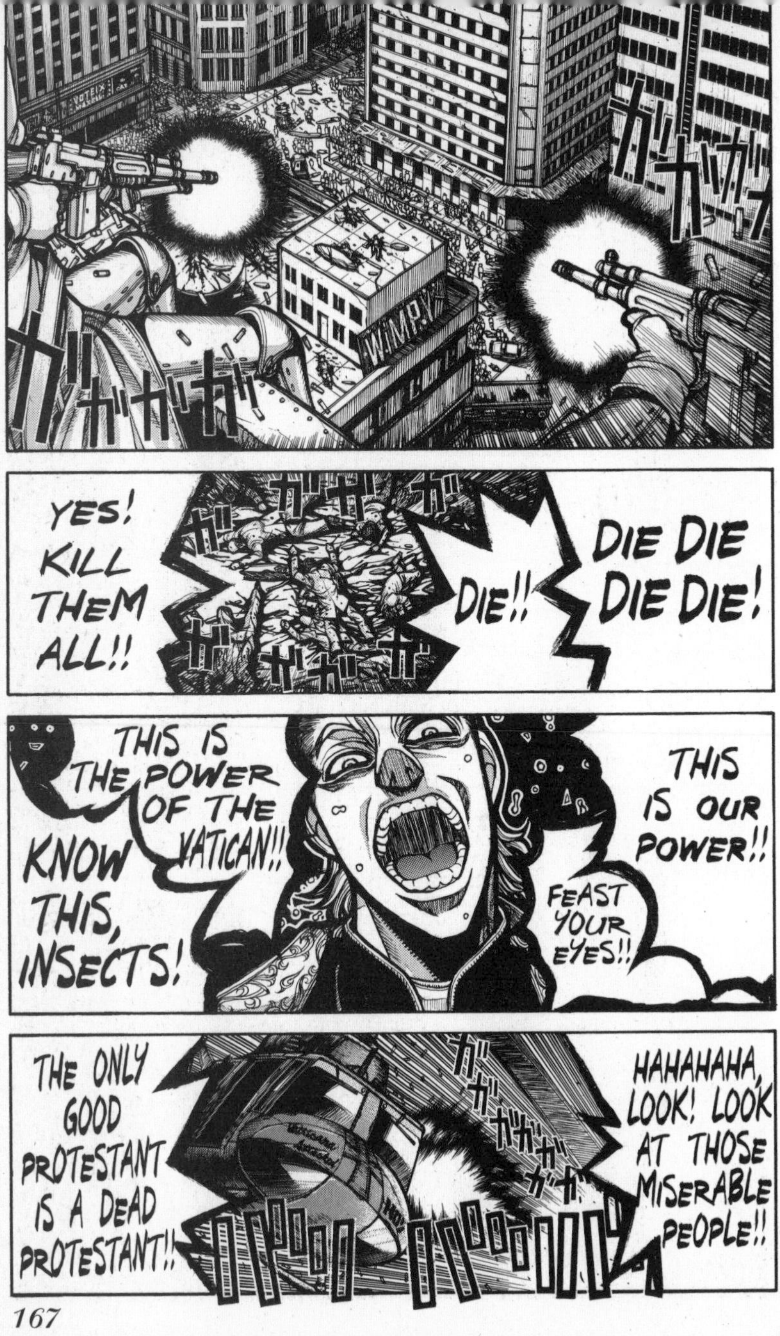
DIE DIE DIE DIE!
DIE!!
YES! KILL THEM ALL!!
THIS IS OUR POWER!!
FEAST YOUR EYES!!
THIS IS THE POWER OF THE VATICAN!!
KNOW THIS, INSECTS!
HAHAHAHA, LOOK! LOOK AT THOSE MISERABLE PEOPLE!!
THE ONLY GOOD PROTESTANT IS A DEAD PROTESTANT!!

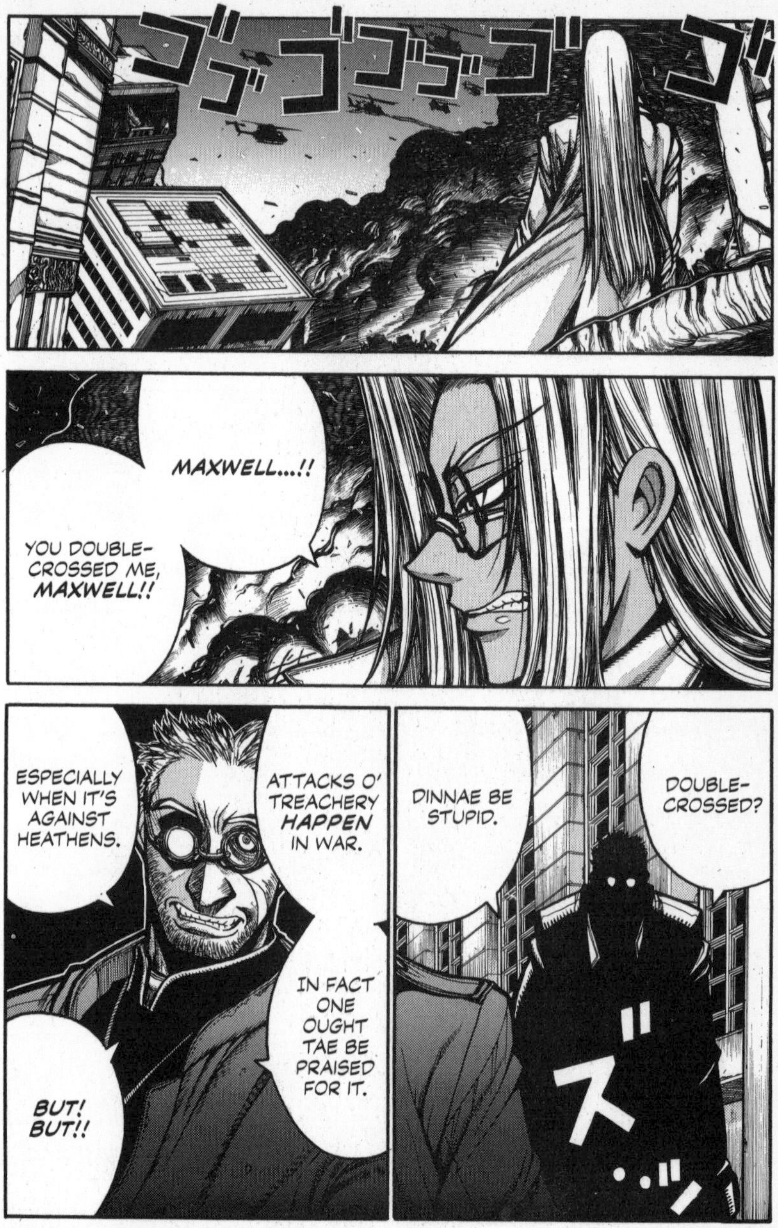
ゴゴゴゴゴゴ
MAXWELL...!!
YOU DOUBLE-CROSSED ME, MAXWELL!!
DOUBLE-CROSSED?
DINNAE BE STUPID.
ズ
ATTACKS O' TREACHERY HAPPEN IN WAR.
ESPECIALLY WHEN IT'S AGAINST HEATHENS.
IN FACT ONE OUGHT TAE BE PRAISED FOR IT.
BUT! BUT!!

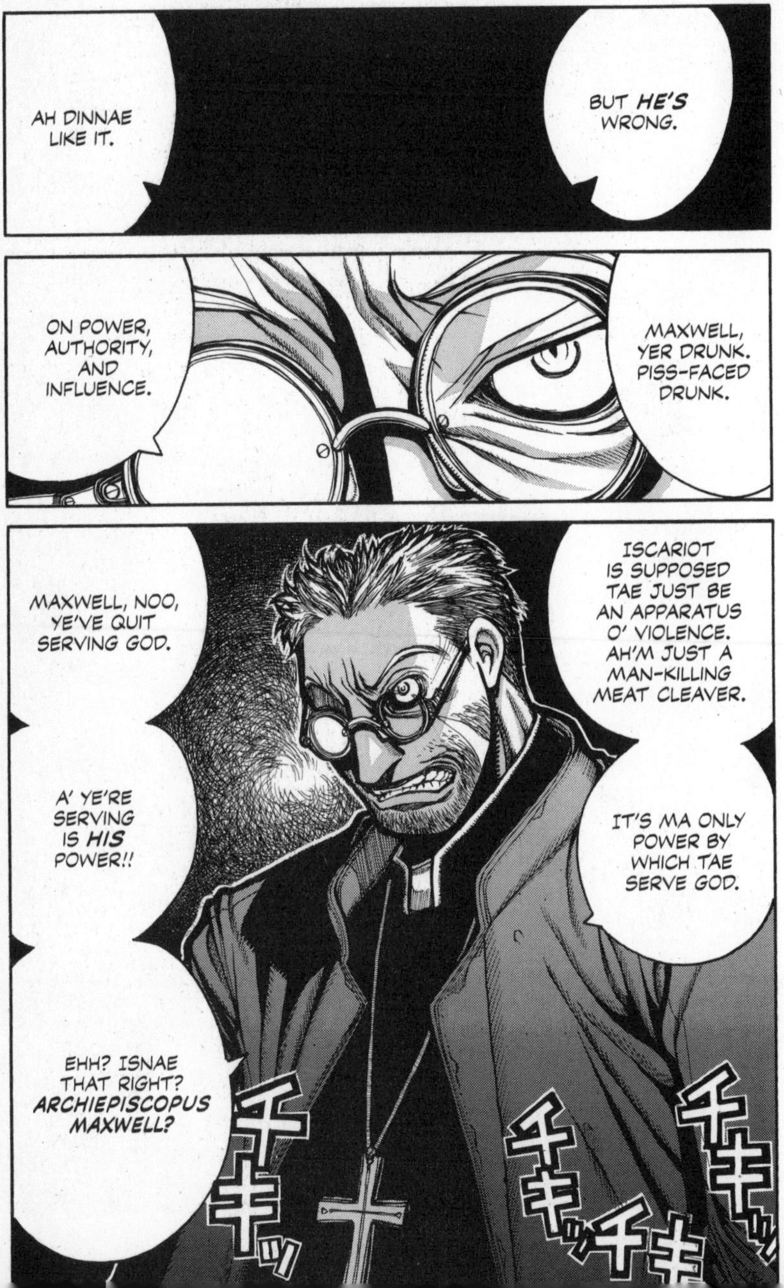
BUT HE'S WRONG.
AH DINNAE LIKE IT.
MAXWELL, YER DRUNK. PISS-FACED DRUNK.
ON POWER, AUTHORITY, AND INFLUENCE.
ISCARIOT IS SUPPOSED TAE JUST BE AN APPARATUS O' VIOLENCE. AH'M JUST A MAN-KILLING MEAT CLEAVER.
IT'S MA ONLY POWER BY WHICH TAE SERVE GOD.
MAXWELL, NOO, YE'VE QUIT SERVING GOD.
A' YE'RE SERVING IS HIS POWER!!
EHH? ISNAE THAT RIGHT? ARCHIEPISCOPUS MAXWELL?

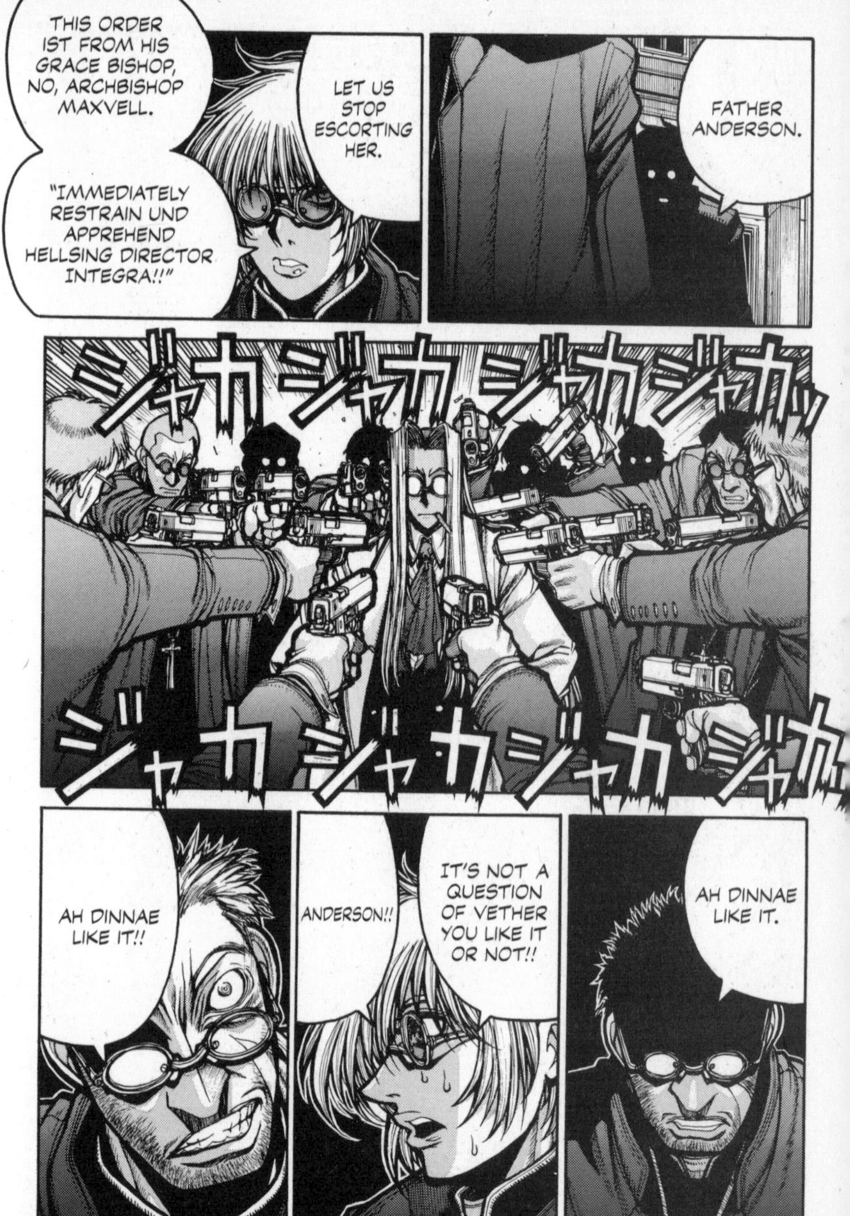
FATHER ANDERSON.
LET US STOP ESCORTING HER.
THIS ORDER IST FROM HIS GRACE BISHOP, NO, ARCHBISHOP MAXVELL.
“IMMEDIATELY RESTRAIN UND APPREHEND HELLSING DIRECTOR INTEGRA!!”
ジャカジャカジャカジャカッ
ジャカジャカジャカジャカ
AH DINNAE LIKE IT.
IT’S NOT A QUESTION OF VETHER YOU LIKE IT OR NOT!!
ANDERSON!!
AH DINNAE LIKE IT!!

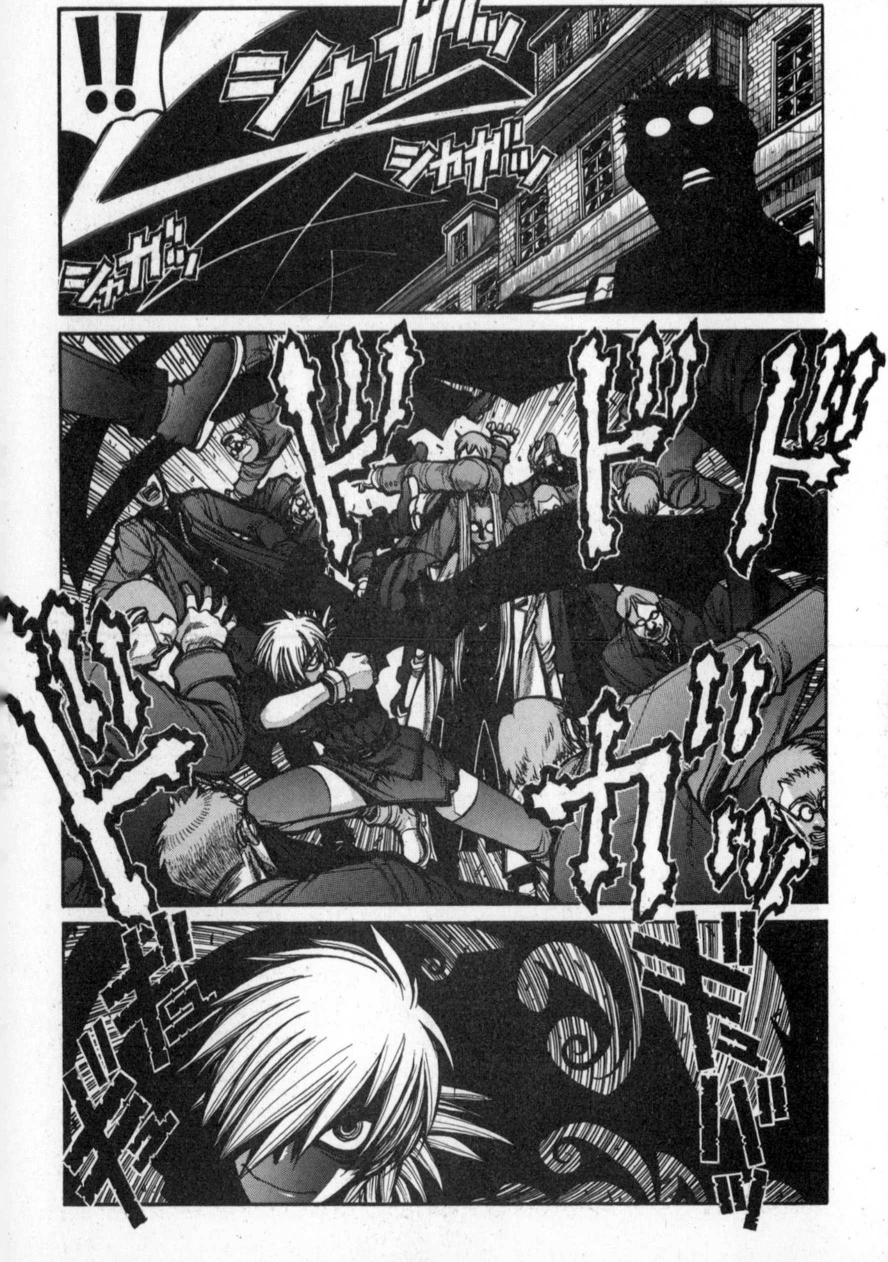

シャガッ
シャガッ
!!
シャガッ

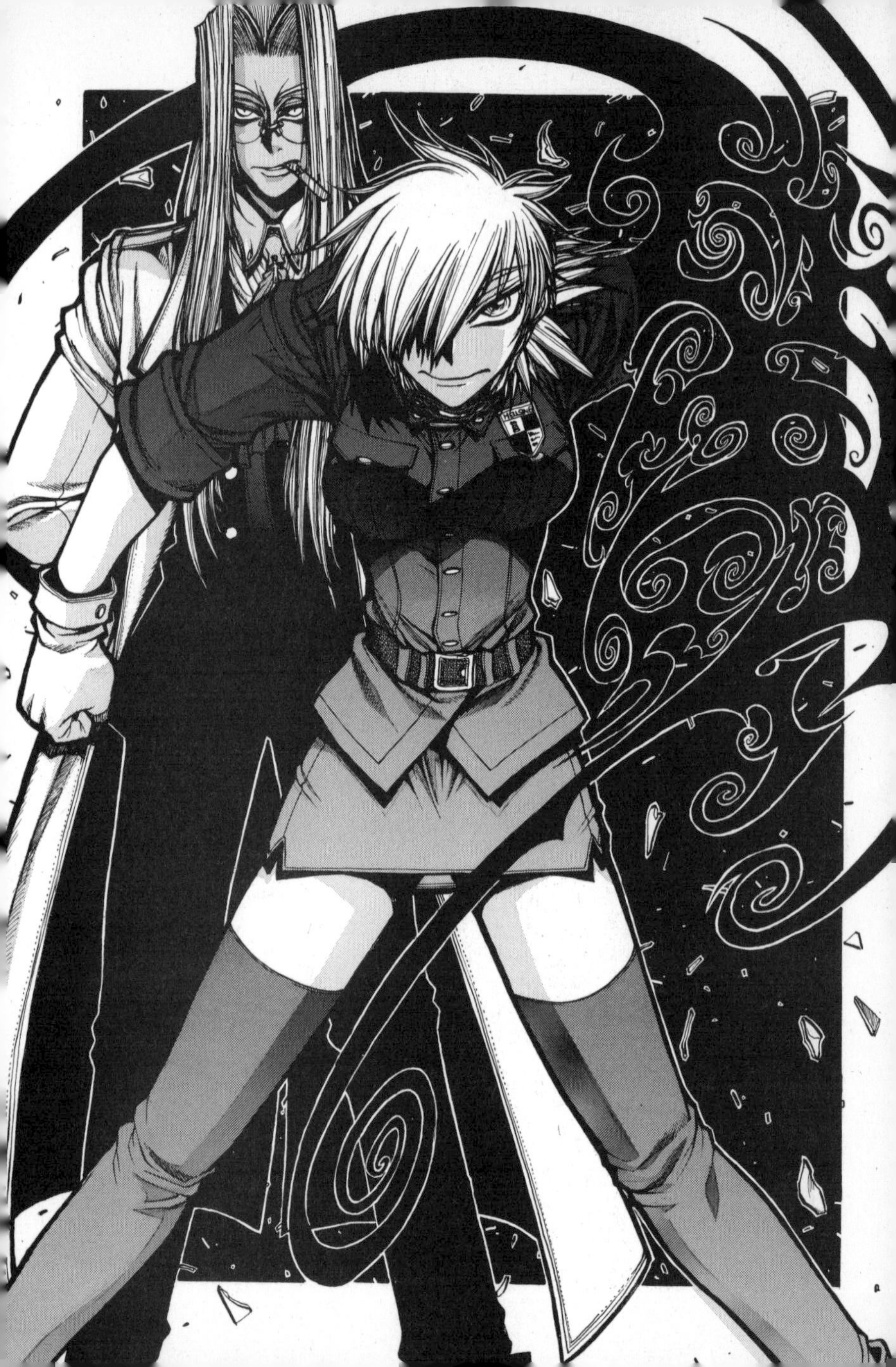

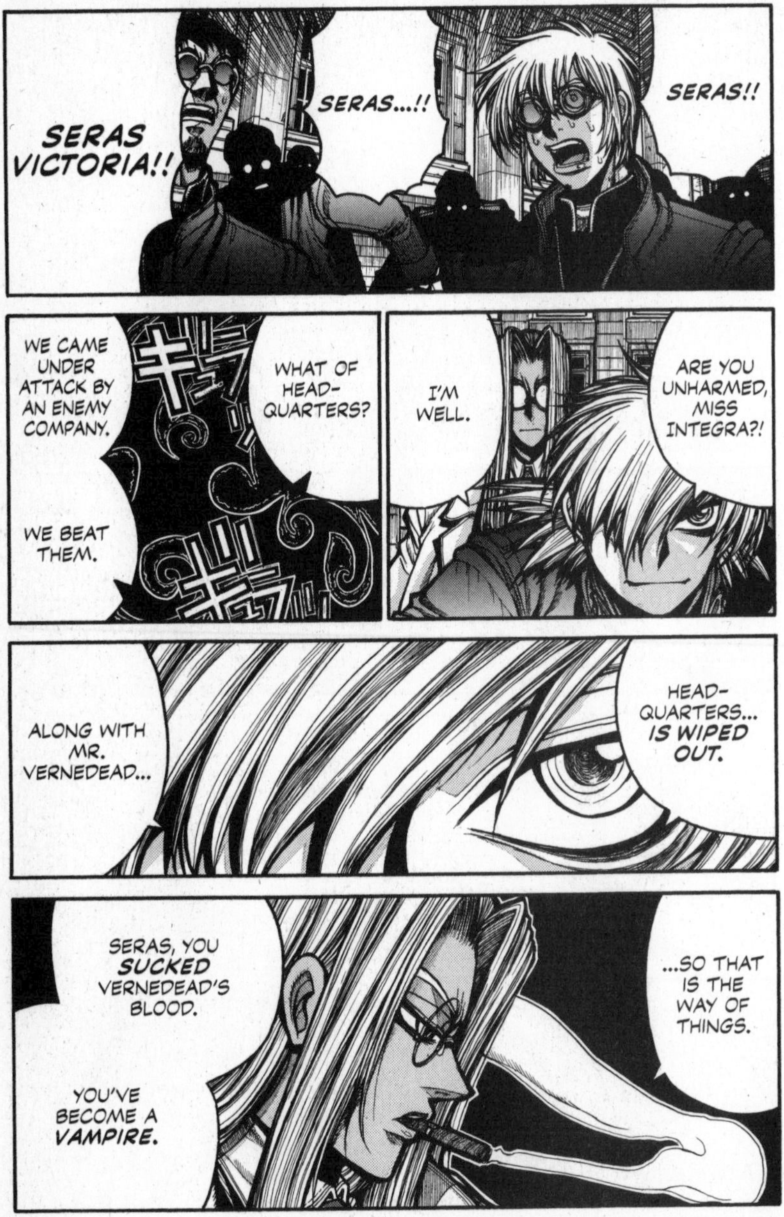
SERAS!!
SERAS...!!
SERAS VICTORIA!!
ARE YOU UNHARMED, MISS INTEGRA?!
I'M WELL.
WHAT OF HEAD-QUARTERS?
WE CAME UNDER ATTACK BY AN ENEMY COMPANY.
WE BEAT THEM.
HEAD-QUARTERS... IS WIPED OUT.
ALONG WITH MR. VERNEDEAD...
...SO THAT IS THE WAY OF THINGS.
SERAS, YOU SUCKED VERNEDEAD'S BLOOD.
YOU'VE BECOME A VAMPIRE.

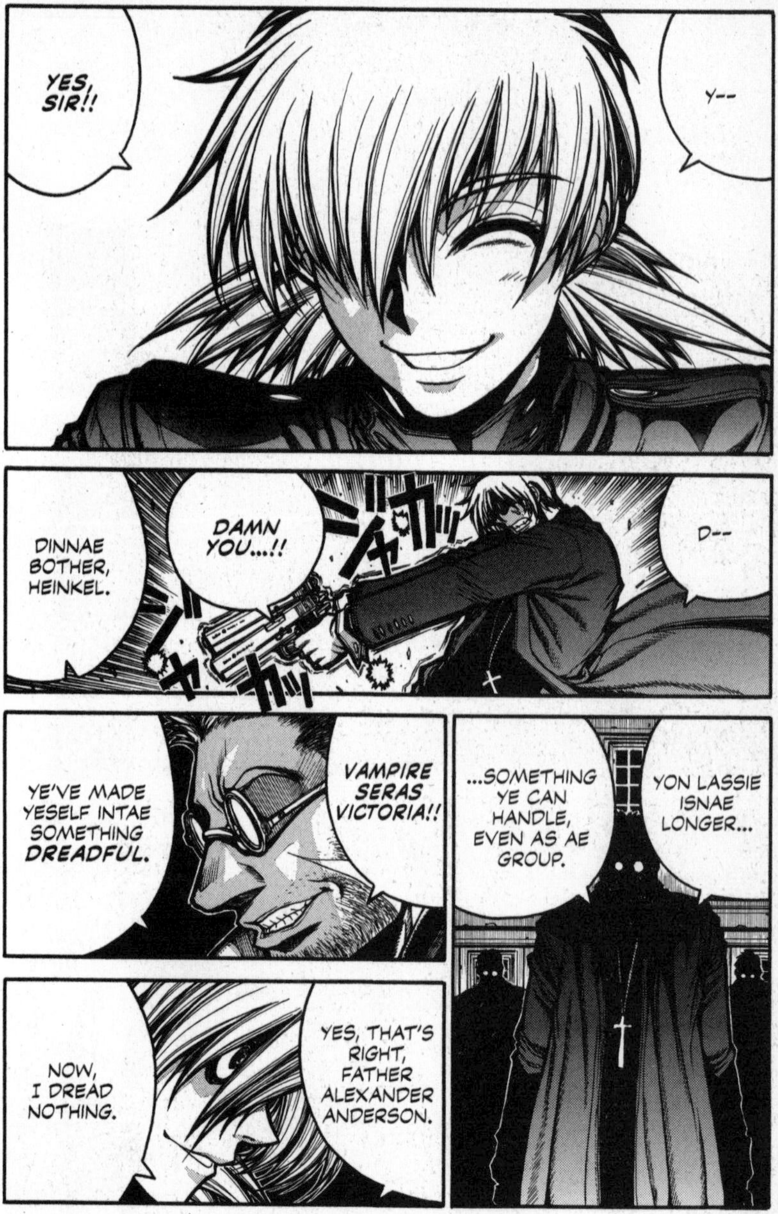
Y--
YES, SIR!!
D--
ジャカッ
DAMN YOU...!!
ジャカッ
DINNAE BOTHER, HEINKEL.
YON LASSIE ISNAE LONGER...
...SOMETHING YE CAN HANDLE, EVEN AS AE GROUP.
VAMPIRE SERAS VICTORIA!!
YE'VE MADE YESELF INTAE SOMETHING DREADFUL.
YES, THAT'S RIGHT, FATHER ALEXANDER ANDERSON.
NOW, I DREAD NOTHING.

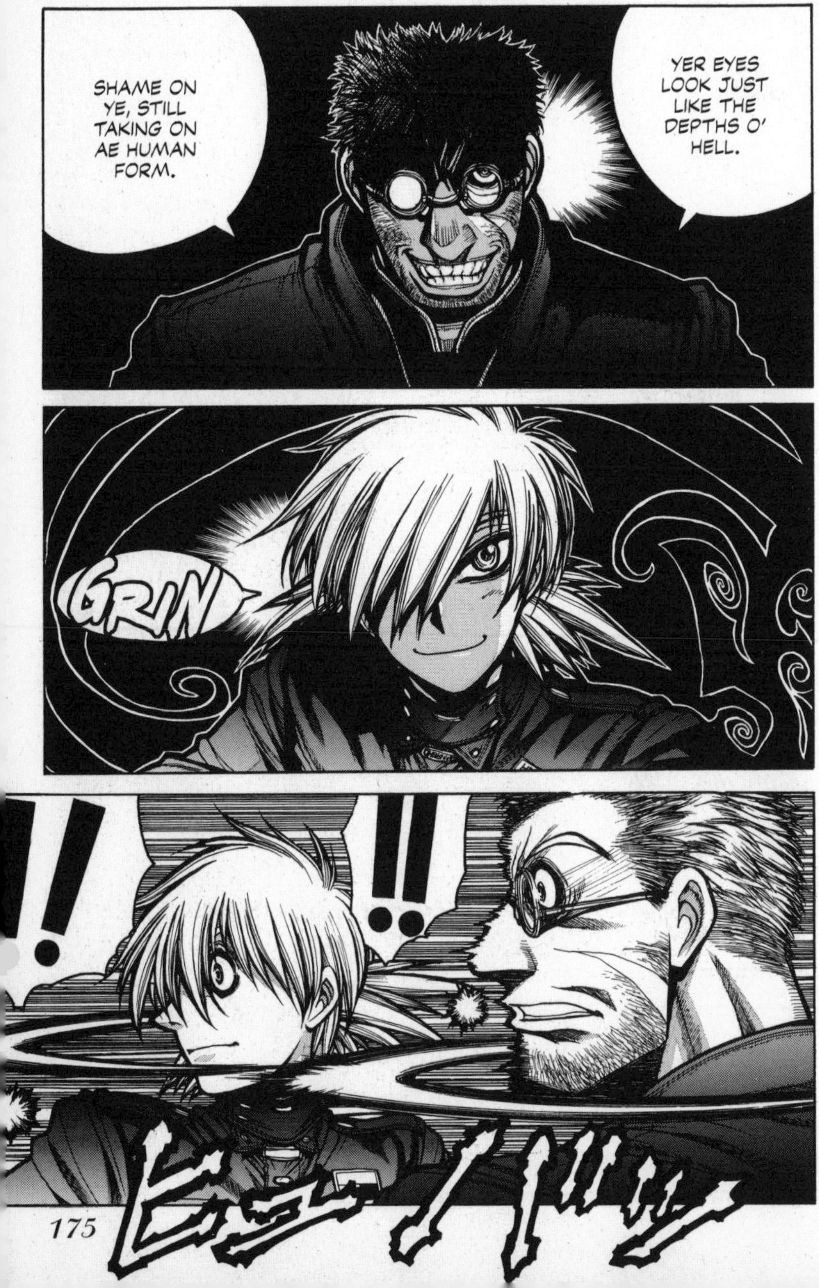
YER EYES LOOK JUST LIKE THE DEPTHS O' HELL.
SHAME ON YE, STILL TAKING ON AE HUMAN FORM.
GRIN

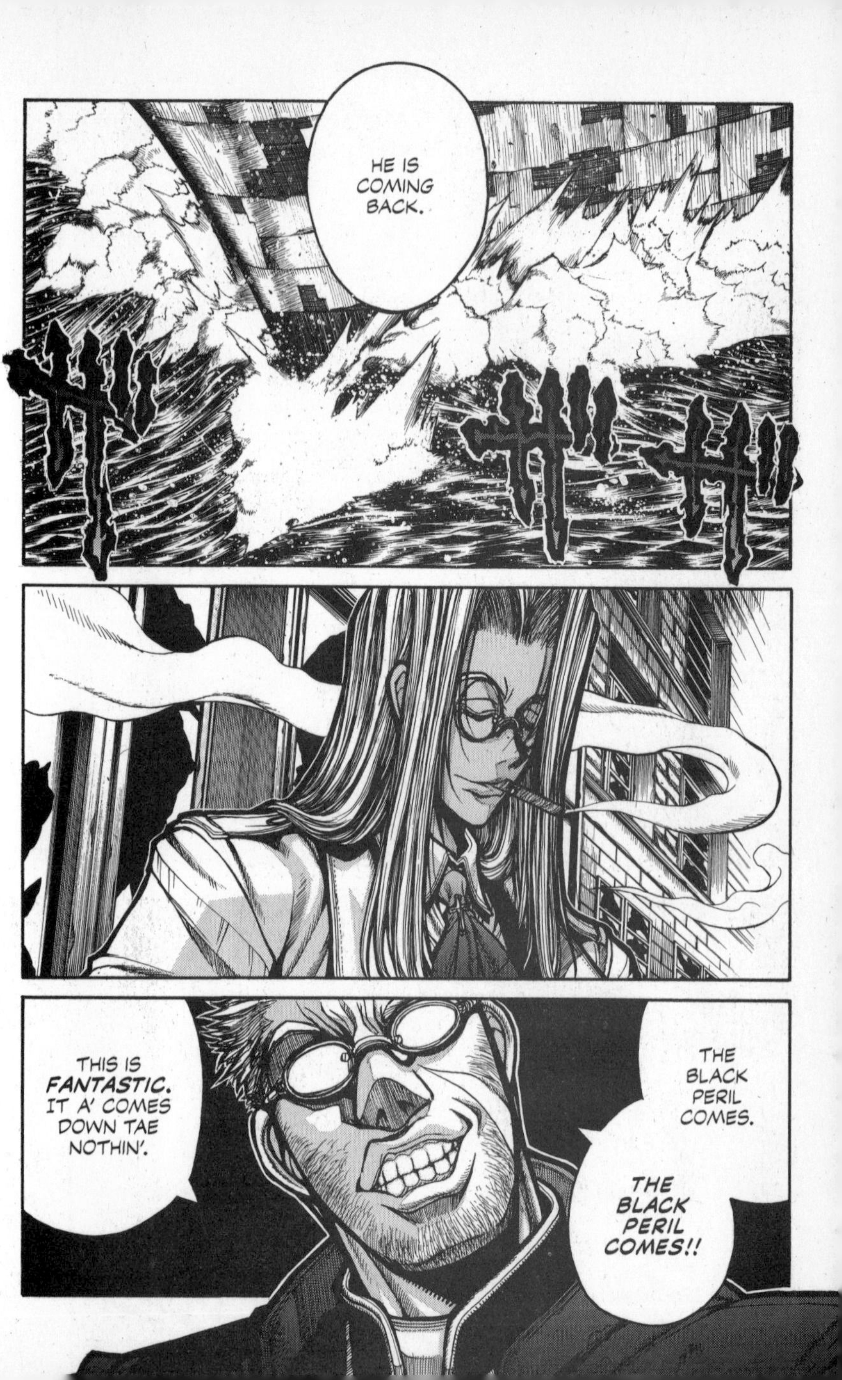
HE IS COMING BACK.
THE BLACK PERIL COMES.
THE BLACK PERIL COMES!!
THIS IS FANTASTIC. IT A' COMES DOWN TAE NOTHIN'.

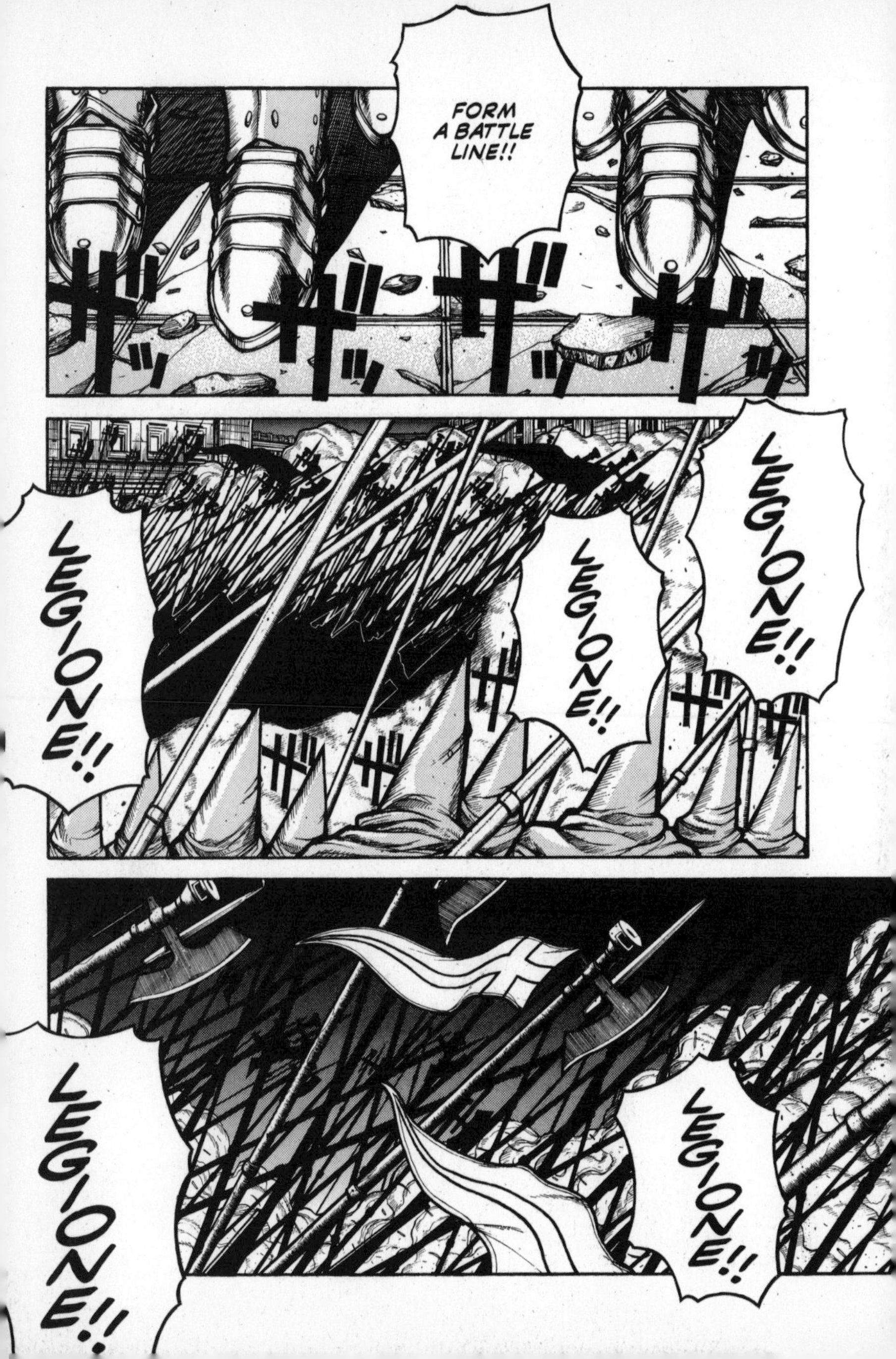
FORM A BATTLE LINE!!
LEGIONE!!
LEGIONE!!
LEGIONE!!
LEGIONE!!
LEGIONE!!

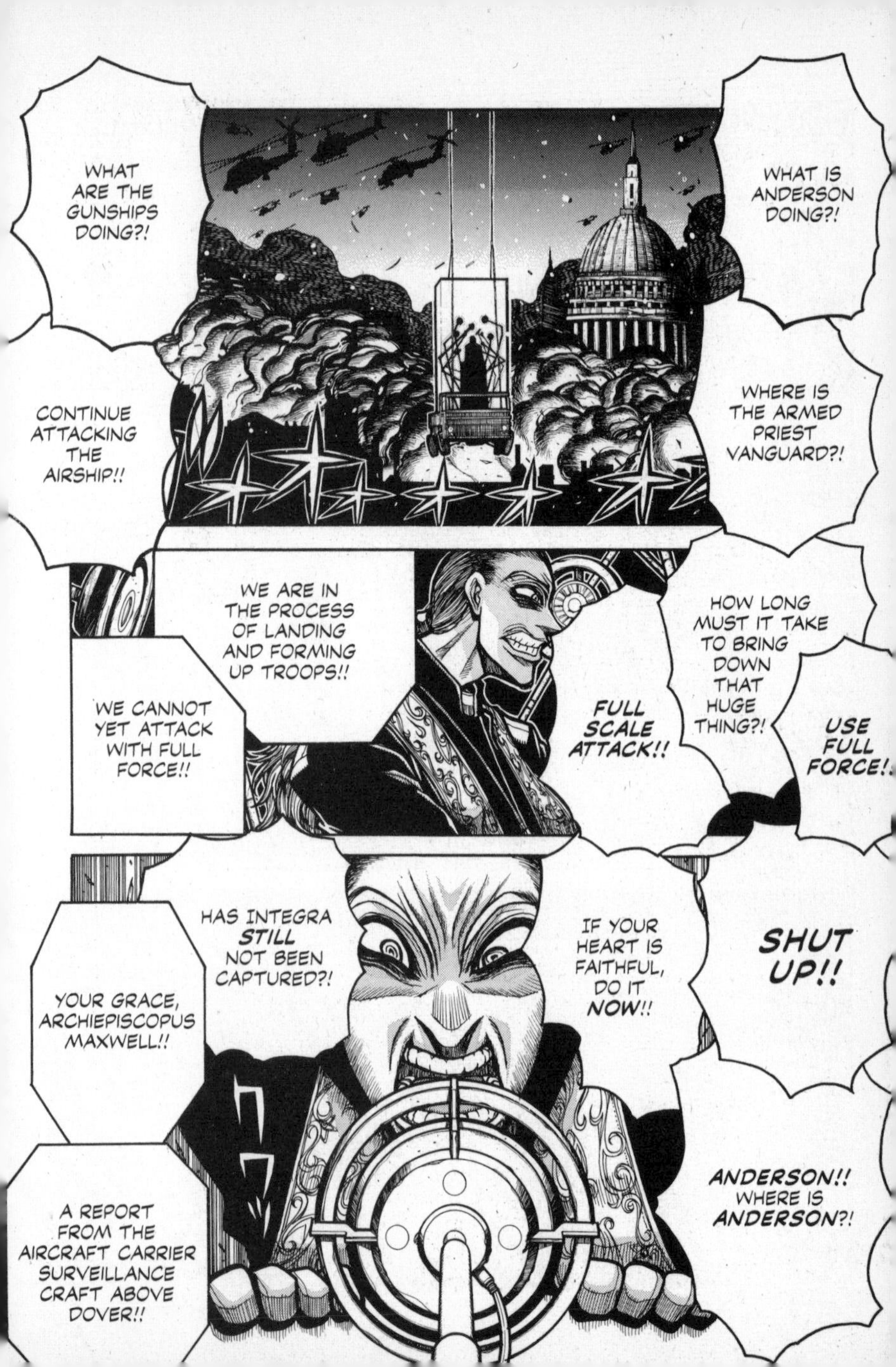
WHAT IS ANDERSON DOING?!
WHERE IS THE ARMED PRIEST VANGUARD?!
WHAT ARE THE GUNSHIPS DOING?!
CONTINUE ATTACKING THE AIRSHIP!!
USE FULL FORCE!!
HOW LONG MUST IT TAKE TO BRING DOWN THAT HUGE THING?!
FULL SCALE ATTACK!!
WE ARE IN THE PROCESS OF LANDING AND FORMING UP TROOPS!!
WE CANNOT YET ATTACK WITH FULL FORCE!!
SHUT UP!!
IF YOUR HEART IS FAITHFUL, DO IT NOW!!
HAS INTEGRA STILL NOT BEEN CAPTURED?!
YOUR GRACE, ARCHIEPISCOPUS MAXWELL!!
ANDERSON!! WHERE IS ANDERSON?!
A REPORT FROM THE AIRCRAFT CARRIER SURVEILLANCE CRAFT ABOVE DOVER!!

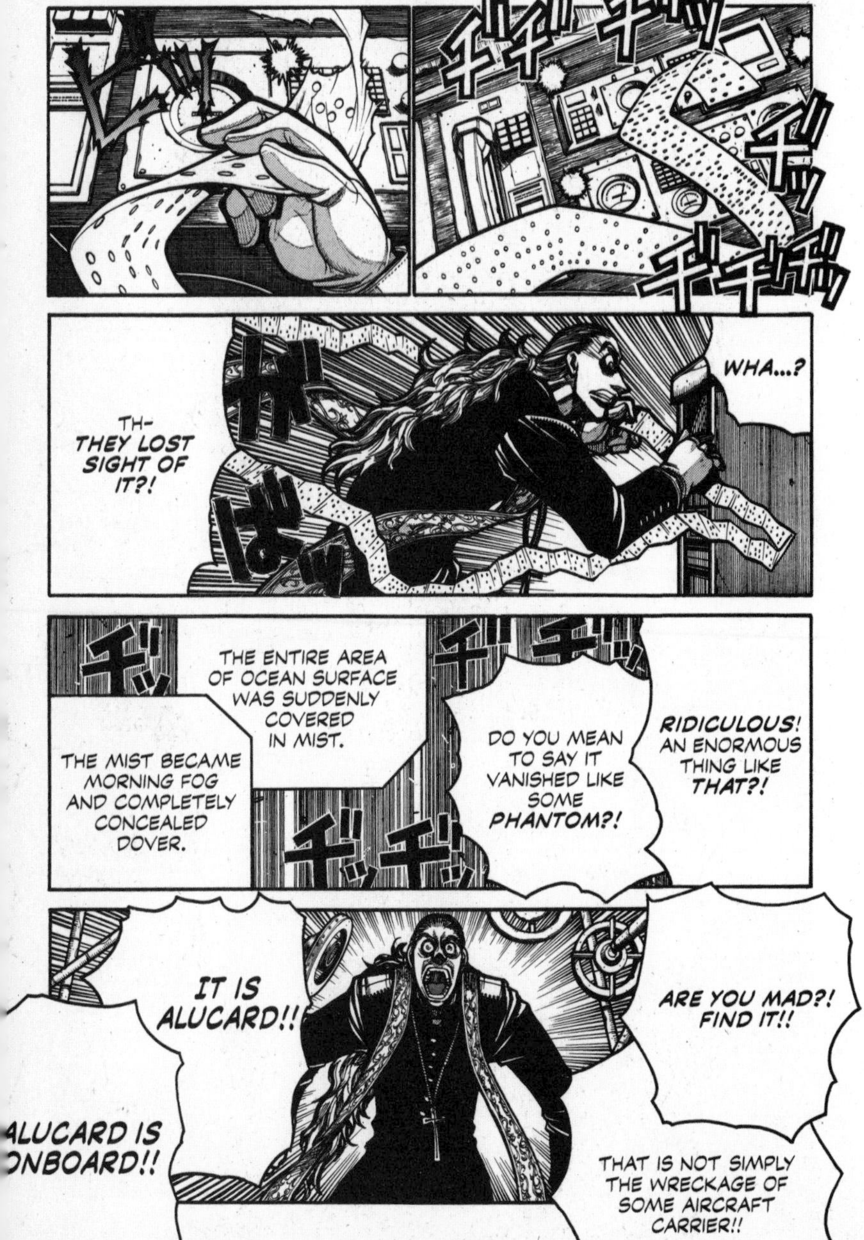
WHA...?
TH- THEY LOST SIGHT OF IT?!
RIDICULOUS! AN ENORMOUS THING LIKE THAT?!
DO YOU MEAN TO SAY IT VANISHED LIKE SOME PHANTOM?!
THE ENTIRE AREA OF OCEAN SURFACE WAS SUDDENLY COVERED IN MIST.
THE MIST BECAME MORNING FOG AND COMPLETELY CONCEALED DOVER.
ARE YOU MAD?! FIND IT!!
THAT IS NOT SIMPLY THE WRECKAGE OF SOME AIRCRAFT CARRIER!!
IT IS ALUCARD!!
ALUCARD IS ONBOARD!!

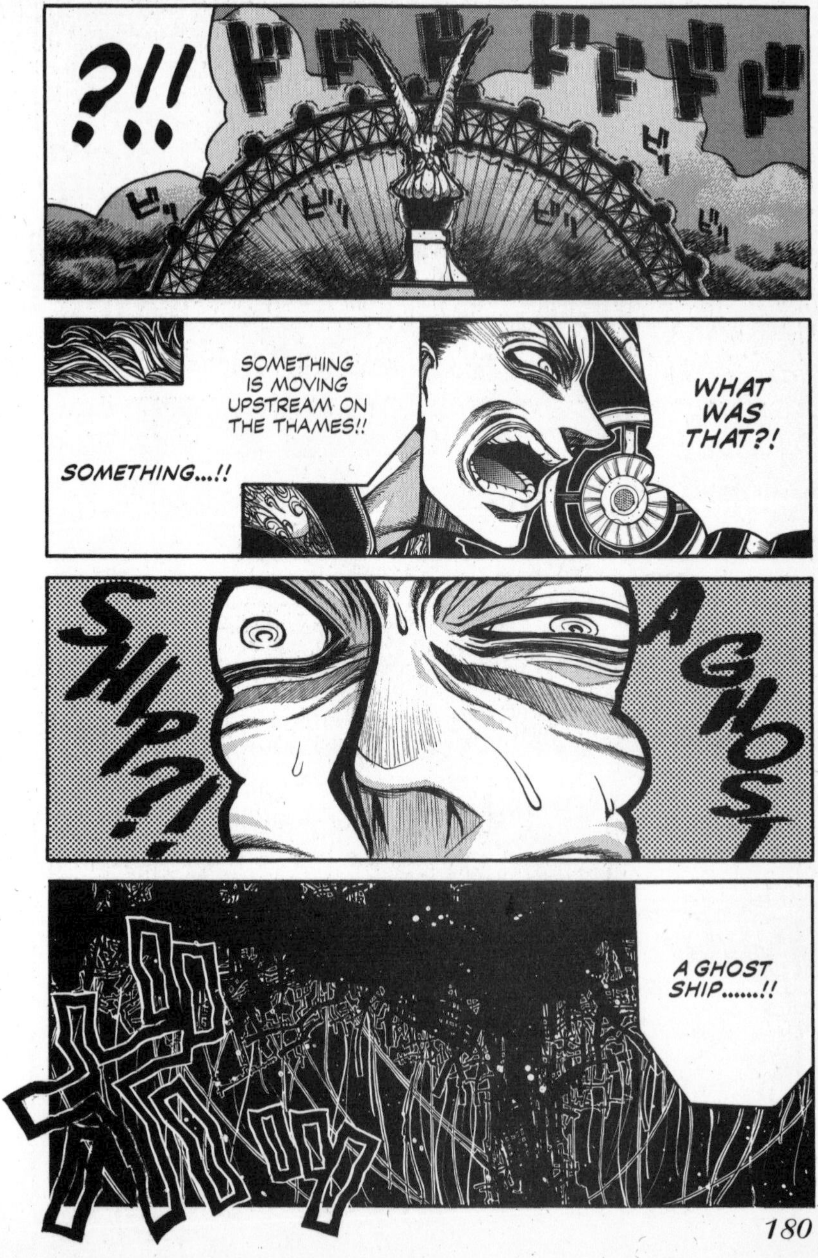
?!!
WHAT WAS THAT?!
SOMETHING IS MOVING UPSTREAM ON THE THAMES!!
SOMETHING...!!
A GHOST SHIP?!!
A GHOST SHIP......!!

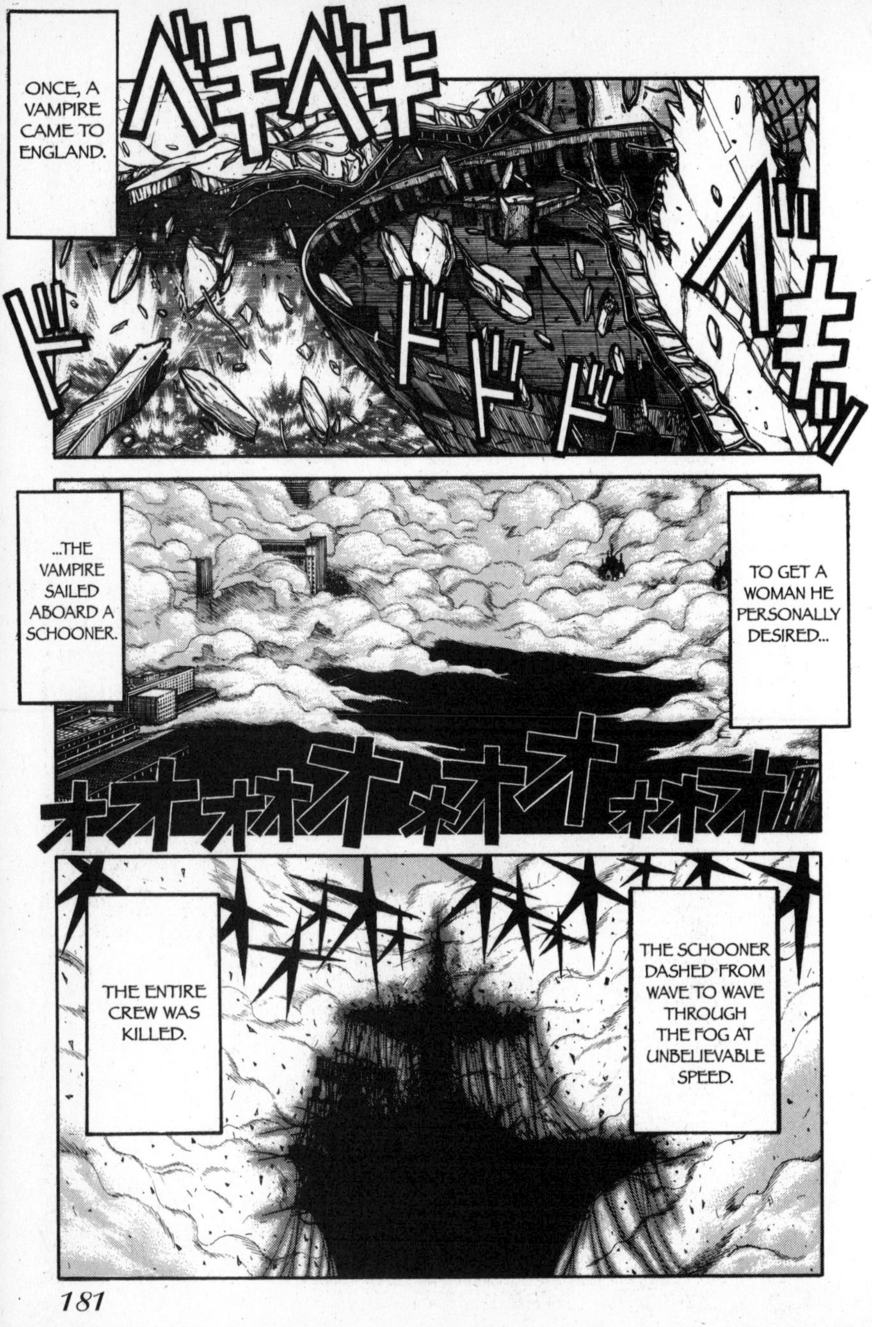
ベキッ
ベキベキ
ONCE, A VAMPIRE CAME TO ENGLAND.
TO GET A WOMAN HE PERSONALLY DESIRED...
...THE VAMPIRE SAILED ABOARD A SCHOONER.
THE SCHOONER DASHED FROM WAVE TO WAVE THROUGH THE FOG AT UNBELIEVABLE SPEED.
THE ENTIRE CREW WAS KILLED.

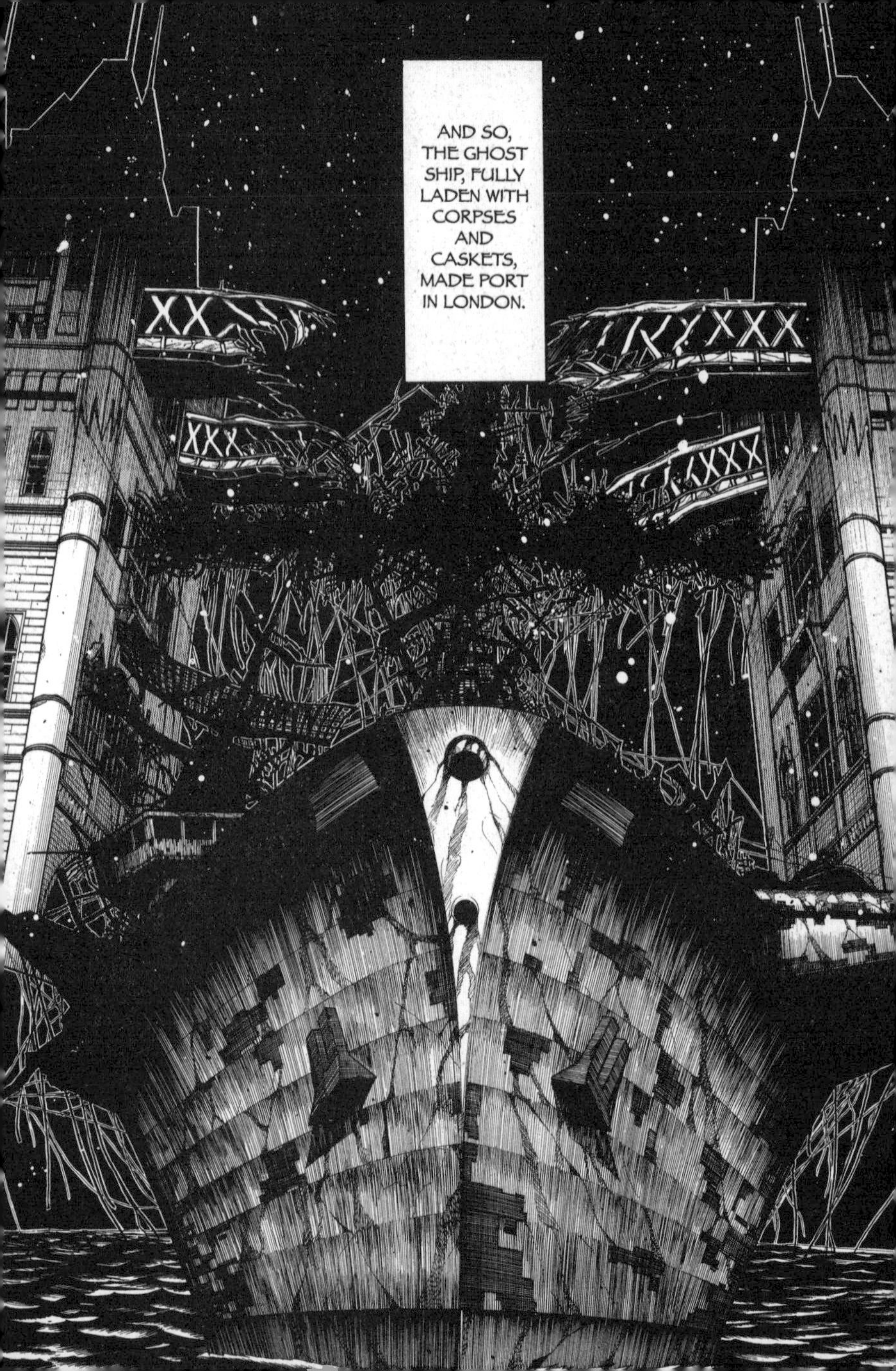
AND SO, THE GHOST SHIP, FULLY LADEN WITH CORPSES AND CASKETS, MADE PORT IN LONDON.

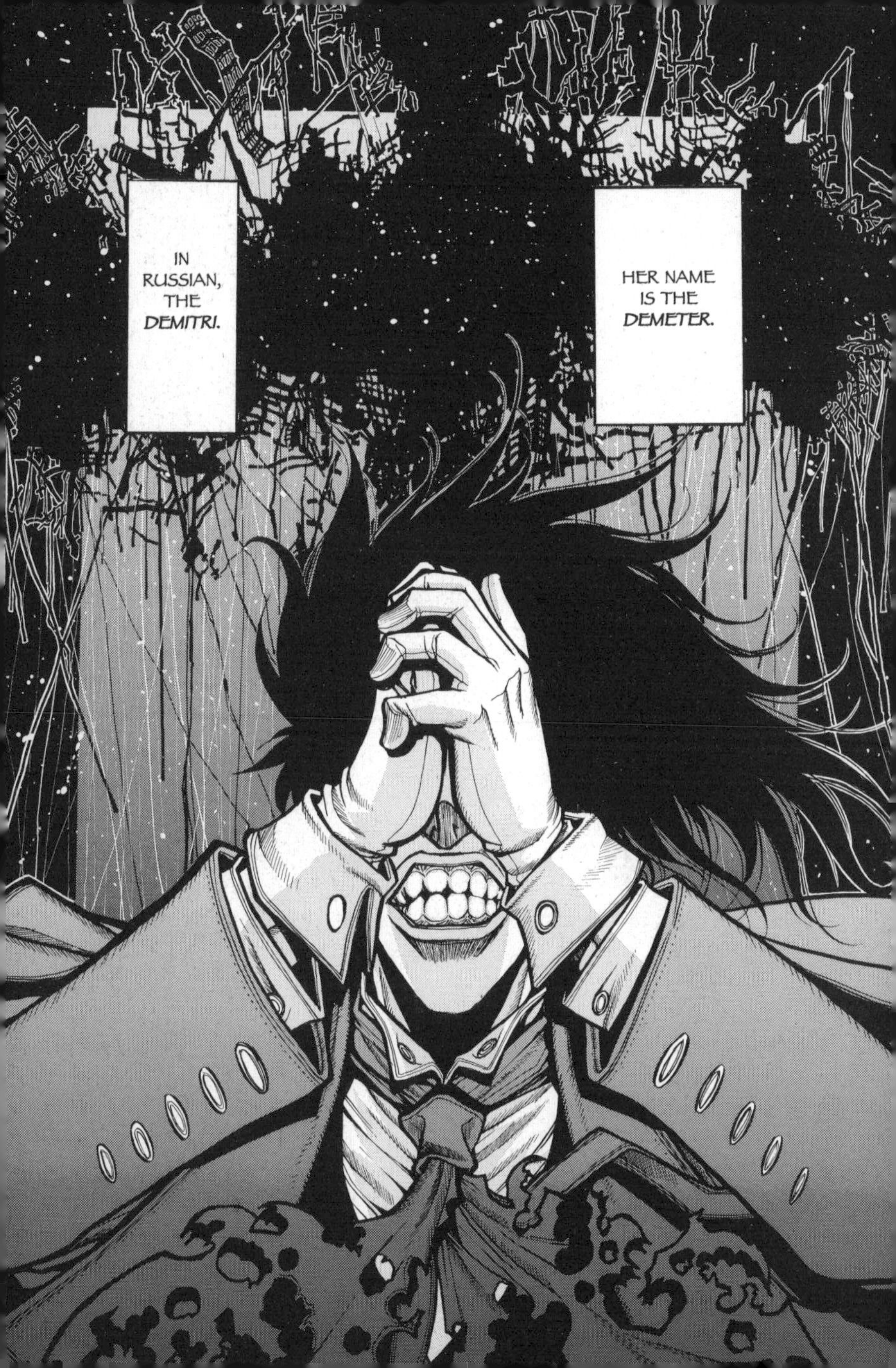
HER NAME IS THE *DEMETER*.
IN RUSSIAN, THE *DEMITRI*.

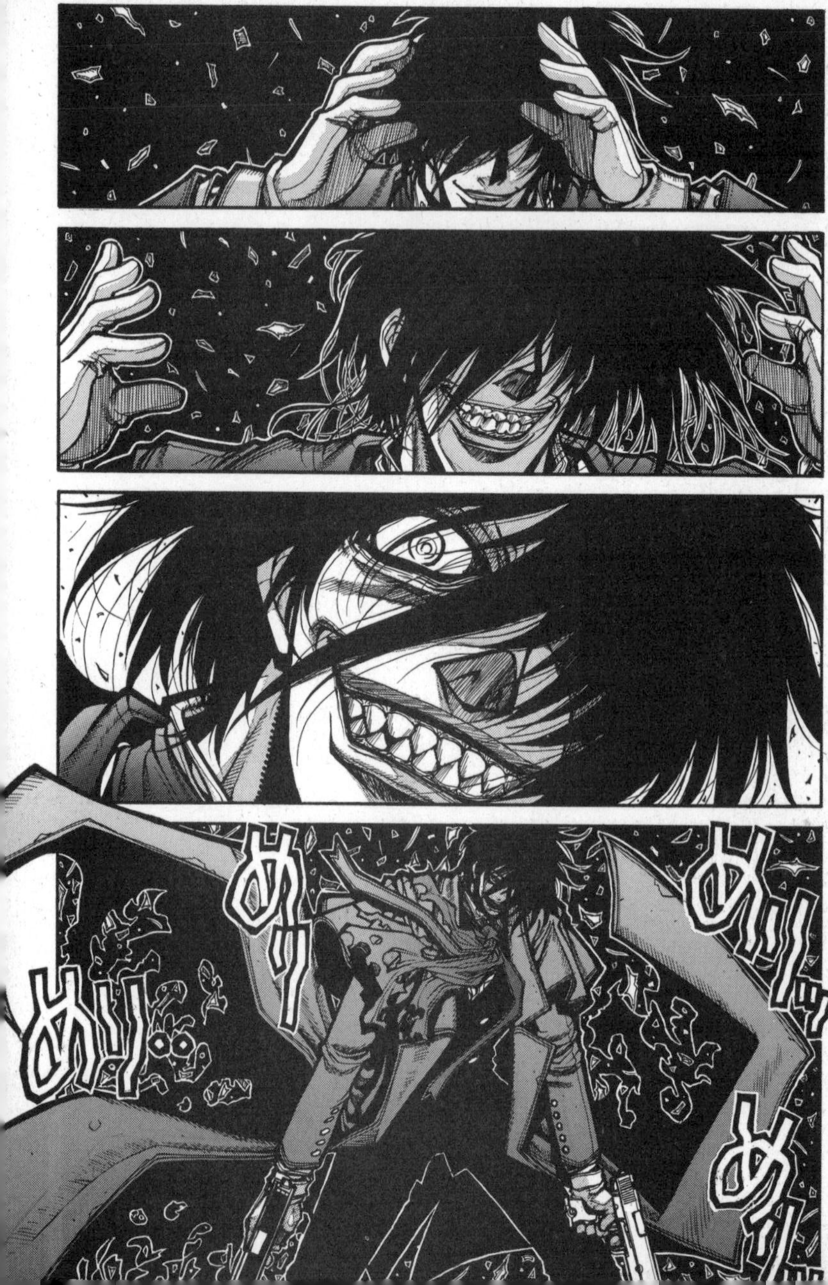
めりッ
めり
めり
めり‥

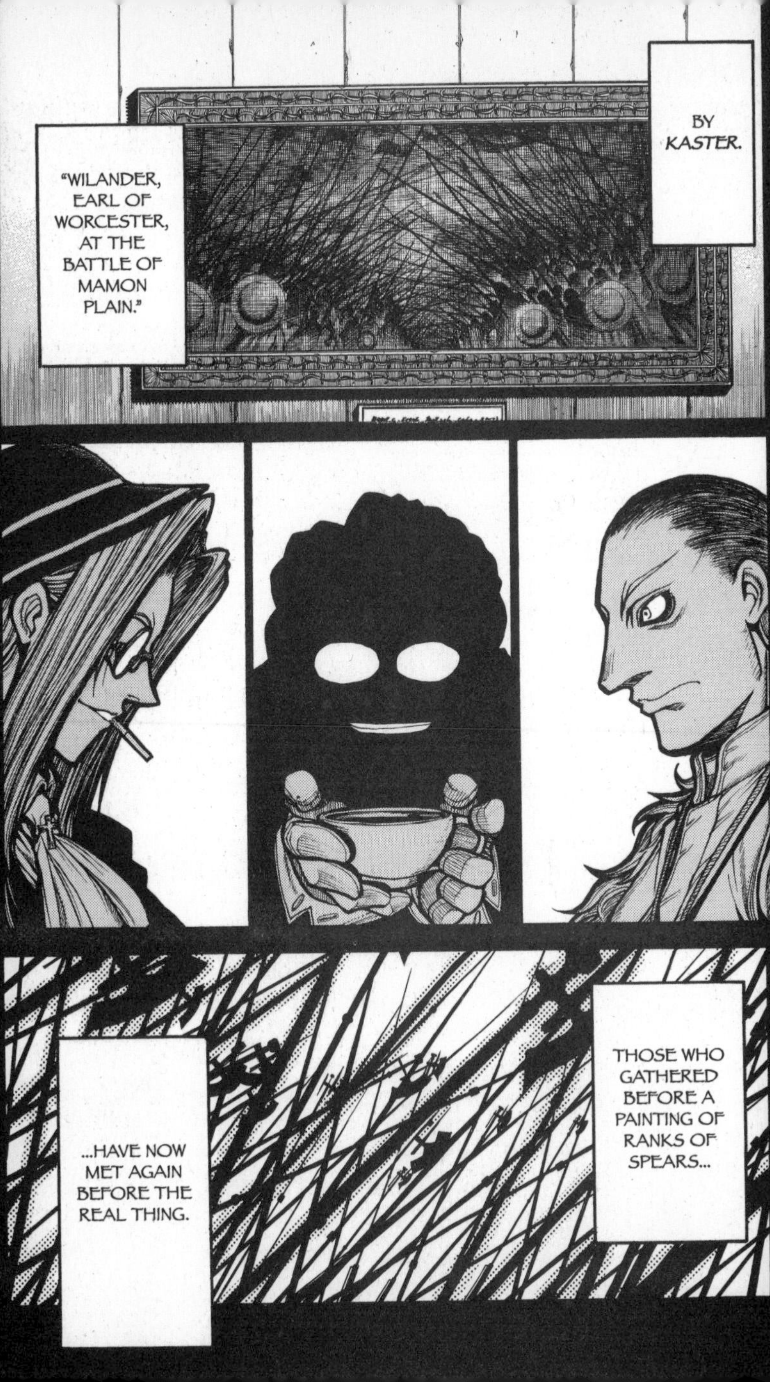
BY KASTER.
"WILANDER, EARL OF WORCESTER, AT THE BATTLE OF MAMON PLAIN."
THOSE WHO GATHERED BEFORE A PAINTING OF RANKS OF SPEARS...
...HAVE NOW MET AGAIN BEFORE THE REAL THING.

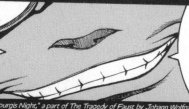

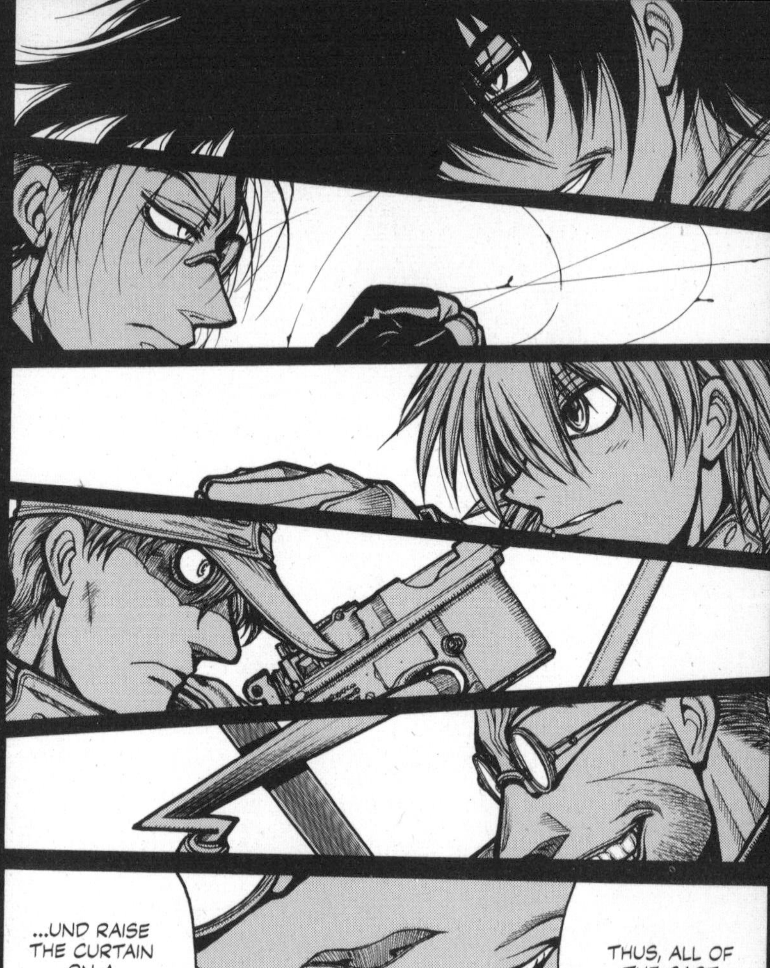
THUS, ALL OF THE CAST TAKE TO THE STAGE...
...UND RAISE THE CURTAIN ON A WALPURGIS* AT DAWN.

ORDER 10/END

Note: This is a reference to "Walpurgis Night," a part of The Tragedy of Faust by Johann Wolfgang Von Goethe.

TO BE CONTINUED

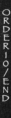

HONEST, REALLY.

CURE GRAY

KOHTA HIRANO, SO HAPPY ABOUT
THIS VOLUME GOING ON SALE THAT
HE'S PAINTED HIS ENTIRE BODY GRAY
AND IS TRYING TO GET HIMSELF RIGHT
IN THE MIDDLE OF PRETTY CURE.

HAILING FROM ADACHI WARD, TOKYO

HOBBIES
+
BEING OBNOXIOUS, BEATING OFF.

FAVORITE MAID NO. 3
+
SHIRLEY

FAVORITE MAID NO. 2
+
EMMA

FAVORITE MAID NO. 1
+
ETSUKO ICHIHARA

*NOTE: SHIRLEY AND EMMA ARE MAID CHARACTERS FROM
EPONYMOUS MANGAS BY KAORU MORI. ETSUKO ICHIHARA WAS
A LEAD ACTRESS IN THE (JAPANESE) FILM BLACK RAIN.

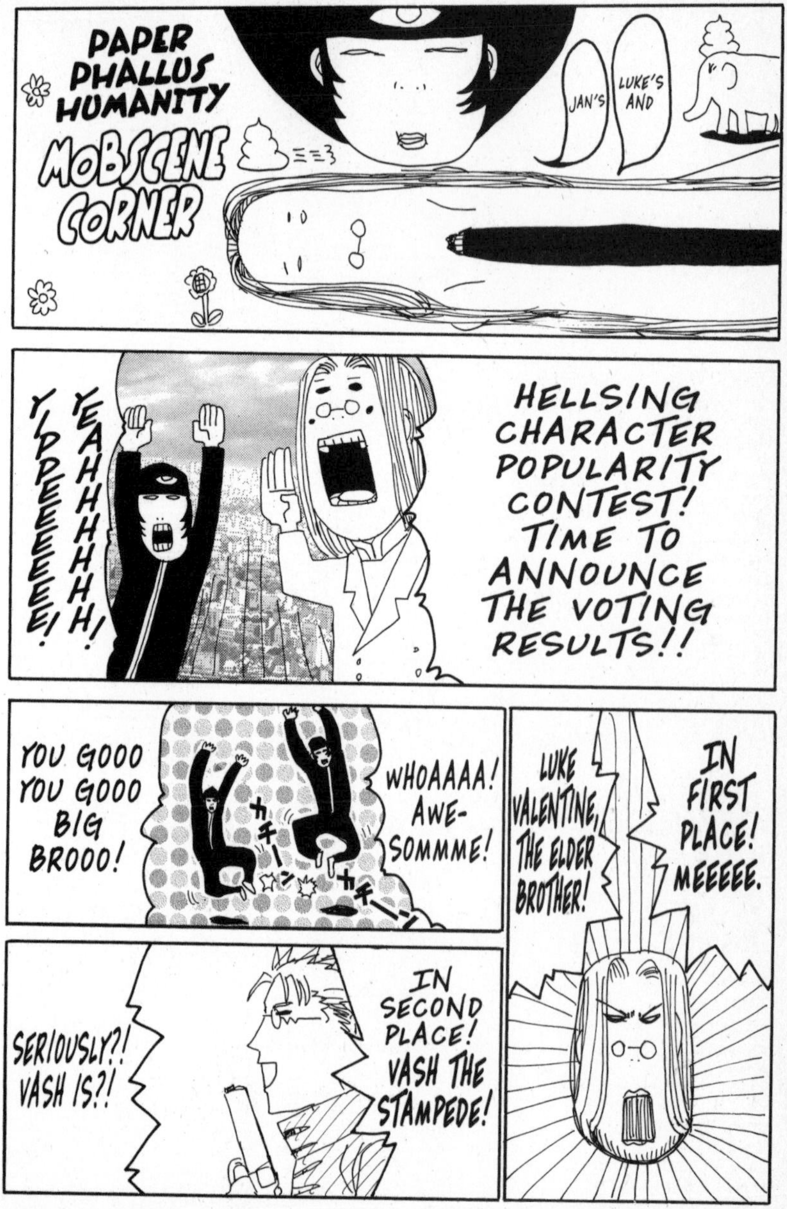
LUKE'S AND
JAN'S
PAPER PHALLUS HUMANITY
MOBSCENE CORNER
HELLSING CHARACTER POPULARITY CONTEST! TIME TO ANNOUNCE THE VOTING RESULTS!!
YEAHHHHHHH!
YIPPEEEEEEE!
IN FIRST PLACE! MEEEEEE.
LUKE VALENTINE, THE ELDER BROTHER!
WHOAAAA! AWE-SOMMME!
カチーン
カチーン
YOU GOOO YOU GOOO BIG BROOO!
IN SECOND PLACE! VASH THE STAMPEDE!
SERIOUSLY?! VASH IS?!

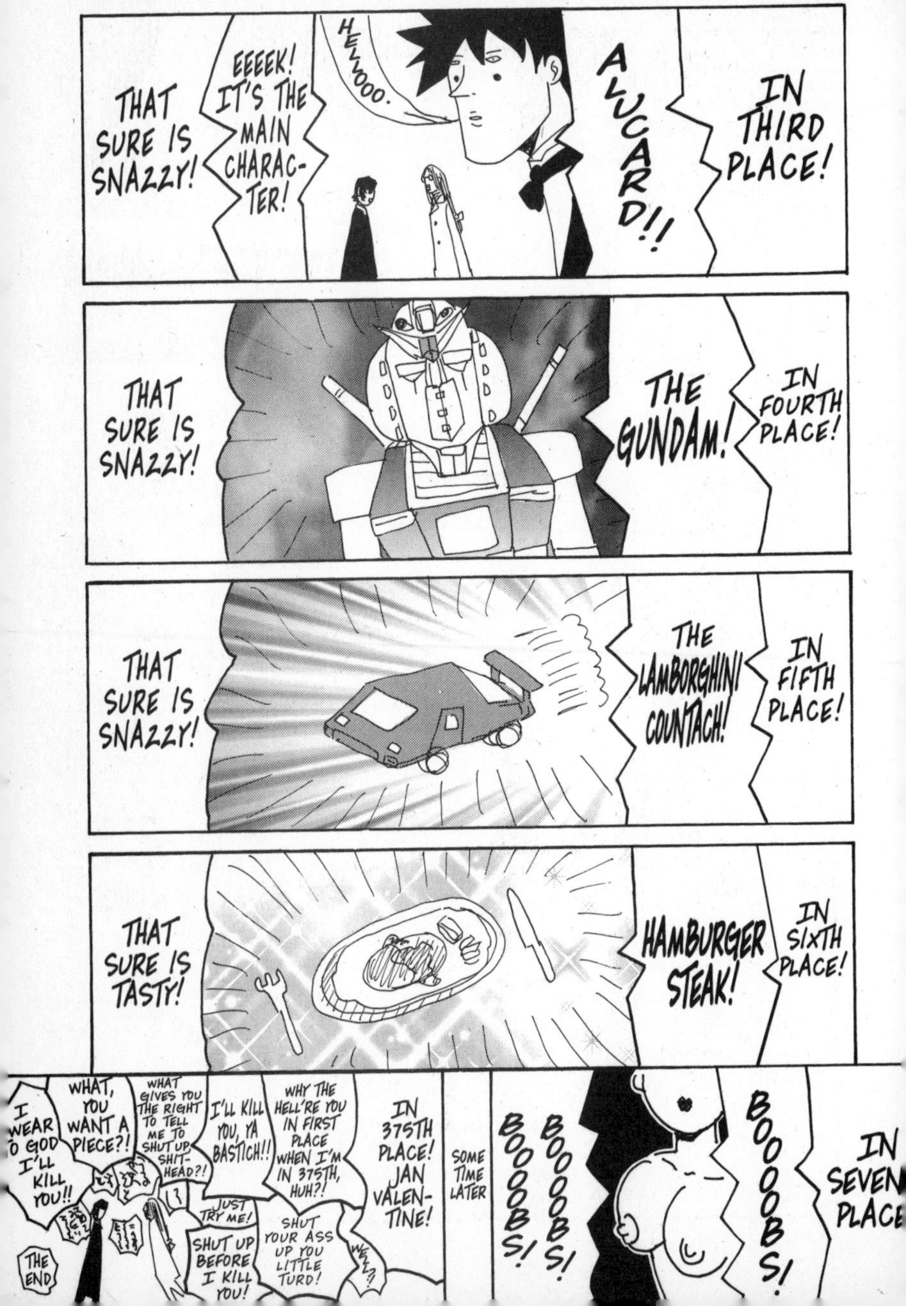
IN THIRD PLACE!
ALUCARD!!
HELLOOO.
EEEEK! IT'S THE MAIN CHARAC-TER!
THAT SURE IS SNAZZY!
IN FOURTH PLACE!
THE GUNDAM!
THAT SURE IS SNAZZY!
IN FIFTH PLACE!
THE LAMBORGHINI COUNTACH!
THAT SURE IS SNAZZY!
IN SIXTH PLACE!
HAMBURGER STEAK!
THAT SURE IS TASTY!
IN SEVEN PLACE
BOOOOOBS!
BOOOOBS!
BOOOOBS!
SOME TIME LATER
IN 375TH PLACE! JAN VALEN-TINE!
WHY THE HELL'RE YOU IN FIRST PLACE WHEN I'M IN 375TH, HUH?!
WEH?!
SHUT YOUR ASS UP YOU LITTLE TURD!
I'LL KILL YOU, YA BASTICH!!
JUST TRY ME!
SHUT UP BEFORE I KILL YOU!
WHAT GIVES YOU THE RIGHT TO TELL ME TO SHUT UP, SHIT-HEAD?!
WHAT, YOU WANT A PIECE?!
I WEAR O GOD I'LL KILL YOU!!
THE END

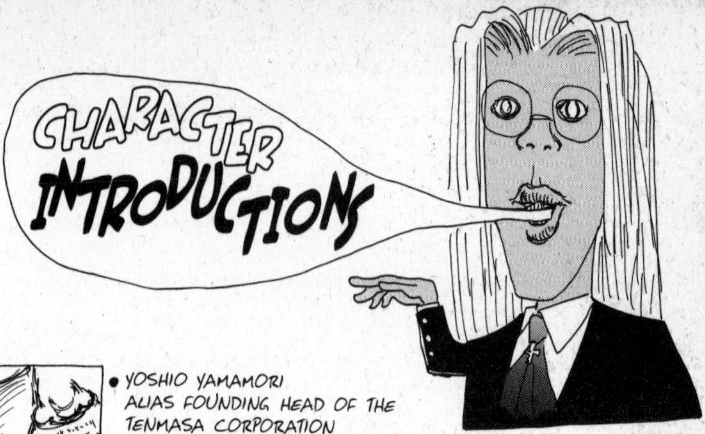
CHARACTER INTRODUCTIONS

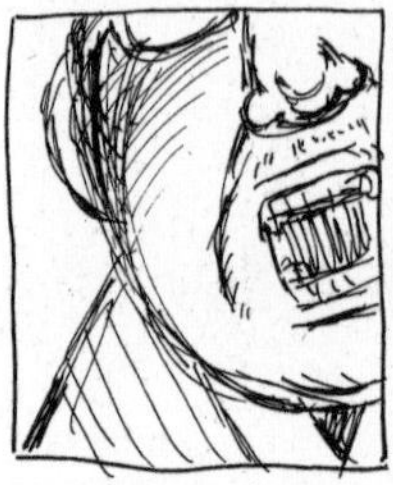

- YOSHIO YAMAMORI
  ALIAS FOUNDING HEAD OF THE TENMASA CORPORATION
  "WHAT'RE YOU TALKIN' ABOUT?! DON'T GIVE ME THAT CRAP!"
  THE FOUNDING HEAD OF THE TENMASA CORPORATION, ETC. BEING THE HIROSHIMA YAMAMORI GANG, ETC. ORGANIZATION, HE MORE OR, ETC. COMPLETING HIS DUTIES, ETC.

- CAPTAIN VERNEDEAD
  ALIAS CAPTAIN LUNA. MISS LUNA. STOP, MISS LUNA, WE MUSTN'T. HE GOT HIS KISS AND THEN DIED. HE WAS SUPPOSED TO DIE SOONER, SO HE DID REALLY WELL CONSIDERING. PLEASE GIVE HIM A HAND.

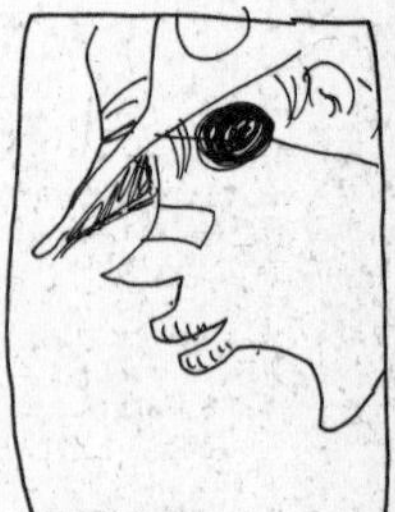

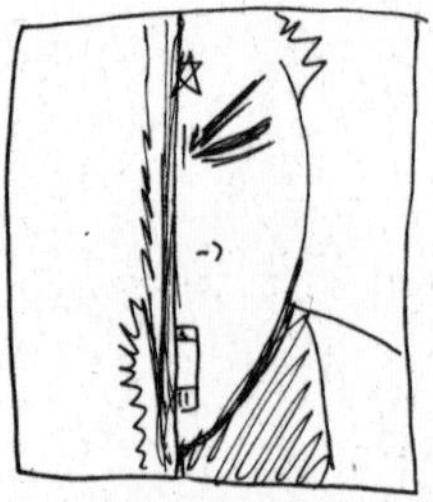

- ZORIN BLITZ
  ALIAS RIN. RIN'S WINGS. TOMINO.
  CAUSE OF DEATH: EXCESSIVE GRATING.

- WALTER (YOUNG)
  HIS YOUTH HAS BEEN RESTORED. HE REMINDS ME OF THE PRESIDENT OF JAPANET TAKATA.

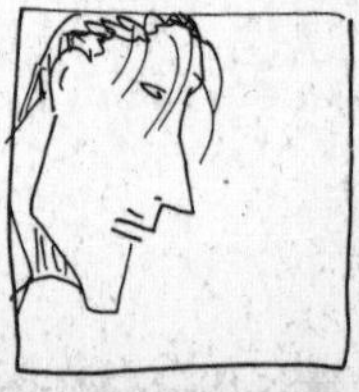